A Small War in Eden

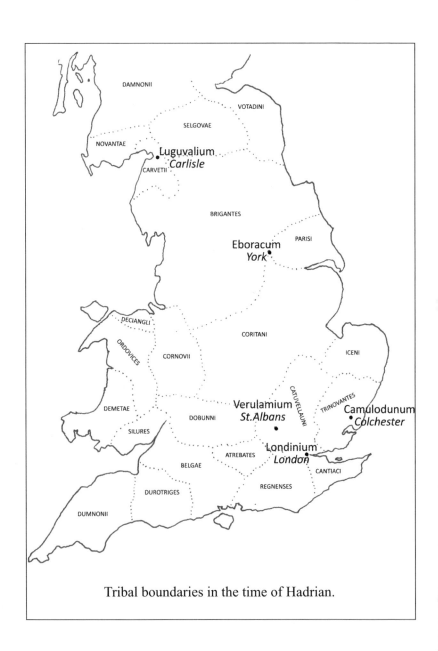

Tribal boundaries in the time of Hadrian.

A Small War in Eden

A Tale of the Eden Valley

JOHN M. HUGHES

HAYLOFT

Published by Hayloft Publishing Ltd., 2019

A CIP catalogue record for this book is available from the British Library

ISBN 978-1-910237-44-1

Designed, printed and bound in the EU

Hayloft policy is to use papers that are natural, renewable and recyclable products
and made from wood grown in sustainable forests. The logging and
manufacturing processes are expected to conform to the
environmental regulations of the country of origin.

Climate neutral
Print product
ClimatePartner.com/12667-1903-1003

The additional carbon offset project
supported is Forest Protection, Pará, Brazil.

Hayloft Publishing Ltd,
a company registered in England number 4802586
2 Staveley Mill Yard, Staveley, Kendal, LA8 9LR (registered office)
L'Ancien Presbytère, 21460 Corsaint, France (editorial office)

Email: books@hayloft.eu
Tel: +44 (0)7971 352473
www.hayloft.eu

To Margaret with my thanks for unstinting help, and a willingness to forgive me for turning an original idea for a short story into something that turned out to be a little longer.

Too many people have contributed information and ideas for me to thank them all by name, but my very special thanks go to Tim Padley at Tullie House Museum in Carlisle for his considerable assistance, and to the staff at Dumfries Museum for their help. Thanks also to those who read the book in its various manuscript stages for their helpful suggestions, corrections to matters of fact, and willingness to smile sweetly when I thanked them but went my own way. I have tried but failed to find the copyright owner of the cover photograph to thank them personally for this lovely image. And, last but but by no means least, my thanks are due to my Latin teachers at Alleyn's College in London, who not only got me through my Latin 'O' Level, but who made me love Vergil as well.

Roman place-names and their English counterparts..

I

Anno 870 Ab Urbe Condita, in the consulship of Imp. Caesar Traianus Hadrianus Augustus III and Publius Damusius Rusticus

(119 AD)

It began – when, exactly? That depends on your point of view.

For some, it began when two tribes combined to raise the great stone circle that men today call Long Meg and her Daughters, and a man named Urien stole Blanaid, the wife of his brother Lugos, and at last murdered his brother. And that ancient story goes on to tell how dead Lugos was transformed into an eagle and became a god of the sun, but in the fullness of time Blanaid shrivelled away to become an owl and Urien dwindled to a face sometimes glimpsed in the leaves of the forest.

For others, it began some 76 years ago, when the Emperor Claudius invaded Britain with four legions, among them the Ninth – Legio IX Hispana, to give them their formal name.

For others again, it began some time in February, when two cohorts of infantry were posted to a former cavalry fort by a little town with the strange native name of Luguvallium, charged with upholding Rome's name and power here on the edge of Caledonia.

But perhaps it really began on a dirty April day just nine days short of the May Kalends when a man was murdered on the road a little way to the south of the town. It happened like this…

First, the weather: cool, with unseasonably heavy rain coming in from the south-west. Low cloud, the hills to the east almost invisible, and the paving of the road slippery and puddled. In short, this is not a day for travel.

Next, the victim: a man, alone except for a donkey, his hood over his face against the foul weather. There are few signs of wealth, though an observant eye might look at the cut of the hood or the silver trim on the shoes and consider him at least not a poor man.

Then, the place: not too close to the town and its Roman camp – perhaps a couple of miles away – where the road crosses over a beck on a wooden trestle. Here there is room for the thieves to hide themselves under the very deck of the bridge, and the rushing of the water, swollen by several days of rain, covers any sound they might make.

Last, the thieves: two men, the one dressed in dirty homespun, the other in little more than a barely-tanned sheepskin. Neither has shoes. Their hair is matted and greasy – the one fair, the other dark – and one of them has a knife; the second, who has a cast in one eye, is clutching a jagged piece of rock which he will use as a club.

And so it happens, messily and noisily on the deserted road. The victim, unsighted by his hood and the rain, is taken completely unawares, but somehow manages to unsheathe the dagger concealed under his cloak. The man with the knife takes a wild sweep at the traveller's throat, but his bare feet slip on the wet slabs and the blow goes awry.

Now the second man has grabbed the traveller's cloak from behind and pulls him back off-balance; and the donkey, suddenly aware of danger by its very side, gives a startled *hee-haw* and takes off at a brisk canter, hooves clattering along the road.

A few moments more and the fight is over: the traveller tumbles onto his back, his dagger flying out of his hand as he falls. Winded, he tries to scramble to his feet, but all the advantage now is with his assailants. One kneels on his chest and batters him about the face with the rock while the other holds back his head by the blood-stained hair and manages at the second attempt to cut his throat.

Now there is a long moment of silence; the thieves, winded by their exertions and with their hearts racing, look at each other in triumph. Then they pull themselves upright, drag the battered corpse off the road and under the bridge, confident that the rain will soon wash off the blood. Squatting down, they pull off the victim's cloak, then grab his arm-purse and tip its contents into the red mud between them.

Gold gleams in the shadows, some of it the minted coins of one emperor or another, some of it little unminted bars; and silver and copper pieces as well. They let the metal trickle between their fingers, grinning at the way it catches the light. And then they laugh at their success and its promise of bread and beer for each of them, and perhaps a woman as well.

It is, inevitably, the donkey that betrays them. After the first mad rush of panic the beast has regained its nerve; it pauses, turns uncertainly and begins to retrace its steps to where it last saw its master. It stops by the bridge and lets out a puzzled bray, fetching the murderers out from their hiding place with the sudden realisation that there is more wealth to be had in the animal's panniers.

The donkey proves harder to trap than its master. As one man grabs at its halter it turns to face him, then lashes out with its heels at the other as he circles behind. So much noise do they all make, shouting and braying and banging that at first none of them hears the little patrol approach. But here it is, just a tent-group of eight men with an *optio*, an under-officer named Eburnus, in charge; for them, a dull day dragging up and down the road in the unceasing rain suddenly becomes more interesting.

The two men are overpowered and on the ground in moments, one of them gasping for breath after a solid blow to the stomach, the other laid out unconscious after near-throttling. A quick search reveals the corpse, and the optio details two men to chop down saplings with their swords for a makeshift bier. Finally the troop, more used to handling donkeys than either of the thieves, trusses the unconscious thief across the beast's back and heads off to camp, dragging the second man gasping behind them at the end of a rope.

They all know what this means; for the troops, a word of commendation from the camp commander; for the traveller, a decent funeral, and perhaps, if anyone can find enough about him, even a letter to his people telling how he met his end – and for the thieves, crucifixion.

II

Perhaps the story should begin that same evening, when a tall man with a Caledonian accent shoved open the door of Bran and Morrig's inn in the little town, pushed back his hood, glanced around and asked, 'How much is the girl?'

Bran wiped his hands on his apron and glanced briefly at the questioner; he was tall, with little flesh on him, and perhaps in his sixties.

'Her? And just you? Four coppers if you're quick, six if you want to take your time. And you pay me first.'

The coins clinked into his hand. Bran peered at them for a moment: bright copper, quite a new minting, and probably short-weight. 'She's all yours. Behind the curtain there, all right.'

He gestured towards the draped alcove, then shouted to the scrawny black-haired girl who was swabbing a table at the back of the room. 'Messalina, get your skinny backside over here. And be nice to the man, he looks like he could do with a spot of comforting.'

The girl gave him a dirty look, then slouched over to the little cubby-hole, pulling up her tunic as she went, then turned and shot a quick wink at the drinkers before tugging the curtain nearly closed.

Bran watched the curtain move for a few moments, then wandered over to the best-lit table the Eagle could offer, where two soldiers were gambling with three dice. They'd been in for most of the afternoon and had reached that happy stage of drunkenness where they were best friends with each other, with Bran, and with all the other customers; Bran knew just how quickly that mood could turn, especially where dice were concerned.

'It's a three,' muttered the first. 'Look, One, Two Three.'

His friend didn't seem so sure. 'A two, so I'm out.'

With the extreme patience of the drunkard, the first said again, 'Can't be; you can't get a two with three dice. Look, One, Two, Three.'

'I said it's a two. Want to make something of it?'

'Jupiter, man, can't you count? Or are you just looking for trouble?'

The second soldier began to stand up. His movements were unsteady, but his hand was on his dagger. In an instant Bran grabbed at the sleeve of his tunic, which was still damp from the day's rain.

'If you want a fight, get out. You can have wine and the girl here and you can gamble your pay away if you want to, but you do your fighting somewhere else, all right?'

The man hesitated for a moment, then rose to his full height, pulling clear of Bran's grip; his dagger was now half-way out of its sheath.

'I don't need any bloody Briton to tell me and my mates what to do, right. I come in here and I put up with your stink and your flea-bitten whore and your greasy wine and I pay for what I take. And if I want a bit of exercise, I'll have that too. So get your hand off me before you end up with your guts all over the floor.'

Bran cast a quick look at the other soldier, wondering if he was of a mind to join in, but he had pushed back his stool with an air of benign drunken amusement. Bran gave a defeated shrug, dropped his hand and nodded his head, all the bravado gone out of him.

Then, at the very moment of defeat, reinforcements arrived from an unexpected quarter. The tall Caledonian was standing at his shoulder, stark naked except for a leather bag hanging from his neck. His erection showed that he had not yet finished with Messalina.

'You heard him. Get out. Or I'll have the pair of you before your feet touch the ground.'

The soldier stared at him for a moment, then swung round, pulling the dagger free of its sheath as he moved; but before he could thrust it home, the tall man had reached forward with surprising speed and buried his long fingernails into the drunkard's wrist in a paralysing grip. With no apparent effort he tightened his grasp, watching the man's eyes bulge as he tried to keep his grip on the weapon. Then with a quick shake the Caledonian sent the dagger flying to the floor before he finally brought the soldier's hand hard against the rough edge of the table-top in a bone-jarring crash. Still keeping his grip, he dragged the cursing soldier half-bent-over through the room.

'You're no' so braw now as you were earlier, my man, are you?' He spat on the floor. 'I know your sort. Call yourself a soldier? I've seen finer wee laddies running round wi' their kecks round their ankles.'

He turned to the man's companion, who was still sitting on his stool with a broad smile on his face, as if nothing that had happened had anything to do with him at all. 'You, take him back to camp with you, and thank your gods you found me in a good humour. Take his knife with you and begone.'

The man rose unsteadily to his feet, his eyes fixed on the Caledonian's erection, then shook his head as if to clear it, took the proffered dagger, grabbed his companion's free arm and pulled him through the doorway. Bran pushed the door closed behind them and barred it, then turned to thank his ally; but the man had already gone back to the little alcove, ignoring the hoots of the other drinkers, and pulled the curtain closed.

Bran was mopping his brow with the greasy cloth that Messalina had used for wiping tables when the Caledonian finally finished his session with her; part of Bran's brain was suggesting that he had taken rather longer than he had paid for, but it seemed unlikely that it would be wise to say anything.

'You have beer?' said the man as he sat uninvited at Bran's side, pulling his woollen tunic down and tying the leather belt around the waist.

'People here drink wine,' muttered Bran, then unwillingly added 'I've some beer in the back that I keep for myself.'

The stranger nodded and smiled widely for the first time, showing a mouth from which all the front teeth in both jaws were missing.

'Do you always fight naked?' said Bran as he pulled himself to his feet.

'Not when I can help it, but it seems to happen sometimes. Get the beer.'

When Bran came back with the big earthenware jug in his hand the man was leaning back against the table as if he didn't have a care in the world, watching Messalina as she carried a flagon round the room filling empty wine-cups. Without taking his eyes off her he took the jug from Bran's hand and poured a deep draught down his throat, hardly seeming to swallow as it went down.

'It's not that I mind wine,' he explained, 'but sometimes you need something with a bit more go to it. It's a fine drop you have here anyway; I'm supposing that your wife would be the one who makes it?'

He pushed the jug into Bran's hand, the motion somehow suggesting that Bran should join him at the table. As Bran raised the jug to his lips, the man leant forward and muttered confidentially, 'You heard about the business outside town today. Roads aren't safe. Still, the soldiers got the bastards that did it.'

Bran nodded. 'Killers, the pair of them. They'll get what's coming to them, anyway. And I brew the beer myself.'

Then he took a deep swig from the jug and put it on the table, wiped his lips with his sleeve, took a quick glance around the room and muttered, 'One of them was one of the old ones, they say. Not someone to cross, if you take my meaning. Not that any of that bothered the soldiers, it seems.'

He turned and spat noisily onto the floor to avert the evil eye.

'The old ones? Druids, you mean? Would that be so? Not that he can ever have been what you might call a member of the college, him being too young and the Romans killing them all wherever they found them long before he'd have been born. But you say that he had a touch of the craft about him?'

Bran stood up; there were some things that everyone knew but that were unlucky to say out loud. But the Caledonian reached out his hand to stay him. 'You have a place where a poor travelling man can sleep, no doubt? I'll be here for a few days, till I've sold the kine I brought down and pastured outside town. Couple of other things to do too. We'll talk later, then. And you'll be after leaving the jug.'

Before Bran could reply the man grasped his hand, and when he released it Bran realised that there was a silver denarius in it. 'You'll be looking at that when the light's better, I'm thinking,' said the man. 'See that you do. And remember that Senorix gave it to you.'

Bran hesitated, then nodded. 'There's good clean straw in the shed at the side. Will you be wanting anything else?'

Senorix considered for a moment, then gestured at Messalina, who was making eyes at him from the other side of the room. 'Aye, you can send the girl over again. I haven't quite done with her yet.'

III

Not the posting I'd have chosen for myself, Marius thought, but it might turn out to be quite tolerable. A good house to live in, an old friend as *primus pilus*, a brand-new little town to watch over, and decent countryside for hunting if I can ever find time for it. Still, better weather wouldn't go amiss.

At least the rain which had been coming down in drenching showers for more days than he had counted had stopped, and the sky showed patches of blue, promising better weather ahead. And the town seemed blessedly peaceful, a place where ordinary civilian life could flourish. He and his men could walk through the streets without attracting either attention or a dagger, note the everyday traffic of the town and savour the homely smells of the tanners, the bakers, the slaughterers.

One day, he thought, there might be a great city here where the road from the south met the military road winding over the hills from the east; for now at least the little native *vicus* which had sprung up south of the camp had taken on a surprisingly organised air, with a busy little forum of its own, a wharf on the river, and the first signs of sensible town planning. He smiled as he imagined it in a future he would never see with perhaps a stone aqueduct and a proper town council, and fine stone walls instead of the timber ramparts that had been hastily erected to protect the place.

He blinked and the vision faded. But even today the little forum seemed to be flourishing; on the north side a sleepy acolyte was sweeping the steps in front of the temple of Mars Victor, and on the opposite side of the square a new *caupona* had opened selling hot food; the tavern next to it on the corner of the square had been there for some time, and the sign was already beginning to look battered; it displayed a crude picture of an eagle and the name *Aquila* in rough black letters.

He walked through the town like this most days, to see and to be seen, in Ovid's phrase. He told himself that it was good for morale, and sometimes admitted that it improved his own morale as well as that of his men. There were too many places in the world where a confident Rome had proudly planted her banners and had then shamefacedly withdrawn in the face of constant bar-barian harassment; here at least Roman ways seemed to be thriv-ing, and peace had brought trade and a measure of prosperity.

Today he was riding, not walking, his unfashionable cob happy to be out on the road. Straight past the forum he went and through the south-gate, past the little cluster of new tombs and then two miles south on a proper road, already busy with little groups of travellers, and even a well-to-do lady borne along in a litter, with a fair-sized retinue trailing after her.

As he jogged along he began to hum to himself, then started to murmur softly the words of his soldiers' newest marching-song. After the first couple of verses he broke off, and the name of his latest administrative problem flashed into his mind: Gracchus.

He had nothing against senior tribunes as a class, but by all the gods of Olympus Gracchus was something else. Sent out to gain practical experience of military life on the edge of the empire, his foppish manners and drawling Esquiline accent had obviously proved too much even for the staff officers at Eboracum; no won-der they'd pushed him off up-country as soon as they decently could.

Almost without realising, he'd come to the point where he would have to leave the road and follow the broad drive-way to the palace – a spacious villa, really – a bow-shot to the east of the highway. A small *vexillation* was posted here, partly as a courtesy to the Queen and partly to act as his eyes and ears around the court. He was quite certain that she understood this and would try to use it for her own ends, and he suspected that enough money occasionally changed hands that he would never know everything that passed. Still, he rather enjoyed teasing out the intelligence they brought him to work out what it was she wanted him to hear and what she would prefer him not to have known.

A sharp salute and one of the waiting men took the cob's reins. Then the gates were thrust open and he was within the – he supposed it would have to be called the garden, though only the gods knew what would flourish in this climate; the chill winds that apparently blew from the north or the east through most of the winter and the westerly gales that he'd been told brought scudding rain from the sea all summer would have made most gardening impossible, he thought.

However they had tried; there were proper gravel paths and borders of herbs, and scattered about were a few statues, inferior copies of decent Greek originals knocked up on the cheap by careless Gauls. There was even a fountain, though there wasn't enough water pressure to make it rise decently, a telling symbol of the locals' famed inability to make anything that actually worked as it ought to. And, inevitably, there was an old oak tree standing in the lee of the walls, with a wide gravelled space around it. Native customs, thought Marius, while admiring the skilful way in which the ancient tree had been incorporated into the scheme of things.

The architect – paid for out of Imperial funds, no doubt – had been sensitive about the site as well; the roof-line of the main building carefully mirrored the contours of the distant hills beyond, and the colour of the neat tiles matched the red sandstone from which most of the palace had been built. This, he reflected, was the home of a Queen who had been brought up in a round hut with a fire burning in the middle and a beaten earth floor; yet she appeared loyal, and it seemed to him that her loyalty had been well-worth the price paid.

He sat down on the rim of the fountain pool and trailed his hand in the cool water; there were carp there and they nuzzled his hand expecting to be fed. From somewhere in the run of low buildings to the right he could hear some men arguing, though he couldn't make out the words; but the main house was quiet and orderly.

'It's a game,' he told the fish, 'all a game. I come here and pretend it's a courtesy call, and then your mistress pretends that she's summoned me for an audience. And there are other men just like me across most of this damp island who play the same game with other little Kings and Queens, and somehow together we govern the province for the joint benefit of Rome and the provincials; and for now at least the gods of Rome and of Britain seem to smile on us all.'

A respectful cough brought him to himself; the major-domo was standing at his shoulder. But instead of the public rooms in the main wing he was gesturing towards the Queen's private quarters on the northern side.

This was new territory; Marius looked with frank curiosity at the way in which the buildings had been artfully folded back on themselves to contain a proper Roman atrium, with another incompetent fountain and pool in the centre, and a suite of rooms opening off it. A currule chair – a magistrate's backless folding one – had been left with apparent carelessness facing the pool, with a low footstool off to one side; neither, he knew, was intended for him. But the message was clear: I am a Roman; I live in the Roman way, in a fine house built for me by the Roman emperor, and I conduct affairs of state in the civilised Roman fashion, even though my compatriots are uneducated barbarians. Treat me accordingly.

Verica knew enough of Roman ways to be sure that he would be kept waiting; not so long as to be obviously rude, but a beautifully timed few moments perfectly calculated to let her visitor know who was the superior and who was the inferior in this complex dance.

A tinkle of gold jewellery and the soft pad of sandalled feet announced her arrival; with the slightest of nods she sat in the currule chair. She was wearing a simple dark tunic, fastened at the shoulders with enamelled dragon clasps in the old British style, but everything else was pure Roman; there was a thin golden circlet on her brow, her flame-red hair was fastened up in the latest fashion, and her gaze was open and direct; in the backless chair she sat bolt upright. Forty-five years old and a widow, thought Marius; but born to rule for all that.

There were two others with her: first, almost treading on her heels, a man who might have been anything from fifty to seventy years old, short-haired and clean-shaven in the Roman manner; Marius knew him as her harpist, and knew too that he was there to remember everything that was spoken between them. In his own judgement the man was fully the equal of his Queen and the superior of everyone else, and he sat quickly on the footstool without even a glance at the Roman. Then there was the inevitable maid, taking up her station behind her Queen. She was, Marius thought, perhaps fifteen years old and plain with it. That made sense; there would be no other beauties beside Verica in this court.

'Καλημέρα, κύριε'

Marius bowed and took note of the unspoken words underlying the Greek greeting – see, I am a proper Roman lady who knows both Latin and Greek – and wondered briefly whether to rise to the bait before replying with a careful, 'Good morning, my lady; you do me much honour this morning.'

'An informal occasion can be helpful sometimes, Commander. And I have something to ask of you.'

Not that informal, thought Marius. She's keeping her feet firmly on the ground as we speak, and as long as a Celtic ruler's feet are touching the earth then everything that happens is official, but he smiled and nodded.

'And I for you also; but that can wait.' Two men would be crucified on the roadside to the north of the camp tomorrow, thieves caught red-handed with a Syrian merchant's purse that they were dividing between them; he had no doubt that Verica already knew all the details since the robbery had taken place barely half a mile to the south of her palace. But courtesy demanded that she should be told and her formal consent obtained. First the courtesy, then the slow public deaths to deter others who might break the Roman peace of this province.

'The markets are quiet,' she said, 'but winter is past and spring is almost here. Within perhaps two or three days my people will begin to celebrate Beltane, and there will be fires lit in the town. They will come from many places in my kingdom to light their own hearth fires anew with brands kindled here at the sacred fire. Those who wish to come must be able to travel unmolested, and your men must see to it that it happens so.'

Her voice was quiet and confident, the Latin unaccented, fluent, better than many of the troops under Marius' command could manage; this woman could as well have been a senator's wife in Rome, born to high rank and privilege, than the Queen of a barbarian tribe on the very edge of the world.

Marius smiled. 'The safety of the roads depends on the swift and merciless taking of thieves and robbers, two of whom are even now chained up in my camp waiting for their crosses; and, by Jupiter, they will not have to wait long. You may depend on my troops to exercise due vigilance; but be sure to tell those who join with you in your festival that honouring the gods does not mean dishonouring Rome.'

Verica shrugged. 'A few miles around the city, there is peace; along the roads, there is peace, and where there is not then your justice or mine will be sure to follow. But how far will your men venture into the forests? How far will you go to the north? Away from your paved roads and the places around your camps, there is only the law of those few of our wise men whom you have left alive, and the customs of my people.'

'For now, perhaps. But a time will come when this whole land will be Rome. Your tribes and your little squabbles over who rules in this valley or that will be ended when that day comes.'

Suddenly bitter, she flashed at him, 'And in Caledonia too? You will rule there, where you set up your camps so brave and proud and then ran away from them when you found that your teeth had taken more than your mouth could hold? Commander, I know your power; but by Belenos I swear that I know your weakness too; and since my safety at the last depends on your men, it is your weakness that concerns me here. Do not you presume to tell me how we shall celebrate our Beltane, and I will not presume to tell you not to nail those robbers you have taken to their crosses. There was a time when my foster-mother had to call for the help of the legions, and all Rome could send were wretched auxiliaries.'

Marius' eyes dropped for a moment to the harpist where he sat on his stool at the Queen's feet. The man's attention seemed to be fixed on a fly that was crawling across the fine mosaic, but Marius knew that every word spoken by either of them would be firmly locked in his mind. It was said that the druids used to spend ten years doing nothing more than perfecting their memories, and for all his Roman haircut this harpist was no doubt as adept as they were in that particular skill.

Thank the gods I know my history, he thought. 'When your foster-mother, the great Queen Cartimandua, called for our help it was in the Year of the Four Emperors, and in truth she was fortunate that anyone could be spared. But that was long ago, and now Rome is at peace with herself.

'And there is nothing in Caledonia for us – no gold, no pearls, no wealth of any kind. And away from those roads and forts which, my lady, we still maintain there, the people are mere painted savages, unworthy of the benefits of Roman life. When we had established those facts, we left them to their own devices. Let them call themselves free if they will; would you, my lady, exchange your life for theirs?'

'Commander, these painted savages of whom you speak so easily came near to fighting your troops to a standstill at Mons Graupius.'

Suddenly she smiled. 'But let us not quarrel; each of us has something that the other needs; and we are both wise enough to know it and to admit it to the other. I ask you again to guard the roads at Beltane; and you know well that if rebellion against Rome were to start here, then I would be its first victim. Commander Marius, I am no Boudicca.'

Marius shrugged. 'We work together for a common aim, my lady. The thieves will go to their crosses at first light tomorrow, and will no doubt take the ferry over the Styx before three days are over. This will not, I think, cause any problems for those who come here to mark your Beltane; indeed, the roads may be all the safer for this show of what the law does to those who break it.'

'You would think so; but it is not always so simple. I do not mean that there would be any sympathy for those robbers whom you took. It is your way to nail them to crosses, but in the days before your people came into the land we would have burned them alive in wicker effigies as an offering to the gods, so in one manner or another both would die for their offence.

'No, Commander, the problem I have to speak to you about goes a little deeper than that, though indeed these two men are a part of it. Come with me; I have something to show you. Iras, quick, stir yourself and open the doors.'

The little maid was already running to open the double doors of what Marius now realised was a private dining suite, all laid out in the proper Roman manner; of a summer's evening it would be pleasant to recline here and listen to the fountain while feasting. At shoulder height to the right of the entrance was a carved bas-relief of three seated Celtic goddesses, the *matronae*; as she passed it, Verica bowed her head in brief homage.

The interior was decorated with fresco-work in what Marius at first took for a series of patterns in which leaves and fruits predominated; it seemed to be a garden scene, and indeed now he looked more closely he saw that there were birds flying above. The work had been superbly done; no doubt it had been another substantial charge on the imperial budget.

'Look at the pattern on the walls, Commander; tell me what you see.'

Marius looked more carefully at the interwoven foliage. Then as his eyes grew more used to the gloom he realised that it could be read in two different ways: what had at first seemed only to show leaves and branches could also be read as a pattern of green faces peering out through the undergrowth, with fresh shoots emerging from ears and mouth.

'Have you ever seen anything like that before, Commander?'

He considered carefully. 'Yes, once in Rome; there was a certain friend at whose house I dined from time to time who had painted on his wall the story of Daphne, who was turned into a laurel bush when the god Apollo tried to rape her. His painting showed her at the moment of change from girl into tree. This is something similar, I imagine, my lady?'

Verica softly clapped her hands together in mock admiration. 'Indeed, Commander; I know the story well.' Smiling she began to recite, '*In nova fert animus mutatas dicere formas corpora.*

'You see, I have read your Ovid. But I think that this is something much older than your story; it is said that it goes back to the time when men such as we are first came to this great valley. There were not many of them, but they were led by a magician, a shapeshifter who, it is said, could take on any form he wished.

She turned to her harpist, who had followed them into the room and was standing close behind her with his arms at his side. 'Gwydion, tell him the story.'

GWYDION'S TALE OF LUGOS AND URIEN

Not yesterday, not yesterday but a long time ago a man came down from the high fells which stand on the eastern side of this valley. He was grieving, for his wife had died a few days earlier and he had buried her on the high moors beneath a cairn of stones according to the custom of his people and whispered the secret words over her body to let her spirit return in some other guise. And now he and his two sons and some two dozen others of less account had set their backs to the high ground and looked over this valley.

The true name of the man is not told in any tale for he told it to no-one, fearing that this might give others power over him; he held himself to be a shaman, wise in the ways of the spirits that live in trees and in rivers and wells, and most particularly the spirits that live in the stars and the moon and the sun, whose power shapes the lives of men.

He thought himself to be a shape-shifter, for he would eat of certain plants that he had prepared in secret and would go alone to a high place away from all others, and there go into a trance; and in that trance his spirit would soar in the air with the eagles, or swim the rivers with the salmon, or roam through the woods with the bears; and when at length he awoke and returned to those who knew him, the marks of his spirit-journey would be seen on his body: scratches of brambles and branches if he had gone with the bears, or the bruises of the rocks if he had battled upstream with the salmon. And men said that he knew ways of healing, and could carve on wooden tokens such signs as would bring health and strength to those wearing them; though men noted that no secret signs had been powerful enough to hold his wife when she had sickened and died.

For all his power, men thought that he looked to be of little account, for he was short and his nose was crooked, as if it had been broken. The hair of his head was sparse, and what there was of it was light as if it had been bleached by the sun. His skin too was fair except on the top of his head, where it was blotched and marked by scarring and the lines of old wounds. But when men saw his eyes they thought less lightly of him, for he seemed never to blink but rather to look into the depths of men's spirits, and to see there much that was hidden even to those at whom he was looking. And men said that he had an evil temper, and was more likely to curse than to bless; and they said too that his curse might be followed by a blow or the secret thrust of a dagger, and so they took care not to come too often to his notice.

Now it is time to tell of his sons, and there is much to be said of them, and of their descendants down to our own day; for they were of two natures, as befitted children from such a father.

The elder was named Lugos, which means Light, for he was fair like his father; and the younger was named Urien, which means High-born; and he was dark like his mother had been. Now it was the custom in those days that when the time of child-birth was on them the women would throw certain herbs onto a fire, and would then breathe the smoke of the burning, for they held that this lessened their pain.

The herb also gave them from time to time the power to see the fates that would govern the life of their child, and of Lugos his mother saw this: that he would find no wife among his own people, that he would be skilful in hunting, that he would find his death at the hands of those whom he loved, and that he would not die from any lawful weapon, nor while he lay on the ground nor while standing, and not on water nor on dry land.

Of what she saw of the fate of Urien his mother said little, and none dared to ask her; only this would she say, that he would hate the people who hated him, and that his death would be a lonely one and far away; but there were those who thought that she had told him many secrets that she would not speak of to others.

Lugos had seen some twelve summers when his mother had died, and Urien two fewer; and it seemed to many that both had mourned her passing more than their father had seemed to do. Lugos proved to be his father's favourite, for he was obedient and willing to learn the ways of the stars and the spirits from his father, while Urien was wild and much given to roaming on his own; and he took little note of the ways of the people, but thought that his own wisdom was greater than that of his father.

From where he stood on the edge of the high fells the man and those with him could see that the valley below them stretched to the north and the south, wide and fertile, with the glint of a great river showing among the oak woods. Far to the south-west other hills rose, and to the north-west there was the distant hint of deeper water, which perhaps might lead one day to other lands; but he put that thought aside for another day. Far to the north there were other hills, dimly seen through the haze of the distance.

As he looked his eye caught smoke rising in some half-dozen places, and he knew that here was the habitation of other men, who might resent or welcome their coming as the mood took them; for himself he cared little what they might at first think, for he knew that he had the power to bend them quickly to his will if only he could speak with them. And yet it seemed to him that the valley was so empty there were many places where his clan could find good game and fishing, and soil deep enough to raise barley, in a place where others would not trouble them perhaps for many years.

Afterwards it was said that although other men might perhaps have nodded with satisfaction, or gestured with their arm towards the land below, the man did none of these things; rather, they said, he stepped forward like one who knows that he has reached his journey's end, who already hears the welcome call of his home.

There was now the task of claiming the new land; not from other men, for there were few nearby, but from those spirits of the place that might look with disfavour on the newcomers. The Shaman knew these well – there were the spirits of the bears and the wolves and the beavers and the otters, and of the adders and the slow-worms, and all the spirits of the trees and the earth and the river and the stones. Of all these, he thought the spirits of the earth and the river the most powerful, for they could bring sickness and wasting diseases if they were not appeased, and could drive the game away and make the barley shrivel up or rot or be blasted by mildew. But for all these things he knew the words to say.

Of the establishing of their place in the valley little is said, and there is perhaps little to say. With their bronze axes the younger men cut down trees and made a clearing on a rise within a bend of the river at a place that their Shaman had chosen for them, where there would be little danger of flood. They stripped the branches from the trees and thorny shrubs and wove them into a strong fence to protect the landward side of the clearing from any animals that might stray there, trusting to the depth and strength of the river and the steepness of the bank to keep that side secure. Then they raised huts, strong and round and thatched with saplings; and they took fire from the fire-pot that they had carried with them in all their travels and carried it around to each of the huts; and then the Shaman made his dance and said his words to make it safe for the men and women and their children to live there.

Some two years went past while they lived in peace and fished and hunted; and they cleared space for a field and planted barley there; and the women bore children – who lived or died as the spirits of the place chose – and they considered themselves happy and blessed, though they were few in number.

They found, as they grew used to the place where they were, that there were other clans of the same people as themselves living nearer than they had supposed, speaking a language that was close to their own; and slowly they began to trade with them, passing back and forth objects of bronze – which they greatly valued – and trinkets of jet and of bone. And after some time, some of the young men of the group brought back girls from this village or that, and they all swore oaths to the spirits of the place.

The Shaman became known among many of the clans for his healing powers; for it was said that he knew all the herbs that can be used to heal, and that the spirits of the forest had told him where to find them and what their powers were, and had taught him too the songs to sing and the dances to make while they were burned on the fire, so that the ash might be rubbed on the bodies of the sick; for that is the way that healing was done in those times.

Further off there were other people too, whose language the Shaman and his people did not understand, and whom they despised, for they were shorter of stature, and they used only tools of stone and knew nothing of the making of bronze. And they avoided them, and made the sign of the evil eye if they saw them by chance in the forest, though in truth their ways seldom crossed.

So things might have lasted for many a year more. But when Lugos was sixteen years old and his brother Urien fourteen it happened that one day they were out together hunting hares; they had been the same way the day before, setting snares that they had made from withies and had fastened to the ground with strong pegs of alder; and now they were eager to see what their traps might have caught.

When they looked they found that some snares had caught nothing – which was indeed to be expected – but that where others had been there was now nothing to be seen but some disturbance to the ground, as if both snare and prey had been taken away. At first they thought that a fox or a wolf might have happened on the place and taken the hare for itself; but Urien, who could read the signs on the ground with great skill, said that he could in one place surely see the press of a heel such as might be made by a child, 'and so someone else has been here before us and has robbed our traps.'

Lugos, whose eyes were less on the ground than his brother's, had answered that his words were true, 'and I can see the face of the thief, and it is not unsightly.' But by the time Urien looked up, the face had disappeared from view.

The brothers saw no more of the thief that day nor the next, but as time went by Urien felt eyes upon them more often than not, and they were not the eyes of the animals of the valley; and their snares were often empty or stolen when they came to look for them. But it was only after some ten days had passed that they came out of the woods one day onto the banks of the river and saw a girl of some fifteen years bathing there where the water was shallow; and as she turned to face them, unconcerned about her nakedness, neither of them doubted that she had meant them to find her, nor that hers were the hands that had robbed their snares, and hers the eyes that had watched them from the undergrowth. And she was of the other people, the ones who knew nothing of bronze and with whom they held no trade.

She showed that she had a power of her own, for even as they looked, she flung herself backwards into the deepest part of the river where the current was fierce in the autumn rains, and disappeared below the surface, and they caught only the briefest sight of her swimming there as easily as an otter. But they did not see her leave the river; neither did they dare to jump in themselves and fight against the current.

Lugos rubbed his hand over his face and looked at his brother and said, 'Whoever she is, and of whatever people she comes, I will surely have her for mine.' And Urien said nothing; but his thoughts were the same as his brother's.

After that they saw her often, but always from a distance; if they were in the valley then they would look up and suddenly see her on some ridge high above them, outlined against the sky; if they were hunting high on the edge of the fells, then she would appear on the riverbank far below; and always she was out of their reach. Wherever she was, she seemed to take no notice of them, though they both guessed that she had some magic that would tell her of their plans before even they had settled them for themselves. Neither spoke to their father of what had happened; and when a time came that they did not see her for many days together, they thought among themselves that perhaps some accident or sickness had befallen her and they would see her no more; though neither of them spoke of the matter to others.

The Shaman was skilled in watching the looks and hearing the words of others, and especially of hearing the words they did not say; and so one evening he came to his elder son and said to him that the time had come for him to take a wife, 'and indeed I think you have found yourself one; and as your mother foretold, it will not be of your own people.'

Lugos at first said nothing, and it was only after his father had mockingly said, 'Do you want no wife? Is no-one fitted for you? Must I take the flowers of the broom and the oak blossom and the meadowsweet and make you a fitting wife out of them with my words?' that Lugos spoke at last of the girl he had seen, and said that he had not been able to come close to her, but he said nothing of his brother.

'She will come,' said his father. 'I have flown with the hawks and I have seen her; and at evening tomorrow she will come here; for I have spoken the words to make this happen. And this time she will not run away.' He smiled as he said these words, for Lugos had said nothing of their first meeting at the riverbank. But it is said that afterwards the Shaman looked sad, as if he could see a great trouble appearing from afar.

The next morning he sent both Lugos and Urien far away down the river, for he knew that their meeting would not be as Lugos had seen it in his thoughts; for at evening a man and a woman came to the village not with others in their company but alone and thin and dazed with sickness; and they were of the stone people. And they were brought to the Shaman as he sat staring into the fire that burned night and day at the door to his hut; but for a while he said nothing to them but rather looked deep into the flame.

At length he rose from his trance; and the sick man and woman stood before him, both of them bowed with pain; and by signs – for they had no language in common – they gave him to understand that they had come to him for healing; and they gave him also to understand their names; and the man was called Math, and his wife Arian. Even in their sickness it was plain to all who saw them that they were of importance among their own people.

The Shaman seemed to take little heed of them, but instead smoothed a level place on the earth in front of him, and brushed it clear of twigs and leaves, and showed them that it was empty, and gestured to them to fill it. And so they understood that he would do nothing without some gift; and they laid on the ground such gifts as they had – arrow-heads of stone, finely made, indeed, but of little value – and gifts of fox and beaver-pelt. And these the Shaman glanced at and put to one side, refusing them as of little worth; and it was plain to those who saw him that he knew of a better gift that they still had to offer. And so the man and the woman stood in their sickness, until at last they spoke low words the one to the other, as people who know they must agree to a bad bargain for there is no other to be had.

So at last the man called out aloud, like one calling a hound; and there was an answering call from some distance away; and at last the girl whom Lugos and Urien had seen came and stood there; and she was their daughter, whom they had brought as their gift, though indeed they had not offered her at the first.

The girl also was not as Lugos and Urien had seen her before: her hair, which had been fair and long, was bedraggled; and her face was besmirched with smoke, like one who has spent much time hunched over a small fire; and her eyes were red, though whether it was with fire-smoke or with weeping no-one could tell.

The Shaman took her firmly by the hand, and drew her into the space that he had cleared on the ground; and he looked hard into her face; and she found it hard to answer his gaze. At last he shook his head, like one who is not entirely satisfied by the bargain he has made; but for all that it was plain that the sick man and woman would be given his help.

This was the manner of his proceeding: he told three men who were standing nearby to dig two shallow pits and then to set up two shelters of branches, one over each pit, covering them with turves, and at the entrance of each he had a fire lit of rowan and pine, which men call a wend-fire, and also had many herbs which he believed the spirits of the place were fond of burned on them.

He had great stones heated in the fires, and then when they

were hot enough he had them pushed into the pits; and he had the man and the woman take off their clothes, and he set the man in one shelter and the woman in the other, and threw more herbs into each fire. And the man and the woman began to feel violently hot from the action of the heated stones and of the fire at the entrance of the lodge. Then he began to sing and to dance around them, until in the end both the man and the woman fell into a deep sleep. Still he danced and sang to the spirits for a long time, until the autumn stars came out in the sky and wheeled over their heads while all the time the girl whom he had taken in payment stood disregarded at the entrance to his lodge, and said nothing. And no-one dared say anything to her.

When morning came, the Shaman came to an end of his dance and stood like one who has been struck, and as he did so the man and the woman who had been asleep awoke; and the fever that had been upon them both had passed, leaving only a great weariness. In that first light of dawn, Urien and Lugos returned from their hunting, and the other young men of the people with them; and they found the girl standing by the Shaman's lodge as she had stood all night, shaking with weariness.

Lugos remembered his father's words, that she would not flee from him this time; so he took her by the hand and led her into the hut that he had made as his own, and he lay with her whether she would or not for she was too tired to resist him. And no-one knew whether she was willing or otherwise, but none would say anything against what he did; and Urien watched his brother, and men said that it was then that the great hurt began to well up in his heart.

Now Math and Arian returned to their own people leaving their daughter behind and saying nothing to her, for it seemed to them that they had lost her for ever. Some of Lugos' people counted her as his wife, remembering his mother's words that he would find none among his own people; but he had said no oath for her before the spirits of the place, and so there were others who accounted her no more than his whore. Lugos treated her kindly, and remembering his father's word that he would make him a wife from flowers, he called her Blanaid, which means flower; but her name among her own people, no-one knew or asked.

Some began to whisper against their Shaman, that he had driven too hard a bargain with Arian and Math for they feared that he had created an enmity between their people and his own; for although the stone-people who had lived in the great valley before their coming were unused to bronze and only of small stature, yet it seemed to many that they were more numerous than all the villages of their own kind. The Shaman kept his own counsel.

Now Blanaid began to learn Lugos' language, so that she could speak to him and understand him when he spoke to her; and she learned quickly, so that very soon she was able to grasp the meaning of everything he said to her. It seemed to many in the village that although she had come unwillingly among them, yet she had in the end taken her fate in her own hand. As the year turned to summer she bore Lugos a son, and Lugos named him Llyr; and the spirits of the place let him live.

As for Urien, at first he went hunting with his brother as before, and if there was any coolness between them it did not show in anything he said; and if there were those who noticed that his eye frequently rested on Lugos' wife, Lugos himself seemed not to be aware of it. Blanaid gave no sign that she had seen his eye fixed on her.

After a while Urien went hunting only rarely. Instead he went out to the fields that the men of the village had cut out of the forest; one of these was close by the river-bank, and the soil there was rich and fertile. Urien took special note of the barley that had been planted there, which the women of the village ground down to make flour; and it may be that he remembered the ways that he had been told by his mother about the making of barley-beer;

for from the first the spirits of the place blessed his drink and made it ferment, so that it was very strong. In the evening many of the men of the village would come to his hut and drink his beer, and talk of this and that, and sometimes become drunk; but Urien was careful in his drinking; and it was seen that Lugos never came to drink with his brother.

It happened that one hot summer day in his hunting Lugos came to a place where he had never been before, half a day's travel from his village; and there he saw a strange thing. For the forest in this place was sparse, as if it had been cut down long before and had not regrown; and towards one end of this clearing was a great standing stone, that looked as if it had been placed there not by men but by the hands of giants; and the lower part of the stone was buried deep in the earth. Lugos understood that this was a place sacred to the spirits; and he looked with reverence at the stone, and bowed before it, and remained there a long time in silence.

After a while he laid his palm on the stone, half fearful lest it should move beneath his hand; and although the day was hot and the air still, yet the stone was cool as if the sun had no power to warm it; and Lugos knew that there was a deep magic within it. He stayed there all the rest of that day, and into the night; and when the darkness came and the moon shone over the clearing he felt sure that he had seen the stone move in its place, as though it were awakening and stretching like one who has been long asleep. He bowed again before it, and remained there awake the whole night.

The next day Lugos went back to his village, and told his father what he had seen, and how he knew that the spirits were strong in that place; and his father considered the matter carefully. And after some days he sent word to the other villages of his people asking them what they knew of the standing stone that Lugos had seen; but none of them had heard or seen the thing, for it was not in a place to which any of them went to hunt.

Lugos spoke to Blanaid of what he had seen, and of the great power that he had felt in the stone; and she told him that her own people knew of it; and that it had not indeed been raised there by the hand of men – not even by the Ancients who had lived in the land long before the memory of anyone living and who were skilled in many wonderful arts; but, she said, it was told that there had been once a great sorceress, skilled in shape-changing and in other magical arts; and that her magic had been so powerful that even the spirits of the place would flee from her. But she had not the power to stay young for ever; and so in despair that a time would come when she would die, she had at last changed herself into the great stone, so that she would stand for ever in the clearing she had made; and through all ages to come she would watch over the people of the valley, and would see them born and flourish and die, while she remained for ever unchanging. And when he heard this story, Lugos understood the great power that he had felt in the stone; and he told his father what Blanaid had said to him.

So a scheme was born in the Shaman's mind, to honour the sorceress and so to harness her power and it may be to bend her magic to his own ends. And he sent messengers out to all the villages of their own people round about, telling them of what he planned to do and calling on them to help, with many promises of blessings to come on them when once the work was done.

This was the work that they did: with great effort they brought more stones, not so tall as the sorceress nor so well-shaped, and they set them up in a ring with the Sorceress standing alone some distance away, so that she might hold court with them and so that they might pay her homage. And the work of finding and shaping and bringing the stones and setting them into a great circle so that they filled the clearing took three summers and three long winters to complete.

Indeed, the work would have taken much longer but that after some time Blanaid's people, led by Math and Arian, appeared and showed themselves willing and eager to help; for it was plain to them that in this way they would share in whatever blessing was to be found in the work. They had among them a skilled man who had made a pipe from some animal's bone; and as the others heaved the great stones on their wooden rollers, he would play to them, setting a time for their efforts. And from afar it might appear that the stones moved themselves to the rhythm of his music.

At length the work was completed, with no fewer than seventy great stones brought down from the hillsides and dragged into place; and when that was done, the Shaman gave orders for another such circle to be built nearby, and though that was a much smaller one yet the work of bringing the stones and setting it up was not much less, for the land must be cleared of trees and undergrowth, which had not been so for the great circle; and for that work, another two years was needed. And it became plain as the work was carried on that the spirits of the place were indeed pleased – or it might be that the Sorceress felt herself honoured and so extended her protection to them – for there was little sickness among those who came to work at the stone-moving, while the others who had not come but had stayed in their villages often sickened and grew weak as they had before. The people understood that the place among the stones was sacred, and went there only rarely, and never alone.

When at last the work was completed, the Shaman led both peoples – his own and those of Math and Arian – in a great cleansing of the places; and he set up wend-fires at the foot of each of the stones, with the greatest fire at the feet of the great Sorceress, and burned herbs on each of them; and when the fires burned low, he took the ash and smeared it on the arms and faces of all that were there, bidding them not to wash it off for it would, he said, give them protection as long as it was there. But he did not make any sacrifices of men or women or children, nor yet of animals, for that was not the custom of those days; and, indeed, he knew that any such act would bring doom on them all from the vengeful spirits of those who had been killed.

The stones still stand as the Shaman had ordered them to be placed, with the Sorceress at the head of the greater array, so that people may know that this story is true, though many of the stones have crumbled into dust in the centuries that have passed. But still the people of the valley bring offerings and place them around the stones; and there the Sorceress stands, watching the people of the valley come and go.

With the great work accomplished the Shaman now stood as the acknowledged head of all the peoples of the valley northward from the Sorceress and her retinue, until the river at last turned its course west and flowed through confused and changing channels to the sea. And the people of the valley grew in prosperity and health, and the spirits of the place were good to them, and they counted themselves blessed. They cleared the forest and planted more fields of barley; and some of the grains they ground to make flour; but more and more they brought barley to Urien, and he made barley-beer, and men held that he was possessed of a great magic that he had inherited from his father, although in truth the craft of brewing had been taught him by his mother.

In all this time, Lugos and Blanaid passed their time together with some contentment; and Math and Arian saw that their taking of their daughter to the Shaman, which had seemed to them a matter of great shame, had instead brought peace and plenty to the land.

Llyr grew up strong and healthy; his mother would often talk to him in the language of her own people rather than that of her husband; and he learned many crafts from her. Lugos continued in his hunting.

Now one day while Lugos was hunting and Llyr was asleep, Urien came to her hut bearing a beaker of barley-beer; and it seems that he told her that the brew was blessed by the spirits so that it would make men laugh and sing and forget their weariness, and he gave it to her to drink; and that was the first time that she had taken such a drink.

Of what passed in the hut nothing can be said, for none but Blanaid and Urien knew and they told no-one; but men guessed that she had become drunk and that he had taken her as if she was his wife, remembering his thought of many years past when he had first seen her in the woodlands. Blanaid showed no shame for what she and Urien had done, but rather began to look for other chances when her husband was hunting and her son asleep, so that they might meet away from other eyes. No-one dared to speak to Lugos of what they imagined, so that he went hunting as often as before with no idea of betrayal in his mind.

In time Blanaid bore another child, a daughter, and she was named Branwen, which means White Raven, for her hair was dark but her skin was as white as the snow which sometimes lit up the high fells in the wintertime. And if there were those who thought that she did not look greatly like her brother Llyr, but rather that she had something of the appearance of Urien, they kept their counsel to themselves. Still it seemed that Lugos saw nothing, but was happy in his hunting – of what the Shaman his father thought no-one knew.

Then at the last the thought came to Urien and to Blanaid that they had no need to hide away from Lugos, for they might easily come upon him when he was alone in his hunting and kill him; and then there would be none to hinder them. Urien bethought him of the words that his mother had spoken when Lugos was born and that had been remembered and often told in his hearing, that no lawful weapon could kill his brother, and that he would not die either in water or on land; and so he considered for a long time how it would be best to carry out the deed.

When it seemed to him that he had found a way that would answer, he went to his brother and said that they should go hunting together as they had done when they were boys together; and Lugos agreed, for he was without guile and thought no ill of his brother nor of his wife. And so on a warm day of spring they set out, and climbed the edge of the valley to the fells on the eastern side, for there was good hunting of deer and other game there.

As the day passed on they saw little enough game, and nothing that would have been worth the hunting; and when Lugos would have turned back, Urien called him ever on, saying that it was shame to leave their sport when they had at last come out together after so long apart; but at the last, when Lugos would have turned homewards regardless of his brother's urging, they found the track of a fine stag and followed it ever higher before they lost it in the gathering darkness.

Now they found a place where they could sleep under the over-hang of the high cliff; and Lugos said that he would keep watch first, for they had brought no fire with them to keep themselves safe and their people then had not the knowledge of the making of it. After Lugos had watched a while, Urien awoke and said that he would now keep watch in his brother's stead; and at first he watched the stars as they wheeled in the heavens, and considered in his mind whether he would indeed do what he had planned. At the last he made up his mind that he would not kill his brother, and nor would he return to Blanaid.

Even as he came to this thought, he saw in the first light of dawn a white owl sitting at the entrance of the cave with its eyes full on him; and in its talons was a snake. And suddenly the owl flew away, leaving the snake on the ground. And a madness came on Urien, and he grasped the snake behind its head and placed it on his brother's neck as he lay sleeping; and the snake fastened its fangs into his brother's throat, and then hastened away into the darkness; and Urien heard the cry of the owl, as if it had suc-ceeded in its purpose.

Lugos was not dead, and he staggered to his feet and held out his hands, imploring his brother to help him. Urien, torn between pity for his brother's pain and anger at his own deed, but still want-ing Blanaid for his own, grasped his brother by the shoulder and flung him out of the entrance of the cave, where he stood for a moment and then fell down the sheer edge of the fell. And when Urien looked after him, he could see him lying a long way below, and not moving; and he thought that his brother was dead.

Now he loosed his hair in token of mourning; and it may be indeed that he repented of what he had done. When the full light of day was on him, he returned to his home and told all whom he met that Lugos had been bitten by a snake while they were sheltering, and that his body lay at the foot of the fell.

His father looked for a long time into his eyes, and then asked him what sort of a snake it was that came upon them in the cold of the night, 'for such a thing was never known before.' He turned his back on his son and flinging his cloak around his shoulders he ran through the gate of the village. And there were those that saw him who swore that as he ran his shape changed and became that of a hawk, and that he took to the air in search of Lugos, though none now can say if this was indeed so.

Whether that was true or not, there was no doubt that before much time had passed he had found his son where he lay, and there was still life in him; and he took certain herbs from his pouch and pressed them against the wound in Lugos' neck; and he took his son in his arms and held him tight, as he did so a gentle rain began to fall.

Urien did not wait for his father's return, but went to Blanaid and took her by the hand; and she took up Branwen in her arms; but Llyr she did not take. They went at first with no fixed place in their mind, but as they went it seemed to them good to find a spot where they might be safe from the Shaman's anger, and so they went to the sacred place among the standing stones, and put themselves under the protection of the great Sorceress and the other stones which paid court to her. And there they waited for whatever might befall of good or ill.

No tale tells how long the Shaman sat on the earth with Lugos in his arms while the rain fell upon them; but at the last Lugos took a long breath and died. In the moment of his death his father saw his own folly in taking Lugos in his arms while the rain fell on them, for in this way his son had died neither standing nor lying, neither on dry land nor in water, and killed by no lawful weapon; and that he had indeed been killed by those whom he loved, the Shaman now had no doubt; and he went in his anger to find Blanaid and Urien.

It was no long searching before he came upon them as they waited for him in the great ring of stones; and as he drew near they invoked the holiness of the stones and even taunted him that he dared not shed their blood, and that of Branwen, in so sacred a place. The Shaman bowed down before the great Sorceress, and then stood facing the three; and there he put a great curse on them.

This was his curse: that they should wander through the earth and find no-one to give them succour; that they should seek peace and not find it; that all men should know of them and shun them; and that at the last they should not die as others die but move for ever in the silence of the groves, and that men would fear them and their haunting. Then his eyes saw Branwen, and he relented a little of his curse, so that she might have the common life and death of men, though she would have but little of their fellowship as long as she lived.

Urien and Blanaid and their daughter left the ring of stones; and it is said that Blanaid faded away as she grew older, and in time took on the likeness of that owl that had brought the snake to Urien in the cave; and still in that guise she roams the wood and calls out in her grief.

Urien too faded, becoming no more than a spirit in the greenwood; and from time to time – and especially in the springtime – men would see his face, ringed around with leaves, looking upon them from the depths of some thicket. As for Branwen, she did not share the fate of her parents but grew and married and had children of her own in due time; and her descendants are alive to this day.

As for Lugos, when his father returned to find his body he found that it had gone, but that in its place was a great eagle; and the eagle cast its eye upon him as if it would say Farewell and then with a great beat of its wings went soaring up to meet the sun. And the Shaman knew that Lugos had not died as others do, but had become one with the spirit of the sun. And he bowed before that great god, and went back to his own people, and no tale tells of him after this.

IV

'A fine story. So Urien kills Lugos and takes his wife, and as a punishment both Urien and Blanaid are changed into different
shapes, and Lugos becomes one with the sun. And that is the story
told by this most beautiful mural. But then, why did you have
Urien painted in your mural rather than Lugos? Why do you not
celebrate the great sun himself rather than the powers of deceit
and darkness?'

Verica turned, leading the way back to her chair. Once seated
she gave Marius almost a shy look, as if admitting to something
she would rather not say.

'It is our way, Commander, though you do not yet understand
it. Perhaps it is because we are people of the northern lands, and
are more used to dark days and nights than you are. In Rome you
celebrate your New Year in March, when the days, though short,
are already getting longer; we celebrate ours at Samhain, when it
is already dark and will soon be darker still; and just as you say
that the unconquerable power of the sun is already manifest during the darkest days of winter, so we say that the power of darkness is already afoot in summer, when we celebrate the August
Kalends.

'Be that as it may, we think that the spirit of Urien lives on in
the woods, just as Lugos lives on in the sun above; and so we pin
Urien down, paint him in a picture, put him where we can see
him. For in these northern lands the spirit of the wild woods is
still strong, and it is not a spirit to trifle with. I think that is something your countrymen found in the Teutoberg forest, and found
it again in Caledonia where the primeval forest spreads from sea
to sea in an unbroken range.'

Marius thought for a moment in silence. 'But what has this to do with us now? As time goes on, no doubt many woods will be cleared, for the man with the axe is always stronger than the tree he faces, and so it may be that a time will come when this spirit of the woods will lose his power, while the sun above will reign unconquered.'

'Your troops captured two men, yesterday, Commander; two undoubted thieves and murderers, and tomorrow you say you will crucify them at first light and leave them to hang there until their bodies rot to pieces and the crows feast on them.

'For all I care you may do that unhindered, for I will have no murder among my people. But I tell you that I know a little of these two, and most especially I know of the one who was dressed in a sheepskin, he who has a cast in his eye.

'Where he comes from at first I neither know nor care, but I know that for some years he has lived hidden in the woods not five miles from here, and that the common people believe that he can do magic, and can call up spirits to do his bidding. The people call him Urien, though whether that is his true name or not I cannot tell; but among the poor and dispossessed there are those who think that he is a god reborn, and so I warn you that when you hang him on his cross there may be those who think that you do ill.'

'You believe that people may think that a naked homeless wretch nailed to a cross is some sort of god? Surely not.'

Verica gave a wintry smile. 'I think, Commander, that what you find so incredible has already happened many years ago in another troublesome province; it would be as well for both our sakes to avoid it happening here, would it not? And so I advise you not to put the name of Urien at the head of his cross, only that the man is a thief.

'And if any trouble begins, I would counsel you to deal with it firmly, or things may quickly get out of hand. We mark Beltane with fire, Commander, and there are so very many things that can burn, are there not?'

Marius paused for a moment. 'I will think about what you say, and speak again to my officers. But remember that I command only two cohorts – fewer than a thousand men even if we were at full strength, which we are not – and many of these have been posted here and there to camps up in the hills to the east of us, and along both sides of the estuary of the Ituna, and even up into southern Caledonia, while others patrol the roads for perhaps twenty miles around. And there is your honour-guard as well, of course. With the men I have, I will do what I can.

'But at all events we are agreed that the murderers must die. And now I must ask you to forgive me, but I have many things to see to, not all of them connected to this affair.'

Verica smiled and nodded, then clapped sharply twice to summon her major domo.

Deep in thought Marius bowed and followed the man to the gate. So the maid was called Iras, was she? An unlucky name, some said, and famously the name of one of Cleopatra's maids who had died at her mistress' feet. Am I to be Antony to her Cleopatra he thought. Well, she is beautiful and rich and clever enough. After a moment's thought he dismissed the idea with a shrug. Not everything good was meant to be; but perhaps in another world…

At the gate he paused while the cob was fetched, and spurred down to join the road. It was busy still with travellers taking advantage of the first dry day for perhaps a week: a farmer driving half a dozen sheep to market, a heavily-laden wagon drawn by two oxen creaking slowly northwards to the town, urged on by a boy poking a stick up the beasts' backsides. The road, Marius thought, would stay as safe as he and his little contingent could make it, and next morning two men would be hung up to die to make his intention plain. He suspected that his tribune would rather enjoy it.

After he had left, Verica sat for a long time in silence. At last she turned to Gwydion with a smile. 'A fine man, is he not? There are many things we can agree on, I think, though surely not all.

'Some of these Romans are like fish, Gwydion. You lure them, trap them, net them, and at last they become as tame as the carp in my pool. But perhaps this one is different; so instead of fishing, I shall play him at *gwyddbwyll*, and we shall soon see which of us is the stronger.'

'*Gwyddbwyll*, my lady? Which side would you play in such a game? The side of the King, looking only to be secure? Or the side of the Attacker, hunting the King down?'

Verica laughed. 'Perhaps we shall play more than one game and see who wins the rubber. Or perhaps just one. Then I shall be the King, Gwydion, and we shall soon see if he is able to track me down, and perhaps capture me.'

She looked up as the first drops of a sudden shower began to spatter the ground around her, then rose abruptly and swept indoors. Gwydion watched her for a moment and then followed her, his face troubled.

V

A.D. VI Kal. Mai – April 27th

Rome, and blessedly warm. And Cinna and his wife were there, smiling while the steward ushered him through the atrium with its splashing fountain and tame doves, and into the dining room. And there to his delight was the gorgeous mural of Daphne and Apollo, the girl's arms transformed before his eyes into branches and her frightened face into leaves.

He turned to Cinna with a graceful compliment. 'How beautiful it is.' And Cinna bowed with pleasure, and his wife turned smiling to face them both. But now her face was the smiling face of Verica, and the dining room was no longer in Rome but unmeasured leagues away in Britannia.

And then Marius was awake. A faint red glimmer under the edge of the door showed that the lamp was still burning in its alcove beyond, but no light from outside showed around the wooden shutter that covered the window.

He lay unmoving. It was so real. What did it mean he wondered. He shook his head as if to dislodge the image of Verica and tried to guess the progress of the night by the faint sounds: a tawny owl calling far away, then the advancing and retreating thump of boots on the camp's wooden walkways as the sentries did their rounds, and from the camp sickroom someone briefly coughing. Then finally he heard the hesitant stirrings of bird-song announcing the first fading of the darkness around.

Almost time to get up, he thought, but still lay there for a little longer, listening as the birdsong slowly grew louder and more confident. Then there were other sounds, human and much nearer: whispered talk, the scrape of steel on flint as more lights were lit, the innumerable small sounds of the household waking up to the new day.

In a single fluid movement he pushed back the bed-cover and

sat naked on the edge of the bed, feeling for his light sandals with his feet, careful to ensure that it would be a lucky day by slipping on his right sandal before the left.

He stood up, stretching with his hands behind his head, then clapped twice, firmly. Almost at once the door opened with a slight scrape and Cybele came in, still rubbing the sleep from her eyes, and pushed the door closed with her shoulder. She was now, he guessed, perhaps fourteen years old. He had sent his steward to buy a girl for him not long after arriving, and he bore with good humour the ribald songs of the camp about the arrangement; he suspected that they would have been more shocked to discover how infrequently he had slept with her. Jupiter and Mars, why can't she wipe that miserable look off her face?

He bent briefly over the copper bowl that she held out, scooping up the water to wash his face, then spat into it to clear the taste of the night from his mouth. He turned away from her, letting her slip his fine woollen robe around his shoulders, then turned back to let her kneel and fasten his sandals.

'You have a visitor, Master,' she said. 'Aelius Asellio was scratching at the door as soon as I lit the first lamp.'

'Asellio? So early? Tell him to come up.'

Cybele favoured him with her customary scowl, then bobbed her head in acknowledgement. But she had hardly turned when the door swung open and a broad-shouldered man in his late forties entered. Marius smiled to himself; Marcus Aelius Asellio was not a man to waste time kicking his heels in the entrance hall.

Despite the hour he was immaculately dressed and looking as smart as a legionary on a statue; only the livid and puckered scar of a sword-cut clear across his face made it plain that he was no mere parade-ground soldier. This was his commander's Primus Pilus, the senior centurion with more than twenty years' experience fighting Rome's battles everywhere from Dacia to Germania, and a habit of beating order into the men with his vine-staff, reminding them as he did so that no treatment he could mete out to them would compare with what the barbarians would do if they got a chance.

'Centurion, you have everything in order?' The question was superfluous; everything that Marcus Asellio put his hand to was always handled competently and with the minimum of fuss.

Marcus smiled and nodded. 'Yes, sir. The punishment squad will be getting those thieving bastards on the move already, and I've put a few of our lads on a watching brief along the road just to make sure that nothing happens that might disturb the peace, if you see what I mean. If there's any trouble we'll get a squad along there and break a few heads, but we've not had any sign of anything yet. Anyway, it looks like it'll be raining again before long, and there's nothing like a good Britannia downpour to keep the troublemakers away. Too bloody lazy to fight unless they can do it in the dry, if you ask me. Which is strange, when you think about it, considering just how much it rains round here. Oh, and our famous senior tribune's hanging around keeping an eye on them; thought you'd like to know.'

Marius nodded, unsurprised. 'What about the fellow they killed? Did anyone find anything out?'

The centurion sniffed. 'I went right through his things, sir; good stuff by the look of it. Some gold, a fair bit of silver and some expensive-looking brooches and pins. Just a lot of ladies' gewgaws with garnet and lapis lazuli really. Foreign-looking stuff – Syrian, one of the jewellers said – but I hear that's the fashion these days. Exotic.' He wrinkled his lip in distaste.

'I sent three of our best lads into town with it yesterday and had them ask questions at a couple of the jewellers' stalls, and they got a decent offer for most of it so they passed it right over then and there. Won't be what it's really worth, but it's the best we'll get, I should say. Anyway there's plenty to pay for a decent funeral for the poor bastard and a bit left over for whoever it belongs to now. No name, though, so we'll probably never know who he was.'

'Any sign of religious connections? We owe him a proper send-off, after all.'

The centurion caught Marius' eye and grasped his unspoken thought: Let's show the men that if the worst comes to the worst, they'll get a proper send-off too because that's the last thing any-one can do for them.

'Elagabal would be a good guess for a Syrian, sir; if that's what he was, anyway. Sun god, apparently, sort of their version of Apollo. I'm sure he'd be willing to look after the poor bugger on his way to the underworld or whatever; if the blessed sun ever shines on us again with all this rain, that is. Too wet for the funeral at the moment anyway; you'd never get the pyre going, not even if you used plenty of oil to start the fire off.'

Marius nodded. 'Right, we'll have to keep the body cool for a few days. The money had better stay in the strongroom and we'll see if anything comes to light. You never know, some other mer-chant may show up who knows something about him, and if not then come the end of the year we'll just add it to the funeral club money. Anything else I ought to be worrying about?'

'Only the festival really, sir. I'm just nervous about the natives getting over-excited. We've seen it before; starts with a drunken fist-fight, then someone gets stabbed, our lads step in and before you know it there's a full-scale riot going.'

Marius shrugged. 'I can tell you, Marcus, for all the ambitions I had as a young man I never thought I'd end up running a police force in a provincial town in rain-sodden Britannia. Still, better nip any trouble in the bud rather than end up fighting a full-scale street-battle after things have got out of hand. Better pick half a dozen steady lads who won't get into anything they can't handle and have them patrol the streets in pairs. Tell them to keep it low-key – we don't want to provoke anything. That's all.'

Aelius Asellio saluted smartly and left, and a moment later Marius heard his boots clatter down the stairs.

Cybele was still standing there unmoving, the copper bowl clutched tight in her hands. Marius turned and tried to coax a smile from her. 'You must be used to the rain, Cybele; miserable, isn't it?'

Hesitantly the girl answered, her Latin still a little stilted as though she were translating from her own language as she spoke. 'Rain like this is not usual, Master; not day after day after day with hardly a break in the clouds. I think our gods are offended; perhaps when they see the fires at Beltane they will let the sun shine again. Or perhaps they are telling us that they want proper sacrifices, sacrifices like we used to offer them.'

Marius frowned. 'Men and women burnt alive at the command of some unwashed Druid? That will never happen where Rome rules, not even if Deucalion's Flood were to threaten to come again.'

'Not always the fire, Master. The druids used to know which sacrifice was needed. The gods and goddesses of the rivers ask for sacrifices too.'

'Offered at the water's edge with the victim's blood running into the stream? Or trodden down into some marsh? Yes, I've heard of such things in Germania, and in Gaul as well. It will not happen again; there are new ways now, and the gods of this province will have to come to terms with them.'

Cybele looked askance, but made a brief bow in silence. Marius gave her a curt nod and headed downstairs with the girl close on his heels.

At the foot of the stairs his steward Flavius was already waiting. Marius nodded to him too, this time the friendly nod that recognised the long years that Flavius had served his family – indeed, to Marius' mind the man had hardly changed from the stooped, balding but good-humoured fellow he had known as a child. He remembered with embarrassment how after his father's death he had offered to give Flavius his freedom, and how the man had reacted with shocked outrage, as if he was being dismissed and sent away.

At last now he could turn his attention to breakfast: hot oatmeal washed down with a cup of mint tea. And then from the tiles overhead he heard an all-too-familiar drumming sound, warning that the rain had once again started to fall.

Oh for warm, dry Rome. But the face was Verica's.

VI

In the little lean-to shed behind the Eagle, Messalina began to stir, wakened by the drumming of rain on the roof and the first sounds of the new day – a crying baby, two cocks crowing, voices of women fetching water from the fountain in the forum. Senorix had fallen asleep lying on her left arm, and gently she tried to wriggle free without disturbing him.

But he woke just as she was about to sit up. 'Where are you going, girl? Sneaking off? Come here.' He pulled her down, but she shook her head. 'I can't stay. Master and Mistress will be wanting me to fetch water and get their breakfast.'

Senorix gave her a wolfish grin. 'Let them wait.' He reached out and cupped her breast in his hand, but she pushed him away. 'They'll hit me if I keep them waiting. Or perhaps Mistress will scratch my face again.'

She stood up and brushed straw off her legs and hair, half-pulled on her tunic as she went to the door, then suddenly turned with a grin, 'Oh, go on, then. Just a quickie, mind.'

As Aelius Asellio had promised, the punishment squad had begun their work before first light. There were four of them, and they set to their task with a will, hoping to get the worst of the job done before a crowd had gathered.

They pulled the killers screaming out of the cellar where they had spent the time since their arrest, kicked them into silence, and dragged them through the mud to the whipping posts standing ready at the back of the parade ground. Quickly they bound them to the posts by their wrists, fastened so high that their feet barely touched the ground and their faces were pressed again the wood.

The *optio* in charge stood back for a moment, as if considering whether there was any fight left in the men, then pulled back the head of the taller of the two and spat copiously into his face, watching as the spittle ran down his chin.

'Not much of a day for it, lads; it's crosses for the pair of you, but don't worry, we'll make sure that you get everything that's coming to you. Gods, you don't understand a word I'm saying, do you? Well, you'll get the drift soon enough.'

He turned away in disgust. 'Right, you, get those things off them.' he ordered, motioning with his head at the youngest member of the squad. 'There's nothing there worth having, just cut it all off.'

In moments the men hung naked and shivering with cold and terror in the dawn light; and as they waited, the spring rain began to fall again.

'Pretty little flowers, aren't they? Olympus, don't they ever wash? They stink the place out. Right, let's give them something to dance for.'

The killers were twisting their heads, trying to see what was about to happen, but Marcellus, the squad's whip-man, stepped up smartly behind them, took a deep breath, and began to lay the knotted cords around the dark-haired man's shoulders.

Blood flowed almost at once, running mingled with the rain down his back. Now his partner made frantic efforts to free himself from his stake, twisting and scrabbling with his bare feet at the ground. But Marcellus was taking his time, carefully opening up the shoulders of his first criminal, working with the quiet satisfaction of a man dispensing justice and enjoying himself at the same time, ignoring the pleas and screams.

'And now it's your turn,' he muttered at last, turning his attention to the second. 'This is nothing compared to what comes next, you murdering little bastard.'

Again the blood, the screams and entreaties; but the second man was weaker than the first and lapsed quickly into unconsciousness.

The optio laid a restraining hand on Marcellus' shoulder. 'Gods, aren't they pathetic? Happy to slit someone's throat when they thought they could get away with it, but look at them now. But we don't want to kill him here, do we? Make it too easy, that would.

'Right, lads, let's get on with the job. Cut them down and we'll get moving. And if that squint-eyed little thug doesn't wake up, get a branding iron and burn him until he does.'

But the man was already groaning back to consciousness as the ropes around his wrists were cut, though within moments he collapsed face-forward into the mud.

With practised efficiency two of the squad were already fetching the cross-beams. Unceremoniously they dropped them onto the men's shoulders, ignoring their screams as the rough timber pressed against the wounds left by the whip, and then pulled their arms back and tied their wrists to the wood. Then both men were hauled to their feet and hustled through the camp.

They were driven the long way around, staggering under the weight of the timbers but kicked and beaten if they hesitated or stumbled; first a complete circuit of the camp as the troops jeered and the gouts of blood fell on the already-soaking ground, then out and through the North Gate and onto the highway.

A little way along the road and the dark-haired man lost his footing on the wet road and collapsed full on his face, breaking his nose and smashing his teeth; for a while he lay senseless on the ground, blood pouring from his mouth, while the little group waited and the rain fell. Finally he stirred into consciousness and was at once dragged to his feet and pushed on his way.

Within a quarter of a mile they reached the execution ground. An expectant crowd was already gathering despite the early hour and the rain. News of the forthcoming executions had spread quickly, and a good crucifixion tends to bring out the curious, the bloodthirsty and the idle, as well as those who regard it as a sensible way of preventing future crime. They stood perhaps a hundred strong, men and women and even a few children, their heads and shoulders shielded from the weather by their hoods.

Afterwards, most of those watching at the beginning remembered two things especially: the sounds, and the smells.

The sounds first. The mechanical sounds, of course – the thumping of hammers, the creak of wood. Then the natural sounds: the sighing of the wind and the relentless drumming of the chill rain, soaking cloaks and tunics and flesh.

Then the human sounds: the steady voices of the squad, the stream of one of the soldiers pissing against the foot of the first cross to go up, the mutterings and shouted curses of those watching. And then the animal sounds: the stray dogs barking, the distant sound of sheep on a hillside and cows lowing in the market.

Above all of these were the inhuman, ghastly sounds of two men who would scream in agony, one breath after another until, perhaps after three or four hours, their voices failed them and there were only groans, and after that only rasping breath, until at last, perhaps after another day, even that would fall silent. The optio, it was plain, was a man who knew his work and did it well: here there would be neither quick deaths nor blessed unconsciousness to ease the pain. And so the message goes out to the crowd: this is the penalty for murder and theft: avoid it.

The smells were worse.

First there was the unmistakable stink of fear; then of blood, of mud and vomit and piss and shit. Before Beltane was finished those venturing on the road northwards from the town would hurry past the hanging bodies, faces averted, making the sign against the evil eye and muttering a prayer to the gods to save them from any such fate.

Few stayed for long in the crowd watching the scene; a few with delicate stomachs left quickly while others waited only until both crosses had been hauled upright and dropped into their sockets before they bustled off to attend to the ordinary business of the day, perhaps promising themselves that they would pass by again later when time served. It did not seem there would be any need to hurry back.

But as some left, others arrived. Perhaps news of the crucifixion had only now reached them, or perhaps they were travellers coming to the town, unaware of the scene being enacted not far from the North Gate. A few of these – those that could read and understand Latin – noticed the word *latro* – thief – daubed onto the board above each killer's head; and a very few perhaps wondered why it was that on neither cross had the name of the victim been added to the placard. The first morning passed amid blood and rain, and the punishment squad begin to relax; and finally the watching crowd began to thin out while above them the slow agonies continued. Death was content, it seemed, to bide his time.

Around noon the rain slackened a little and the crowd began to grow once more; the hanging victims still moved in spasmodic jerks, but their heads were bent forward and their groans were quieter. In the last hour or so both had fouled themselves in their agony, and the stink still hung in the air.

Despite the smell the little execution party broke out their lunch rations and now stood at ease munching bread and cheese and a few olives; the optio broke the seal on the little flask of sharp wine hanging from his waist and passed it around the troop. After each man had taken a gulp, the optio held out the flask towards the nearest of the crucified men, waiting until he saw the man's one good eye fixed on him.

'Want some, do you? Come on, it's yours for the taking.' He laughed as a spasm passed across the tortured face, then slowly and deliberately tipped the flask, shaking out the last few drops of wine onto the ground. Then he laughed and turned with exaggerated sympathy to the crowd. 'None left. What a shame. Perhaps he'd like to drink my piss instead.'

He knew it was a mistake as soon as he spoke the words; where before the little knot of watchers had been almost completely silent there was now a sullen muttering, though he was unable to catch the words.

'All right, shut it. Just shut up and watch the show, all right.' He turned back to the hanging man, and as he did so a stone came flying out of the group and caught him on the shoulder.

It was only a little stone, the sort that might have been picked up at the wayside, and the *optio's* thick cloak saved him from even a scratch, but his temper suddenly broke and he turned again to the crowd; this time his Spanish sword was in his hand. Behind him he heard a soft sigh as his men too drew their blades, automatically falling into formation behind their officer with their backs to the crosses.

By now the crowd was perhaps a couple of hundred strong, and the optio suddenly realised that more stones would quickly bring his little squad to their knees. But Marcellus had thrust his sword back into its scabbard, had pulled the whip from his belt and was beginning to advance on the crowd, swinging the lead-weighted cords around his head as he did so.

The threat was all that was needed; sullenly the crowd drew back, leaving a clear space perhaps two spears' length around the squad. The *optio* held out his sword, then thrust it back into the sheath with a flourish, as if to draw a line under the incident, though he still kept his hand on the hilt.

There was a moment's silence, broken only by the hiss of falling rain and the groans of the men on the crosses. Then suddenly the one whom the optio had taunted spoke, loudly and clearly – not the voice of a man dying in agony but a firm voice that carried clear across the execution ground; and to the *optio's* amazement he spoke in good Latin, without a trace of the nasal British accent.

'Three times, and the third will be the greatest. Three times, and the third will be the greatest.'

He paused and then spoke again, this time in what the soldiers recognised as the local dialect, and though they could not interpret the words they all realised that he must be saying the same thing again in the language that most of the onlookers could understand.

The optio scanned the faces of the crowd wondering what they would make of the sudden outburst, but they seemed as uncertain as he was. Without turning away from the crowd he glanced over his shoulder; but the man had collapsed again, as though the effort of speech had drained his last strength; already he was sagging low, and in his throat there was the tell-tale rattle that warned he would soon be dead.

The optio turned his head to look at the second man, but he seemed lost in a private world of agony, unaware of anything that had happened.

'Right, lads, looks like one of them's getting ready to go and introduce himself to Charon; best keep a close eye on the crowd till he goes, they don't seem to care about the other one.'

'Shall I break his legs?' muttered the whip-man. 'Speed things up a bit? Give him a last little taste of what happens to murdering bastards before he goes off and explains himself to Rhadamanthus?'

The optio hesitated for a moment, uncertain of how the crowd might react; then he nodded. 'Just the talkative one,' he added, 'the other can stay up there and wriggle as long as he likes.'

The man lifted his whip again and with great deliberation smashed the heavy handle against the crucified man's knees, first the right and then the left. Each blow brought a scream of agony from the man, and a murmur arose again from the crowd. But within minutes a bloody froth appeared on the victim's lips, and then a tinge of blue about his mouth. As the crowd and the soldiers watched he gave a final convulsion, then the last of his breath left his body in a long-drawn-out gasp, and he hung motionless and silent.

'One down, so to speak, and one to go. Thought he'd last a bit longer, but these Britons aren't as tough as they like to think. Gods, I've seen Gauls and Germans last three or four days up there, not peg out after a few hours; where's the fun in that? Still, perhaps his mate will do better.'

His hood over his head, Senorix wandered among the booths in the little forum until turning a corner he spotted a giant shoe hanging over one of the shops. To his surprise there was a woman sitting behind the counter, perhaps fifty years of age and with a weather-beaten face.

She glanced up from her work and smiled at him, then waved him to one of the stools that had been carefully pulled under the awning to keep them dry. 'I make good boots and shoes. Look at this.' She held up the little ladies' shoe that she was working on, the calf-skin delicately punched with flower designs. 'Nearly finished now. Just needs my maker's mark burned into the sole. Too pretty to wear in this rain, though. Now, what can I do for you?'

Senorix was already fingering the leather samples on her counter-top. 'How long to make me a decent pair of boots? And how much?'

The relief squad arrived in the late afternoon – a pair of hard Dacians and a couple of raw local recruits who needed blooding, with the smart new tribune Gracchus in charge. The optio, who shared his commander's view of the man, rather suspected that he had volunteered for the job and would give it his meticulous attention; within minutes of his arrival he was studying the hanging body of the first thief, and was even feeling the muscles in the man's legs for the onset of rigor mortis.

'All yours now, tribune; one down and one to go. I'd keep half an eye on the crowd too, if I were you; they've been pretty quiet most of the time, but they looked like trouble once or twice.'

The tribune gave a superior smile. 'So I hear; the Commander would like a little word with you when you get back to camp; just you, optio, and right away if you please. He said that the others can get straight to the bath-house and clean up, but there's a couple of points he'd like to clear up with you right away. I really can't imagine what that's all about.'

The condescending smile suggested that the tribune knew perfectly well what was in Marius' mind but preferred to keep it to himself. He turned back to the dead man on the cross and started to study the wound in his feet where the massive nail had gone home, then turned back. 'Don't let me keep you, will you? I'm sure you can't wait to get back.'

'Pompous bastard,' muttered the whip-man as the squad trailed back to the camp. 'Thinks he's in the Senate already, doesn't he. Bastard.'

♕ ♕ ♕ ♕ ♕ ♕ ♕

It was late in the evening when Messalina brought the last few empty wine-cups into the little washroom at the back of the Eagle and dropped them with a careless splash into the wooden tub on the floor; then she wandered back into the main room and started to gather the little clay lamps which were still flickering in their niches high on the walls, carefully snuffing each one as she picked it up.

Holding the last lamp high to give as much light as possible she made sure that the bar across the door was firmly in place, and then checked the shutters. Then she yawned, tugged off her grubby tunic for a pillow and lay down in her little alcove, leaving the curtain open so that her master would not suspect that she had run away if he should choose to look in.

She gave a last glance around the room to be quite sure that she was alone, then dug her fingers under the straw mattress until she found the little crack in the boards; there. She pulled them apart with her fingernails and fished out from underneath the cloth bag with her precious stash of coins in it, a few tips from her customers and the odd coin that she had sneaked from the change when she had been sent out shopping. Today there would be nothing to add to it, but it gave her comfort to know that her cache was safe and undiscovered, and she ran the thin coppers between her fingers as eagerly as any Greek banker counting his gold.

Reassured that nothing was missing she held up the lamp in her left hand, wet the thumb and forefinger of her right and prepared to pinch the wick; but before she could do so there was a sudden thunderous knocking at the door, five sudden hard blows that seemed to set the whole room shaking.

Frightened she sat up. 'Who is it?' she called.

No answer, just a repeated knocking, five spaced beats that rattled the door.

She hesitated; she dared not open the door, and yet she knew Bran would certainly give her a black eye if she kept one of his friends standing in the street. Silently she slipped out of her alcove, leaving the lamp still standing on the floor, and started to tiptoe towards the sound; then, on an afterthought, she turned and picked up her tunic where it was lying crumpled at the end of her bed. For the third time there were five hard blows on the door, and this time at last there was a voice.

'Wake up in there. Let me in, you idle little tart. Do I have to rouse the whole town?' And again, five deliberate blows on the door. A little emboldened, Messalina called out, 'Who is it? What do you want?'

'I want to come in, you stupid whore. Now open the door before I kick it down.'

She pulled on her tunic and crept closer to the door; there was a peep-hole in it, but when she stood on tiptoe to see through it there was nothing visible except the glare of a torch.

Nervously she laid her hand on the bar which kept the door closed, but still didn't dare to lift it. She was still wavering when she heard the stairs at the back of the room creak and Bran came down, carrying in his right hand the fine bronze lamp from his bedroom; he had pulled on his ordinary clothes and was carrying a blackthorn cudgel in his left hand.

He stood for a moment, considering. 'Lift the bar, girl, let's see who it is.'

Messalina eyed the cudgel then hauled the bar out of its sockets. Almost at once the door burst open and Senorix strode in, a lighted torch in his hand and a wild look in his eye.

Bran looked at him in unbelieving fury for a moment, then grabbed the torch and stamped it out on the floor.

'In the name of all the gods, what are you playing at? Drink and whore all you like, and stay up all night to do it, but the rest of us have to get some sleep. And I don't need you to burn the place down, either.'

Senorix gave him a cross-eyed look and then burst out in a wild laugh. Drunk as a senator, thought Bran. 'Messalina, take him out to the shed and stay with him until he goes to sleep. No, stay there all night and keep him company again, he pays good money even if he can't hold his booze.'

Senorix looked as if he was about to argue, then gave a little bow. 'Aye, she's a good girl, and a good earner for you I dare say. Perhaps I'll buy her from you, she knows some tricks that would make me a rich man back home.'

He flung his right arm around Messalina's shoulder, reaching down to squeeze her breast. She stifled a yawn then dutifully giggled and put her left arm round his waist.

Bran watched them out of the door, then slammed it shut and banged the bar back in place; then he picked up the last clay light that she had been carrying, snuffed the wick, and looked carefully around the room by the gleam from of his own bronze lamp.

The little bag of coins still sitting on the mattress in Messalina's alcove caught his eye and he stepped over to see what it was; he picked it up, shook out the little heap of coppers, counted them quickly, and took them up the stairs with him, vowing as he did so that his slave would have a painful lesson to learn in the morning.

VII

A.D. VI Kal. Mai – April 28th

In the end, though, it was Morrig, Bran's wife, who took upon herself the disciplining of Messalina. Herself raw-boned and big-built, she had quickly become jealous of the little slave, certain that she was playing around with her husband when business was quiet. When Bran told her what he had found, and – worse – when she had to cook the morning's porridge herself because Messalina was still out in the shed with Senorix, she was filled with a cold fury; and while Bran would have contented himself with giving the girl a few strokes on the legs with a hazel-switch, she had other ideas in mind.

None of this showed in her face when Messalina finally came yawning through the door just as Morrig was clearing the por-ridge-bowls away. Instead she gave the girl a smile. 'I have some shopping to do,' she said. 'You will come and carry the basket.'

With no breakfast inside her, and the smell of the porridge all around the room, Messalina's heart sank; but she lowered her head obediently and waited for her mistress.

Once out in the street, Morrig motioned the girl to walk beside her rather than the customary two steps behind, and then began to talk confidentially to her.

'Did you hear about the crucifixions, my dear?'

'Yes, Mistress.'

'A terrible business. One of the men died quite quickly, I hear, but they do say the other is still hanging on. This will be his second day; all that time on the cross, knowing that he is dying; really ter-rible.'

Messalina nodded, wondering where the conversation was going. For a while her mistress was silent as she looked round the stalls on the little forum. Then she went on, 'The crows took out the eyes of the first man after he was dead, you know.'

The girl shuddered at the thought, but her mistress went on, 'And with the second one, they didn't even wait for him to die. Yesterday evening it was, they just came and pecked his eyes right out as if he were a sick lamb in the field. Can you imagine such a thing?'

Again Morrig was silent as she poked around the stall, making a show of looking at the radishes on one stall, and then at the sheep's cheese on another.

'I suppose I shouldn't feel sorry for them, though. The signs on the crosses said what they'd done. *Latro*, it said. Do you know what that means, Messalina dear?'

'No, Mistress.'

'Well, my dear, it means thief, because that is what happens to thieves, you see. They are nailed up naked on crosses for everyone to see, and the crows peck their eyes out, and then in the end they die.'

This time Morrig stopped in front of a butcher's stall, with bloody and fly-blown sides of beef and pork hanging from hooks. She felt some of them critically, waving the flies away with her hand, then went on conversationally, 'And you are a thief too, Messalina, are you not, stealing money from your kind master and mistress? Perhaps I should take you to the soldiers now and ask them to strip you and whip you and nail you up beside the other thieves?'

A look of horror passed over the slave-girl's face as she remembered the little bag of coins. In an instant she was kneeling on the sodden ground where the blood had dripped from the carcasses, clutching at Morrig's knees in terror.

Morrig felt a sudden thrill of power, but still went on smiling sweetly. 'Stand up, my dear. There will be no cross for you; not this time. But your master and I are very angry with you; we have taken you in, fed you, clothed you, given you shelter; and this is how you repay us for all that we have done. Because you see, Messalina, without us you would have nothing at all – no food, no clothes, nowhere to go when the winter comes. Perhaps we should brand you on your face as a thief – think of that burning iron on your cheek, Messalina. Or your breast perhaps, that would be better. And then just send you away. No one will take in a thief, you know, so you will starve on the street.'

Messalina was now grovelling on the ground, hysterically kissing Morrig's feet, and begging, ' No, Mistress, don't burn me, Mistress, please don't let me starve.'

Morrig paused to drink in the full pleasure of what she was doing, then went on, 'No, Messalina, this time we shall forgive you once we know how sorry you are. So I shall beat you until I think you are truly sorry enough. And hush that terrible noise; there will be no wailing in the street, not unless you want a double beating; I don't want some sobbing wretch walking around here with me and making everyone stare. You will be silent and dry your eyes until we get home, and then I shall give you plenty to shout and cry about.

'Your master shall hold you down while I beat your skinny little backside so hard that you will think of it every time you lie down for the next week. And in your line of work you do have to lie down such a lot, do you not, my dear? I do hope for your sake that none of your customers complains.'

And then, as another thought occurred to her, she went on conversationally, 'Of course, we shall leave the door open while you're being beaten, so people can come to watch. Some men like that sort of thing, you know. There's always quite a crowd when someone gets fastened up to the whipping post in the forum. You can hear the screaming from miles away. But first we shall walk around and look at all the stalls, and you will be my obedient slave and smile at me politely, and all the time you can think of what will happen to you as soon as we get home.' Again the sweet smile as she bent down to haul Messalina to her feet.

For the next hour Messalina trailed miserably around the little square behind Morrig, her shoulders hunched and forcing back her tears whenever they threatened to burst out. Only once did Morrig buy anything, not even bothering to bargain for it, a smart little leather pony-whip from a stall selling bronze horse-charms and odds and ends of tack. She swished it experimentally through the air four or five times, then gave it to Messalina to carry with a look that left her in no doubt of what it would be used for.

At last they turned back to the Eagle. There were two men in there already, old cronies of Bran called Crotos and Apuleios, both with their faces deep in their wine-cups; Bran had a besom in his hand with which he was clearing the rubbish from the floor and sweeping it out onto the street.

'Well, I think we're all ready now, aren't we,' said Morrig. Lean right forward over that table, Messalina; and Bran, my dear, will you stop your sweeping and stand over there at the other side and hold her hands? The time has come for her to learn her lesson.' She turned to the two drinkers, adding, 'You gentlemen can watch what happens here to thieving little sluts.'

With her left hand she pulled up the girl's tunic; Messalina tried to turn around to watch her, then started to sob loudly, begging for forgiveness and promising that she would never steal again. Morrig simply ignored her and tapped the pony-whip against her backside, provoking a louder wail, then lifted it high, ready to deliver a blow with all her considerable strength.

'That yelling's no cure for a hangover I can tell you.' Senorix was standing in the open doorway, one hand clutching his head. 'I've no doubt the girl deserves it, but would you mind holding on until the pounding in my head stops?'

Morrig looked at him in annoyance, still holding the whip high.

'Deserves it? The slut ought to be happy she's only getting a beating and nothing worse, little thief that she is.'

'The beating's one thing, it's all the yowling that goes with it that's bothering me,' said Senorix. 'Can't it wait a little? Get me some beer to settle my head first. And anyway, I have a tale to tell.'

Bran let go of Messalina's hands and she stood up uncertainly. Morrig reluctantly shrugged, then muttered, 'Well, it'll give her longer to think about it. Go on, you lazy little whore, clean your face and go and fetch the water from the fountain; do you think all your chores are going to do themselves?'

Messalina stood up, wiped her face with her sleeve and tugged down her tunic before running out of the door, brushing against Senorix as she went. Only when she was safely out in the street did she realise that he had pressed something into her palm as she went past.

Making sure that no-one could see her she peered between her fingers. There was a bright copper *duponius* there, a whole half-*sestertius*, more money than she had ever had for herself in her life. Hiding it tightly in her fist she hurried round to the back of the Eagle and picked up the water pitcher.

Inside the tavern, Senorix sat down and put his elbows on the table, all signs of his hangover vanished. 'Bring the beer first,' he said. 'Then I'll tell you a story.'

VIII

Morrig hesitated, weighing up in her mind whether to stay or bustle upstairs; it had the air of men's business about it but somehow also of money, and the money-box was her particular kingdom. Senorix raised a quizzical eyebrow at her and pushed up on the bench to make room. 'You seem like a lady who knows money when she sees it,' he smiled. 'Just the person we need, a very Juno keeping an eye on all her husband's affairs.'

Bran's brow knotted for a moment, uncertain whether the reference was to Jupiter's famous girl-chasing or to cash, but Senorix clapped him on the back with a grin, showing the great gap where all his front teeth should have been. Then he drained the jug, wiped his mouth on his hand and went on, 'Now man, did you do as I said and take a good look at that coin I gave you when I arrived?'

'I look at everyone's money,' muttered Bran. 'You should see the rubbish some people try to buy wine with.'

'And you saw nothing about it? Man, you should look at what's in front of your eyes. Do you still have it about you somewhere? Ah no, it'll have gone to this fine lady here to put safe away I'm thinking.'

'It's with the rest; it seemed good.' She turned to Senorix, ready to accuse him of cheating them and then boasting about it, but he gave her a good natured wink and pulled up the leather bag that hung from his neck under his tunic and tipped the contents onto the table.

'It's no matter, there's more here just as good,' he said. 'Some from the same minting, too.' He spread out the silver with a quick movement of his hand, picked up one of the pieces seemingly at random and scooped the rest back into the bag, glancing as he did so at the faces around him and noting how Crotos and Apuleios were both staring fixedly at the coins.

'Look at that now, all of you. A bonny thing, isn't it? See, there's a man's face on the one side – and whose would that be, d'you think? – and on the other side there's a picture of a little naked laddie sitting on a globe with stars all around him.' He sighed, almost regretfully, then went on,' Aye, it's a bonny thing to be sure.

'Now, whose face are you supposing that would be on there? Or perhaps there's one of you can read what it says round the edge? Come on, either side will do.'

Morrig took the coin and tipped it so that the light from the doorway fell on it more clearly.

'The words are all run together,' she muttered, then went on, 'The Divine Domitian, is that right?'

'Aye, that's right; he put his name on both sides so there'd be no question about it, it seems. Not a man to cross, by all accounts; they say he murdered his brother who was Emperor before him, and that wasn't either the start or the end of his villainy. Still, there's this to be said of him, he put more silver in the coins than they used to do, and a poor man has to be grateful for that.' Senorix reached across and took the coin back from Morrig and then slipped it back into the bag with the others.

'For a poor man, you seem to have a lot of them.'

'Well, I work hard for what I have, trading my kine up and down between here and Caledonia; but I got this pretty piece and its fellows on the same day I lost my teeth, and whenever I bite into a crust of bread I try to tell myself that I got a good exchange.'

He paused and glanced at the empty jug, then passed it back to Morrig. 'You must pay the singer for his song, they say.'

Without a word Morrig passed the jug straight across to Bran, who hurried from his seat to refill it, then brought it back still foaming from the jar.

Senorix waited until he was sure he had everyone's attention, then went on almost as an aside, 'You see, that little lad on the coin there sitting on the world and playing with the stars, you'd think it was just a pretty fancy; but the people who made that, they really think these things.'

He gave what might almost have been a shy smile before adding, 'I was a pretty fine-looking man back in the days when this money was new-made; and there were a few thousand more who looked no worse, I dare say. How many? They talk of thousands and tens of thousands, but I was never one to count them.

'And the people who think that they sit on the world and play with the stars, well it seems that all that they had wasn't enough for them and so they wanted what little we had as well. And me and the other lads, we didn't take kindly to that way of seeing things.'

'Mons Graupius,' muttered Bran.

'Aye, that's what they call it now; far up in Caledonia, where there was nothing for them but the dreadful fear that someone else might have something that they did not.

'It was a proper battle, too, the sort of pitched set-to that there's not been since I was a bairn. But the Romans were spoiling for a real fight, and I dare say that the know-it-all senators back in Rome had been telling the governor over in Londinium that all it needed was one more big push and he'd have the whole island in his grasp.

'Perhaps he even believed that himself. For certain he'd laid the ground well enough, with a whole fleet of ships bringing up men and supplies, and auxiliaries of every sort from just about every corner of the Empire: sling-shot men and cavalry and archers, and a good number of proper legionaries to put a bit of leaven in the lump. The Ninth were there, with the others – I'll always have a special spot in my heart for them.

'So there we were all ready to have it out once and for all. Our lads were all lined up on this hillside, with the Romans down below in the glen; and their only way up was through bracken and briar and gorse and heather; and there was a wee burn that cut down through the space between us that they'd have to cross before they could come to grips. And the ground was too rough for them to be able to bring up their big catapults; too rough for our chariots, too, and though a few of them went racing up and down to show willing, once things got going we never saw them again.

'The great pine forest came down behind us, so the Romans wouldn't have known for sure if we had more men hiding there in reserve; and it left us a clear space to retreat if we needed to. I knew nothing about strategy or tactics then, but it seemed a pretty good spot to me. Gods, I was green back then.

'We even had speeches before we set to, though I was so far back that I couldn't hear what was said right enough; something about the Romans turning the land into a desert and calling it peace, if I remember right. And the Romans had their holy chickens out, running around and pecking at the grain they threw down; we all had a good laugh when we saw that, and some of the lads started cackling like hens at them.

'Then they shooed the birdies back into their coops and came at us, right up the hill and over the burn as unstoppable as the tide coming up the beach. Twenty paces away they stopped and flung their spears at us and then linked shields the way they have, and waited while their sling-shot men pelted us with stones.

'That was hard to take; the lad who was standing to my right who'd been laughing and clucking away at the Romans a few moments before went down like a felled tree, and lay gurgling and thrashing about with a stone sticking half out of his forehead. That's when I had the first idea that this wasn't going to be the wonderful victory that I'd been expecting.

'Not that we didn't show up well, mind. One group of our men was ordered round to go forward and try to turn their flank, but their cavalry were on them as quick as lightening and put an end to that; and so we had no choice but to set to, man to man and sword to sword.

'There were perhaps only a quarter as many of them as there were of us, but by all the gods there was enough good blood shed that day to turn that hillside into a quagmire; and most of that blood was ours, for there was no doubt that the Romans fought stronger and with more discipline than we did. They say that men who've been in a battle can still hear it and see it in their dreams years later. If that's true, then I thank all the gods that it hasn't happened to me, and I pray that it never will; but the smell, now, of the pine of the forests and the stench of sweat and the blood mingling with it, that I'll carry to my dying day.

'I was one of the lucky ones, or the wise ones as it may be; I ran away and hid in the forest while I still had the use of my legs. I was ashamed of it then, but as the years have passed the shame of it has grown less. And the strange thing is that when enough of us had turned tail and bolted, there was suddenly no-one left for the Romans to fight; it was just them and the dead alone, with the forest all around. Oh, they came looking for us right enough, but they found no-one.

'In the end I think it was the forest that beat them, all those unending leagues of pine and birch; but whatever the reason was, within a couple of days they struck their camp and marched back south again, as if they'd done whatever it was they'd set out to do. So I suppose you could say that we won by default, though there were plenty of brave lads who never lived to see the day. It seems that it's not easy these days to tell your victories from your defeats; but it was their general that got given a triumph in Rome.'

'And the teeth?'

'I was coming to that, and the money too.'

Senorix picked up the jug of beer and raised it to his lips, then put it down again untasted, and shook his head slowly at some secret memory. Then he went on, 'I supposed that some great general would say that his men regrouped and harried the retreating invaders; but the plain truth of it is that a bunch of us lads came together in the forest and decided to follow them, just wondering if we might be able to pick off a few stragglers. Maybe there were twenty of us, maybe a few more. Perhaps I was hoping to get my honour back after running away; perhaps we all were.

'We weren't exactly equipped for a fight; most of us still had swords of some kind, but they were pretty poor stuff compared to what the Romans were carrying, and of course none of us had any sort of armour at all. And all we had for food was the remains of the girdle-cakes that our mothers and sisters had baked for us days before. By all the gods, we were a pretty hopeless crew as we sneaked around in the forest, trying to fool ourselves that we were brave.

'Two days we followed the soldiers as they clumped their way back south to their forts, and we saw at once that there was no chance of catching anyone unawares; tight formations they had, a proper rear-guard, their wounded carried on litters slung between horses, and a general who seemed to be everywhere at the same time, riding up and down the line from dawn to dusk, chivvying his men into order, never stopping for a rest or a drink or to ease his aching limbs.

'I watched him from the trees, and as I did so I learned a lot about soldiering from him. The gods know he'd killed enough of those who were dear to me; but for what happened afterwards I'd share a drink with him any day and bear him no ill-will, though I much doubt if he'd return the compliment.

'Then late in the afternoon of the third day, we got lucky. The army was fording a wide burn, high up at the upper reaches of Bodotria where the trees come right down to the road, and a proper professional job they made of it, with scouts sent ahead and cavalry to guard their flanks, and some of their sling-shot men ready to let fly if even a squirrel came near. And we sat up in the trees, my friends and I, and watched and wondered, and felt our stomachs rumble for hunger.'

Senorix paused and stood up. 'You can have the rest of the

story in a minute. I'm going out for a piss.'

He pushed through the door into the street and squelched down the muddy alley at the side and turned to face the wall. A little further down the alley, Messalina was busily stacking empty amphorae, but when she saw Senorix she hurried to his side.

'Master...'

He hushed her and finished his business, then pulled down his tunic and turned to her. 'Your mistress won't forget your whipping, you know. You still have that to look forward to, girl.'

Messalina dropped her gaze and nodded. 'Thank you for the money, Master.'

Senorix held her tightly by both wrists. 'I have another coin like that for you, if you can earn it.'

The girl's eyes opened wide. 'Oh yes, Master. What do you want me to do?'

'When your mistress gives you your whipping, you must take it in silence. It won't make it hurt any less, and it may even get her angry enough to make her beat you all the harder; but if you can take whatever she hands out to you without yelling and screaming, then I'll give you as much again. It's your reward for showing you can be brave. And now learn the sense to hide your treasure somewhere where your master and mistress can't find it.'

For a moment he still held her wrists tight; then with a grunt he let go of her and turned back down the alley, leaving Messalina staring after him.

IX

The little group around the table was still sitting unmoving as Senorix sat down again and went on with his tale.

'It was plain that there were that many of them that they'd take a while crossing that burn, and as troop after troop went over the water you could see the mud on the banks get more and more churned up. The whole land round there was what we'd call a carse, fine and dry in the summer, good enough to plant barley on maybe, but sodden wet in the winter; and the autumn was well on by now, and the ground was softening up nicely.

'But for all the mud, they kept going just as they'd kept coming up that hillside after us; and then it began to rain, a downpour that soaked us to the skin as we roosted up there in the trees like birds. And as the rain fell, the burn began to rise, and the mud got worse, and you didn't need to understand their language to tell that things weren't going right down below, with oxen and donkeys and men slipping and sliding in the filth, and a lot more shouting and swearing than we'd heard in all the days before.

'But they got on with it for all that, and then just when they were almost done, one of their carts – the last but one, as it happens – got stuck fast in the ford. There was a bit of a wait while they unhitched more oxen from the cart in front that had just got over, and they fetched up men to stand in the water and shove as if their lives depended on it; and the upshot of that was only that the axle broke and the whole thing tipped on its side, with the rising burn getting stronger against it all the time.

'There was a big, beefy centurion in charge, and he didn't hesitate for a moment. A couple of quick orders and the men started unloading everything and handing it all up onto the bank. When they'd done they tried to give the broken cart a quick heave-ho down the stream to clear the ford, for there was still the one wagon and the rear-guard waiting to get across.

'The more they pushed and swore, the harder that wagon got stuck; and the burn was rising all the time with the rain still coming down, and some of the men were finding it hard to keep on their feet in the current. The centurion wasn't too troubled, though; he had some rope brought up from somewhere, perhaps ten fathoms of it or so, and had the men tie it round their waists to stop them from being swept away; and then he made the only mistake anyone had made all that day and called some of the rear-guard forward to help.

'By now the light was starting to go down there under the trees; and we lads could see that the good order I'd been admiring was fraying badly at the edges; their minds were dead-set on getting the ford clear, and everything else was forgotten in the rain and the rush.

'We lads looked at one another and we nodded and we crept down from the trees and came up on that last wagon that was waiting on our side; and in all the downpour no-one saw us until we were right onto it.

'I cut the driver's throat myself, a fat little fellow with yellow hair; he was the first man I ever killed. I can still see the look on his face when we crept up out of nowhere. And then the few soldiers who were left on our side of the ford started to lay into us, and someone sounded a horn to warn the main troop.

'By now our blood was up, and we fought like wildcats. One fellow came right for me, but I managed to get inside the swing of his sword and grabbed him round the body; in a moment he'd shortened his grasp and smashed me full in the mouth with the pommel, then as I reeled back he turned the sword to run me through.

'I was on my knees spitting out teeth, but I managed to launch myself at his legs and brought him down; then I knelt on his arms and strangled him there in the mud; it seemed to go on for ever, and before I'd quite done the sling-shot men on the other side were starting to let fly at us, but the ford was blocked and they were all safely away on the other side.

'It would have been folly to stay, so the half-dozen or so of us lads who were still left standing grabbed what we could off the wagon, great bags of it that weighed like lead, and faded away into the forest.

'Before long some of their men had managed to get through the ford despite all the rising water, and we heard the yells as they finished off those boys of ours who hadn't made it away. And then they came looking for us, swords drawn; but the forest is our place, and though they hunted till the light was quite gone, they had no hope of finding us.

'When the moon rose in the middle of the night we took a look at what we'd got; I was hoping there'd be something to eat, and so was everyone else, I'd say. But it was just money, silver coins like the one I showed you earlier with the wee lad sitting on top of the world. So we set to to carry it away with us, and by the time the sun rose we were ten miles away and starting to feel safe. And that's the whole story of it.'

'Stolen money, then?' said Bran. 'No luck comes to those who keep it, they say.'

'Spoils of war, man; they'd had plenty of ours in return, and I'd paid out a good deal in blood and teeth. And anyway, I'm respectable now, and I trade kine up and down between here and Caledonia, and I nod and smile at the Romans who keep the road safe for me and they nod and smile right back at me. Money, they say, has no smell, and that's the end of my story.'

Morrig sniffed sceptically. 'Only a fool believes every traveller's tale. But I've heard worse, I'll give you that. So where does this cattle-trading take you next?'

Senorix gave her an indulgent smile. 'Believe it or not, my drowrie, just as you fancy. Still, I'll be biding here for a few more days if you can put me up that long; I've a fancy to take in the

Beltane feast up in the hills, and then I'll be off again. Anyway, if that *caupona's* open yet next door I'll be off for some breakfast now.'

Still smiling he stood, made a little half-bow, and sauntered through the doorway. Behind him, Bran, Crotos and Apuleios exchanged a quick glance.

'Found the money-tree somewhere though, hasn't he?' muttered Crotos.

Morrig shot him a look of pure venom. 'His money stays his, except for what he pays out here. Unless you want to join those two outside the North Gate?'

Crotos shrugged but said nothing, and Morrig went on, 'There'll be no thievery here, and you'll remember it if you want to keep your skin in one piece. And that reminds me…'

She picked up the pony-whip, lying where she had flung it on the floor. 'Get the slut,' she told Bran. 'She's had long enough to think about what's coming to her.'

Bran went out and came back a moment later gripping a very subdued Messalina by the arm; but to Morrig's growing bafflement the girl took her punishment with nothing louder than the occasional whimper. At last Morrig flung the whip down in a fury, grabbed Messalina by the hair and shoved her into the back room. 'Little thief.' she muttered as she returned, and then turned to Crotos and Apuleios, her brow black with anger.

'And have you two paid for your drinks?' she demanded. 'Then you can get out.'

Senorix brushed the last crumbs of breakfast from his lips and looked slowly around the forum. There they are he thought. But even the words entered his mind, Crotos and Apuleios seemed to sense his eyes on them and slipped away into the crowd.

He turned to the *caupo*, the proprietor, with a satisfied smile. 'That was good. Best I've had for days.' Then he stood up, turned his back to the forum and slipped a couple of coppers into the man's hand. 'A couple of lads were over there watching me a moment ago; what's the gossip?'

'From the tavern? Crotos and Apuleios?'

He grunted and spat on the ground. 'Nothing better to do all day than hang around getting drunk on credit until Morrig turns them out. Bran's a good chap, but he lets them get away with murder. Well, that's his problem.'

Senorix nodded. 'There's folks like that wherever you go. Life's too easy for some; anyway, I've got some shopping to do.' He clapped the *caupo* on the back and wandered over to the stalls, smiling quietly to himself and thinking, bait the hooks, trail them in the water, and wait for the fish to bite... and I think they're nibbling already.

X

Verica leant back on the cushions of her carrying chair, pulled back the curtain and cast a worried glance at the rain. But despite the weather, the Beltane Eve festivities would go ahead as planned.

The procession was moving slowly up the slope of the great range of hills that bordered the valley on its eastern side. At this place in days long-gone, the story said, Lugos himself had changed into an eagle at the very moment of his death, soaring up into the sun, and now at the cross-quarter between equinox and solstice both Sun and Moon would be honoured with fires lit on sacred hills the length and breadth of the world; but no fire was as sacred as this one, lit at the very place of Lugos' passing; and here the Goddess of the Spring, crowned in flowers, would be pursued and taken again by the God of the Forest.

Verica leant out of the chair and gestured to Gwydion, who was keeping an easy pace by her side, though where the path was roughest he leaned against the rough stick in his hand; a leather bag was slung over his shoulder.

'Gwydion, look back and tell me how many are following.'

He paused to take a quick glance at the line of followers, then drew nearer to the chair and answered, 'More than I can count, my lady, despite the rain. I have made sure that there will be plenty of oil for the fire, but they will not find it easy to light their own brands from it and keep them alight until they reach their homes.'

'Then we must look for the help of the gods themselves, Gwydion. My son made sacrifice to the Matronae at first light this morning, and he thought that they smiled on him as he did so.'

'Indeed, my lady.' He hesitated, then added, 'But there are those who think that your son should be here with you, ready to share with you in the lighting of the Beltane fire and at your choosing to take the part of the Forest God. Some worry that he has taken the ways of Rome to his heart rather than the ways of our own people.'

Verica frowned. 'I have taken much from Rome myself, Gwydion; and I think they have not found it cheap to deal with me. I am no innocent like Boudicca, who thought in her folly to challenge Rome when she could not match Rome's strength; I can ride Rome's horse and my own at the same time and steer both to my own ends, and they will never even know that I have done this. Surely the best victory is when the vanquished does not even know how much they have lost? And I tell you, the old ways will never end, no matter how much Rome may bluster.'

Gwydion fell silent and drew his woollen cloak tighter about his shoulders. Now they were higher the rain was giving way to a soaking mist, and even inside his fine boots his feet were sodden. He wondered how the great crowd of those who were following would fare, barefoot for the most part, and dressed in little more than simple homespun. He knew how they had looked to the coming of spring, to the hope that the winter's rains would somehow end with the changing of the seasons, and he wondered again what the gods had in store for them.

The bearers were becoming noticeably out of breath now, and finding it hard to keep their footing on the wet path; Verica's chair swayed as they walked, and although her face was calm she clung firmly to the edges of the seat.

At last they reached the summit of the hill. Here was a great level space perhaps a hundred paces in every direction, bare of trees and bushes; it had been kept clear for as long as either memory or song could tell; and in the middle of this platform was a great tangle of branches, piled up perhaps three times as high as a man. Set off a little to one side was a smaller pile of tinder, lichen and moss and shavings of wood, all carefully kept dry under a bower of withies roofed with turf.

At the edge of the clearing Verica's bearers set down her chair. She stood imperiously and looked about her; and as she did so the rain suddenly slackened and then stopped altogether, though raindrops still pattered to the ground from the trees all around.

She hesitated a moment, then pulled back her hood, letting her red hair fall free about her shoulders and turned in delight to Gwydion.

'The gods truly are with us tonight, Gwydion; we shall set such a bale-fire ablaze as will be seen from the stars themselves.'

'And from the town also, my lady; there will be many eyes looking to us tonight. And look, the mist is clearing below.'

It was true; the soaking fog which had wrapped itself around them as they climbed was thinning even as they watched; the great valley was opening beneath them, and the distant hills to westward were showing stark against a brooding sky. The first stars were showing, bright spots against the darkness, and the first glow of the gibbous moon was showing above the trees to eastward. Soon the whole shining celestial road of Caer Gwydion would be visible, the great glowing pathway of the gods splitting the sky between moonrise and sunset on this most sacred of nights.

And then below, just between where the Ituna flowed towards the sea and the new town stood, there was a sudden pinpoint of fire. Verica looked questioningly at Gwydion. He pushed the wet hair out of his eyes and blinked twice, trying to fix the exact spot of the blaze in his mind.

At last he smiled. 'The fire is a little to the north of the town, and I think even a little to the north of the Romans' camp as well. Surely it can only be a funeral pyre, my lady. It seems to me that at last they have set the blaze to consume the body of that merchant who was murdered on the road. Perhaps without knowing it they do honour to our gods as well.'

Verica nodded and smiled. 'You see how they give their blessing to us without meaning to. It is good to have such unknowing friends as these.'

Now the clearing was filling with those who had made the climb with them, perhaps four or five hundred men and women, some holding pots in their hands in which they would carry the blessed new fire down to their homes and hearths, while others held branches which had been dipped in pitch. Most were also carrying wooden rattles, though a few had hand-drums slung around their waists, and one was even carrying a sistrum, no doubt stolen long since from some Egyptian shrine. Chattering animatedly they ranged themselves around the wood, waiting for the moment when the great blaze would be lit.

Verica watched them, and then suddenly remarked, 'Surely those Greeks were right who said that fire makes up a fourth part of this great frame of things, Gwydion; and tonight I feel that fire coursing in my own veins. Gwydion, I am fire. And like the fire, I consume whatever I wish; see, I take everything the Romans are fools enough to give me, and still I remain what I am.'

'And the Romans, my lady? If you are fire, what are they?'

Verica laughed. 'Who knows; some no doubt are this and some are that. But of this I am very sure – their commander Marius is surely of the earth. He has no imagination, no fancy. Earth, Gwydion, no more than that.'

Gwydion bowed his head but said nothing. 'May ill-luck not come of it,' he muttered to himself, remembering that whenever fire and earth meet, the earth is always the victor at the last. But Verica seemed almost possessed by a sudden wildness, like one who has drunk too much wine.

Pushing the ominous thought to the back of his mind Gwydion began giving instructions to those in the royal party who were carrying great amphorae of olive oil on their shoulders. Under his instructions they began to spread the oil onto the waiting timber, some of them clambering up high into the tangle of branches to ensure that everything was properly soaked

At last the task was done. Gwydion quickly pulled a scrap of cloth from his sleeve, wrapped it around the head of the stick he was carrying, and poured what was left of the oil onto it. Then he and the others stepped back, letting Verica herself move forwards until she was standing by the little heap of tinder. Wordlessly she knelt, holding a piece of yellow flint in her left hand and a dagger in the right, and began to strike sparks, each one glowing briefly before fading.

Then suddenly there was a tiny wisp of smoke rising from the moss, and from the throats of all who could see it came an involuntary gasp; the bale-fire had taken, and the gods would look down and see it.

Gently Verica blew at the little flame until it began to leap through the moss and the shavings. Then she held out her hand to Gwydion, motioning him to bring her the oil-soaked rag which he had wrapped around the head of the stick he carried. She thrust this into the new fire, waited until she was sure it had caught, then stood, lifting the blazing brand high above her head. She stood so for as long as a man might take ten breaths, turning around so that all could see her.

'Beltane is here.' she cried. 'The earth is fruitful again. The fields will bear our crops. The fire within us grows stronger, and love is reborn. King and Queen of earth and sky walk again among us.'

With the torch still lifted high Verica strode around the great pile of logs, her gaze fixed now on the crowd gathered around. Suddenly she paused in front of a slim girl of some fifteen summers whose rain-soaked dress outlined the shape of her body.

'Child,' she said, 'what is your name?'

'Barita, my lady,' she answered, colouring as she spoke.

'Will you be our Queen at this Beltane? You know the ritual, surely?'

The girl responded with a shy nod, but at a nudge from the older lady standing by her gave a firm 'Yes.' Gwydion proffered the bag he had been carrying, and Verica took from it a little chaplet of flowers, bluebells and primroses, the first of the year's blooms. Motioning to the girl to kneel on the wet earth, she placed the flowers on her head as a crown.

'Here surely is our Queen.' she called, and then walked on, this time looking at the young men.

This time her glance lighted on a lad of some sixteen years, dark-haired and thick-lipped.

'And your name, lad?'

'Motius, my lady. Yes, I know the ritual and I will be the Forest King.' There was a knowing laugh from those nearest to him and he cast his eyes downward and blushed, suddenly conscious of how his eagerness would appear.

'Then we must crown you also, Motius. Kneel and receive the mark of your office.'

Again the bag was held out, and this time Verica drew from it a pair of stag's horns, mounted on a leather strap. Placing it on the boy's head she called out, 'They are crowned. Flowers for the fair and horns for the strong.

'The fire within us grows stronger.' she called, and as she spoke the words the newly-crowned Queen began to run sunwise around the logs, dodging in and out of the throng. Motius followed, always keeping several steps behind, careful not to get too close, while the girl wove her way in and out among the watchers.

'The fire within us grows stronger.' called Verica for the second time; and now she stepped forward and thrust the burning brand into the centre of the log-pile. As she did so there was a great roar from those gathered around as they took up the shout, 'Beltane is here. The fire within us grows stronger.'

As the oil caught, the fire suddenly roared and sparks rose high into the air; within moments the wood was ablaze, and the scent of pine and oak began to fill the clearing.

Still Barita and Motius danced around the fire, never more than a few steps apart but never quite touching. Three times in all they circled the new blaze; and at the end of the third turn, Barita finally paused, offered her lips to Motius, and let him embrace her. The first kiss was modest; the second passionate; in a few moments more the young god and goddess were pressed against one another on the ground, while those around sounded their rattles and beat on their drums, ululated and clapped and hooted encouragement to them, knowing that this mystic mating would make their crops plentiful and their animals fruitful.

The night was deepening now, and slowly other pairs began to embrace until at last, in the space around the fire, hundreds of men and women were coupling on the ground, while those who were more modest slipped under the trees for their more private lovemaking. At last only those who were widowed like Verica or sworn to celibacy like Gwydion were left, staring into the fire and perhaps seeing in its pulsating colours the images of old loves or of loves yet to come.

An hour passed so, or perhaps two; then, almost reluctantly, the couples began to rise, though they still clung to one another. Slowly they came forward to the fire, dipping their own torches into the blaze or collecting glowing embers in their fire-pots; then, the great ritual completed, they began their long walk back to the town or to their farms or hamlets in the great valley below.

High on the hill the only sounds now were the crackling of the fire, the occasional settling of the logs, and the whispered conversations of the lovers who still lingered by the fire. Then the calm was broken by a woman's scream followed by two more, piercingly loud, then the cracking of branches in the undergrowth and more screams, now interspersed with sobs as a girl ran into the clearing from the forest, stark naked except for the shift that she pressed against her body. And as she ran, a white owl wheeled over her head, and vanished into the darkness on the other side of the flames.

XI

Senorix slowly awoke in the little lean-to shed behind the Eagle and lay unmoving in the gloom. Sleepily he began to piece together the events of the last couple of days, then on a fancy took out of his money-bag the little gift he had bought at the jeweller's stall a few days earlier and studied it carefully in the dim light.

It was a brooch with an intricate design of an owl in silver and lapis lazuli – from somewhere far away, the jeweller had said and I won't be getting any more like that. As Senorix looked at it, a jumble of memories of the Beltane Eve celebrations the night before ran through his head – No, he corrected himself, two nights before. He wondered how he had ever got back here afterwards? And what by Belenos happened to yesterday? Ah well, he thought, the gods themselves look after drunkards.

The gods. That was it. There was an owl there too, flying over the clearing, and then the crazy woman swearing she had seen the leafy face of Urien peering through the undergrowth. Well, Beltane Eve was as good a time for the gods to appear as any other. Take your omens where you find them.

He put the beautiful trinket back in his bag. For a lady? Lucky girl, the jeweller had said with a grin, and he had answered with a knowing wink. Yes, he had thought, for a lady, but not in the way you're thinking.

He lay for a while listening to the sounds of the town, then got up, washed his face and hands at the fountain on the forum and bought two flat loaves from the baker, tearing pieces off and eating them noisily as he walked around.

Now he had two calls to make: first, to pick up the fine new pair of boots that had been promised for today; and then a quick settling of accounts with the butcher who had taken six head of cattle from him just nine days before the kalends. Then, tasks accomplished and with the boots slung around his neck and the new money safely stowed, he set off on an errand that he had long been looking forward to.

Time was getting on now – it would be somewhere around the third hour, he guessed – but there were still a few travellers around the South Gate. They were a decent enough group, it seemed: a fat, bald man with a fine bass voice who seemed determined to get everyone to join him in singing obscene verses, a pair of look alike tinkers who were probably brothers and who trudged on in silence, bent low beneath carrying-sticks from which dangled all kinds of household pots and pans which rattled as they walked, and a tall rake of a man sitting on a donkey although his feet almost trailed along the ground. All-in-all, Senorix told himself, as typical a set of travellers as you could find anywhere in the Empire, though he carefully excluded himself from that calculation.

Outside the town where the road ran close to Verica's palace Senorix waved his farewells to his fellow-travellers and set off up the driveway. The gate was open, as he had expected, giving a good view of the courtyard and gardens beyond; the little honour-guard of Roman soldiers was keeping a desultory watch on the entrance, but they did no more than nod casually to him as he walked past and through the gateway.

Senorix dropped his new boots onto the ground and looked around. As he had half expected, a crowd of perhaps fifty men and women was gathered around the oak-tree in the corner of the garden, most of them squatting or standing on the gravel; under the branches Verica was sitting in her currule chair, her chin resting on the knuckles of her right hand as she gave all her attention to the two men standing submissively before her; off to one side, her little maid stood with her head bowed. Gwydion was standing at her shoulder, and as Senorix watched him he leant forward and whispered something into Verica's ear.

The Queen listened carefully, then nodded. In a clear voice that left no doubt of her authority she spoke up, addressing the older of the two men first.

'You have come here because your father has died and so his property is to be divided between you and your brother, as is indeed our custom. But you have a third brother, older than either of you, who has turned merchant, and to whom a third of the property is also due, though he is not here to claim his portion.

'This, then, is my judgement. To you as the oldest here I confirm the right of *dadanhudd*, so that you may light your fire on the hearth of your father's house and claim it as your own. Apart from the house, to each of you here I give the right and the ownership of one third of the land while you live, one third of the cattle, one third of the slaves and one third of the crops of last year that may still remain in your barns, the younger of you to choose his portion first as the law requires.'

She turned to the younger man, and went on, 'You may build your own house on the land that you have chosen for your own, and as a sign that you and your brother are joint inheritors you will light your first fire from the fire burning on your brother's hearth, and you will both swear over that fire that you will live close in brotherly love.

'When the third brother returns from his travels, he may take up his own third of the inheritance if he wishes, though he must see me so that I may know of his purposes; until he returns you must farm his portion and care for it as if it were your own, dividing its produce evenly between you, and upon his return he must give to each of you one quarter of his gains from his travels as recompense to you for guarding and farming his land. If he does not agree to do this, then he has no further claim on the property.'

She paused, glancing at both men to see their expressions, then went on, 'If you have any dispute over the division into thirds that I have decreed, then you must take it to your neighbours to settle, each of you choosing one man to give his judgement and those men choosing a third between them, to judge in honesty and peace; but if either of you should move any of the ancient land-marks then a curse will rest on you and the land will give you no sustenance, a murrain will strike your beasts, and your barley, your oats and your wheat will fail. This is my judgement, and so it will be remembered.'

The men bowed, the customary bobbing of the head that ac-knowledged the Queen's authority without any trace of servility, then turned and walked away, both apparently satisfied with the judgement. Senorix watched them go, then squatted down on the edge of the group to watch more of the proceedings.

Over the next hour or so, Verica dealt with perhaps a dozen cases. The first was apparently the most trivial, involving the ac-cidental killing of a man's cat, allegedly a famous mouser, by his neighbour, which he claimed had left the rats free to pillage his barns, and for which she awarded him six copper coins; the sec-ond, a plea for divorce by a woman who claimed that her husband had not been able to satisfy her in bed for over six months, was met with a good deal of ribald laughter from the crowd, though Senorix noted that Verica kept a straight face throughout the case and granted the divorce without any hesitation as soon as she heard that the husband in question was not prepared to speak up in defence of his own manhood.

At last the little crowd of litigants had faded away completely except for four men; Senorix guessed from their demeanour that two of them were regular visitors to Verica's court, men used to the traditions of the law and to giving help to those who asked them. More formally than any who had been before them both representatives set out their case, the first asking for compensation for the death of a man who had been killed by his neighbour's bull and the second admitting that the death had indeed happened but claiming that the victim had brought his fate on his own head by persistently baiting the animal from the other side of a gate until finally the enraged beast had broken through and gored and trampled him to death.

Verica listened carefully to both men, then asked a number of questions about the animal concerned, occasionally turning to Gwydion to ensure that her understanding of the law was correct.

'It is plain that the man brought his own death upon him,' she finally announced, 'so no compensation is to be paid to his family; nor must his family pay compensation to the man whose bull he baited, causing it to turn wild and intractable so that its owner lost much of the use of it, for it is clear that it should have been tethered so that it could not break free. For my part I claim no payment from either party for the death of the man, for he acted in the folly of the moment and not in malice. The law is the law of the people and not of my making, but even if it lay in my power to do so, I would make no change in it. That is my judgement.'

The two parties made the usual formal bow, though it was plain that neither was fully satisfied with the ruling; but when Verica lowered her voice a fraction and added, 'Now go and live together in peace.' they took a hasty departure, still muttering among themselves.

Verica glanced around and saw only Senorix waiting. 'Do you come for judgement at our Court of Beltane?' she asked.

'No judgement, my lady,' replied Senorix with a much deeper bow than was necessary, 'only a request that you should know me.'

Verica paused for as long as a man might take three or four breaths, staring at his face, then shook her head in disbelief. 'Senorix?' she muttered at last, 'Uncle Senny? Really you? I thought you had long gone to your place among the stars.'

'It's a long time since anyone called me that – and I was never your uncle, you know, my lass.'

For a moment Verica bridled at the unaccustomed familiarity, then smiled. 'A childish fancy. But how many years is it since I saw you last?'

'A long time indeed. But not so long since I saw you, my lass. I was on the hill-top with the others when you lit the Beltane fire, though you never saw me. Indeed, you had many other things on your mind I should say.'

Verica nodded, then stood up abruptly. 'The chair adds some style to the proceedings, but it certainly does nothing for my back. There, you can see how old I've become since we last met.'

'None of us are what we were, my lass. But 'tis a fine chair for its purpose. I heard somewhere that it's meant to keep a judge from falling asleep in the middle of the case, and I suppose that those who invented it thought that a bad back was little enough to worry about. But you have no need of such a thing, surely, you who give judgement in the old way beneath that fine oak of yours.'

Verica smiled. 'Walk with me around the garden a little – or would you prefer a drink? I can have wine fetched, and I think that there will be *mulsum* to drink soon. Walk with us, Iras.'

'Honey and hot wine mixed? Fine enough if you have a bad throat, I dare say, but too sweet for my taste, lass. But it will give me pleasure enough to walk with you and see your garden.'

For a few moments they strolled among the formal planting in silence, with only Iras and Gwydion the harpist following a few paces behind; then Senorix murmured, 'How long since we last talked, you and I, and you just a little lass? And that was a long way away, as I recall.'

'Over by the eastern sea, indeed. Do you remember how we would walk on the beach, and you taught me to skim stones over the waves? But I could never do it as well as you, however hard I tried.'

'There are better things to do with one's life than skimming stones, lass, and it seems to me you have found them.'

Verica smiled to herself. 'Gwydion would remind me that the gods bring us joys and griefs together, and the greatest joys and the greatest griefs walk hand in hand; and there is truth in that saying. But the gods give us many gifts, and I have learned to seize them with both my hands, and to hold them fast with all the strength they have given me.'

'And so, my lass, I see that you live in a fine house that the Romans built for you, but still light the Beltane fire as our fathers have done since the days of Lugos himself; you sit in a Roman chair and yet pronounce your judgements from under an oak tree according to our own law, as the old ones did. You live in two worlds, my lass.'

'I do, and I am wise to do so. I have no quarrel with Rome, but the old ways are familiar to me and there is a secret place in my heart which knows that they are good and will endure, perhaps even longer than Rome herself endures. We shall not cease to honour our gods, Senorix, nor to practise our ancient customs.'

'Even honouring the gods has its dangers, my lass; we had a taste of that when the Beltane fire was lit, I'm thinking.'

Verica shrugged. 'A crazy woman shouting that she saw the gods? Such things have happened before, and will no doubt happen again. Once the hysterical fit was over she was soon calmed.'

Senorix paused in his walking and turned to face Verica. For a moment he hesitated as if unsure how to continue, then went on, 'Hysterical? Are you truly sure of that? There are those who would say that she saw the face of Urien himself among the leaves, and that Blanaid herself attended him in her form as an owl; the owl, indeed, I saw myself, as did you and many others who were there. And I must tell you that many in the town talk of this already, though not all have heard it.'

'Yes, hysterical,' Verica insisted. 'It is surely no act of the gods that an owl should fly in the woods at dusk of a spring evening.'

Senorix shook his head. 'I take my omens where I find them. I have seen signs, and heard things spoken, that leave me thinking that the world is about to change. I'm no *veleda*, dipping into the future in my trances; but I make no doubt that you have heard what that crucified murderer shouted out before he died.'

Verica, who had paused beside Senorix, resumed her slow walk along the garden paths. 'Yes, I have heard; that foolish old prophecy that no-one can put a name to, that there will be three great wars against the Romans, and that the third will be the greatest. What of it?'

'There are those who say, my lass, that Boudicca's war was the first, and that the campaign in Caledonia which ended at Mons Graupius was the second. It may be that the time of the third has now come. And, my lass, I see you riding on two horses at the same time, and I fear you will fall.'

'And that is why you have come to see me after so many years? Senorix, you are telling me as much of the truth as you think I would like to hear; but I remember from long ago that you have little love for the Romans, and I do not think that you have changed in that.'

Senorix gave her a wry smile. 'The years have given you wisdom, my lass, and you see clear to the heart of me. To tell truly, yes, I wish they were long clear of this island, with their bragging ways and their bullying manners, and the thump, thump, thump of their hobnailed boots.

'But in Caledonia things are changing; they may not say so aloud, but one at a time these Romans are abandoning their forts, always moving their line a little further to the south. Tell me, my lass, did you ever hear of a man called Fabian, a famous general of theirs?'

'The one they called the Delayer? Senorix, I know as much of Roman history as the Romans themselves, perhaps more; I read everything I can, in both Latin and Greek; and where I do not understand, I ask whoever I can until it is clear to me. So yes, I well know your Fabian and how in a time of great danger he kept his army always away from that African Hannibal who had invaded Italy, harrying him all the time but for ever avoiding battle.'

Senorix smiled again. 'I should not underestimate you, that is plain to see. At all events, that is how things are now in Caledonia:

there is little fighting – a skirmish here, an ambush there it may be, enough to prevent the Romans from foraging far from their forts, and so a little at a time they retire. I think they will not take back the ground they have relinquished so easily.'

Verica shook her head. 'And do you have a part in this harrying you talk of? I think that you do. And see, you do not deny it.

'This Fabian of whom you speak so highly; do you not understand that for all his skill it was not through him that Rome won the final victory, but only because of the despair and folly of Hannibal's own countrymen? You tell me not to ride two horses, and yet you take as your own model these very Romans whom you profess to dislike so much. Senorix, I fear that you delude yourself in this matter.'

'You cannot argue with geography, my lass; slowly, so slowly they move southwards like a retreating tide.'

He smiled. 'You know how the tide runs in the estuary of the Ituna, my lass – it comes in faster than a man can run, but then turns and goes out so slow that you can hardly see the change. So it is with the Romans in Britain. When that slow tide ebbs as far as here and the last legionary has tramped away noisily to the south, what will you do then? For that time may come sooner than you think. And I think that our gods may be appearing at this time to give us both warning and heart.'

Verica considered the words in silence, then answered hesitantly. 'I am not impious, Senorix; I believe in the gods and I know that they hear our prayers and repay us for our sacrifices. But I see no sign of the future that you claim is coming; if indeed I should see it coming from afar, then I shall remember what you have said and thank you for it.

'But enough of this drear talk. You have told me nothing of yourself. What have you been about in all the years since we last talked together? Are you married? Do you have children of your own? Surely you would be a good father; I remember well how kind you were to me when I was little.'

'No wife and no children, my lass – at least no children that would recognise me, though I may have many by-blows in the brochs and homesteads of Caledonia. The settled life is not for me, or not yet, and I still roam far and wide buying and selling kine; and I won't deny the other thing you have laid to my charge.

'But sometimes of an evening I own that maybe my old bones are becoming too weary for that life, and so you may yet hear that I have built my own bothy and raised a brood of my own by my own hearth. But I see that our walk around your fine garden has brought us back to your gate, and so I shall take my leave of you. But I must not forget that I have a little gift for you. Here. Wear it and remember me.'

With a smile he pulled out the little lapis and silver owl brooch and presented it with an exaggerated bow. Verica took it and looked at it curiously. 'It's beautiful. From somewhere far in the east, I should think; I shall wear this always in hope that we shall meet again, and I shall indeed consider what you say. And so fare you well, my own old Uncle Senny.'

Senorix bowed again, then gave Iras a broad wink. On an impulse he took Verica's hand and kissed it. Then, without turning back he scooped up his new boots from where they lay on the ground and set off back to the road, walking briskly and humming cheerfully to himself.

Verica watched Senorix stride through the gateway, then turned to Gwydion, who was standing silent a few feet away.

'So ends our Beltane court. Have I given judgement fairly and according to our law?'

Gwydion smiled. 'In every case, my lady; though I think the last is the one that will trouble your thoughts in the coming days.'

'I know you of old, Gwydion, and I know that it is not the man killed by the bull that is uppermost in your thoughts.'

'Indeed, my lady.'

He smiled again, but this time it was the sad smile of a man who remembers the past with a pang of regret. 'Senorix was always a good friend of your father's, my lady. I knew him today at his first coming in, and asked myself more than once what was his business here.'

'My father? To both my fathers, rather. And after my first father died, he was a good friend to me too. But I do not think it was only his friendship that brought him here today. Does he really believe that the gods were there at the lighting of our Beltane fire, and that I did not know them?'

Gwydion considered, his brow creased. 'That, my lady, is a judgement that I shall not make. But I think he wishes you, at least, to believe that they were. And I think he is right when he says that the rumour of their presence will indeed spread through both town and country, slowly and hesitantly at first and then with ever more certainty as the days pass. It would be as well to be ready for this.'

Verica gave a brief nod of agreement. 'Well, if the gods are truly here, we should prepare to acknowledge them and welcome them among us. If they are not, then the story will soon die of its own accord when some new wonder catches the peoples' fancy.'

'Remember, my lady, what we know of the gods. They may come to warn, or to impel us to some action, or even it is said to delight in the company of a human lover; but most of all, they come looking for sacrifice. Little enough blood has been given to them of late, and I fear that they grow thirsty for more.'

'Oh, you are like Senorix, Gwydion; you come with warnings of the terrible things that may happen. May, may, may. And because you talk about the gods you dress your warnings in high-flown language like some seer pronouncing a ban; but here the earth does not shake under our feet, there are no fire-mountains ready to pour their brimstone on our heads, the people are content and, for all I know, the gods are happy for it to remain so. Come back down to earth, Gwydion.'

Gwydion stood his ground, shaking his head. 'My lady, you indeed honour the old ways, the ways you learned from your father and that he had learned from his fathers before him…'

'And from you too, Gwydion. When I was a child I loved to hear you singing the old tales, of how the gods moved among us when the world was young, taking the shapes of cats and bears and wolves and eagles.'

'Do not forget owls, my lady; the owl that comes so silently at night to feed on the blood of the little creatures that neither see nor hear it coming, so intent are they on their own little world, their paths through the forest, their young and their mates. The owl cares nothing for these others but seeks only to satisfy its own appetites. Truly is it said that Blanaid, who could not contain her lusts, lives for ever in the form of an owl, such an owl indeed as you and I saw flying at our Beltane fire.'

'So what advice do you give me? Can we avert this trouble you hint at, or should we try to ride out whatever storm may come?'

'My lady, the gods have their own ways, and when they wish to drink blood no act of ours can slake their thirst. If it is blood that they seek, then no other sacrifice will move them, and no prayer will stay their hand. But truly I hope it will not be so.'

Verica, who had listened with her face cast down, suddenly laughed. 'Then we should enjoy our lives while we can. Though I have no wish to die, Gwydion, for life is still very sweet.'

She gave a regretful shrug and went on, ' If only the Cauldron of Rebirth that you used to tell stories about were still true today as it was in the old times, so that everyone who dies could be cast into it and come out again as strong and young as ever they were before.'

'The tale of the Cauldron, my lady, is very truth and not some fable for children; if you think so then you think awry. For know that the Cauldron is this world, and that those who are cast into it in death will indeed spring up again, as young and healthy as they ever were; all of us have this fate, my lady, that we shall be reborn whether we wish it or not.'

Verica paused, looking around the young gardens of the

palace. 'But not in this time I think, Gwydion, not in this time nor this place, and both are so dear to me...'

After a moment's silence she went on in a suddenly firm voice, 'I must know more – I shall go and see *her.*'

A frown crossed Gwydion's brow. 'Is this wise, my lady? What will the Commander say when he hears? He would think her a *maga* – a witch.'

'He shall never hear of it. We shall go in secret tomorrow early, you and I; and Lugos shall come too, it is long since time for him to know of such things.'

Gwydion shook his head. 'If your mind is set on this, my lady, then we must go indeed; but not tomorrow, I beg you. We are all still tired from our exertions on Beltane Eve, and I for one fear that I lack the strength for another such journey so soon.'

'Then the day after. I will wait no longer.' Verica shivered and clutched her wrap to her shoulders. 'How cold it seems suddenly. Let us go in.'

XII

By the time Senorix reached the Eagle, the rain had begun again and the place was already full with men who had clearly decided that they might as well enjoy a drink in the dry as carry on working in the wet. Glancing around the gloom he saw Crotos and Apuleios sitting hunched on a bench by the back wall, while Bran was walking around with an amphora in his hand busily refilling wine-cups, but pointedly ignoring his friends.

With a weary sigh Senorix squeezed himself between the two men, then called to Bran for wine. Bran looked distractedly at him, then muttered, 'Your money's good, but if you-know-who sees those two drinking on tick I'll never hear the end of it.'

'Make it my treat. Just add it to the bill.' He turned to Crotos and slapped him on the back. 'Come on, man, you listened to my tale of woe patiently enough, so now it's time for me to hear yours. Wet your throat first, then off you go. A good tale of misery and injustice, eh, that's what I'd like to hear.'

Crotos looked at him blankly for a moment then began to speak, the words suddenly tumbling out as if he had long rehearsed them in his head. 'It was my land, my home. Up on the hills, in a place where the air's sweet. Good tilth, too, fine grass for sheep and cattle, sheltered, with plenty of clear water at hand. My father's before me, and his before him. Thank the gods the old man never lived to see it happen… one day they came and took it, just like that. There must have been fifty or more of them; they burned the house to the ground and drove us off like dogs – me, my mother, the farm-hands, everyone. The bastards. Orders, they said.'

'Our Roman friends? They did that?'

'Took the land for a new camp, didn't they? Even changed the name. Brovonacis we called it – Bravoniacum, they call it now. Left us to beg, or starve. Did for my old mother, it did. Bastards.' His face was dark now with bitterness, but Senorix simply shook his head in apparent amusement.

'Tush, just look at you, man. They take away your whole country and you do nothing but shrug and say, "That's the way the world is" but let them rob you of your old round hut and a few miserable acres and it's a whole different story.' He turned his head and spat on the floor.

'Easy for you to say, you've made your money already. And what about my mother? I want *galanas* for her.'

'Blood feud? Fair enough. That's the old law right enough. So it's all up to you. You know your rights. Revenge, that's the thing. So how many of them have you killed so far?'

Apuleios leant over and rested his hand on Senorix' arm. 'Easy on him. He's only a farmer, you know. It's one thing to keep your sheep safe from bears, another to go round cutting soldiers' throats.' He shuddered as the thought of the two thieves on their crosses flashed through his mind.

'Only a farmer? Ah, that would explain it then. And what about you? What do you do, apart from spending your days boozing on tick with your friend here?'

'This and that. Nothing...'

'He's a guide. He knows all the paths along the shore and up and across the estuary – where the quicksands are, where the cockle-beds grow, how to take the short path across without getting drowned.'

'It's not something you learn just once.' There was pride in Apuleios' voice. 'The channels keep shifting all the time, and what was firm footing yesterday'll see you drowned tomorrow. So you pray to the god there to keep you safe, and you take note of all the signs he sends you.'

'Ah,' Senorix nodded, 'a man of rare skill, then – someone who knows where there are bodies to rob and when he can do it safely.'

There was a long moment's silence before Apuleios shrugged. 'So if I take what the god gives me, what's wrong with that?'

Senorix seemed deep in thought, but after a moment he roused himself. 'Good man. Always grab what the gods send, or they'll see you havering and change their minds. But it seems you have no quarrel with the Romans, for all that your friend's complaining enough for the both of you.'

Apuleios shook his head gloomily. 'My quarrel's right outside the North Gate. A fine wide road for folks like you to come and go as they please, and let the poor shore-guide starve. A few years back you'd have paid for my help or you'd have drowned; now you stride up and down and never think of the way things were.'

Senorix nodded thoughtfully. 'Ah, the world's changing, right enough, and some folks are sure to be left behind. Left you high and dry, did they?'

Apuleios looked at the floor and let Crotos answer for him. 'He still gets a retainer; not enough to live on, though. Got him on a leash, they have – not worth staying, not worth leaving.'

Senorix clapped Apuleios on the shoulder. 'So you're still on the books? Perhaps things'll look up one day? Think of the future, lad, not on what's behind you. Hey, while I think of it, where's herself this evening?'

'Which one? The gorgon or the tart? Same answer, I suppose; she dragged the girl out to keep her company while she went to visit an old biddy she's been friends with for years, somewhere near the South Gate. Left him to do all the work on his own, didn't even leave the girl here to lend a hand. Still, he'll get his own back soon enough, I'll wager he'll be off fishing tomorrow.'

He lowered his voice confidentially and went on, 'Don't think he catches much, but ask yourself, would you hang around if you had Morrig for a wife? And she's got it into her head that he's got a girlfriend around somewhere. No way. He's learned his lesson now – give him half a chance and he's out on the river in his little coracle, with a bit of sheep-fleece over his head to keep him dry.

Better be wet and happy on the water than dry and miserable at home, that's his motto. And if he does feel the itch, then he's got the little tart all ready at home. A quick knee-trembler with her outside in the alley-way, that's all he dares do when the gorgon's around.'

Senorix grinned. 'And folk wonder why I never got married. You know, it occurs to me that I might be able to help you – not a word to Bran and herself, though, this is special for the pair of you. Wrongs ought to be righted, I say. I'll think it over, you'll hear from me one day soon, make no doubt of it. Now drink up, and then we'll have another one.'

XIII

Early next morning as he lay in the dark warmth of the straw in the Eagle's shed, Senorix was woken by the rain beating on the boards of the roof. Next to him, Messalina stretched, then opened her eyes, yawned and pressed herself against him.

'Not now, lass; time for that later. I have to say, you earn your keep well enough.'

'Mistress doesn't think so.'

Senorix grunted. 'Your mistress is a nasty old cow, and you can forget I said that. But we all have our own mistresses to follow, and I suppose I've seen worse than her.'

Suddenly remembering, he asked, 'Did you take your beating quietly like I told you to?'

'Yes,' she squirmed as she remembered it. 'You were right when you said that it wouldn't hurt any less. And then she pulled my hair and pushed me around. And right in front of Master's friends, too.'

Senorix yawned. 'Then I owe you your money, right enough. Have you a better place to hide it now?'

'I think so. But I'm not telling.'

'Smart lass.' Senorix fiddled with the money-bag which he still wore while sleeping and pulled out a coin. 'That's a *duponius*, by the feel of it; keep it safe in your hand. Your left hand, lass, I've got work for the other.'

Later, lying back and still apparently on the edge of sleep, he suddenly added, 'Remember now, no more stealing – and especially from the soldiers, they might not take kindly to it. Still, I suppose they don't tip badly.'

Messalina considered for a moment, then turned to lie on her stomach. 'Some of them are nice; they give me tit-bits, sometimes, and teach me a little Latin; rude words, usually, I think.

'But some of them pull my hair, or say horrible things, or twist my tits, or make me do things I don't like. They're worse when they're drunk; sometimes they can't do it properly then and they get angry. Not like you.' She giggled and wriggled close to Senorix, then went on, 'But I suppose that they've paid so they can do what they like. And all some of them want to do is talk. About where they've been, or where they're going, and about how brave they've been, sometimes. I'd rather they got on with having me.'

'More fool them. Any special favourites?'

In the darkness Messalina pouted. 'I wouldn't tell you if there were. But most of them don't stay around here for very long; they keep sending them off to some other camp and bringing different men here instead of them. Bravoni something. They have a special name for doing that, but I can't remember it.'

Senorix considered briefly. 'Troop rotation, is that it?'

'That's it. Do you like the soldiers? You seem to know a lot about them.'

'A bit of a hobby of mine, that's all. I can tell you know a lot more about them than I do.' He lay back, listening carefully to Messalina's chatter until finally it slowed and died away; but just before sleep took her again he whispered, 'I like to hear you talk about the brave soldiers and everything they've done. If I come back this way one day, perhaps I'll give you a nice tip if you'll tell me more of those stories.'

Instantly Messalina's interest was aroused. 'How much? Can I have the money first?'

'Ah, lass, you've already had plenty of cash from me this trip, there's no more now. But it's a promise: if I come back, and if you can remember some of the things that they've said, I might let you have – oh, even another *duponius* or perhaps two. But I'll know if you've been making things up, lass, so don't even think of trying it. And it's our secret, remember. If anyone finds you've been talking to me about them, then the beating you've had today will seem like a lover's tickle, I promise you.

'And now, I've a long journey ahead of me and people to talk to before I go, so I'll get back to sleep if it's all the same to you. Turn over lass, you make a fine soft pillow for a poor old man who's a long way from home.'

Marius shoved his porridge bowl away with a frown, waved away the slave who had stepped forward to take it and hushed him into silence. Moodily he stared at the table and tried to work out exactly what it was that seemed subtly out of place in his house; but the harder he tried to put his finger on the fugitive thought at the back of his mind, the further it seemed to slip away, and he turned his attention to the day's tasks.

Beginning of the month – that means reports. He quickly scanned through it so that he could show that everything was on an even keel, muttering the details to himself as he did so – one recovering from a broken leg, another coughing up blood and unlikely to make it past the end of the month, and five – why so many? – sick with eye problems.

He opened a fresh tablet and smoothed down the wax, then rummaged on the shelf to find his copy of the figures he'd sent at the beginning of April. He stopped and scratched his head as he spotted something he'd meant to check last time but hadn't got round to. Perhaps Marcus Asellio would know about it?

The centurion answered the summons with his usual promptness, but still felt the need to apologise. 'Sorry for the delay, I was checking spear-shafts in the armoury. Got a bit of a problem there, I'm afraid, sir. A lot of them are only good for firewood. It's this blessed damp, it gets into everything. We're going to need to sort that out, so I was thinking we'd send out a party into the forest for timber, if that's all right with you sir?'

'Good idea, Marcus; but not today, I think. I'm just filling in our returns for Eboracum; look, it seems as if we've been paying some local contractor or something five sesterces a month, but I'm damned if I know what for. Do you know what this is about? Some convenient little scam that someone's hoping I won't find out about, perhaps? Or something left over from when the cavalry were here?'

He pushed the tablet across and waited while the centurion read it. 'Ituna guide five sesterces. Yes, sir, I've heard about that. It's all above board, though come to think of it I'm not sure we ought still to be paying out.

'You were right about it being a hangover from the cavalry; it seems the prefect commanding the Ala Gallorum Sebosiana who were here before us wanted to be sure that his men could cut straight across the Ituna Estuary if he needed to reinforce the forts along the north shore; it's miles shorter than going up on the road and cutting across.

'The estuary must be a mile or more wide in places, but apparently you can walk or ride all the way across if the tide's right. But I hear there's quicksands that keep shifting around, so unless you've got a good guide it's a death-trap. We've been keeping some fellow on a retainer, five sesterces a month. Don't know when he was last used, though.'

Marius nodded. 'Thanks. I'll check into it and see if we still need him. While you're here, there's something else I wanted to ask.'

He broke off and glanced at the slave waiting impassively by his side. 'Tell you what, why don't we walk round the town together. Beltane's brought all sorts of people into town, it'd be as well to keep an eye on things.'

They were safely through the camp gate before Marius spoke again. 'No secret's safe from slaves. Now, man-to-man, what do you make of our smart young Tribune? You've watched him with the men more than I have.'

'Gracchus? All right, I suppose. Like you'd expect, really.'

He hesitated, then grinned. 'Permission to speak freely, sir? Right, he's bloody good and he knows it; but there's something about him that rubs me up the wrong way, if you know what I mean. Perhaps it's just the way he talks; I never could take that accent. Still, on the face of it I'd say we're lucky to have him; seems a bit odd that the brass in Eboracum could do without him, really.'

'Ambitious?'

'Goes without saying. Britannia would be a good posting for him, especially if he can get some real field experience while he's here.'

He glanced round the bustling forum and shook his head. 'Not much sign of that happening here, though. All seems placid enough to me. Hang on, though, what's that fellow up to?'

An excited-looking man in native dress was standing by the fountain and holding forth to a cluster of perhaps half a dozen idlers, but when he noticed Marius and Marcus watching he first dropped his voice and then stopped altogether and walked quickly away. As the little crowd dispersed Marius collared one of the audience. 'What was all that about?' The man searched for the Latin words, then said simply, 'God coming. Here.'

Marius and Marcus exchanged a cynical glance; probably the same old Eastern hokey they'd heard so often in Rome. 'Coming here, is he? In person? Better see he doesn't cause any trouble when he comes, then.'

They turned away and strolled on in silence for a moment, then Marcus Asellio went on, 'You don't suppose our Tribune could be someone's eyes and ears, do you? A spy in the camp?'

'I'd wondered the same thing. Then again, why choose us? There's dozens of garrisons like ours all over the island.'

A sudden thought entered his mind. 'You don't suppose he's checking out our readiness for a push up north, do you? The full reconquest of Caledonia. Now that would impress the Senate when he's up for a consulship in a few years' time. Well, I suppose we'll know soon enough.'

'A push up into Caledonia? That might be interesting.'

Marius sighed. 'In theory we control the whole of Britannia; the real truth is that up in Caledonia we have almost no influence at all once you get away from our forts and the roads that link them, and the Queen wasn't slow to remind me of that a few days ago.

'You know the theory as well as I do, Marcus: set up towns, let the natives make a bit of money from trading, then get them relaxing in the bath-houses and watching a few superannuated gladiators whack the blazes out of each other in a smart new arena, and before you know it they're starting to speak Latin and wanting to go on trips to Rome. It's a sound policy; it's worked everywhere – well, everywhere outside Judaea, I suppose, until the Divine Vespasian got those fanatics sorted out. I suppose it'll be the same in Caledonia; they'll come round in the end; everyone does sooner or later.'

He gestured towards a couple of empty stools outside the little *caupona*. 'Let's have a bite to eat, good street-food instead of what Licnos serves up for me every day.' With a wry smile he went on, 'Do you remember what the Divine Augustus said when he saw someone tucking in to his packed lunch at the Games one day?'

'Something like, When I feel hungry, I go home, wasn't it?'

'That's it. All very well for Emperors. Let's see what they've got.'

But Marcus Asellio shook his head. 'Not for me if you don't mind, sir; I ought to get back to the armoury and finish checking out the spears. If you're right about you-know-who's ambitions, we might need them sooner than we expect.'

Marius watched him go, then glanced at the board hanging from a pole sticking out at the side of the caupona. It seemed that the *caupo* prided himself on his artistic ability: pictures of various dishes had been daubed up on it, and strings of onions and garlic hung alongside. But of the man himself there was no sign, so

Marius called out, 'Bread and sausage; any good?'

There was a muttered answer from somewhere inside, and the man appeared wiping his hands on his tunic; a barefoot girl of perhaps seven or eight came out behind him and stood watching Marius with intense curiosity, her left hand clutching her father's clothes, her right fingering the amulet that hung from her neck.

'Sausage? Our speciality. Good pig-meat, chopped, with pepper. Best you'll ever have. But we don't do the bread.' He nodded towards the baker's stall on the other side of the street. 'They'll see you right. I'll get you some wine from next door if you want. Only rot-gut, but what d'you expect? If you get a belly-ache after, just don't blame my sausage. Huctia, get a beaker of wine from next door, then fetch some bread. And make sure it's fresh.' He gave the girl a gentle push towards the Eagle, then wiped his hands again and looked proprietorially around the square. 'Nice to have it dry. After what we've been having I thought it was never going to stop.'

Marius agreed, wondering briefly if the man was going to stand there making conversation while he ate, but after a moment he wiped his hands on his tunic again and turned to the bowls of food keeping hot on the counter, whistling through his teeth as he stirred them with a wooden ladle.

Marius watched him until the little girl reappeared, gave him a grave look and handed over the brimming wine-beaker. Then without a word spoken she backed away, ran across to the baker's stall, and picked out a flat bread from the basket on the counter, holding it up so that the baker's boy would see her and score it up. Then she scampered back, eyeing Marius the whole way, and pushed the bread into her father's hand.

Marius gave the wine a cautious sniff, then took a sip; it seemed just as bad as the man had said, but at least it would take the dust of the street out of his throat.

'Garlic with the sausage? Or onions? No extra charge.'

Marius nodded his head absent-mindedly, his attention caught by two men walking across the forum and arguing with each other, their arms waving passionately.

'Here you are.' The bread and sausage arrived on a well-scored wooden platter. The meal smelled and looked better than he had expected, though he was surprised to see that the sausage was curved rather than straight.

The *caupo* followed his gaze across the forum. 'Will you look at those two? Spent all morning in the Eagle, they have – nothing better to do than hang around arguing and getting drunk all day. There's plenty of work for them if they could be bothered to roll their sleeves up. Hey, you two, you still owe me from last week, remember?'

Marius wrapped the steaming sausage in the bread and bit gingerly into it. It was surprisingly tasty. 'This is good. They'd pay good money for this in Rome.'

But the caupo was still staring in disdain at the two men as they elbowed their way through the crowd. 'It's all The Romans did this, and The Romans did that with them, saving your presence sir, but I've told them, there's no need to mope, there's money to be made. Not that they'd listen.

'See that one on the left? Best guide there ever was over the estuary and up into Caledonia; but the Romans took his living away with their blasted road, that's all you ever hear from him. Good-for-nothing now, the pair of them; fed them both on tick last week, I did. Should have had more sense, but I'll get my money off them in the end, don't you worry. And talking of money, that'll be three coppers if you please.'

Marius fumbled in his arm-purse for the coins, then muttered half to himself, '*Lupus in fabula* – talk of the wolf and lo he appears. I bet that's the man we're paying a retainer to. What's his name?'

'That'd be him all right, sir; Apuleios the Guide we used to call him; Apuleios the Drunkard now, more like.' He leant over confidentially. 'Wouldn't catch me boozing like that, not even with the wine-shop right there next door. No stopping some people, is there? Anyway, I'd best leave you to your dinner. Come on, Huctia, let the gentleman enjoy his food in peace and quiet.'

It was early afternoon before Senorix had gathered his few possessions into a leather bag, aware that Morrig was keeping a very sharp eye on him. Finally he pulled on his new boots, wincing a little at their stiffness.

'Just what I need to keep my feet dry on a wet journey. Right, my good lady, that's everything I think; if there's anything I've left behind, you'll keep it for my coming back, I'm sure. Now, what do I owe you?'

He listened with a slight frown while Morrig itemised his bill, rattling the beads up and down her little wooden abacus as she did so, then whistled in mock surprise.

'As much as that, you say?'

'You've drunk plenty while you've been here. Good beer costs money to make. And treating those two good-for-nothings yesterday as well; I'd steer clear of them and their sob-stories if I were you.'

'Ah, everyone's got a tale to tell; I'd told them mine so it was only fair to let them tell me theirs, after all. And I'm thinking a fine, strapping lady like you would have an interesting story to tell too. And that husband of yours as well, I dare say. Which reminds me – where's himself disappeared to today?'

Morrig spat noisily on the floor. 'That useless waste of space? Off with his fancy-woman, if you ask me. He says he's going fishing, if you can believe that; one day I'll catch him with her, and when I do, I'll scratch her eyes out, so help me.'

Senorix smiled. 'Ah, that's the ticket. I do like a lass with a bit of spirit. Anyway, I'd best settle up and go.'

With a deliberately audible sigh he counted out the money on the table, shaking his head regretfully as he did so. At last he pushed the little pile over to Morrig with a shrug. 'Well, that's good money I'll never see again.'

Morrig scooped it up and counted it, then counted it a second time before slipping it into the leather money-bag hanging from her waist. 'For a man who's a long way from home, you've taken your time about leaving.'

'Ah, there's nothing as sweet as someone who's sorry to see you go. But I'll not be travelling far today, you see. Start off gently, that's my motto. Still, I've had good entertainment here, I'll grant you that.'

He shouted out to Messalina, who was busying herself cleaning beakers in the little scullery at the back and sniffling quietly. 'Hey, girl, come here and give me a kiss before I go. Make it a good one, you might never see me again.'

'You'll do nothing of the sort, girl. He's had everything he's paid for. Get on with your work and stop your moaning or I'll give you something else to complain about.'

'Let the lass channer. I'm thinking you laid into her pretty hard, after all. Black and blue she is.'

'Nothing more than the little slattern deserves.'

But Senorix stood up, quickly put his arm around Morrig's waist and kissed her firmly on her lips before sauntering out of the door, leaving her staring red-faced after him.

※ ※ ※ ※ ※ ※ ※

On his way back to the camp Marius paused for a little while, watching two little girls sitting by the side of the road, completely absorbed in playing cat's cradle. He smiled as they passed increasingly complicated figures back and forth between them, until finally one of them made a mistake and the whole intricate creation collapsed, and both children broke into howls of laughter before starting again. As he turned away, one of them caught his eye and smiled shyly. The blessings of peace, he thought. May they never be forgotten.

As he walked on, a sudden thought struck him. I knew there

was something wrong this morning, but I couldn't put my finger on it. Cybele. She was grinning from ear to ear this morning. What's got into the girl, he wondered. Well, whatever it is, it'll wait until I've finished with those reports.

A little more than a mile beyond the North Gate brought Senorix to what had once been a passable ford over a tidal creek, though now it was crossed by a single wooden span. Tucked down in the lea of the bridge stood a cottage, home to the old woman who in earlier times had steered a leaky coracle across the channel when the water rose, and who now ran a profitable sideline in some fiery spirit that she brewed herself. He shouldered open the door and sat down uninvited at the table that made up most of the furniture.

She peered at him through the gloom and smoke. 'You're back then? Thought to see you sooner.'

'I had business. More than I'd expected.'

'Speak up. Ear's bad.' She indicated her left ear, cropped and torn by some event long ago. 'Town all right? Drink and whore to your heart's content?'

Senorix grunted. 'You know me too well. Ach, the place is full of men with no spirit and women with too much. Are you keeping well yourself?'

She shook her head. 'Midwifing's not all it's cracked up to be.'

Senorix cocked his head on one side. 'Lose a baby?'

She looked at him bleakly. 'Yes; and no, as it happens. Helped one little babby into the world, and then smoothed his poor mother's road out of it. I just hope the lad comes to a better end than some I've known.'

She was silent for a long moment, then shook her head. 'Grieving does little good. You'll be after your things? All ready for you. Sword's hanging over the door, bay horse is at pasture. Want them now?'

'In a wee while; let's the pair of us have a sup of that poteen of yours first; I think we can both do with it. Then whistle up the old nag and I'll be off. I have a hard ride still to do before sunset.'

A little later she watched him mount and clatter away across the bridge until he was lost to view. She shrugged and turned indoors, muttering to herself. Help the newborn into the world, and ease the living out of it; and I see further than he thinks. And I know a warhorse when I see one. Old fool. Nothing personal.

XIV

It was quite dark before Marius could at last sit down to supper. A long spell in the bath-house had helped him relax and he quickly threw on a house-robe and lay down to eat, aware that he had spent longer in the hot-pool than his slaves would have expected.

He was paying for it now: Licnos had made a fine nettle flan which would no doubt have been delicious half an hour earlier but now tasted lumpy and a little stale. The second course – fish stew with dumplings – was better, though, and by the time he was tucking into a pudding of his favourite honey-cakes soaked in wine he was feeling at ease with the world.

The wine was good, too, unwatered, a fine old dry Falernian that he had paid far more for than was sensible and which he kept locked away for his own personal use. All the way from Latium, he thought, warm and carrying with it all the scents of a Roman summer; and how different from the stuff that the tavern was serving up.

At last he put down the cup by the side of the couch and turned to Flavius, 'Where's Cybele?'

Flavius frowned. 'She should be making sure that the lamps are all trimmed and lit, sir, but now you mention it I haven't seen her for an hour or so.'

He turned to one of the slaves clearing the low table. 'Find her and bring her here; and make sure she's got a clean face before she comes in.'

It seemed, though, that his steward's worries were unfounded, for Cybele appeared almost at once, her face showing signs of a recent scrub but her hands still black from the lamps.

'Kneel down, girl, that's right.'

Her face now level with his, Marius looked closely at her; the broad smile of the morning had faded somewhat, but she still looked happier than he had ever seen her.

'Tell me, Cybele, are you happy here?'

To Marius' astonishment, Cybele's face suddenly crumpled into horrified tears. 'Master, don't sell me. Don't make me go to work in a brothel. I'll work harder, I promise, I'll do anything you tell me. See, how hard I've been cleaning the lamps.' She held out her hands to witness her efforts while the tears streamed down her face.

'A brothel? What on earth put that into your head, Cybele?' Suddenly at a loss, Marius turned to Flavius. 'What's this all about?'

The steward coughed apologetically. 'I caught her idling around this morning, sir; I'd set her to cleaning the privy but half an hour later I found her just sitting outside with a silly look on her face, and the privy untouched. I gave her a good hiding but she still looked as useless as a wet hen, so I warned her that if she didn't get her ideas straight then you'd be sure to sell her next market-day. I didn't say anything about a brothel, though.'

He wouldn't have needed to, thought Marius; the brothel was the common destination for disobedient or idle girls, and Cybele would have taken it for granted that she would end up there. There seemed no need to disabuse her, he thought; the idea might make her more tractable.

'Well, Cybele, you know what happens to lazy girls; now dry your eyes and be quiet.'

Cybele continued to sniff but wiped her face and nose with her hands, leaving black soot-marks across her cheeks.

'Now, what were you mooning about for when you have work to do? Everyone here has to work, and that's what I bought you for. I can understand that you don't like scrubbing out the privy, but it has to be done and you must take your turn with the others; and if you are not obedient to your masters there will be no place for you.'

He paused and looked closely at the girl's eyes; he knew men who would simply have knocked her to the floor with a single blow for such disobedience, but there was something in her manner that made him want to understand what was going on in her head. And still under the grime and the tears he could trace the remains of that smile.

'Are you playing about with the men, Cybele? Have you let someone have you? Answer me, girl.'

That at least got an answer. 'No, Master, only you. Two months ago. Not since.'

Jupiter, Marius thought, she's keeping count. He shot a quick glance at Flavius, but the man's face remained impassive.

He tried another tack. 'Cybele, were you angry that on Beltane Eve you couldn't go to the special fire with the others?'

She shook her head and went on innocently, 'No, Master. I just said the special words quietly to myself while I was lighting the lamps in the evening, and then I burnt a little lamb-fat in them for a sacrifice, everybody does it, and I took it from my supper, I didn't even take it from the kitchen.'

Special words and a sacrifice. Forcing himself to speak calmly Marius went on, 'Cybele, is that some sort of magic? And you did it here in my house?'

She shook her head in horror. 'No, Master. Just a sacrifice to our gods. That's not magic. It does no harm.'

Marius glanced at his steward again. 'Flavius, do you know anything about this?'

The man shrugged. 'Who knows what these stupid Britons do when they're on their own? If I'd known about it I'd have stopped her, but they have their own ways and sometimes I don't have a clue when they're up to something.'

He was right there, Marius thought; but the time for pleasant speaking was clearly over. 'Cybele, if I thought you were trying some sort of witchcraft I wouldn't sell you, I'd have you crucified; do you understand, nailed up outside the town? Witchcraft can hurt me, my men and their families, the Divine Emperor himself even. Pray to your gods if you will, but let me find you trying to cast some spell and straight to the underworld you will go.'

Now the girl's shoulders were shaking in real terror. 'No spell, Master, no, I promise. I only prayed, Master, like we always do at Beltane. I never knew that the gods were really going to come.'

Marius sat up in surprise, suddenly remembering the man who had been haranguing his little group of hearers in the town earlier. 'What do you mean? When did the gods really come? Where?'

'Not here, Master; at the Beltane fire on the hill. Everyone knows about it.'

Marius paused to take stock, then spoke very slowly and clearly. 'Everybody knows about it, do they? Well, I don't, so let's start at the beginning; who told you about this?'

But Cybele was sobbing and staring at the floor. Marius sighed and turned to Flavius. 'Get Marcus Asellio here. He'll probably still be in the bath-house. I want him to hear this.' Then as the steward turned to the door he called out, 'And the tribune, too; there's something going on and I'm going to get to the bottom of it. And you, girl, hush that racket.'

Cybele made an effort to control herself; she lifted a tear-stained face and wiped her streaming eyes first with the back of her hand then with the bottom of her tunic; but she was still weeping when Marcus and Gracchus clattered into the room, both in various stages of undress.

'Sit down, gentlemen; I'm sorry to spoil your evening, but I hope this won't take too long. There's some silly rumour running round the town, and I want to get to the bottom of it.'

Marcus gave a rueful smile; the dice had run well, but at least the interruption meant that he had his evening's winnings safely tucked away in his purse. He sat solidly on one of the dining couches, letting the tribune perch on the edge of another one; neither man seemed altogether sober.

Marius reached out and put his hand under Cybele's chin.

'Now, tell these officers what you told me, Cybele. The whole truth about your Beltane sacrifice, and how people are saying that the gods came. If you tell us everything truthfully, then I promise that you won't be punished. But I'll know if you're lying, remember.' He took his hand away and carefully wiped it clean on the bottom of the couch.

Slowly Cybele began to retell the story, looking from time to time at Marius for reassurance. When she had finished he asked her again, 'Now, who told you this stuff? The truth, now, Cybele.'

She hesitated, then muttered, 'It was one of the carters who come into the camp, Master. I don't know his name. He said everyone knew about it.'

'And when was that?'

'Very early this morning, Master, just after the gates had opened. It was the man who brings the eggs every week. And I was so pleased to hear about it.'

'Did he tell you how these gods of yours had come, Cybele?'

'Oh yes, Master. He said that a woman had seen them first, but that afterwards everyone had; first there was Urien, all covered in green leaves, and then Blanaid in the shape of an owl, just as the story says.'

Marius raised a sceptical eyebrow. 'Why would they come here, Cybele? If the gods choose to come, they come in state to their temples, not in disguise to some bonfire up in the hills.' He paused, then went on thoughtfully, 'Do these gods of yours even have proper temples, Cybele? Or just some sacred grove – somewhere where the druids used to sacrifice to them, perhaps?' He hesitated, then went on, 'Does this have anything to do with that thief we crucified a couple of days ago?'

Cybele shook her head urgently, terrified again by the repeated mention of crucifixion. 'No Master, I don't know anything about him, I swear. And there are – were – no bad sacrifices to Urien and Blanaid, only to the gods and goddesses of the streams and the waters.'

She was silent for a moment, her shoulders shaking. Then she spoke again, hesitantly, as if uncertain that it was wise to talk but fearing the consequences if she kept silent.

'They say that there is a place that was sacred to them, where there are great stones all in a circle. South of here, Master, a ride away I think. But I was never there, Master, and I never heard of sacrifices there either, though…'

'Go on.'

'I heard about it a long time ago, Master. Long before you bought me. Everyone in the town would know about it. They say that country girls take flowers there in springtime and lay them in front of the biggest and oldest of the stones; they say that it was once a witch and that she still has power to…' Again her voice tailed away.

Marcus suddenly laughed out loud. 'Find them a man? Is that it?'

Cybele half turned to face him and nodded miserably, then wiped her nose with the back of her hand.

Marius glanced at the other two, then said to Cybele, 'If you've told us the truth then you have nothing to be afraid of; but if I find that you've lied, you will be punished or sold. Now go and get on with your work.'

Cybele bobbed her head in acknowledgement and ran out; behind her as she fled she heard a roar of laughter.

'I can't say that I've ever known country girls to have any trouble finding a lover.'

'Ah, sir, these are British girls she's talking about, not our forward Italian sort. Modest, sweet and not very clean. So naturally it takes them a bit more effort.'

Marius smiled. 'Right, gentlemen. This business of the gods could turn nasty if it's allowed to spread among the people unchecked; on the other hand, if we make too much of a fuss about it, we'll perhaps only be stirring the pot and making things worse. I suggest we keep a watching brief, come down hard on any disturbances, but otherwise let it just fade away; these things usually do, in my experience.

'This shrine and these stones, though; they might be worth checking over; what say we ride over there in the morning and take a look, though it's probably nothing to get too worked up about. Oh, and before I forget, Marcus – I found out a little more about that guide we've been paying a retainer to. Seems he's most famous for his boozing these days. If we ever need him, let's hope he hasn't drunk himself to death first.'

After the others had left, Marius sat for perhaps half an hour thinking about what Cybele had said. Finally he gave a sigh, drained his wine-cup and called to Flavius to say that he was going to bed.

One lamp was already burning when he reached his room, but he had thrown off his robe and climbed between the blankets before he noticed that Cybele was kneeling silent and naked at the foot of the bed. Irritably he shook his head, turned onto his right side and was asleep in moments.

It was perhaps three or four hours before cock-crow when he was awakened by the too-familiar sound of the rain drumming on the tiles above his head. He peered around the room, but Cybele had gone.

XV

A.D. IV Non. Mai – May 4th

The summits of the hills behind Verica's palace were barely out-lined in the dawn light when three people crept out of the postern, hooded and bent low to avoid the scudding rain and to lessen the chance of being seen by the little courtesy guard of soldiers shel-tering by the main gate. They picked their way eastwards first through the open pasture of the valley where the shapes of white-faced sheep loomed in the darkness, and then into the fringes of the forest climbing up the valley side, beech, elm and oak growing together in a tangle of branches.

Only when they had walked and stumbled for perhaps half a mile in the darkness did they stop to catch their breath. It was drier under the trees, and the tallest of the three pushed back her hood, shaking her head to free her long hair.

'It will be easier now; you both have your swords ready?'

'Yes, my lady, though I scarcely know how to use it,' answered the first man. 'My training was in other things.'

The other man gave a grin, his white teeth flashing in the faint light. 'Mother, you're safe with me. No robbers will dare come near us, and we're an easy match for wolves or bears.'

'Then we must hurry; we have a long way to go, and the rain will hinder us. And Lugos, though your sword is a comfort to me, I hope you will not need to use it.'

'Lugos?' The voice was half amused, half petulant. 'Lucos is what everyone calls me.'

'In Rome maybe; not here. Here you are Lugos, and here there is work for you to do.'

The young man shrugged. 'If I'm willing to drag myself up into the hills in the rain to see this wild woman of the woods of yours, then at least call me by the name I prefer. Rome is the future, mother, and you know that well enough; why do you keep clinging to the old ways as well?'

Verica shook her head in silence, then turned her back on the other two and began to stride up the long hillside. Behind her, her son walked with an easy pace, while Gwydion followed in the rear, panting a little as the climb steepened.

For much of the morning they tramped on in silence as the day slowly brightened. In the hills the rain gave way to a drenching mist, though Verica seemed sure enough of her way not to hesitate for a moment; five times they came upon mountain becks rushing down their own little valleys, and each time neat stepping stones in the water showed that they were indeed on the right way.

Perhaps an hour before noon as the little party emerged at last into open country they could hear away to the left the first sounds of human activity since they had left the palace, the chip, chip, chip of picks on stone, then the rumble of cart-wheels and the bray of asses.

'Our Roman friends are very busy here,' said Verica, pausing for the first time. 'They have mines for lead that go nearly fifty fathoms into the hillside, I've heard it said, with great bronze mirrors to cast light into them. But those should be a mile or more away from our way, so we have nothing to fear.'

Lugos rested his left hand on her shoulder then laid the forefinger of his right hand on his lips. Then, shaking his head gently he pointed away to the south. 'Latin,' he whispered, then stood with his head cocked to one side.

After a few moments all three could hear the voices; there were two men at least, perhaps more, and sometimes there was the telltale crack of a branch underfoot; it was clear that whoever was approaching had no thought or need of silence.

'Back,' murmured Verica, and the little group carefully retraced its way through the bracken, gently lifting the stalks back into place behind them. Once under the cover of the trees they stopped again, crouching low; Lugos was fingering his sword, but

Verica shook her head urgently and the lad grinned at her and winked, though he still kept his hand on the pommel.

At last a man came into clear sight about a bow-shot away, followed by three more, with a couple of long-haired British hunting dogs at their heels; Verica guessed that they were a forage party, or perhaps just a group of friends heading homeward after a morning's hunting. Two of the men were carrying loosely strung bows and the other pair had spears sloped across their shoulders, with the bodies of perhaps a dozen hares hanging from each. All of them were laughing and joking together, talking in harshly accented Gaulish Latin.

'From the mines,' whispered Gwydion in Verica's ear. She hushed him with a wave of her hand, and he stepped back, cracking a twig as he did so.

The noise was slight enough and should have been lost in the soft patter of rain on leaves, but one of the dogs suddenly stopped and gave a soft whine.

The group's leader paused. 'There's another one. Come on, Tetricus. Last one of the day.'

He turned to scan the forest, ready to order the dogs forward, but his friends just laughed. 'Leave it, we've got plenty already. You're not going to share them with the mine-slaves, are you? Time to get dry in front of the fire.'

Tetricus was not to be so easily persuaded. Crouching and resting his left hand on the shoulder of the nearest dog he began to step carefully through the undergrowth, peering to left and to right as he went. Verica felt Lugos' grip tighten once more on his sword, and again she shook her head urgently. At her shoulder Gwydion was calmly muttering a charm against discovery.

Then as she was at the very point of stepping forward into the open and making herself known with her haughtiest stare, Tetricus suddenly gave a rueful laugh and turned back to his companions. 'All right, you win. Don't complain that you're hungry tomorrow, that's all.'

Verica and her companions remained unmoving while the hunting party continued on their way, and only after all sound of them had faded from hearing did Verica at last relax.

Lugos gave a little chuckle. 'Mother, you are a Queen but you hide from these men like a runaway slave. You should let me teach them their place.'

'And have it known that I have come up here? What we are doing here is no business of theirs, and I will not have them sniffing around like their hunting dogs until they find…' She let her voice trail away, then went on, 'things that are no concern of theirs.'

Lugos lifted a lazy eyebrow but said nothing, but Gwydion nodded. 'We are very near now, but the place is so secret that I am sure that no-one could find it unless it were betrayed. But the day is drawing on and we should hurry while we can.'

The slope was downward now. Soon a tiny stream appeared, barely a rivulet, making its own little channel in the hillside. Verica turned to follow it as it pattered over the stones, deepening and becoming stronger almost with every stride.

'We must go wet-shod here,' she murmured, and stepped firmly into the cold water. The two men followed, walking first ankle-deep as the stream found its way between two grey boulders and then turned abruptly to the left into an unexpected rift in the hillside.

Now they went in single file, their arms stretched out on each side to steady themselves against the sides of the cleft, stumbling over the rocks as they went. For almost half a mile their road lay along the stream until it suddenly made a turn to the right, tumbling over a little waterfall and vanishing from sight. Here the ground opened out into almost a small meadow rising above the water, with two goats tethered nearby, chickens scratching around their feet, and at the far end a well-tended little garden. On three sides the cliffs rose around them, standing perhaps three or four times higher than a tall man, their tops crowned with ancient oaks.

The three travellers climbed up onto the drier land. Verica stood for a moment in puzzlement, scanning the base of the cliffs;

behind her, Gwydion was muttering another charm, while Lugos stood stock-still with an amused expression on his face.

'It is so long since I came here,' Verica murmured, 'and she was not young then. Perhaps she has gone away, or died. But then whose goats and hens are those; and who tends the garden?'

'Welcome, friends. As you can see, I still live and breathe.' The voice was so close at hand that all three started in alarm, and Lugos spun around with his hand again flying to his sword.

And now they saw her; she was, they might suppose, some seventy years old, but still tall and straight, with long, finely-combed grey hair. A grey woollen cloak, almost the same colour as the cliffs themselves, covered her from crown to toe, and behind her was a tall cleft in the rocks from which she had clearly just emerged. Now she smiled broadly at them, showing a mouth full of firm, white teeth. 'I have so few visitors that I have become a poor hostess. But not all guests would be as welcome here as you are, my lady.'

She gestured towards a large flat rock standing in the middle of the little enclosure. 'Sit and rest. There is good water here for your thirst.' She turned deftly, picking up a little wooden cup from the cleft behind her and offering it first to Lugos. 'You drink first. For I think that this wild woman of the woods is not as you expected.'

Lugos blushed but mastered himself in a moment and accepted the cup with a little bow. 'You cannot have heard me, so how did you know my words?'

'Young man, they were written plain on your face from the moment I first saw you. And it is, after all, my business to see what is truly there. So few do. You should know my name; I am Niamh.'

Lugos spread his hands in a gesture of amused resignation and turned to his mother. 'It seems you told me the truth.'

Verica smiled. 'She can tell you some things that are true and many that are, well, less certain we might say; and she will let you decide which are which.' She sat beside her son, leaving Gwydion still standing at her shoulder. 'Niamh, do you know why we have come?'

'For the same reason that anyone still comes to me: to know what the future holds. It is a strange folly that while everyone imagines that they can act freely themselves, they also imagine that the future is fixed; do not expect me to resolve that riddle.'

'But you can still see further than most,' Verica insisted; 'I have known you do so before. If you can clear a little of the mist that lies ahead of me, that is all I ask. Can you do this?' She smiled sadly. 'We have already had a full day's travel this morning, and must retrace our steps before evening comes.'

Niamh considered for a moment. 'He knows,' she said pointing to Gwydion, 'that since the Romans slew the druids there are fewer ways in which I can divine the future. If we had a victim here then we could sacrifice him in the old way and so summon the gods; but the gods do not always come, and besides that takes much time to prepare. And I have my divining cup, but again the images that come to me there are often mysterious and hard to understand.

'The last way has more dangers than either of the others, but it is more certain; it is for me to enter the world of the gods. Oh, that is easy enough – their world lies so close to ours that the immortals themselves can come and go as they please; but to come back is less sure. I might go there in my mind for a seeming morning only to return and find that my body has been locked in sleep here for twenty years or more. If I am to venture there, I need some token that will give me safe passage back, something that has itself been near to death, for nothing that speaks of death can be borne for long in that place. Have you such a thing?'

Verica shook her head, then looked questioningly at Lugos and Gwydion. 'It seems that none of us has anything of the kind, and that our journey has been wasted.'

She stood up and as she did so the light suddenly caught the little lapis brooch that Senorix had given her, which she had used to fasten her cloak. Niamh stepped forward, her hand reaching towards the pretty thing.

'This will be what I need. It reeks of death. Can you truly not feel it?'

She touched it with her fingers and shuddered. 'This came from a man who was murdered, and not long ago nor far away. How did you come by such a thing?'

'It was a gift, given only a day or two ago; I had thought it was given honestly.'

Niamh nodded. 'I am sure it was so; you should not blame the giver. Rather, thanks are due to him for without this we could go no further here. Quickly, take it off and let me hold it.'

Verica loosened it with suddenly clumsy fingers. 'Here you are. What will you do now?'

Niamh took the brooch, gingerly at first then grasping it tight in her right hand. 'I shall sit there in my little cave, and you will think I do nothing. Do not call to me, for I shall not hear you. It may be that soon we shall be able to see a little further through this mist of yours.'

With a smile she retreated to the cleft from which she had come. Lugos watched her go, then after a short pause he jumped to his feet and strode to the mouth of the cave and looked in. For a moment he stood there in puzzlement, then shaking his head he came back to the others.

'She is not there. She has gone somewhere. Is there a secret way from the back of that little hollow?'

Verica smiled and shook her head. 'She is still there, but you have not the eyes to see her. Look more closely; she will have faded right into the rock, for now she is barely in our world at all. Go, look again.'

Doubtfully Lugos did as his mother said, staring into the darkness for a long while, before coming and sitting by his mother again. 'Yes, she is there, but with that grey cloak of hers she seems one with the cliff. No-one could find her unwanted.' Then as the thought suddenly struck him he asked, 'She has given you her advice before, it seems?'

'Yes. She has foretold your fate, and that of your brother as well. But that was twenty years or more ago.'

'You have told me nothing of this. What did she say?'

Verica laughed. 'Suddenly you believe in Niamh because you hear that she has spoken about you. No, I shall not tell you what she said; you must find your fate by living it.'

Lugos looked as if he were about to argue, then shrugged and let it pass. 'I remember that you asked her what we should do when she took this journey to the world of the gods so I do not think that you have seen her do this before.' He paused, letting his unspoken question hang in the air.

Reluctantly Verica nodded. 'You are right. Your fate and that of your brother were foretold in the old way. Your father had a man in his charge who had gone mad and had killed his wife and children. That was in the times before the Romans had begun to mine near here, so we could ride up with no fear of discovery. We fed him his *viaticum*, his food for the journey, and brought him here along the little stream the way we have come today. He came consenting, not knowing the fate that awaited him; then together we killed him, the three-fold death that I make no doubt you have heard of. His blood, or a part of it, fell into the stream as a fitting sacrifice to the gods, and Niamh watched him die and then the gods spoke to her in a trance. He was standing not far from where you are now when the dagger struck him.

'And I held and pulled the rope around his neck as he fell and drew it tight; then we forced his head into the water, so that he was strangled and drowned and stabbed. It was – interesting. And after his death we all took him and stamped his body into the little marsh below there where the stream flows, so that the sun should never shine on his shame. No doubt his bones rot there still.

'Gwydion reminded me yesterday that the gods thirst for blood. See you do not forget it.'

Lugos nodded, apparently unconcerned, though Gwydion

standing silent by noticed that the lad took the chance to move away from the fatal spot as soon as he easily could. For a moment the silence of the meadow was broken only by the chatter of the stream as it plunged out of sight, and then from somewhere in the distance came the shrill repeated call of a curlew.

Verica smiled and nodded to herself at the memory, then cast a questioning look at her son. 'You did not feel the blood in this place when we arrived, Lugos?'

'No; but then I have seen so much blood spilt in Rome that perhaps it means nothing to me any more. At least there they kill people openly, not hiding death away in secret places like this.'

'Oh, Rome has its share of secret shrines where many have died, I promise you Lugos. And it was never our way to kill for entertainment alone, there is that at least to be said for us.'

Suddenly philosophical, Verica went on, 'You know, it was the folly of the Jews to think that their god was somehow just or honourable; but in the end they understood the truth, that he wanted blood just like all the others. And so it was that when their temple sacrifices ended he soon turned his back on them, did he not?

'Worship and fear the gods, Lugos, but never, never be so foolish as to trust them. Is this not good advice, Gwydion?'

'Indeed, my lady. I hear that this god of the Jews has turned his attention to finding other people to worship him, and now has all the blood he could wish for from these new followers.'

Verica smiled grimly but before she could speak she saw Niamh emerging silently from the rock. Now her hair was dishevelled and her face was ashen and drawn.

Verica and Lugos both jumped to their feet, but Niamh held out her left arm to fend them off. Carefully she walked to the flat rock and sat down on it. Then she opened her right hand, took out the little lapis brooch and laid it beside her.

Verica knelt in front of her. 'What happened? What did you see? Can you tell us?'

For a long moment Niamh was silent, her eyes cast down. At

last she spoke, her voice sounding as if it was coming from a great distance. 'I have no riddles for you to untangle today, my lady. The gods are meeting together in council. Make no doubt of it, much blood will be shed.'

Verica took two or three deep breaths before she spoke. 'I feared as much. Can you tell what the outcome will be?'

Gradually the colour was coming back into Niamh's face. After another long pause she gave a wan smile. 'Now I could riddle,' she murmured. 'Hear me do so: those who think to gain will lose all, and those who fear they will lose will be the gainers.'

Suddenly she shook her head in distaste. 'No, though what I have said is true, yet I will not play with words. War is coming, and much that is good will be destroyed. That is all you should know.'

'Then what should I do? What should any of us do?'

Now Niamh stared at her with an expression of utter amazement. 'What should you do, my lady? You truly ask me what you should do? Why, do that which is right, of course. I can tell you nothing more.' Then in a single harsh movement she took the brooch and thrust it back into Verica's hand.

For a moment Verica stood irresolute. 'Now go.' said Niamh in a voice so loud and fierce they could scarce believe it came from one so old, 'Go.' Then she bowed her head and sat in silence.

☙ ☙ ☙ ☙ ☙ ☙ ☙

It was in silence that they trudged most of the way home, dog-tired and disconsolate, with the fresh rain falling still about them. Then, with a perhaps a mile of the journey left and the shelter of the woods just past, they heard the sudden clatter of hooves and three men came riding hard out of the mist, heading north. Gwydion and Lugos put their hands to their swords, but the first rider hailed them in surprise and reined to a stop, while the others brought their horses to a stand a little distance away.

'My lady,' said Marius, leaning forward on his cob's heaving neck, 'I had not thought to find you abroad in such foul weather.'

XVI

Before Verica could think of an answer, Lugos stepped forward, pushing his hood back from his head as he did so and lifting a hand in friendly greeting.

'Commander Marius, I think – we've met just a couple of times.'

'The Queen's son? Lugos, is that right?'

'I prefer Lucos, Commander; but yes, that's right. You and your friends seem to have had a hard ride in the rain?'

If Marius noticed the way that his question had been turned back on him he gave no sign of it. 'Duty sometimes gives us strange tasks.'

'Us too, Commander; my mother has certain religious duties which take her attention, as you will surely understand. This unending rain has driven us out to make prayers and offerings to the River Goddess, though whether that lady will choose to listen no-one knows. Our devotion often goes for nothing, it seems.'

Marius nodded curtly. 'True enough, the gods often seem to take and give nothing in return. But time goes on, and we must head home. But forgive me my rudeness – these men are my tribune Gracchus and Marcus Asellio, my primus pilus and my old friend as well.

Verica had already recovered her composure. 'Why not come to dinner, Commander? Surely that would be more pleasant for you all? You can rest your horses, use the bath-house, relax for a little while. One of your honour-guards at the gate can carry a message to your camp and tell them not to expect you till morning.'

Marius hesitated, then nodded. 'Yes, why not? We can carry you the rest of your way; my lady, will you ride pillion with me, and the others can ride with my men?' He fixed his eye on Verica, watching closely as her troubled expression was suddenly replaced by a smile.

'Why not indeed, Commander? They say that only a fool checks the saddle without inspecting the horse, but here both are surely sound enough.' She grasped the pommel and swung up easily behind Marius, tucking her wet cloak and skirts easily around her and wrapping her arms around his waist, then turned and laughed at Gwydion and Lugos.

'Ease your legs, come on. Why not ride with our friends?'

But Gwydion shook his head. 'No, my lady, I shall plod home on these same feet that have borne me the rest of the way today. You ride if you wish, but I shall walk.'

Lugos paused, looking from one to the other. 'Then I shall walk with you; it's only a mile, and we can hardly get any wetter than we already are. And a fine dinner with friends will give us something to look forward to at the end of our hike.'

The two watched as the horses cantered off towards the palace, then trudged after them in silence. Only after they had covered perhaps half the distance did Gwydion finally speak.

'You did well; your mother was taken unawares – we both were. I wonder what they were doing?'

'Ask them at dinner,' Lugos laughed, then suddenly stopped before going on in a more subdued voice. 'The *veleda*, what did she see? What made her drive us out? Do you know?'

Gwydion smiled grimly. 'Niamh saw her own death, I think. Perhaps it is not so very far off; who knows how far she can see when the trance is on her? But I do not think that death for her will be as it is for others. Those who walk with the gods have a different destiny.'

'For a seer she spoke very plainly. Does she always do so?'

Gwydion took his time before answering. 'The words with her are always plain, but sometimes they have a deeper meaning that only time reveals. But few go to ask her advice now, hidden away in the hills with the Romans all around – they would think her a half-druid at least, and they have no love of that kind as we all know.'

'Well, I will not give her away.' Lugos thought for a moment, then went on, 'Do you know what fate she saw for me and my brother all those years ago? Or at least do you know why my mother will not tell me what it is?'

'Yes, I know what it is and why she will not say. And where she is silent, I must be too. But this I will say, that although it is not a fate she would wish for you, it is not a bad fate – indeed, I think it is one that you would happily choose for yourself even if the gods had not laid it down. And I shall not speak of your brother's fate either.'

Lugos nodded. 'I miss him, you know, and I think mother misses him even more, though she never seems to speak much of him. Rome is not so far now as it used to be, only a few days' ride on good roads through Gaul and over the passes into Italy, and then down through the warm sunny land to the Great City herself. How long before we feel the sun on our backs again here, Gwydion?'

'If the River Goddess has heard what you said it may not be for some time. She will not take kindly to you talking so loudly of offerings and prayers when we have not made them. The river is a jealous goddess, you know.'

'Then I shall make them tomorrow, and make them specially generous to make up for my fault. Will that do?'

Gwydion nodded absent-mindedly, but still muttered under his breath, 'It is blood that she wants; and I think she will have it before very long.'

It was, Marius admitted to himself later, a far better dinner than he would have had at home, with no less than ten courses ranging from delicate candied rose-petals to stuffed larks and a whole roast boar, no doubt killed earlier in the forest. Fine bronze lampstands had been carried into the dining room and in the light of the flickering flames the murals that he had first seen a few days earlier seemed to shift and move; there were two braziers to provide warmth in the cool of the evening – clearly the furnace which in winter sent warm air through the hypocaust had been allowed to go out. Marcus Asellio would certainly regret his decision to ride back to the camp rather than enjoy this fine hospitality.

The wine, too, was excellent – far better than he could have afforded, and served in handled silver cups, with an incised design. He squinted at his own in the dim light, trying to see what it depicted, and suddenly became aware of Verica's eyes on him.

She smiled. 'You like my *kantheroi*, Commander? I think you will find nothing like them anywhere else.'

Marius silently noted the Greek term, and raised the cup in salute. 'Truly they are very fine, my lady, and do good justice to the wine within. I was trying to decipher the motif, but my eyes aren't what they were. A mythological scene, I presume?'

'Not especially, as it happens; a man, a woman, a tree and a wineskin, with a frieze of vines above them, that is all. So they can be anyone you wish – Mars and Venus, or Dido and Aeneas, or Antony and Cleopatra, or even you and me. The choice is yours, Commander. But you must all have had a hard day's riding. Tell me about it.'

To his surprise Marius found himself colouring. Her arms had been wrapped tight around his waist and her face laid against his back as they cantered home. Ah, in a different world… But he nodded and took a deep drink from his cup before answering.

'I'm afraid you must bear the blame for that, my lady; or Gwydion, at least. His tale of the great stones left me anxious to see them for myself, and having done so I must agree that they are truly magnificent, far beyond my imaginings. If the story Gwydion told us is true, they must have been there for centuries; long before Rome was founded, perhaps even before Troy fell.'

Verica gave a wry smile. 'Oh, we barbarians do have our skills,

Commander – though I doubt if we could raise such things today. But you must know that there are innumerable such shrines in Britain – indeed, there is a fine one on a hill-top not very many miles to the west of us – and I hear there are many others beyond the sea. And each one was raised as a mark of man's devotion to the gods and the great heroes of times gone by.'

'And each one has its own story, no doubt?'

'Ah, if he were here Gwydion would be able to tell you many such tales, but after today's travels he prefers to lie sneezing in his bed. I have heard him tell some of them long ago, about stones that rise from their places on moonless nights and go to drink at the river nearby, or stones that no-one can count, or that have a great treasure buried beneath them, or that mark the burial place of some great hero or prince. Whether his stories are true or not, I think the stones will stand long after the tombs of Rome's emperors have turned to dust.'

'That may be, but they will not outlast Rome herself. Rome is for ever.'

'*Imperium sine fine*?' Verica smiled. 'That was the promise to Aeneas for his descendants, was it not?'

Marius nodded. 'And so you will know, my lady, that when Aeneas was shown the place where great Rome would one day be built, the spot where Capitoline Jove's temple would rise was a thicket of thorns, and the site of the Forum was a mere cow pasture. With the blessing of the gods Rome has grown from nothing to greatness, and her growth and splendour will never end.'

'Rome has grown great indeed. But if only Gwydion were here he would say that everything in creation moves in great cycles, as the stars turn in the sky, and that Rome's Forum will be a cow pasture again before the end comes.'

Gracchus could contain himself no longer. 'Rome will outlast even the pyramids, let alone some barbarian stones. But even so, they troubled me.'

Marius raised a questioning eyebrow. 'Troubled you? Why?'

'Unregulated worship, sir; we've seen the problems that can bring in Rome, where every crazy sect has set up shop. Oh, this seems to be nothing at the moment, just a place where country people bring flowers and stuff, but it might become a centre of unrest if we don't keep an eye on it.'

Marius glanced at Verica and Lugos. 'Have you ever thought of that? That the place – or other places like it, perhaps – could be a focus for some sort of trouble?'

It was Verica who answered. 'Commander, there are dozens of such places within thirty miles of here, though it's true that this is the most impressive. It would be impossible to watch them all for signs of trouble; and even the power of Rome could hardly pull all the stones down. Sowing Carthage with salt was one thing, to destroy all these would be a far greater work, and I think it would be for no benefit. And Commander, I do not think Rome has enough soldiers to do this anyway?'

Lugos broke in. 'On the other hand, Commander, perhaps there is something in what the noble tribune says. His concern, I think, was not for the stones themselves, but for the fact that people go there to worship and sacrifice with no supervision, sometimes in ones or twos, and sometimes in twenties or thirties.'

Gracchus nodded. 'Exactly. Rome herself knows how dangerous such places can be. Commander, you will remember what used to happen at Diana's temple at Lake Nemi until Nero himself finally brought it under proper state supervision. There was open murder there, repeated bloodshed, with the very priest himself a runaway slave and a killer who went unpunished. And he called himself a king, no less.'

'Rex Nemorensis. Yes – until someone else came to take over the post and bumped him off in turn,' remarked Marius dryly. 'Unusual, but at least it was traditional; I would have thought that you would have honoured the ways of our forefathers a little more, Tribune.'

'The goddess and the ways of our forefathers are honoured

there still, Commander, but in a more civilised way, with a proper temple and a salaried officiant. Why should we not do much the same here?'

'A salaried priest out there at the stones? Can you be serious? Who would pay him?'

Gracchus smiled. 'No, my lady, not at the stones; the country people need to learn that the future is in the great towns and cities that we Romans are building, and to forget their uncivilised ways. Why do we not build a new shrine here – in the town, I mean – where we can keep an eye on things? If we do it tactfully enough the old place will be forgotten in a generation.' And, he thought to himself, there will be no taste of the druidical about it.

'Forgotten?' This was Lugos. 'I can't see how anyone could forget those thumping great stones. But perhaps you're right; it would certainly be better to educate people away from these country shrines. What do you think, mother?'

Verica pushed the hair away from her eyes and considered, then started to speak but hesitated. She turned her wine-cup in her hand for a moment, looking hard into it as if she was searching for an answer in its depths, then slowly nodded.

'I see no harm; our gods should be honoured everywhere, not left as a relic for the farmers and shepherds and country girls. And it must be a place of sanctuary as well, so that those who call on the divine powers cannot be taken away by force. Suppliants are always sacred to the god, are they not? Remember how when Troy fell, the Locrian Ajax dragged Cassandra from Athene's shrine, and the evil that flowed from that. But Rome will have to pay for it.'

Gracchus winced and turned to bring Marius back in to the conversation. 'Well, Commander?'

'Such shrines are usually supported by those who worship there,' he said pointedly, 'but perhaps in the first instance we could erect at least a decent altar on some of that empty land behind the forum; surely some of the wealthier merchants in the town would be willing to stump up a little cash for that, especially as they'll stand to make a tidy profit from anyone coming in to worship? A temple might follow one day if funds allow. And, as you say, supplicants there would be under the god's protection.'

He smiled as a thought occurred to him. 'The rites would not be such as to cause any offence, of course?'

'To Lugos we only offer flowers,' said Verica.

'And maidenheads as well, from what I've heard of the goings-on on Beltane Eve.' That was Gracchus again, speaking now a little too loudly in his cups.

Marius moved in smoothly to cover any embarrassment. 'Such things are common enough; the rites of Egyptian Isis are well-known, and our own Lupercalia is hardly the most modest festival you could imagine.'

'And we all know of the rites of the followers of Phrygian Cybele, who castrate themselves and dress and behave like women.'

No sooner was Cybele's name out of his mouth than Gracchus realised what he had said and blushed scarlet. Marius half rose from his dining couch with a face like thunder, then forced a smile and took a deep drink from his cup. Then he glanced at Verica's face to see whether she had understood the gibe, but her expression was impassive and gave nothing away.

'My friend has had a hard day's riding today, my lady; you will allow him to withdraw for the night?'

Verica smiled and nodded. 'We have all had a hard day, Commander, and a wet one as well.' She waited while Gracchus rose from his couch and bowed stiffly to her before leaving, then went on softly, 'That man has a mouth that will get him into trouble, I think.'

Marius shook his head angrily, then made a conscious effort to control himself. 'Or make him even richer. The people of Rome love a man who will speak his mind and tell it like it is, no matter what sort of rubbish he comes out with. In twenty years' time Gracchus will have a fine political career, and we can only hope that he learns to keep his mouth shut in the meantime.'

'And he has forgotten his Hesiod. Παντα ρει.'

'All things pass? I wonder if he has ever heard the line.' He glanced at Verica, and she noticed – or perhaps only imagined – a sudden warmth in his eyes. Then he shrugged and took another draught from his cup. 'But despite that, he's made a good suggestion, and I think we should act on it. I will make sure that a suitable place is found and cleared for it, and then when a suitable altar has been made we can have decent rites of dedication for it and all will be well; perhaps your son here would feel honoured to take up duties there from time to time.'

Lugos smiled. 'Officiant at a shrine which carries my own name? A rare distinction.'

Verica shook her head. 'Commander, such an altar should surely commemorate some particular blessing that the god has granted, and it is for those who have benefited from it to pay for both altar and dedication.'

The fine wine had lulled Marius into a state of happy acquiescence. 'That is true, my lady; and now I will vow to have such an altar made myself, if only the god will send us fine weather. What greater benefit can any of us ask for?'

Verica's eyes opened wide. 'Commander, that would be truly generous, and would do much honour to my son and to our god. Such an altar would certainly be welcomed by all our people.'

Marius drained his cup, then nodded. 'Well, if the sun shines and the rain stops for as long as it will take for the altar to be carved and the land cleared for it, then I shall stand by what I have said, even though I said it after drinking too much of your excellent wine. And perhaps my tribune will find it to his benefit to contribute something to the costs of the altar as well. If the rain ever does stop, that is – hear how it rattles on the tiles.'

He yawned and shook his head to clear it, then went on, 'Be that as it may, I thank you indeed for your hospitality, my lady, but I am not as young as I used to be and I find that I need my sleep.

Will you please excuse me?'

Verica smiled and nodded. 'Of course, Commander. For my part, I find that sleep is sometimes slow to come, and then the night can seem so very long; but tonight I shall rest happily, knowing that if your vow does indeed bring better weather, then everyone for miles around will bless you.' She inclined her head as Marius rose and watched as the major-domo bowed him out, then turned to her son, who was yawning on his couch.

'A day of turns and reverses. Before noon we hear that Niamh foresees blood, and I think Gwydion is of the same mind, but before we go to our beds we see that our Roman friends are ready to raise an altar to our own gods. You will see, all will be well yet.'

XVII

A.D. III Non. Mai – May 5th

Verica stirred as Iras swung open the shutters and the warm spring sunshine flooded in; somewhere nearby a blackbird was singing, and from further away came the mournful notes of a cuckoo.

She sat up, looked hard for a moment at the bright light, and then laughed softly as memories of the previous evening flooded back into her mind.

'What time is it, girl?'

'Nearly the second hour, my lady.'

Verica shook her head to clear it. 'After yesterday's exertions I think we all needed our sleep. Our guests – are they still here?'

Iras shook her head. 'No, my lady. I saw them ride off almost as soon as it was light.'

Verica caught the wistfulness in her servant's voice. 'You thought they looked brave, child?'

Iras blushed in silence and bowed her head. Verica smiled and went on, 'Brave indeed, and their leader more than most. Ah, what fine oaths he swore last night. And I think the gods have taken him at his word.'

'My lady?'

'No matter. Is Gwydion about yet?'

'Yes, my lady; he said he would speak to you as soon as you wish. He looked rather…' She hesitated, then went on in a puzzled tone, '…well, rather dirty, my lady.'

'Indeed? I wonder why. Come, girl, dress me quickly. Fetch me my fine green silk from the great chest, and my sandals with the silver clasps. And then call the other girls to put up my hair and paint these lines out of my face and make me look young again.'

Another hour had passed – an hour of careful powdering and

painting and curling – before Verica could finally look with satisfaction at her reflection in the fine bronze mirror. Then she rose from the little drum-stool, cast a last triumphant glance over her shoulder at the sunshine-filled courtyard beyond the window, and swept down the corridor to her private sitting room, the silk gown whispering about her and Iras pattering along behind.

Gwydion, his face and tunic filthy with soot, rose as she entered and bobbed his head in greeting. Verica stopped, put her hand under his chin and laughed, then caught herself and shook her head.

'Gwydion, Iras told me you were not your usual clean self today, but I must not smile at you; after all, I am the author of all your discomfort. Did you truly have a terrible night? And after such a hard day before it.'

The harper grimaced. 'It was like Annwn itself, my lady, filthy and hot and smoky, and with nowhere where I could stretch out my old body. I wriggled in between the pillars as best I might, and thought I might never free myself or breathe wholesome air again. There are no words in any language to describe it. My lady, I need a bath as never before.'

'And yet here you are waiting like a brave soldier to make his report before you leave the battlefield. Well, tell me what you heard while you were crouched down there in the hypocaust.'

Gwydion nodded, his eyes shining. 'There were angry words, my lady; it seems that the Commander had taken deep offence at something the tribune had said to him. The name of Cybele was mentioned more than once, and in terms which suggested that the Commander knows her well; but who she may be – if not the Phrygian goddess of that name – I cannot say.'

Verica frowned. 'There was some such remark at dinner; I did not know what to make of it, but it was plain that he was – well, angered by it. Go on.'

Gwydion hesitated for a moment. 'You know, my lady, that those who eavesdrop may not always hear things to their own credit?'

'So it is said, Gwydion, but after yesterday's toil I am past caring. Tell me truly.'

'The words were those of the tribune, Gracchus. That man has a very distinctive voice.'

'He is high-born, Gwydion, and thinks everyone else is beneath him, and every word he speaks makes his disdain clear. So what did this tribune have to say?'

'The words were these: Why should we Romans, who govern the whole world, have any dealings with this woman and her little kingdom. She calls herself a Queen, and governs hardly more than one valley and its little tribe of barbarians, and yet we build her this villa – which she calls a palace – and treat her with as much honour as if she were the governor of a province. She is nothing.'

He paused and glanced up, but Verica laughed. 'At last, a man who tells the truth. I like him better already. Did the Commander answer him?'

'Yes, my lady. He spoke of treaties, of Rome's word given, of what would happen if the Great City should be seen to retract its promises. I thought that he would speak about you too, my lady, but he did not. Perhaps in his heart he believes what his tribune said.'

'And what else?'

'He said that for his part he would do as Rome does, and honour his vows, and then he spoke of raising an altar in the town. He did not say why. There was nothing else of note before they slept. And the tribune snores.'

'Then I must tell you more. He has promised to raise an altar to Lugos if the god brings us fair weather after all this rain, Gwydion. And the immortals have taken him at his word, it seems, and sent the very weather that will make him honour his oath.'

Gwydion nodded. 'Then you and the gods have done well between you, my lady. But although the gods will be thankful for the altar, remember that they can be fickle, too. Do not presume too much on their good humour. Remember what Niamh saw. But it may be indeed that we have some time of peace left us, and for that we should be grateful.'

Verica stood for a moment turning his words over in her mind, then glanced away through the window into the garden beyond. Everything stood out clear in the bright morning light, and even the distant hills to the west were visible in the clear air. As she watched a little group of house-martins swooped across the basin of the fountain, their voices one shrill scream. The gods hear our oaths, she thought, then they put us all to the test. Well, let it be as they would have it.

She turned back with a smile. 'My dear Gwydion, you have endured true hardship; no soldier was ever more faithful to his night-watch. Now take yourself to the bath-house and have some-one scrub away all your grime and your pain. And only name your reward for what you have done, and you shall have it, I swear.'

'A reward, my lady? Only that you never ask me to do this again.' Again he bobbed his head, then turned and limped through the door.

Verica watched him go, and smiled to herself. So he never mentioned me? But, Gwydion, you could not see his eyes as I could, and anyway it would have been beyond your craft to read them. And so I think you understand him very little.

☙ ☙ ☙ ☙ ☙ ☙ ☙

In the unexpected sunshine Senorix rode easily, his sword slung across his back and his pack hanging from the horns of the saddle. He had spent the last night with some cottars who had made him comfortable enough on a bed of bracken and had refused to take any of his Roman money in recompense for their trouble, or indeed for the breakfast of oatcakes which they had shared with him, though he suspected that their store was slight enough. What does Rome mean to them and their like? he mused. A road, stretching endlessly away, a distant name, perhaps soldiers sometimes trooping past, nothing else; for them, the world goes on unchanging as it has always been.

But a mile or two further on it was plain that change had happened here too. On his way south a few days earlier he had ridden past a long-abandoned Roman signal tower that had stood by the side of the road, perhaps a relic of Agricola's campaign that had ended at Mons Graupius.

Now, though, the great timbers supporting the beacon-platform had been dragged down and lay flat on the ground – heavy work for a team of oxen, that – and all the metalwork had been stripped away and filched. Most of the lighter woodwork had been carried away too, though the still-smouldering remains of a fire showed where the less useful stuff had been set ablaze.

Senorix smiled to himself and remembered his words of a few days earlier: slowly, so slowly they move southwards like a retreating tide. And now even the fine road he was riding on seemed to bear out the truth of his words; though it still ran on as straight as ever, grass was beginning to force its way through the gaps between the slabs and there were few travellers; now Senorix rode more carefully, alert to every sound, and with his sword close at hand.

After perhaps two hours' riding he left the paved road on its embankment and turned his horse away to the north-east, heading along an ancient trackway which followed the line of a stream cutting down from the hills. Wild garlic was flowering all along the edge of the water, and he put back his head and breathed in the powerful scent.

Once out of sight of the road he paused, pushed back his hood to feel the blessed sun on his face, then swung down from the saddle, knelt by the river and cupped the water in his hands to drink and to splash over his face. From somewhere on the other side of the stream came the call of a curlew, repeated three times; then an answering call from further along the track. He smiled, pulled himself back into the saddle and resumed his journey.

The track seemed to be busier than the road had been, for after perhaps another mile a man riding a shaggy native pony trotted out of the forest and took up station a bow-shot behind Senorix, never coming closer but never quite out of sight. Then before long they overtook another man riding in the same direction, who glanced at them over his shoulder then set his pony's pace to match theirs.

Senorix grinned widely and looked back at the rider following him; but the man was bent right forward over his horse's mane and took no apparent notice of him. Senorix reined back, and the others slowed too; then he urged his horse into a gentle canter, only for the others to quickly match his pace.

The valley was wide and grassy, and the stream was shallow, picking its way between flat water-worn stones. There was a ford here, easily passable in almost all weathers; but it seemed this time there would be no easy crossing. For as Senorix and the others approached, a dozen men galloped out of the woods on the far side of the stream and took up their position right across the track; they wore armour and helmets in the Roman fashion, and carried swords and spears.

As Senorix watched, the rider ahead of him spurred across the stream and took up his station with the others.

With a quick movement of his arm Senorix drew his sword and held it high above his head. Then ululating wildly he pushed his horse into a thundering gallop and charged into the ford.

XVIII

For perhaps two hours Niamh had sat silent and unmoving in the sunlight at the entrance to her little cave, lost in deep thought; her eyes were closed, and she seemed hardly to be breathing. Finally, as if coming to a painful decision, she stirred, reached into the cave for a turned beechwood bowl and stood up silently.

With the bowl held in both hands she stepped across the little lawn to where the beck plunged over its fall. Here was a pool, wide but shallow, where the stream eddied and backed before sliding out of sight, and in it she dipped the bowl, filling it to the brim with clear water. Then she retraced her steps to the cave and slipped inside, setting the bowl softly on the ground.

Gently she knelt by it, her body blocking the sunlight so that the bowl was in deep shade. She waited until the water was quite still then with one hand still on each side of the bowl she leaned forward and stared into the depths. As she did so she began to sing wordlessly to herself, her voice surprisingly deep and resonant in the narrow space.

Behind her back the shadows moved slowly as the sun arced across the sky; but it was long before Niamh moved again, kneeling upright though with her hands still clutching the sides of the bowl.

Carefully she stood up, holding the bowl, then carried it gently back to the stream. With almost ritualistic care she tipped the water back into the beck, then wiped the bowl dry with her sleeve. Only when that was done and the bowl was back on the floor of the cave did she shake her head sadly; then she carefully wiped the tears from her eyes. So it has happened she thought. And the other, who will come in my place – who is she? Where is she now? Well, I shall know everything in the gods' good time.

As Senorix charged across the ford, the waiting band opened to make way for him, then whooping loudly the whole party galloped down the track for perhaps another mile, swords and spears held high.

At last the trees on both sides gave way to a sunny meadow with the river running along the south side, and here Senorix reined back, then wheeled his horse and brought it to a stamping, steaming stand. But the others rode on, still shouting and brandishing their weapons, until they had disappeared into the trees at the far end of the open ground. Now a broad-shouldered man perhaps 35 years Senorix' junior stepped out from among the trees and hailed him; he was deeply tanned and his thick red beard was dressed in two long plaits.

'You'll be wanting a bite and a sup? We'd almost given up expecting you.'

Senorix slid down from the saddle and stretched theatrically. 'Took me longer than I expected, Iatta. I'll tell you all about it later. Here, take my saddle, will you?'

He unfastened the girth and lifted the saddle free, then, leading the horse by the rein, he walked to the edge of the river with Iatta at his side and sat himself down on one of the boulders at the waterside to watch the horse drink. On the opposite bank now stood a perfect replica of a small Roman marching camp, complete with earthworks and palisades.

Senorix looked at it with admiration. 'Your new lads have done well. How long did that take them?'

'Longer than I'd have liked, to tell the truth; but the building of it teaches discipline, and now it's done we can use it for battle-practice. And it's a secure place for our quarters, too. Ah, I'll get them all licked into shape before too long. Everyone of them has a blood-quarrel to settle, they're eager enough to start cutting throats, but if we make them wait too long they might just start cutting each other's.'

'So you set them to work on that old signal-tower?'

'Yes, they did a fine job there; and there was plenty of good ironwork free for the taking; we filled five kegs with those great nails they use, and there was a lot of other useful stuff as well. We couldn't have built the camp without it.'

'That was a fine ambush they'd set up – I'd have been cakking my keks if I hadn't known what to expect. But you see, I knew they were there before I ever came to leave the road. And a curlew's calls in woodland, indeed! Still, it was pretty good going for all that. Now, where's that drink you promised me? And someone to rub the horse down too, it's been a long trip for us both.'

Soon Senorix was chewing his way noisily through half a loaf of barley-bread and washing it down with buttermilk, all the time keeping one eye on the lad grooming his horse and nodding with approval at his gentle handling. At last he wiped his mouth and grinned.

'It was a strange time, Iatta. Perhaps you've heard something of it? How the gods came when the Beltane fire was lit?'

'Only a rumour. Is it true? Did you see them yourself?'

'It was a woman saw the face of Urien first, all covered in leaves and peering through the forest at the end of the clearing where the fire was; and then Blanaid appeared as an owl, and I saw her clearly with my own two eyes as she flew above us and away into the night. The gods are moving, Iatta. And when they move, we must move too. But then, I think these new lads of yours are straining at the leash.'

Iatta nodded. 'They are that. But tell me, how sure are you about the gods? Was it real? Or just something you'd like to believe?'

'To speak truth, Iatta, at that moment, I was sure. Afterwards, you start to wonder. But for all that, enough people do believe it, my lad. It was the talk of the town. Though the Queen wasn't as convinced as I'd like.'

'Ah, so you met the Queen as well?'

'I did. She held court at Beltane in the old style under an oak tree though she sat herself on a Roman chair to do it. She lives in two worlds, Iatta, as did her foster-mother Cartimandua before her, yearning after the old ways while welcoming the new. I don't know what the end will be for her; but she is no-one's fool, Iatta. I knew her long years ago when she was a child newly fostered away in Brigantia, and there among strangers she learned soon enough how to use her wits and her looks to get whatever she wanted.

'And the Romans know it, and pay court to her; they have built her a pretty new palace with fountains and a garden; and she flatters them, and speaks fine Latin and plays the Roman Matron to perfection. In truth I think she is more than a little in love with what they have given her; and yet if I do not misread her she would throw it all away with little more than a sigh if fortune's wheel took that turn. She will be no ally, Iatta, but I think no enemy either.'

'Are the Romans strong there in the town?'

Senorix considered what he had seen and heard. 'The cavalry have moved on somewhere – I remember them from Mons Graupius, Iatta – and now there's a foot garrison of a couple of cohorts drawn from who knows where, well-enough commanded it seems but stretched thin. The soldiers behave as soldiers will, they get drunk and fight and sleep with the girls, but for all that they complain about their pay, Iatta, they have money in their fists and spend it freely enough, and so they are welcomed if not loved.

'And merchants come and bring wine and olives and other things from far away, and the people buy them and become accustomed to them, and so day by day they grow Roman without knowing it.

'Remember this of the Romans, Iatta – there are not very many of them, and so they govern by alliances, by making others turn Roman, until in the end if they're not stopped that little handful of men will own the whole world and fill their own purses with all the profit from it. But it's all a trick, Iatta; when Boudicca burned Londinium, the echoes of her triumph were heard in Alexandria and Athens: a fine new province almost lost, Iatta, and to a woman at that. Brutal bitch that she was.

'And so we draw them out, Iatta, stretch them thinner yet, set their teeth on edge, make them fear the green woods and the god who lives there, make them shed their blood in the rivers and streams. Well, that's been my dream all these years.'

Rubbing his beard Iatta said, 'Not many of them? Not many of us, either. I have about four hundred here, and in other places perhaps another two thousand that we've trained together, you and I. What's that against a legion?'

'A legion? Now that's a fine thought, Iatta. How would it be to destroy a whole legion? If we can do that then who knows what triumphs we might have.'

Iatta raised an eyebrow. 'That's a tall order. And how would we to do it? We may have spirit, but as I say we lack numbers. Though it's a fine thing to fall in battle and have your name sung at firesides and feasts, there's not many who'd consent to being nailed to a cross if the enterprise fails. No bards sing of that, my friend.'

'Iatta, think of how Boudicca started. She took the Romans unawares, marched on Camulodunum and razed it to the ground while Paulinus was off in Cambria looking for druids to kill, then she did the same in Londinium; and all the while the Second Legion were keeping their skins whole somewhere out west, and who can blame them.

'Do as she did. Take them unawares, Iatta, that's the secret.'

'They got her in the end, though.'

'Indeed they did. The Ninth Hispana again, as it happens.'

He shrugged. 'Odd how the Ninth keep coming into the story, isn't it? They were in at the very start, when that old fool Claudius was looking for an easy triumph to show that he was a bigger man than great Julius himself, then after they'd thrashed the Iceni they turned up at Mons Graupius. It was their auxiliaries that caused all sorts of mayhem round Eboracum in the Year of the Four Emperors.

'We need numbers, you say? But Boudicca had them at Verulamium, and relied on them to fight a pitched battle – big mistake, Iatta, and she paid for it with her life, and thousands of others' as well. Mons Graupius was the same thing all over again just a few years later. We line up over here, they line up over there, and we try to slog it out man-to-man. And we lose every time.'

'So what's in your mind? I know you of old, you've got an idea in that wrinkled head of yours.'

Senorix nodded, almost absent-mindedly. 'We've harried the Romans here in Caledonia for years, you and I and others of the same mind. And then I had this fancy – perhaps the gods put the idea in my head – to see Verica again before I died, and so I put myself in the way of doing it, and of taking in the Beltane fire at the same time.

'Ah, the Beltane fire. Did the gods show really themselves there? Whether they did or not, I can't get rid of the idea that they want us to take the fight further south, where they're all sitting comfortable and secure.

'I was thinking about it as I rode up. There's a string of forts and fortlets along the north coast of the Ituna estuary; they're isolated, no proper road, just forest tracks. Now, a relief column from the town could either come up the great road and then turn west – but that's most of a day's march, you see – or they could cut the corner, go straight over the river. It's quite fordable if you know the way, but there's quicksands here and there, and the tides are tricksy. The garrison are no fools, they've got themselves a guide all ready for the crossing, they even pay him a spot of pocket-money to keep him sweet. I met him in the tavern there, and a more thirsty man you never met, especially when other people are paying. I can turn him, Iatta, I'm sure of it. He's killed before, if I'm any judge.

'So, Iatta, I need you to find me a place that will suit; one within fire-signal distance of the town, but far enough west that they'll send their column straight over the river. We can blood these new lads at the same time, if you can hold them back that long.

'Find me that fort, Iatta, and get word to me when you're done. I'll stay here in your fine new camp for a day or two, then head back down south. I used to know that part of the world like the back of my hand when I was younger, but not any more; even the names of places have changed, and there are roads in places you'd never expect to see them. I need to have it all at my fingers' ends again, hold it plain in this – what did you call it – wrinkled head of mine?

'So south I'll go, spend a night or two travelling around, talking to folks here and there. And then I'll head back to the town; there's a drinking-place on the forum there, the Eagle they call it. Send me word there when you're ready, Iatta, and I can work on the fellow I'm thinking of. There are other things there to keep me entertained as well.'

XIX

'Is it a girl? It usually is.'

Marius shook his head in bewilderment. 'What do you mean?'

The stonemason pushed back his curly brown hair and smiled, then ticked off points one by one on his fingers. 'First of all, it's not official, or you'd have had one of your soldiers do the work, the ones that do all that carving on your milestones and foundation stones and the rest.

'If it's not that then it's something personal. You're not giving thanks for getting through a battle in one piece, 'cos there haven't been any round here for a while; and you don't look as happy as someone who's just been left a farm in Tuscany by his favourite aunt, so it's not that either. And you don't look as if you've been at death's door and want to thank the gods for helping you cheat the ferryman, come to that. So I say that you've managed to sweet-talk a girl, and now you want the gods to know you hold them responsible.'

Marius grinned. 'I see. No; clever, but wrong. But it's personal all right, which means I'm paying for it myself – so don't try padding the bill. You know what I want, anyway?'

'The usual formula, I suppose. Sandstone incense altar, inscription on the face to read *To Jupiter the best and the greatest and to the great god Lugos, whatever-your-full-name-is willingly and deservedly fulfilled his vow.*'

'That's about the shape of it. Are decorations extra?'

'The basic price includes two carvings as specified by the client.' The mason smiled with self-satisfaction at negotiating the formal Latin. 'Pomegranates is usual, or a man's or woman's face.'

He waved his arm to show some simple sketches scratched onto the plasterwork at the back of his workshop. 'Like those. Or you could have a seated or standing figure, man or woman; that costs more, but I can do you either if you want. Children come cheaper, of course. We do a quite a few of those for tombstones.'

Marius considered. 'Pomegranates – they're for eternal life, aren't they? Doesn't seem quite the thing here. No, just put a man's face on it, under the inscription, to stand for the god. And how about a couple of thunderbolts at the top? For Jupiter?'

The mason grinned. 'I'll throw them in for the same price. To you, just five sesterces.'

'Make it three.'

'There's a lot of lettering there. You want it to look tidy, don't you? Nice even lines? Takes time, that does.'

'You're not doing Trajan's Column.' Three sesterces.'

'Four. Look, I'm not short of work, you know.'

Marius nodded. 'Four, then. How long will it take?'

The man considered. 'Can't get it started before next Moon Day; I've got other stuff here that needs doing.' He gestured at the half-finished tombstone on the bench. 'Can't keep the dead waiting, or they might get offended, and then where would any of us be? Let's say Jupiter Day next week to be sure.' Without bothering to turn away he spat copiously into the yellow sandstone chippings which littered the floor.

'Jupiter Day it is then. Make sure you keep to it.'

The mason grunted non-committally then rummaged among the detritus on the bench before pulling out a battered wax tablet with a stylus attached to it by a fraying piece of garden twine. 'Put your name on there, nice and clear so I can read it. Oh, and it's half the money up front and half on collection, all right?'

Marius smoothed out the wax at the top of the tablet and carefully incised his name, MARIVS VITELLVS DECIMVS then drew a box around it and held it up for the man to see. 'Clear enough?'

He squinted at it, turning the tablet to catch the light. 'It'll do. Leave it with me.' He tossed the tablet back on the bench and waited while Marius counted out the coins onto the bench, then scrabbled round for a piece of broken pot on which he laboriously scratched 'M V D IIS' and pushed it across to Marius. 'There's your receipt; I'll have it back when you pick the work up.'

Then without a further word he pulled a chisel out of a fold in his apron and started to chip away at the half-finished tombstone. Marius watched him for a few moments, then nodded and turned on his heel.

Once in the bright sunlight outside the mason's little shed he stopped and mopped his brow; the sky was a pure cloudless blue, and there seemed to be no wind. The gods were certainly doing their best to earn their new altar, he thought; and she will be there at the dedication. He smiled ruefully when he saw how his imagination was running away with him, then turned towards the forum, curious to see how much business was being done there. On the way he paused to glance at a poster painted on a wall offering a substantial reward for the return of a runaway slave, and to briefly watch a group of little girls crouching on the ground and playing knuckle-bones together.

The market-square was, he was pleased to see, surprisingly busy; the open space in the middle was almost covered with stalls, mostly selling local cheeses, cheap geegaws, bits of horse tack and such-like; there were two bakers, a couple of butchers, a barber busily scraping away at the chin of a skinny lad in his twenties, a shoe-maker measuring a fat old woman's feet, and – rather to Marius' astonishment – a well-fed and prosperous-looking banker, who had set up his strong-box in one corner of the square and was jingling coins in his hand while offering – according to his business-patter – large loans on very favourable terms. Marius looked round and spotted four very heavily-built slaves loitering around the temple of Mars Victor; clearly the man had brought his own enforcers with him. Marius grinned to himself; Greek business-practices had, it seemed, even reached this forsaken end of the Empire.

A woman's sudden loud wail made him spin round; it was

repeated four or five times, then joined by other voices, male and female, and finally by the clanging of cymbals.

He relaxed; only a funeral. He waited as the cortège passed by on its way to the South Gate and the town's tombs along the road beyond; four or five hired mourners screaming and clashing the cymbals, the women beating and clawing at their bared breasts in front, then the dead woman – little more than a girl, it seemed to Marius – carried aloft on a bier borne by four sturdy young men, and then finally the family, heads piously covered, variously loudly weeping or mute with shock, and followed by half a dozen silent slaves. One of them, he noted, was carrying a tiny baby in her arms; death in child-birth, then. At least the youngster was alive. He cast his mind back to the half-finished tombstone on the mason's bench, then muttered the traditional *Dis manibus. Ave atque Vale.* at the departing procession.

He was taken aback to see that even the noisy funeral procession had hardly affected the chatter and the buying and selling in the forum; a few people had looked around, more it seemed out of curiosity than anything else, but most had simply kept on with their business, turning their backs firmly on the commotion.

Unbidden, his mind turned to the girl on the bier. Who was she? More to the point, where was she now? Negotiating with the ferryman? Walking among the shades of the underworld? Did she remember the world she had left behind and the child she had carried, or had she already drunk the forgetful waters of Lethe?

'All right, sir?' It was Marcus Asellio, out on his own tour of inspection in the town.

Marius passed his hand over his face, then smiled at his centurion. 'Funeral; young girl. Shouldn't bother me, Marcus, I've seen plenty dead, and killed a few myself one way or the other. But Hades, man, when one of us goes down there at least the rest of us give him a proper send-off; no-one here seemed to notice except the family.'

'Civilians, sir. Natives, too. Every man for himself with them.

No discipline.' He grinned. 'Just as well, really; if they ever got organised they could give us all sorts of trouble. Luckily for us that doesn't seem very likely.'

He nodded at the forum crowd. 'What was it the man said, sir? Bread and circuses? Don't even need those here. Give 'em proper square houses, a nice bathhouse and a chance to make money, and they go as docile as a pet lamb. Let's hope it lasts.'

But one person had followed the procession with wide-open eyes. Messalina had heard the clang of cymbals as the cortège passed the door of the Eagle, and stole out unobserved into the street to watch it pass. She stood there barefoot while the dead girl was carried past, borne aloft on her bier, then slipped back into the doorway as the mourners carefully averted their eyes from her.

Once the funeral party had gone by Messalina crept out again into the street, mesmerised as much by the music and the sight of the hired mourners as by the pale corpse. Without quite knowing why, she began to follow the little group, keeping to the edge of the roadway and trying to make herself as inconspicuous as possible. Only when the last of the accompanying slaves had padded through the South Gate did she stop, then turned sadly away, only to come face-to-face with Morrig, who had seen her slip out and had followed her.

She squealed in a mixture of fright and pain as she felt Morrig's iron grip on her arm. 'What's this? Running away?' The question was followed by a blow to the face which sent Messalina sprawling into the gutter.

'No, Mistress. Mistress, please don't hit me.'

Grimly Morrig bent down to grab her arm again and hauled her back to her feet. 'Slut. Idling instead of working. There's another good whipping waiting for you when we get home.'

'No, Mistress, please. It was the funeral; the dead girl looked so pretty and sad, I just had to follow.'

'The funeral?' Morrig's voice was brimming with contempt. 'You ran away because they were burying some rich girl with a lot of fuss and fiddle-faddle? Listen, slut. Your sort have nothing to do with funerals. When we're done with you, it'll be a place on the dung-heap for you, where the street dogs can come and pull you to pieces. Do you think the Elysian Fields were meant for little animals like you?' She grasped Messalina's hair and pushed her head down, then walked her along the street bent almost double, pausing from time to time to shake her roughly.

Finally at the door of the Eagle she let her go, then before she could straighten up gave her a vicious push that sent her sprawling onto the floor. 'And shut up your racket. As if I didn't have enough to do without running after you. And where's that blasted husband of mine got to? Olympus, what a wife has to put up with.'

Bran had taken advantage of his wife's absence to slip out into the forum, and was now standing at the side of the shoemaker's booth, trying to look inconspicuous but with his eyes constantly returning to the imposing form of the Greek banker while he listened mesmerised to his patter and to the jingle of the gold in his hand.

At last the man's eyes lighted on Bran, and he smiled warmly and nodded as if acknowledging an old friend before turning away again. After a little while he turned back towards Bran, apparently surprised to see him still there, and giving another genial smile. Finally he made an expansive gesture with his arm, inviting Bran to the little stool waiting at his side.

Now hooked as firmly as any trout, Bran walked over, sat down and listened spellbound.

'A man of substance, I see. And a man who can see opportunities when they appear; so few people do. It's a pleasure to make your acquaintance. My friends call me Glaucus; now tell me what I can do for you today?'

XX

The sun was already high in the eastern sky when Verica and her escort left her palace. Three – she herself, Lugos and Gwydion – were mounted, while her guard marched beside and behind her.

As the party joined the great road she turned to Gwydion, who was riding at her left shoulder. 'Despite what you say, Gwydion, today I shall ride. That carrying-chair is fine enough, but Marius and his friends will be mounted and I shall greet him from my saddle, not look up to him from the chair. And I think my horse is finer than that old cob of his.'

Gwydion shook his head. 'My lady, every farmer's daughter can ride. You should remember your place.'

Verica laughed. 'Every farmer's daughter, Gwydion? And I was a farmer's daughter myself before I came to higher things as you know full well, and I was on and off my pony's back before I could walk. Off more often than on, to tell the truth, but I mastered him in the end.'

She turned to Lugos. 'But perhaps you would have been more comfortable on foot. A toga is hardly riding gear. Gwydion is right, I suppose; today we must be formal and put our discomfort out of mind.'

Lugos grinned back at her. 'I brought three togas back from Rome, Mother, and I've hardly worn one since; I should have had someone check the chests, every one of them has had the moths in.'

'It looks smart enough, no-one will notice. Remind me, you have been part of a dedication ceremony for an altar in Rome I think you said?'

'Only a little one for the dining club I was in, in the convener's garden. A quick ceremony, some prayers and a couple of libations – what a waste of wine – and it was done and we could get down to the serious work of eating and drinking and talking.'

'And now your brother is doing the same, no doubt; I hope he isn't getting mixed up in anything foolish. If only he would write.'

Lugos laughed. 'You know what he's like, Mother. You won't hear from him until he needs more money, and then it'll just be Send me a draft as soon as you can. PS I'm fine.'

'He has gone to learn Roman ways, not to spend money. To learn about government and law, to watch trials in the Forum, and to read the poets.'

Lugos caught the change in her mood. 'He could have learned all those things without leaving home, Mother. You are better-read than most people in the Great City, and you speak better Latin and Greek too. At least I was well-taught when I arrived there, not left to wander about with my mouth open like some country bumpkin from Latium. But no-one can live in Rome without money, and without spending it freely. Even the slaves there have money to spend.'

'And masters who borrow it from them, I've heard.' She shook her head. 'Let's hope your brother is better-behaved than that.'

Lugos shrugged and carefully changed the subject. ' When we held that dedication in Rome we didn't even bother getting an augur to come, so Jupiter knows what the gods will have made of it. Will the Commander be bringing anyone to tell the auspices? These military men like to do things properly.'

Verica winked at him and gave a sidelong glance at Gwydion. The mention of a Roman augur had brought a flush of anger to his cheeks, but he said nothing. Verica's lips twitched into a mischievous smile as she turned back to Lugos.

'Of course there will be an augur there; how else could Marius determine the will of the gods? No doubt he will be able to read the omens with great skill.'

That was too much for Gwydion. 'I have heard much of these

Roman augurs, my lady, and the way they shape their questions to get the answers they want, and ignore any signs that they find inconvenient. You know yourself how truly to find the will of the gods, my lady, and my aching bones still remind me that you did so not long ago.'

Verica smiled. 'They say that two of a trade rarely agree, Gwydion. I am curious to see what this augur will say, and whether the gods of Rome will bless what we do. And the Commander would not insult us or our gods by giving us an altar unsanctified by his own customs. We will talk no more of it.'

Gwydion bowed his head in acceptance, though it was plain it was done with bad grace; but Verica accepted the gesture with a radiant smile, then turned to wave cheerily at the crowd of people streaming along the highway towards the town, many of them wearing chaplets of flowers or carrying posies of meadowsweet and yellow or orange poppies in their hands.

After a few moments of silence she went on, 'But whether any of us like the augur or not, there will be plenty of our people there to see him perform his rites. Though for all the Commander says, I do not think that they will stop making their offerings at the stones. That goes too deep into our blood.'

Lugos gave his mother a sideways glance. 'You don't like the man very much do you?'

'Like him? I suppose that he's better than that prefect that was here before him; no matter how many baths he took, he still stank of horse.'

Like him? she mused. I've met him half a dozen times and I feel as if I've known him all my life. The old story, and the old folly. Berenice and Titus. Antony and Cleopatra. I hope I'm wiser than either. But for all that it will be fine to see him and speak with him again. She broke out of her reverie and saw that Gwydion's eye was fixed on her. *Did he read my thought? Well, what if he did?*

At the south gate a Roman honour guard was waiting to escort the royal party, twenty legionaries in their parade uniforms with the signifer proudly holding up his banner at the front. Verica accepted his salute with a gracious smile, choosing to ignore both Gwydion's scowl and Lugos' wide grin, and the party clattered slowly up the street, the guards pushing back the growing crowds as they went.

Straight across the little market square they went, Verica acknowledging the smiles and cheers of the onlookers, though Gwydion still had a face like thunder. And there was the altar, wrapped around with a linen cloth, set up on a cleared patch of land just to the north of the forum, and round it were clustered Marius and his tribune with perhaps another thirty men. All except Marius were in their dress uniforms, but he was wearing a civilian toga, perhaps to show that this was a personal rather than official ceremony. They were all on foot too, Marius' cob nowhere to be seen. More soldiers were helping to keep the crowd back, cudgels at the ready, and as the Queen and the others approached they opened ranks to let them through.

Verica reined in half a dozen paces short of the altar, bobbed her head to Marius in a gesture that made her condescension perfectly obvious, and waited for him to bow deeply in return. Satisfied, she sat still while Lugos and Gwydion dismounted, then let Lugos cup his hands around her foot to help her down from the saddle, though it was plain that she could have jumped down easily enough on her own.

'Καλημέρα, κύριε. A fair day for our appointment. Let us hope that all the gods will smile on it.'

Marius raised an eyebrow, then decided it would be politic to respond in kind. 'Καλημέρα, γυνή. A fair day indeed. And the people seem pleased to have this altar here; my men had a bit of trouble carrying it down here earlier, there was such a press of people wanting to see it and touch it, and the lads had to break a couple of heads before we could clear the way. In the end we covered it with this cloth until the time was right.'

Verica smiled. 'Of course. You have cleared a fine space here.'

'Indeed; not all for the *templum*, of course; the augur will need plenty of room, my lady, to watch the skies; who knows what signs the gods may send? Now you are here there seems no need to wait any longer – this crowd can hardly grow any bigger.'

He pulled a fold of his toga respectfully over his head and waited while the others did the same; Verica too pulled her scarf over her hair and Lugos drew up a fold of his toga in a gesture that was quite as natural as Marius', though she noted that Gwydion remained obstinately bare-headed.

At Marius' sign the augur stepped forward and began to mark out the sacred space around the altar with his staff, muttering his incantations as he did so and prompted from time to time by an assistant holding a scroll; Verica guessed that he was more used to forecasting the result of a battle than dedicating an altar. She glanced sideways at Marius, then murmured 'These are secret rites, are they not, Commander? Is it wise to have them written down?'

Marius shook his head. 'Not written in any way you or I would understand. I've seen that scroll before, and I can't make out a word of what's written on it. But Acestes is a good man, he doesn't play any of the old augur's tricks to make sure that he only gets the right answer. Course, he'd be a fool to do that before a battle anyway.'

Verica watched closely as the rites unfolded, straining to pick up any of the words spoken; when she glanced back at Gwydion she noted that while his face still displayed a mask of pure contempt, his eyes were fixed on the augur; she was sure that afterwards he would be able to match every one of his intricate movements. Then suddenly the augur threw his staff on the ground to signal the end of the secret part of the rites, then picked it up again to mark out his chosen quadrant of the sky.

That done he now spoke clearly, though with a strong Greek accent. 'For you, sir, and for you also, my lady, and for all the people of this town and region, I have invoked the great gods of

Olympus. Know that nothing that passes in this world is unmarked by them, whether hidden underground or done beneath the open sky. Know, too, that they will assuredly show us their approval of our invocations and our homage by some clear sign in this portion of the heavens that I have chosen. Far-seeing Jupiter does not lie.'

Acestes signalled to his assistant to roll up his scroll, and stowed it carefully in the folds of his robe. Then he settled down calmly to watch, supremely confident that the gods would send an answer.

For perhaps as long as a man might count to a hundred there was no answer from the heavens; then, in the clear sight of every man and woman watching, a magnificent eagle came swooping over the rooftops, flew silently right across the marked quadrant, and then vanished from view over the town walls.

Acestes smiled with triumph and turned to Marius. 'Jupiter accepts the altar, and sends his eagle to let all men know of this. The gods are truly great.'

Marius turned to Verica. 'Jove's own eagle. What do you say to that, my lady?'

By way of answer Verica turned to Gwydion. 'Well, Gwydion, you have seen it for yourself. Was that indeed Jupiter's eagle?'

'His or Lugos'. For our gods answer too, and a wise man will heed them when they speak.'

Marius acknowledged the comment with a smile. 'There are indeed many gods my friend; and why should they not be allied together for the good of all our people? And so we can sanctify the altar to both Jupiter and Lugos with a good heart. Still, we'd better take a look at it first.'

He stepped forward and pulled off the cloth that covered the altar, then stood back to let everyone see it clearly. Both Verica and Gwydion bent down to examine the inscription and the carving of the god's face, and the Queen ran her fingers along the incised letters. 'This is good work, Commander. It must have cost you a pretty penny.'

'I vowed to have it made if your god would give us good weather, and so he has done. And so we are all blest – my men who are able to go about their work free from the never-ending rain that rusts their swords and spears and makes travel difficult, and the farmers and merchants of your land, my lady, who can carry their goods and plough their fields and sow their seeds and so keep us all from want in the months to come.'

He signed to Gracchus to bring forward his flask of oil and carefully poured it into the hollow at the altar's centre.

'My lady, will you join me? We shall honour the gods together.' He motioned to Verica to stand opposite him and to put her hands flat on the level top of the stone, then intoned in a loud voice, 'Jupiter, Best and Greatest, and Lugos, great god of the sun who gives light and sustenance to all the people, we dedicate this altar to you, willingly fulfilling our vow, and calling all people to honour you here and to bring you their gifts of flowers and oil. This place is now a sanctuary to the gods, and those who come here are under the gods' protection.'

As he said the words a great sigh went up from the watching crowd. For a moment he stood there with his head bowed unmoving, apparently deep in quiet prayer; opposite him, Verica was silent, her head bent, her hands pressed tight on the stone. Then in movements so slight that only Gwydion noticed, both Marius and Verica moved their hands a fraction forward until they touched; for perhaps a dozen breaths they stood like this, hands touching, though barely, then as they lifted their heads, they glanced into each others' eyes.

At last Marius smiled and stood upright, lifting his hands to the sky in the traditional gesture of invocation. Then he pulled the fold of his toga off his head and murmured, 'Now it belongs to the people. And so we must speak to them. Will you do so first, my lady?'

Verica smiled. 'Of course.' She turned to face the crowd, then waited a long moment, perhaps lost in thought, before beginning in a firm, clear voice that carried, apparently without effort, right across the forum.

'My friends, we all know the story of the great god Lugos; how he was first a mortal, like we are, before he was betrayed by his kin, and killed in accordance with the prophecies concerning him; but after he had died he was taken up into the skies, and we have seen today how he still comes in the form of an eagle to assure us of his presence and his care.

'We remembered that god in our Beltane feasts, as our people shall surely do until the end of time; and today also we remember and honour him in this gift to him of this fine altar. Bring here your flowers and your fruits, bring your prayers and offer your vows to the great god, whose shrine shall stand here as long as this town endures.'

As if on a sudden whim she paused, her eyes roaming across the crowd. They alighted on a girl of perhaps ten summers whose mother had pushed her almost to the front of the crowd; her arms were piled high with flowers culled from banks and the margins of fields. With a gentle smile Verica bent down to her, laid a hand lightly on her arm and brought her forward to lay her flowers around the base of the altar, piling them up in a display of extravagant generosity to the god.

'Soon all can bring their gifts and add them to these fine tokens; but first, I ask you to give your thanks to the man who raised the altar at his own cost.'

She signed to Marius to come forward, the gesture conveying effortless superiority, and then stepped back, neatly upstaging him as she did so by sweeping her shimmering silk scarf down around her shoulders.

The Commander was not so easily outdone. An imperious wave brought forward the signifer who had greeted Verica's party by the town gate; then Marius reached across to take the banner from his hand, pointing as he did so to the gleaming row of letters fastened across the head of the pole.

'My friends, you see here the letters by which I and all my men stand: SPQR, the Senate and the People of Rome. You, good people of the town and the countryside about, and all the people of Britannia, are People of Rome, as I am and as your Queen is also. And as people of Rome we delight to honour the gods and to bring them our prayers and our gifts.'

A sudden pattering sound distracted him for a moment: hailstones, small at first but rapidly growing in size, falling out of a seemingly clear sky. Within moments the crowd had begun to thin at the edges and although Marius ploughed relentlessly on with his speech it was soon apparent that he was wasting his breath.

Even the soldiers were now covering their heads from the bombardment, and the ground had disappeared under a white blanket half a hand-width's deep, and abandoned flowers and chaplets littered the forum as the people ran for cover.

Marius turned to Verica with a bitter smile. 'It seems as if your god has a sense of humour, my lady. No doubt he remembers the words of my oath to the very letter. If the sun shines and the rain stops for as long as it will take for the altar to be carved and the land cleared for it, then I shall stand by what I have said. And now that he has his promised altar, he has let the foul weather return.'

Gwydion shook his head. 'Sir, it is not Lugos we have to deal with here. Look at the altar. Look at the face of the god.'

There was no doubt about it; the battering hail had disarranged the flowers and leaves which Verica had so carefully placed about it, and now the stone face that looked out at them peered through thick leaves, seemed indeed almost as though the greenery were a part of it.

'You and my lady raised an altar to Lugos; but it seems that Urien has staked his claim to this as he did to Lugos' wife long ago. And you, my lady, have you not closed your fine gown with that brooch with the little lapis owl on it? See, all three of them are here – Lugos, Blanaid and Urien – and here they will begin their conflict anew. How can the strength of men prevail when the gods decree otherwise?'

Long after the crowds had dispersed, an observer might have seen a tall man walk across the forum and look carefully at the new altar, meticulously studying the way in which the god's face now looked out through the tangled mass of leaves and flowers, before smiling to himself and remarking quietly, 'Take your omens where you find them.'

XXI

As a rule Marius enjoyed having guests at his evening meal; they marked a relaxing end to the day, a time when he could travel in his mind back to some quiet evening in Rome, with no-one to please but himself.

Tonight was different, though; the dedication of the altar and the sudden hail-shower that had ended the proceedings had dampened everyone's mood, and his guests – two of the town's richest merchants – had been uncongenial. After they had gone Marius had stayed on his dining couch, his wine-cup in his hand, staring gloomily at the shadows dancing on the wall, only half-hearing the familiar stamp and repeated challenge and reply of the night-watch on the camp's ramparts.

Finally he turned moodily to Flavius, standing in his accustomed position at his shoulder. 'I shan't need anything else tonight; you and the rest may as well get your heads down. Just leave the one lamp; I'll carry it up with me when I go. And leave the wine.'

For a moment Flavius looked surprised, but he quickly recovered and bowed, then ushered the other servants out. At the doorway he turned and bowed again, then suddenly smiled to himself before pulling the door closed.

Marius reached out a hand to the flagon standing on the table and carefully poured himself another cup of Falernian; setting the cup down he ran a finger along the spout and then licked it. Men, he thought, I can cope with; but who knows what to do when the high gods decide to get involved? We touched hands; right at the moment of dedication, and then our eyes met – and ah, that glance. A woman who is beautiful, intelligent, cultured, rich and powerful. But I think it will not happen in this world; no, not in this world.

His reverie was broken by a gentle scratching at the door. He sighed, then put the empty jug back on the table.

'Yes? What is it?'

He screwed up his eyes as the door opened. 'Cybele? What do you want?'

The girl came round the table and knelt quickly beside him. 'Flavius sent me, Master; he said you wanted me.'

For a moment Marius felt furious. 'Rubbish. Off you go.' Then as the girl made to stand up he suddenly changed his tone; 'No, forget that. Here, have a sip of wine.' He held his cup up to her mouth, tilting it so that the liquid flowed towards her lips. Obediently she sipped it, then wrinkled her nose. 'It's sour, Master.'

'Sour? I've never heard good Falernian called that before. An acquired taste, I suppose. What do they usually give you? Buttermilk, I suppose; or water.'

Cybele nodded, then went on, emboldened, 'Sometimes they let me have beer; I like that.' She looked up shyly. 'Can I try some more, Master? Perhaps I'll like it better now.'

'Wait. After me now.' He took a deep draught, then put the cup in her right hand. 'Now your turn.'

The weight of the cup took her by surprise, and a little wine splashed over the rim onto her tunic, but she quickly recovered and took a sip, followed by a longer drink. Then she handed the cup back with a smile.

'I liked it better that time, Master.'

Marius shook his head. 'Not a taste you should get too used to, Cybele.' On a whim he put down the cup by his side, then reached forward and pulled down her tunic, exposing her breasts. As he did so her head dropped and she gasped. Why not?

'Stand up. Hands by your side.' As she moved he reached forward and pulled her tunic to the floor.

'Now, get up on the table.'

'Master?'

'You heard. Push the dishes out of your way.'

– 174 –

She did so in silence, then lay on her back. What does she think? Marius wondered, then Who cares what she thinks anyway? But when he had finished he saw by the dancing lamp-light that her cheek was moist with tears, and he briefly wondered why.

XXII

When Marius awoke in the morning Cybele was there as usual with her bowl of water and a towel. As she did every day she held them out as he washed his face and rinsed out his mouth, then helped him to dress; but now there was a change in her bearing that he found disquieting.

At a loss, he put his forefinger under her chin and lifted her head. Her eyes were clouded, but her cheeks still carried the marks of tears, and when he looked down he saw that wine-stains from the night before still dotted her tunic.

To his surprise he found himself shouting at her. 'Can't you find something clean to wear, girl? No, don't take it off now. And go and wash your face. Jupiter and Mercury, what is it now? Yes, come in.'

It was Marcus, standing uncertainly in the open doorway, his eyes flicking back and forth between master and slave. 'A letter, sir. All the way from Rome; just delivered. I thought you'd want to see it right away.' He held up the neatly-tied tablets in his hand.

'Yes, of course,' Marius turned irritably to Cybele. 'Oh, get out, girl. And stop slopping water all over the place.' He took the proffered tablets and plumped himself down on the edge of the bed, his fingers tugging clumsily at the knots. Then he opened the leaves and began to read aloud, holding the tablets so that they caught the light from the window and tracing the letters with his finger as he did so: "Cinna to his good friend Marius, greeting. Know, my friend, that I have grave news for you concerning the son of Queen Verica."

Bran paused for a moment to get his breath and wipe his hands on his apron. There must already be a couple of dozen men sitting down and drinking, he thought, and the doorway was crowded with others trying to push their way in. He made a quick reckoning on his fingers: if the money kept on coming in like this, he could buy another girl, perhaps two; of course, then he'd need more space, so he'd need to talk to Bris at his *caupona* next door about renting the little room at the back of his shop – or perhaps he could take over the whole thing, sell food as well as wine, have space for more girls. And the gods were certainly on his side – the sudden change in the weather and the unexpected influx of customers proved that.

Morrig's eyes were on him; he could feel them. Muttering to himself about women and how they don't understand business, he pushed up the sleeves of his tunic and tried to make more space by the door. From somewhere at the back of the room came Messalina's well-practised shriek as someone grabbed her by the breast. Bran shook his head; there was no time for that now; selling wine was where the real money was at the moment. He grinned to himself; real money – at last he knew what that meant.

Did Morrig suspect anything? Did she have any idea that he'd borrowed – he forgot exactly how much, a lot of money anyway – and invested it – well, most of it – in the best stuff that the Gaulish wine merchant could bring him – three dozen amphorae, now neatly stacked under the empty ones in the yard, where they wouldn't attract his wife's notice.

A glow of satisfaction spread through him when he remembered how surprised the merchant had looked when Bran had ushered him round the corner, well away from his wife, to buy something a little special for his best customers. He shuddered when he remembered how much he'd paid for it; but you had to invest some money if you wanted to make more; Glaucus had explained that to him, and it all made perfect sense.

And it was turning out to be true; he was already making more profit than he'd ever made before, and salting the extra money away; his only problem was making sure that Morrig didn't find out about it. As Glaucus had said – and how right he was – women are fine in their place, but they just don't understand commerce.

Of course, he'd have to pay back the loan, but that wouldn't be a problem; he'd been coining it in the last couple of weeks, and he'd had no trouble making his repayments when the man called. Amicus, he said his name was; and he'd certainly been friendly enough. Of course, the words of the agreement were: To be repaid when he asks for it. But that, Glaucus had explained, was just a form of words; as long as the money was coming in and his payments were up to date, everything would be just fine.

Bran promised himself to have a word with Bris later that evening. On second thoughts that might not be a good idea – while the menfolk were pushing into the Eagle, the women and children were probably spending their cash buying snacks next door, better wait until business there was a little quieter, he might get a better deal. How well he understood these matters now.

While Marius was being dressed he sent a messenger to the palace, asking for an audience as a matter of urgency; then, without waiting for the man's return he set out south along the road, clattering along on his cob, with only the tribune Gracchus in attendance. Cinna's letter had reached him in just over a week; he felt sure that any official condolences from the Emperor's office would take longer, given the time that anything except the most urgent matters took to work their way up through the ranks of secretaries and administrators.

At the palace gate they surrendered the horses to a groom. The major-domo was waiting for them, and as they followed him through the garden Marius muttered, 'This time, Tribune, remember your manners. Or I'll have you back in Eboracum before you can blink.'

Gracchus acknowledged the rebuke with a cold smile and a brief nod, then followed Marius into Verica's audience chamber. She was waiting there for them, sitting on the familiar currule chair, a broad smile on her lips; her right hand was playing with the little lapis owl brooch that he had seen her wearing the day before, and the inevitable maid was still fussing with her hair, though she stopped as soon as the others entered and went to stand meekly behind her mistress, her head bowed.

Verica flashed a radiant smile and to Marius' astonishment stood in greeting. 'Commander, why do you do us this honour so unexpectedly? And your tribune as well. Gracchus, I think? I hope you are feeling better today than the last time we met, young man.'

Gracchus hesitated, then murmured, 'Thank you for your concern, my lady. I am much better now.'

Marius drew a deep breath. 'My lady, forgive me for interrupting these pleasantries. I know our coming is an intrusion, and I ask your pardon. Sadly it is not a matter that can wait.'

He hesitated for a moment, looking for a way in to what he had to say. 'Do you remember that I once told you of a friend in Rome who has a fine mural of Daphne in the moment she was changed into a laurel bush? This friend – his name is Cinna – wrote to me a week ago with news that it grieved me deeply to hear.'

He paused again to gather his thoughts, then went on, 'My lady, will you not sit down? My lady, he told me that your son is dead; dead of the marsh fever which takes away so many in Rome. I am sure that the Emperor will write to you himself at the first opportunity; but I could not keep this news to myself and hold you in ignorance of what has happened.' As he spoke he caught sight of little Iras still standing in her place, her face a sudden picture of shock.

Verica was silent for a long moment, then sat down again on

the edge of her chair. 'Dead? Are you sure? Is your friend certain of what he has told you? There can be much room for error in these matters.' She turned suddenly to Gwydion as though appealing for his help, then turned back to Marius.

Marius nodded. 'It may indeed be so, my lady; but Cinna is an old friend – from our days at school together – and I would trust him not to tell me any such thing unless he was sure of it. No, my lady, I fear there can be no room for doubt here.'

Verica's gaze travelled bleakly around the room, as if searching for her son. 'It seems such a short while ago that he was here; and now you come and tell me I shall not see him again.' To Marius' surprise she shrugged. 'I am no Stoic in the matter of death, Commander; I have seen too much of it to take it lightly. And yet my life – and yours – must go on as before. I shall mourn, as all of us will here, Commander, but I shall take to heart Gwydion's promise to me that the dead are born again.'

From somewhere Marius found words that seemed to fit. '*Sunt lacrimae rerum et mentem mortalia tangunt,*' he murmured.

'The world is a place of tears, and the weight of mortality touches the soul. How well Vergil puts it. I truly thank you. And now I think you had better go, Commander, you and your tribune; but I am most grateful to you for bringing me this news as soon as you were able. May we meet next in better times.'

Feeling there was nothing else to be said Marius bowed awkwardly and left the room, with Gracchus on his heels. At the door he paused for a moment, wondering if her composure would break down, but all was silence behind him. He shrugged and followed the major-domo to the gate, then swung up again to the saddle of his cob.

Once on the road the two men rode side by side in silence for a while. Only after perhaps half a mile separated them from the palace did Marius speak. 'Well, Gracchus, what did you make of that? And think before you answer.'

'It shows the power of Rome, sir. What would this barbarian

woman have done in the days before the Divine Claudius brought the benefits of our rule to this island? Screamed, no doubt, covered her head in dust and ashes, scratched her face until it bled, torn her clothes perhaps. But now see how she has learned to control her grief. Even her maid held her composure. We Romans could never have mastered the world if we had not learned to master ourselves.'

Marius looked quizzical. 'Maybe. I have to say she took it better than I'd expected. I wonder if she really believes that nonsense about the dead being reborn? Well, if it keeps her happy I suppose that's something.'

He was silent for a while, glancing around at the quiet countryside. 'She has lost so much in her life, Gracchus. She was born near here, then taken as a child to the household of Queen Cartimandua in Eboracum after the death of her father.

'Cartimandua – now, there's a name to conjure with. I met her once, you know, oh, twenty years ago or more. It's quite a story. She'd given her husband Venutius the push and taken up with his armour-bearer. Anyway, the old man didn't take it lying down; he started a rebellion, and it took all the strength of the Ninth Legion to put it down. It was a typical civil war – the troops went wild, couldn't tell the difference between friend and foe; but for all that, Cartimandua managed to hang on to her throne.

'But it didn't end there. Venutius had survived, and he came back for another go in the Year of the Four Emperors. He'd chosen his time carefully – in all the chaos the Ninth had been ordered away on what were politely described as other duties, and just their auxiliaries were left to manage the defence. If what the legionaries had done a few years earlier was bad, this was ten times worse.

'They went on the rampage, took out their bloodlust on the local population. Those were terrible days, Gracchus. Rape, pillage, slaughter, the lot; villages and farmsteads burnt, the people and their animals put to the sword for no reason at all. Cartimandua herself was pulled out and packed off to happy retirement in a nice smart villa in Neapolis, and that's where I met her. Her little crowd of followers still used to hold court, and one day I got dragged in to a poetry reading there.

'She was really getting on by then, as tight-fisted as the Divine Vespasian and as garrulous as a flock of starlings. But she took a bit of a shine to me, and out the old story came about Venutius and little Verica and how Rome had let her down in her time of need, and all the rest of it. It bored me rigid at the time, but over the last couple of months I've wished I'd remembered more of it.

'Reading between the lines I'd say that Verica would have been around five years old when Cartimandua took her. Perhaps she couldn't have any children of her own; who knows? Whatever the truth of that is, I've wondered if she was really looking to adopt a son – Verica is a boy's name as well as a girl's, you know.

'With Cartimandua out of the way, Venutius was soon back in charge, and thumbing his nose at Rome. And the Ninth's reputation was right down there in the mud; half the people blamed them for what their auxiliaries had done, and the other half hated them for heading off south and leaving them undefended. And our Queen Verica hates them, too; she lived through the killing, saw the worst of it, and those memories haven't faded. It wasn't until about eleven or twelve years ago that the Ninth finally made it back to Eboracum.

'I heard the rest of the story after I'd been posted here. It seems that Venutius kept Verica around for a few years, then as soon as she was old enough he shunted her back here – a convenient marriage to the leader of the Carvetii, the People of the Deer, I suppose. And then a few years ago her husband died too – well, he was a fair bit older than her, I dare say – leaving her with just the two sons.

'So the upshot was that our Verica in short order lost both her natural parents and her foster-mother Cartimandua, and the Ninth, as I say, she loathes with every fibre of her being.'

Gracchus nodded slowly. 'I see, sir. But at least she is our ally.'

'And a damned expensive one, I sometimes think. Just look at that villa we built her – all paid for out of your taxes and mine. But yes, she's pretty reliable; I just hope today's news doesn't upset the apple cart. Best to be positive, though; and incidentally I hear that the Ninth have a new legate, Aninius Florentinus. He's a good man, by all accounts.'

When they reached the gate of the camp Flavius was waiting, and as they dismounted he bustled up to his master with a worried frown. 'Sir, it's your girl, Cybele. We can't find her anywhere. We think she must have run away.'

XXIII

For a while after Marius and Gracchus had gone Verica sat in silence. Then at last she turned to Gwydion with a bleak smile.

'So, Gwydion? It seems that he learned today what we found when we returned from the dedication yesterday, and here he flew like a raven bearing evil tidings.'

She shook her head angrily. 'Ever since I was a child, Gwydion, Rome has haunted my life. It was Rome that unleashed slaughter on the Brigantes; Rome that left great Cartimandua unprotected; Rome that taught my eldest son to forget the ways of his people; and now it is Rome that has taken my second son, my little darling, burnt him to death with a fever.

'My son, Gwydion, my son. Nursed at these breasts, held in these arms. My son. I can see him now, learning to walk, falling, clutching my arm and laughing. By all the gods, Gywdion, this alone would be hard enough to bear; but to crown it all he comes here, so urbane, so, so civilised, with his polite condolences and his poetry and his orator's prattle.'

'My lady, I must remind you that you have heard nothing that Niamh had not forewarned you of those many years ago. And you forbade us to show any marks of mourning, and then received him with a smile as if we had heard nothing. Why was this?'

Verica was silent for a long moment, her head bowed; when she looked up Gwydion saw that for the first time she had tears in her eyes. 'I don't know. Perhaps I wanted him to think well of me. And Niamh? I thrust her warning out of my mind lest remembering it should make it happen. And for what? What good would come of any of it, either for me or my people? And now I hate him and all his kind. And I can do nothing, Gwydion, nothing at all.'

In a sudden fury she grabbed the cushion from her chair and

flung it across the room, then followed it with the chair itself, while Iras cowered in the corner. 'You told me once that the gods want blood, Gwydion. By Toutatis himself, I shall see that they have it.'

After she had stormed out of the room, Iras clutched at Gwydion's sleeve. 'Shall I go to her?'

'Not yet; her anger will burn itself out eventually, and she is accustomed to mastering her feelings. Go to her in a while; rage can be a comfort in times of grief.'

When he was alone Gwydion walked out into the garden and stood by the great oak-tree under which Verica was used to holding court. This is the place of judgement, he thought, and my judgement is this: that she loves him, and thinks she will never have him. And in that, I believe she judges well.

🜲 🜲 🜲 🜲 🜲 🜲 🜲

'No one seems to have seen her, sir. She must have crept out while you were gone. I cried the news in the market-place, offered the usual reward, but there aren't any takers so far. If only she'd been collared or branded.'

Marius shook his head irritably. 'And the gate guards are so used to checking people coming in that I suppose they don't notice anyone going out. I'm sure you did your best, Flavius. Was she kidnapped, maybe? Perhaps some low-life grabbed her and put her to work in some knocking-shop in the town. Take a couple of house-lads and go round hammering on doors till you find her. And Licnos the cook as well, perhaps – he knows people in town and he's a big strapping fellow, you might need him.'

'And if she's left the town, sir? We'll never find her if she's taken it into her head to run to the woods.'

Marius ran his fingers through his hair as he considered what might have happened. 'She knows nothing about the danger, Flavius; she wouldn't last a day. Wolves, bears, boar – *damnatio ad bestias*, eh, Flavius? Stupid little fool.' He shrugged. 'Knock on a few doors in town first; if you can't find her this morning then we'll just have to forget it.'

Flavius hesitated, then went on, 'There's one other possibility, sir; she may have had a helper – some boy from the town that's sweet on her, perhaps? Perhaps that's why she was suddenly so cheerful a few days back? She could have been hidden in someone's house, or anywhere really.'

Marius considered, then nodded. 'That's true enough. Or she could just have been grabbed off the street, raped and killed and then thrown onto some rubbish-heap. All right, you'd better organise a proper search through the town – check the odd corners, places where there's junk lying around, even privies; then report back to me later today. Turn places upside down.'

He shook his head angrily. 'Six hundred she cost me. And she'd have been worth ten times that in Rome, if I'd ever got her back there. If you find her we'll make sure she can't sit down for the next month.'

Exhausted, Cybele sat down by the side of the river and let the water cool her bare feet. Why did I run away? she asked herself. But I daren't go back. Not now.

She buried her face in her hands and began to cry softly. But running away had been so easy. No-one had spoken to her, caught her arm, or even looked at her as she walked through the camp gate; it was as if she was suddenly invisible.

And none of the people in the town had even glanced at her. She'd stolen a piece of bread from the baker's stall in the forum and then sat in the dust and stuffed it into her cheeks, and still no-one had seen her.

Then the open country beyond the South Gate had seemed to beckon her, and the guards had looked right through her as she had hurried past them. And then there were the tombs, lining both sides of the road for perhaps a hundred paces; for a moment she'd thought of hiding in them, like runaway slaves did in stories she'd heard, but then she remembered how dreadful they might be at night, when the spirits of the dead would come back to prowl around their ashes.

Beyond the tombs the empty road stood high on its embankment, running south as straight as a spear, with the open country stretching away on both sides, and sheep and cattle grazing on the lush grass. She could hide there in the woods, and there would be water to drink, and some early fruits to pick, and if she managed to stay safe, there would be nuts later in the year. And her thoughts went no further than that.

All that day Cybele wandered aimlessly south, flitting from tree to tree by the side of the river. There were brambles in places, tearing at her tunic and scratching her arms and tangling in her hair, but carefully she unpicked them and moved on, only half listening now for the sound of pursuit behind her. Three times she cut her feet on sharp stones, and twice she heard men's voices close at hand, and hid until she was sure they had gone.

Night seemed to arrive suddenly, with only a sliver of the dying moon showing but with brilliant stars wheeling across the heavens as she stared up at them. It was colder now, and her stomach was empty – nothing for me to eat all day except for that bread I stole – but she pulled together some bracken and curled up on it and tried to sleep, hoping that she would be safe from bears and wolves.

Afterwards she was never quite sure if the face in the trees, barely glimpsed in the bright star-light, had been real or only a dream; made of leaves, it seemed, staring out at her from the foliage, human and not-human at the same time. She jumped to her feet when she saw it, stifling a scream; but when she summoned up her courage and looked harder there was nothing there but the shifting boughs.

XXIV

For my part, I find that sleep is sometimes slow to come, and then the night can seem so very long. And never, it seemed to Verica, had sleep been slower to come, nor the night longer. Only when the birds had already woken to greet the coming dawn did she at last fall into an exhausted slumber.

And then the dream. Had Marius not brought Vergil to her mind, perhaps a different dream would have come. But now in her fantasy she roamed the Elysian Fields, calling out again and again for her lost son, and not finding even his insubstantial ghost in that realm of the dead, but hearing only the whispered voices of the shades murmuring that she was not the first that Aeneas and Orpheus and Demeter and countless more had all in their turn come seeking the lost, only to discover that none of the dead could return. And she too was bound to stay, for Charon would never ferry the living back across the gloomy Styx. Here she must stay, a phantom among phantoms.

Only for a moment did the horror last. Then in her dream the river was already passed, a strong hand was guiding her through gleaming white gates, and she was awake and back in the world, and the summer sun was streaming through the shutters. And she knew that the hand that had drawn her clear was that of Marius. But in her dream he had drawn her through the Gate of Ivory, where only false dreams can pass. Or so it is said.

When the dawn came Cybele was stiff and cold, and there were insect bites on her legs and thighs. She scratched at them briefly, drank deeply from the river and washed her face, then started southwards again, driven by nothing that she could give a name to. And then, at a place where the river went round in a great loop, she saw a little spring in the bank, with careful stonework around it, and by it were laid some countryman's offering to the spirit of the fountain – cheese and bread and a little posy of flowers.

The river was shallow here and she forded it easily, then greedily she swallowed the bread and cheese, muttering as she did so an apology to the spirit of the place and hoping that she would be satisfied with the flowers alone. Then she went south again, staying in the shelter of the trees the whole way.

She saw the great stones in the afternoon of that second day. They stood some distance from the river, in the middle of a wide tract of open country, but somehow they seemed to call to her, tempting her to leave the safety of the trees.

Breathlessly she walked around them, touching them as she went, feeling their surprising warmth and their indomitable hardness. She began to count them, then lost track and started again, and finally ran out of numbers that she knew.

There at the end was the greatest stone of all, the great Sorceress who had defied death by turning herself into that enormous monolith which reared up twice as tall as a man. Cybele tiptoed towards it, then suddenly realised that there was a woman sitting cross-legged and silent in front of it. Cybele's hand flew to her mouth and she turned to run; but before she could move, the woman spoke.

'So you are here at last, child. I am Niamh.'

For a moment Cybele stood rooted to the spot; then, almost unwillingly, she stepped closer and asked stupidly. 'Who are you?'

Niamh rose easily, moved to within arm's reach of Cybele, then suddenly reached out and caught her by the hair, wrapping it round her hand and dragging the girl even closer. 'I have told you my name. I will have none of your folly here, child. Kneel.'

Effortlessly she forced Cybele to the ground. 'Look at you. A starveling run-away, a dirty-faced little slut, a liar, a thief who can steal from the gods as easily as from men. A nothing. And yet the god has chosen you.' She pushed the girl down further. 'Show respect, child. Kiss my feet. Do it now.'

Trembling Cybele did as she was told. It was a long time before Niamh pulled her upright again and looked into her eyes.

'Obedience is good to learn. Child, who saw you when you ran away?'

Cybele thought for a moment. 'No-one saw me; no-one at all, Mistress.'

Niamh nodded to herself. 'Few can see you when you are under the god's protection.' Still the penetrating stare into Cybele's eyes; the girl tried to look away, and found that she could not. 'And who did you see? Tell me truly.'

'No-one, Mistress. Only you.'

This time Niamh moved even faster than before, slapping Cybele hard across the face, then pushing her roughly down to the ground. 'Fool. Liar. Kiss my feet again. Kiss them until you learn to tell the truth.'

It seemed an age before Cybele dared to lift her head again. 'Mistress? I think I saw someone in the forest. A face in the trees. But then I thought I must have been dreaming.'

Now Niamh pulled her upright again, her iron grip on Cybele's hair not slackening at all. 'A face in the trees. A face made of leaves, was it not so? Give him a name, child. Name the god. Do I have to thrash you until you tell me?'

Sudden inspiration dawned on Cybele. 'Urien, it was Urien. He was in the trees.'

At last Niamh let go of Cybele's hair. 'Yes, child, you have seen the god himself. He has sent you here, though you did not know it; as I have been sent here to meet you.'

Cybele's face was a picture of utter bewilderment. 'Mistress, no-one sent me; I just ran away from my master, and happened to come here.'

Niamh gave a short laugh. 'And I suppose I just happened to come here as well, and happened to meet you? Tell me, why did you run away? Was your master unkind? Were you beaten undeserved? Or starved?'

'No, Mistress; Mistress, I don't know why. I couldn't help myself.'

Niamh nodded and sighed. 'That is the way of the gods, child. We must live together for a while, you and I. Follow me.'

The forest came almost to the edge of the beach, and the air was heavy with the scent of the firs. Over the estuary, away to the south-west, the opposite shoreline was visible as a dark shadow; to the left there was a miniature bay, with half a dozen round huts scattered around the little burn which clattered over the gravel to the sea; and at the edge of the beach itself was a small fort, protected by a simple ditch and a wooden palisade. A signal-tower stood in the middle of the fort, with a pile of timber stacked at its side.

Half-hidden in the shade at the edge of the trees, Iatta and Senorix were considering the possibilities of the place. Iatta was shading his eyes as he tried to make out the forms of the hills on the other side of the firth, but Senorix was running a careful eye over the hamlet and the fort. 'So this is the place, you think? It's been a long enough ride from the town, I can tell you that.'

'The way you came, old friend, is about twenty five miles, and slow going once you've left the road; go straight over the estuary and it's about sixteen or seventeen I'd say and much easier going at that, so well worth cutting the corner. But the tide comes in at an almighty rip. The locals don't seem too bothered about it, though – if you look you can see some folk far out on the sand on the other side. Cockling, I'd guess; they'll be well clear before the tide turns, though.'

'And you'd say that the fort would be in sight of the camp?

That's a fair distance, after all.'

'Signal tower to signal tower, should be a clear line of sight – which you'd expect, of course. Far enough to see the signal, not close enough to see anything else. Will it do?'

'Not bad at all, Iatta. And the village?' He nodded towards the little collection of huts huddled around the fort. 'Many people live there? In the huts, I mean; there seems to be no smoke rising.'

Iatta nodded. 'Yes, a few; fishermen and their families, not more than a couple of dozen or so people all-told I shouldn't think, though they probably find it easier to serve the fort these days. Yes, look.' As he spoke a young red-headed boy, half-naked and bare-foot, toddled out of one of the huts closely followed by a yellow dog. Senorix nodded as he watched the pair pick their way to the brink of the burn, then grinned as the lad lifted his tattered skirts and pissed into the stream.

'Well done, lad. A fine expression of opinion. What about patrols?'

'They're out most days, with a lot of trumpet-blowing and banging about. It may only be a little place but they do like to do it in style. But they're careful too; they'd put up a good fight if we tried to ambush them.' He shrugged. 'But that's not what you're thinking of, is it.'

'Indeed. And how many men are there would you say?'

'Half a century, perhaps; maybe not quite so many but more than you'd think for a place like this. But like I say, they're careful; there's always a good watch on the walls at night. And when they come out they're always dressed up to the nines. All the splendour of Rome, I suppose, just to impress a few fishermen and their women.'

'You mentioned about the tides; how long before the next high ones? In town you don't really notice the moon.'

Iatta gave him a piercing look. 'Not if you're spending your nights with that girl you were talking about. And at your age too. She's too young for you, my friend.'

'Now there you're wrong. The older the man, the younger he needs the lass to be.'

'So you say. Anyway, I'd say it's a new moon in six days or so; that means the biggest tides will start in two or three days, maybe a little more.'

Senorix looked thoughtful. 'I think you have it, Iatta.' He nodded slowly, then said more firmly, 'Yes, you have it indeed.' He glanced at the sun. 'It's getting late; let's find somewhere out of the way to spend the night, then in the morning I think I'd like to take a closer look at that little fort.'

XXV

Senorix awoke with a start. It was already light, and Iatta was busying himself over a little fire.

'What a night, by Esus. Iatta, I'm getting too old for this camping out.'

'Of course you are. Better for you to limp off home and wait by the fireside for Dis to come scratching at the door. Except that you don't want to, not when there's a chance of Roman blood.'

Senorix grunted and then spat noisily. 'You're right, Iatta. Every time I smell those pines I'm back at Mons Graupius. Blood calls for blood, they say.'

He spat again. 'Gods, my mouth tastes as if something died in there. What've you got there?

'There's some bannocks, and there's fresh water in the stream.' Iatta smiled, then went on, 'Sun's well up; looks like a nice day. Plenty of time to finish the scouting and then get back to the others.'

'Water and griddle-cakes. And not a woman worth having for miles around either.'

Iatta looked thoughtful. 'You never used to be so picky. It's that girl, isn't it? The one you were bragging about yesterday?'

Senorix had the grace to look shamefaced for a moment. 'A good lay, that one; knows a thing or two; very practical in that department. Been around a bit of course, but none the worse for that. And I think she'll be useful to us before the game's all done. And afterwards… Well, we'll see. Anyway, let's have some of those cakes you're making before they go cold.'

An hour later he was walking through the little clutch of huts near the fort. As he walked he noted the terrain, the innumerable little dips and rises, the folds and slopes, the patches of turbary land, the whin and the brambles.

There were half a dozen huts in all clustered around the fort, and perhaps another five or six further along the bay with coracles leaning against them; on top of the bank there was a bigger curragh hauled well up beyond the highest tide.

With the air of a man who had every right to do whatever he wanted, Senorix strode deliberately up to the gate whistling through the gap in his teeth, noting as he did so that the nearest huts were almost hard against the palisade, far closer than a wise man would have let them take root; no doubt it was convenient for the little garrison to have their women and drink close at hand.

The guards at the open gate looked smart enough. Not legionary gear, he noted, auxiliaries. Bithynians, he guessed from their weapons, posted far away from their homes in the warm south.

'I want the man in charge. He's in big trouble.'

The burlier of the two laughed. 'He's in trouble? Not half as much trouble as you'll be in if you don't bugger off.'

Senorix looked puzzled. 'I want my compensation. I'm entitled. It's the law. He can't just take my daughter like that. A virgin, too. I've got my rights.'

'Your daughter? Did she look anything like you then?' The guard grinned at his fellow. 'You hear anything about his daughter?' He gave Senorix a long, critical look, 'She'd be about fifty, I'd guess, no teeth, going bald on top; that's about right, I'd say.'

He turned back to Senorix. 'Listen, chum, if she's half as ugly as you, she'd be grateful for a bit of attention. Anyway, the Big Cheese doesn't go for girls, so you can start looking somewhere else. 'Course, if you'd got a grandson it might be different. If he didn't look like something the dog sicked up, that is. Now, go to hell.'

Senorix looked for a moment as if he was going to argue; then he shrugged, muttered 'All right, no harm in trying.' He turned away looking crestfallen; behind him he could hear the two men sniggering. That was easy, he thought. Make them laugh at you and they'll never think to take you seriously. He walked away slowly, noting the little dip that the path skirted, just deep enough for half a dozen men to hunker down in, unseen from the fort. Iatta had done well; there were serious possibilities here.

His friend was already mounted and waiting for him in a clearing perhaps half a mile away. He raised an eyebrow as Senorix swung up into his saddle and received a curt nod in reply.

'It would be hard to take, Iatta, you'd lose a lot of men in the effort, but of course that's not what I have in mind. That smart lad you sent for me; can you send him back to the Eagle with a message?'

'Lad? He must be thirty if he's a day and he's taller than I am.'

'He's old enough to do the job, then. And my friend Apuleios is one fish that's pretty sure to rise to the bait, I'd say.

'Huctia, isn't it? Where's your daddy?'

The child looked up at Bran through serious eyes, then scuffed her feet in the dust. 'Do we have to leave now?'

Bran nodded. 'You're going to live with your grandma, you and your daddy both. You'll enjoy that.'

Huctia considered slowly, her tongue just sticking out through her lips. 'I don't want to go; grandma and daddy always argue, and Voreda's boring. I'd rather stay here. It's fun helping daddy serve the customers; I can count the money for him and everything.'

Determined little girls were alien territory for Bran, but he leant forward and ruffled the child's hair. How hard can it be to run the place? Even this little brat knows all about it. Cook a bit of food, dish it out and watch the money come rolling in. Thank the gods I didn't let the grass grow under my feet. I'm a proper businessman now.

'Don't worry, love; your daddy's got a lot of money now, he's a rich man.' And I'm a poor one, he thought as he considered the three hundred he'd had to spend to buy the caupona, but that won't last for long.

Only an hour after Huctia and her father had left, loading most of their possessions onto the back of a long-suffering donkey and stuffing the rest of them into a bulky back-pack, did Bran realise that he had forgotten to include the fine bronze cooking pots in the deal, and they were now heading away southwards at a patient four miles an hour.

Morrig folded her arms, took up a stance blocking the doorway of the Eagle and glared at Flavius.

'Accusing me of stealing your master's slave-girl, are you? We'll see about that.'

Flavius spread his hands apologetically. 'Not at all, Mistress. We just wondered if she'd come your way in the last couple of days. There's a reward for anyone who can help.'

At the mention of a reward Morrig relented a little, though she didn't move from the entrance. 'Well, we're always willing to help the authorities. But we've already got one lazy, thieving slut eating us out of house and home; what would we want another for?' She gestured vaguely over her shoulder towards Messalina, who was just visible in the dim interior swabbing tables with a rag.

Flavius tried another tack. 'Perhaps your husband could see his way to helping us? Is he here?'

Morrig spat expertly on the ground, just missing Flavius' foot. 'Try the caupona. Either that or he's gone fishing again. That's what he says, anyway, though he never brings much home, and leaves me to look after the Eagle, and now it's the place next door as well. Juno knows where he got the money for it. He's got a fancy woman hidden away somewhere if you ask me, the sort with more money than sense, and he's paying her back in the bedroom. That's what you men always want, isn't it?'

Licnos the cook leant forward and tapped her on the shoulder. 'Actually, I prefer boys,' he rumbled, and gave her a laborious wink.

Morrig stared at his massive bulk for a moment and burst out laughing. 'A pansy, are you? Gods, now I've seen everything. All right, you can come in and look round; just don't break anything, unless you want to pay for it.'

She stood back and let them in, then hurried upstairs to make sure that the money-chest was safe. She listened intently as the men spoke to Messalina, vowing revenge when the girl suddenly started squealing in mock outrage.

Flavius appeared at the top of the stairs and glanced around quickly. 'Not here, then Mistress; sorry to have troubled you. If you or your husband do see anything, be sure to let the Commander know – like I say, there's a nice reward going for anyone who helps us find her.'

Morrig waited until they'd gone, then plumped herself down on the bench by Messalina and began to talk in a conversational tone. 'A runaway slave-girl, my dear, and not branded or collared or anything. She could be anywhere. Perhaps she's been eaten by bears or wolves. How terrible for her master.'

She looked thoughtful for a moment, then went on, 'And supposing you were to do the same, my dear? Why, we'd never find you, would we? Collars don't come cheap, so I think perhaps we'd better have you branded, my dear, just to make sure. I must speak to the smith about it. He'll just lay you over his anvil and brand you right then and there. A nice, deep brand burned right into your skin. No running away for you then.'

She held Messalina's face level with her own, amused by the terror in her eyes, then went on, 'I wonder where would be best for the mark? On that skinny backside of yours, perhaps? Or your leg? Or your arm, maybe? Or your tit? Best to have it somewhere that'll show, I suppose? I must talk to your master about it, then we can have it done tomorrow, or maybe the day after. Something for you to look forward to, my dear. And in the meantime remember, if someone wants to play with you, they pay me first.'

She gave a sweet smile and stood up, then turned and slapped Messalina across the face. 'Go to the caupona and see what your master's doing. Get on with it, slut.'

A sudden clatter of pottery distracted her from her fun; Flavius and his men must be poking around in the stack of amphorae at the back of the alley. Pausing only to aim a kick at the girl she rushed out to see what was happening, but the men had already disappeared, leaving the little gate at the alley-mouth ajar. Cursing, she hurried to see if anything was amiss, then looked at the stack of jars more carefully than she had for several months.

It took her almost half an hour before she was quite certain. When there was no doubt left in her mind she nodded grimly to herself, then walked thoughtfully back indoors and sat down. So her husband took her for a fool, did he? Fool himself. But it would be much more pleasurable to bide her time, to wait for the perfect moment. And then he would pay for it – how he would pay. It would be almost as satisfying as watching Messalina screaming under the red-hot iron.

She stretched back in anticipation and smiled serenely.

XXVI

Apuleios gave the tall man a suspicious glance over the edge of his wine cup. 'Money? Of course I want money. Give it to me now and save me the trouble.'

'Not my money, my friend. The Romans' money. And all yours, as safe as houses.'

Apuleios put down the cup and glanced round. 'Hush. You've seen outside the North Gate, haven't you?' He'd walked past a day or two earlier himself; both of the still-hanging bodies had burst in the early summer heat, and ravens and rats were busy at the carrion.

The tall man shook his head. 'No chance of that, friend. Just a chance to go back to your old trade. A one-off, special offer.'

'Taking people over the firth? Who'd want to do that these days, with that fine new road. Even the soldiers don't want to go.' He spat noisily into the straw on the floor.

'The road, friend, is a long way round, and these people will be in a real hurry. All you need to do is to take them over the firth when they ask you. Most of the way, anyway; the sea-god will do the rest, if you ask him nicely. You can do that, can't you?' The tall man reached over the table and lifted Apuleios' chin. 'Done it before, haven't you? I can see it in your eyes.'

Apuleios pushed his hand away. 'People are careless; don't go where you show them, don't want to wait till the tides are right. Not my fault if that happens.'

'And sometimes they don't want to pay enough, is that right? So you teach them a little lesson? There's a lot of secrets buried in the sand out there, friend, or drifting with the currents. Dead men – and women too – who won't be telling tales any time soon.

Up to you though; keep spending money you haven't got on the woman's rotgut when you could be somewhere out of the way and drinking the good stuff.'

He stood to go, but Apuleios leant over and grabbed his arm. 'All right, how?'

The man turned back and settled down on the bench with a wink. 'Easiest thing in the world, friend. Just wait for the call; they'll come looking for you in a day or two, I should think, so make your bargain and take your payment – but make sure you get cash up front. And then it's all yours; the bodies go to Manannan ap Llyr, the souls go to Arawn down in Hell, and the money – well, that stays snug in your purse, doesn't it. And all at no risk to you. What you do is this…'

Cybele was aching as she had never ached before; after their meeting at the great stone circle Niamh had set a killing pace through the woods, moving so quickly despite her age that the young girl had struggled to keep up, and passing through bogs and becks as carelessly and sure-footedly as if she were walking dry-shod. Never once had she stopped for breath, nor even glanced back to be certain that Cybele was still with her.

Her path had led over the river and then ever upward, leaving the valley far below her, but even as the last of the daylight thickened around them, Niamh had never slackened her pace, indeed she seemed to find an easy path through the bushes and undergrowth, though Cybele was tormented by brambles that snagged her clothes and hair and by sharp stones that cut and bruised her feet.

Only at the very end of the journey, as she stepped into the torrent that led to her secret retreat, had Niamh cast a look back at the exhausted girl, then without a word she had passed along the stream, still moving as easily through the water as if she were walking on firm turf. At last, with the long journey over, there had been nothing for Cybele to eat but some goat's cheese and a few berries, and nowhere to sleep but on the bare ground.

Now Niamh sat bolt upright on the same flat stone where Verica had sat those many days before, while Cybele stood before her exhausted and bedraggled.

Then the questioning began. 'Child, where is Lugos' cloak? What is its sign in the sky? What colours are in it?'

The question took Cybele utterly by surprise. 'Lady?'

'Call me Mistress. And never make me ask a question twice.' A hazel switch had somehow appeared in her hand, and without warning she slashed it hard across Cybele's legs.

Cybele took the sudden pain without a cry, though tears sprang to her eyes. 'I don't know, Mistress.'

Niamh shook her head in irritation, then went on, 'Who is the Mistress of Beasts? Who brings grain from the earth? Who is it who leads the dead home?'

Shaking with fear and weariness, Cybele could only stutter, 'Mistress, I don't know.'

To her relief there was no switch this time. Niamh nodded to herself, then went on, 'Who is the Master of the Wheel? Who rules the sky? Whose chariot sounds the thunder?'

A vague memory of stories from her childhood formed at the back of Cybele's mind. 'Taranis, Mistress? Is it Taranis?'

Niamh nodded to herself. 'So you know something at least; but so little. So why has the god chosen you?' Her voice was suddenly sharp. 'You carry the Roman's whelp; did you know that? And you will bear him here – yes, him – and perhaps you will do so all alone. Some things I can still see clearly, but not all.'

Niamh's voice was suddenly urgent. 'But what can you see? Is that why you have been sent? Fetch water from the stream. In this bowl.' She waved her arm and as she did so the clouds withdrew, flooding the little plain with sudden starlight. Niamh looked up; 'See Caer Arianrhod, where the Great Lady has her home. Fetch the water while the stars are clear.'

Still shaking, Cybele limped to the stream and dipped the little wooden bowl in the water; as she came back the clouds again drifted over the sky.

'Good. Now kneel. Look in the bowl, child. Tell me what you see.'

Shivering with fear as much as cold and hunger, Cybele knelt and looked into the bowl; the ground was rough under her knees and hurt her as she settled down, but fear of the hazel switch made her obey.

'What do you see?'

'Nothing, Mistress. Only darkness. Mistress, it's only water in a bowl.'

Unwarned she yelped as the switch cut her calves, but this time Niamh said nothing. Frightened to move, but starving and dog-tired, Cybele felt her shoulders begin to shake as the long moments passed; she could feel that she would soon begin to sob with misery and fright.

Beside her she felt Niamh stand, felt her raise her arm with the switch for another blow; and suddenly, to her utter amazement, there was a something, a stirring in the bowl, or perhaps it was only in her own beholding. 'Mistress, in the water – I can see a fire.'

'All right?'

Senorix smiled to himself. 'As much as ever. There are two things I hate about this game: the waiting before it starts, and then worrying afterwards about what could have gone better.'

Iatta nodded. 'It's a good plan, though. Just a feint here, then the real blow when they're all looking the other way.' He hesitated. 'D'you think your man down there will be up to it?'

'Ah yes, the human element. No plan ever survives the first contact with the enemy, they say. But yes, I think he hates them enough; and perhaps he loves their money even more; and why should they doubt him, Iatta, so helpful and willing to serve? And he's killed before, I make no doubt of it.'

He stepped cautiously through the trees to the edge of the clearing and looked at the sky. 'Just what we need. No moon, and everything nice and dry. The gods have set the stage, Iatta, and now we have to put on the play.'

He waved forward a group of half a dozen men, all carrying either slings or hunting bows, and with their faces and hands blackened with mud, though even in the gloom their eyes showed bright and eager. 'Follow the path, lads. About forty paces in you'll find a nice hollow to your right; hunker down in that. Once the fires are going well, spread out and wait. I don't think there's any chance you'll be seen from the fort; if anyone else happens on you, feel free to kill them, but by all the gods, do it quietly. I dare say there'll be plenty of yelling before the night's out, but not till I give the say-so. Off you go.'

He waited until the shapes had faded into the darkness, then muttered to Iatta, 'That's the place I'd like to be, my lad, where all the killing is. Well, I'm not as young as I was, and some pleasures fade with age, they tell me.'

Another wave of his arm brought twenty more men out of the forest. 'You've got it easy tonight. Nothing to do at all, unless they think that following us into the forest would be a bright idea. Remember that. No shouting, no yelling; just silent death if they're stupid enough to come close. Cover our retreat if they advance, and hold your ground to the last man if you have to; but I don't expect you'll have to.' He shrugged. 'Anyway, none of us gets to live for ever.'

As the men melted back into the undergrowth, Senorix seized Iatta by the arm. 'You and me, then, lad, and all the gods of Caledonia with us.'

XXVI

'A fire's a grand thing now, isn't it?' Senorix gestured at the flames burning brightly in the stone hearth in the centre of the hut. He turned to look at the little family huddled as far away from him as possible, their eyes filled with terror.

'Don't you be afraid, now. It's not you we're after; just keep nice and quiet and you'll have nothing to worry about. Otherwise, I'll cut all your throats myself, starting with the littlest and working up.' He held up his dagger to show that it was no idle threat.

He went on conversationally, 'It'll all be over in a couple of hours anyway, and think what a story you'll have to tell afterwards. Ah, Iatta, here you are. You dealt with the dog, then. I thought you'd got lost.'

Iatta grunted, then looked around the hut. 'Is that all of them?'

'It seems to be. Just that skinny woman and those three bairns. No man? Hey, you, where's the man round here?'

The woman looked sullen, but muttered, 'Drowned. Half a year ago. He'd have seen to you all right.'

Senorix nodded. 'Dangerous game, fishing. So who keeps you now? Come on, answer.'

'I do what I have to.'

'I thought so. How often do they come? How many?'

'When they want to. Two or three at a time, perhaps.'

Senorix grinned. 'Well, my dear, your entertaining days are over. So just sit there nice and quiet and don't make any trouble, and you'll all be fine.'

The woman muttered something under her breath; Senorix leant forwards, his eyes shining in the firelight. 'Now don't you be saying such things, with the bairns there and all.' He grunted, then went on, 'We'll be staying here, nice and quiet, for a wee while now, so you may as well get some sleep.'

Twice as the night wore on he tossed more wood onto the fire; finally, with the night perhaps two-thirds gone, he nudged Iatta in the ribs.

'Ready, lad?' Iatta nodded.

'Wake them up, then, and we'll begin the performance.' He waited while Iatta shook the sleeping family, then stepped quickly over to the fire and pulled out a flaming brand, held it in his hand for a moment, and thrust it quickly into the thatch above his head, ignoring the woman's frantic screams.'

'That should do the trick. Ah no, no-one leaves yet.'

He watched as the fire spread quickly across the roof and thick smoke began to roll through the hut, then leant into the hearth, pulled out another brand and handed it to Iatta. 'Now – run, and Taranis be with us.'

The watch on the rampart of the little fort were already sounding the alarm as Iatta and Senorix ran through the huddle of huts firing the thatch on each one.

'Blow your trumpets, lads,' shouted Senorix, 'and much good may it do you.'

Within moments the clearing was full of screaming men, women and children, some desperately trying to pull the tinder-dry thatch down, others frantically leading away goats and sheep. Dogs were barking wildly, and somewhere in the confusion a cockerel crowed to herald the unexpected dawn, while sparks and fragments of blazing thatch spiralled upwards, then fell slowly to earth.

Even as they watched the blazing wall of the first hut began to collapse slowly onto the wooden rampart of the fort. 'Building regulations, lads,' muttered Senorix, who had retired to the shadow of the trees. 'You know the rules, but it was just too convenient to have your women next door. Well, now you get to pay for it.'

A half-dressed centurion on the ramparts was directing a dozen men with spears to push the burning wreckage clear of the fort; then, to Senorix' delight, the gates swung open and a party of perhaps twenty soldiers ran out to form a bucket chain between the stream and the huts.

Senorix whistled appreciatively 'You'd think they'd have more sense. Just look at them, a lovely clear target against the light. It's over to your lads now, Iatta.'

Even as he spoke the first arrows began whistling in from the men who had been hiding in the hollow by the path.

Senorix watched critically as the first shots flew well clear of their target. 'Too excitable. You don't get a chance like this every day. They should take their time, Iatta. Ah, that's better.'

Two of the men in the bucket chain had crumpled screaming as arrows took them, one in the back, the other full in the chest, while a third who had caught a stray shot in his upper arm had turned round cursing and clutching the wound. Then another shot took a man on the rampart full in the face, sending him tumbling back out of view.

'That's enough. Now they know they're under attack the discipline will kick in. Ah, see. I told you so.' The bucket-party was already gathering up its dead and wounded and retreating in tolerably good order back through the gate, while inside the fort two men were clambering up the ladder to the signal-tower. Within moments the beacon-fire had been lit, sending out its urgent call for assistance.

Senorix nodded. 'Job done, lads. It wouldn't do to outstay our welcome, you know. The rest of it, we leave to the gods.' As his men melted into the woods he paused regretfully and turned back to face the clearing, still full of villagers and animals milling around, desperately trying to stamp out the burning remains of their homes.

'A few more corpses wouldn't have come amiss; ah, look, there's that fellow who was so rude to me when we met, bad cess to him. You, give me that bow.' He snatched the weapon from the eager young man at his side, strung an arrow and let fly, but the shaft, caught by some random puff of wind, fell harmlessly to the ground.

Senorix spat, then grunted, 'Mustn't be greedy, I suppose. And there'll be plenty more bodies soon, if wind and tide have anything to do with it. To the woods, lad, and Arawn take the hindmost.'

Afterwards Marius felt that he had been awake even before he had heard the pounding feet and the urgent shouts. By the time the commotion had reached his door he was already sitting up and rubbing the sleep from his eyes.

'Jupiter, what's going on?'

It was Gracchus, only partly dressed but looking surprisingly calm in the glow of the little lamp in his hand; Flavius was standing behind him with a gown thrown over his shoulder. 'Fire signal, sir, from one of the Ituna forts; looks like they're under attack.'

Marius swore under his breath. 'What's the time?'

'After first cock-crow, I'd say; no moon or stars, though, so it's hard to judge.'

'Right; situation conference downstairs as soon as I'm dressed; you and the centurions, and a scribe to take notes; Flavius, quick, give me that gown.'

He pulled on the loose-fitting garment, then pushed his feet into his felt slippers, cursing under his breath as realised that his left foot had found its place before his right. Bad luck's the last thing I need now. *Absit omen.*

The rampart, once he reached it, was crowded with men, all whispering with excitement. 'Right, who's on watch here? Who saw the signal first? The rest of you, bugger off and go back to sleep, or I'll find you something to stay awake for.'

'It was me, sir. Arminius, sir.' Marius looked at the speaker, a gangling lad of perhaps twenty summers, hopping excitedly up and down in the torchlight.

An unusual name. 'Arminius? Where are you from, lad? Germania?' Marius spoke with deliberate calm, intent on getting a sensible report rather than a gabble of nonsense.

'Rhaetia, sir. Sir, is there going to be a war?'

'Don't be so bloody stupid. And don't ever talk like that, not unless you want to spend the next month on fatigues. Now, what did you see? Show me.'

The lad took a deep breath, then stepped up to the ramparts and pointed away to the north-west. 'See the light, sir? But there were more fires to begin with, I'd swear it. Just the one to start with, then a lot more close by, and then just the one again.'

Marius shook his head, trying to clear his eyes of the cloudiness that sometimes plagued them when he had not long woken. 'Yes, I see. That's one of our signal towers all right. Arminius, stay here on watch, but make sure you keep your eye on the whole area; if there are any more beacons, or if that one goes out suddenly, I want to be told at once.'

He took another hard look at the distant, twinkling light; was it his imagination or were there still other fires burning close beside it?

'You did well, lad; you have good young eyes.' He clapped him on the shoulder, then turned to stamp hurriedly down the steps.

The little office in his house was already crowded with men, clustered round the wooden table on which someone – he guessed it would be Gracchus – had already stretched out a map and despite the poor light from the flickering lamps was fiddling with a pair of dividers.

'Right, gentlemen, as you know we seem to have a problem; at the moment we don't know quite what it is, nor even exactly where it is – unless one of you has been able to match up the beacon-fire with one of these forts?' He indicated the half-dozen or so little outposts scattered along the north shore of the estuary, then waited for someone else to speak.

'I reckon we can discount the two at the western end,' he went on when no-one spoke up, 'and probably the easternmost one as well; that leaves us with any one of the remaining three. All isolated, gentlemen, none of them with road access, and all of them potentially looking to us to get them out of a tricky situation whatever it might be.'

Marcus Asellio spoke up, his voice slow and careful. 'Do we know it's anything worse than an accidental fire, sir? They should be able to deal with that themselves, they're pretty competent; we've not had any native trouble up there for five years or more, and no reason to expect any, not that I've heard of anyway.'

There was a general murmur of agreement. Marius looked again from face to face: competent men with a couple of hundred years of service between them, not given to looking for trouble but well able to deal with it when it arose. He waited for a long moment, letting them weigh up the probabilities, waiting for them to back Marcus' assessment.

But it was Gracchus who spoke. 'I think we should prepare for the worst, sir. Think how it would look if we didn't.' He paused meaningfully, letting the others follow his reasoning.

So that's the way the wind lies, thought Marius; if we don't shape up to your expectations, your staff friends in Eboracum will hear that we're taking things too easy over here and need a spot of shaking up. Well, I know a trick worth two of that.

'A fair point,' he said aloud. 'As you've reminded us, the worse-case scenario would be that the fort has been over-run or burned to the ground, and the garrison either massacred or taken as hostages. And if that's what's happened they'll surely have taken the *signum* as well; I don't need to tell you the consequences if that was paraded around by an enemy, boasting about the bloody nose they gave us and how we didn't dare do anything about it.

'So, Tribune, let me have your suggestions for appropriate action; we can spare a century at most if you want to organise a punitive expedition, or whatever you think would be most suitable. As long as you bring them back safe, of course.' He gave Marcus Asellio a sideways glance and noticed the grim smile on the man's face.

'I think it would be a mistake to jump in too soon.' This was Eburnus, one of the younger centurions, only recently made up from the rank of *optio*. Marius had noticed his quiet, phlegmatic manner, and been intrigued by it; he seemed to have the useful ability to speak very quietly to the men under his command while still making them eager to do exactly what he said.

'Go on.'

'It could be a trap; there might be an ambush on the road, for instance; we could walk right in to it if we're not careful. I've heard what the noble tribune has said, but Victory loves Preparation, as they say. Anyway, we can't do anything until it's light, and for all we know we could get a message from them in the next few hours. So my voice is for preparation, not action.'

'If there's no message, does it mean that they've not sent one, or that the messenger's been intercepted – perhaps murdered? We can't take the chance.' That was Gracchus again.

Marius accepted his point with a nod, but added, 'Either way, we can't do anything until dawn.'

He paused, accepting that in the last analysis the choice of what to do was entirely his own. *If I bugger it up, though, it'll be the end of my career for sure. Well, that's how the dice fall.*

'A century, then. Ask for volunteers; there'll be no shortage. They eat before they go – it's no fun fighting or marching on an empty stomach – but I'd like to see them in marching order by the end of the first hour; light marching order, no point in loading them up. You, Tribune, will be in command. Take the auguries before you go, of course; it always heartens the men. And you'll need a centurion to act as your Number Two.' He glanced round the room. 'Eburnus, here's your chance to show what you can do.'

Eburnus gave him a huge grin and murmured his acceptance. *I remember when I was as eager as him,* Marius thought. *Let's hope it all turns out well.*

'Tribune, I think you were working out distances earlier; did you come to any conclusions?'

Gracchus nodded. 'We'd be faster if we could go over the river directly, sir, rather than the long way round; and we'd avoid any chance of ambush in the rough country on the other side. That means ships, I suppose; is that possible?'

Marius shook his head. 'There's none of our navy triremes

around, so there's only little coracles and fishing boats to be had. But it doesn't matter; you can cut straight across the firth on foot; they used to do it all the time before the road was built a few years back.

'It's perfectly passable with a good guide, and it so happens that we've still got one on a retainer; I saw him in the town a week or two back, Apuleios or some such. Get someone out to find him and bring him in – promise him a good rate if he does the job well.' He hesitated, then went on, 'Knock up the taverns first; I gather he has a reputation there.'

Gracchus struck the table with delight. 'Strike hard where they don't expect it. That's the Roman way.'

Marius had a sudden vision of his men strung out across the estuary, trapped and with the tide on the turn, but dismissed it from his mind as Marcus Asellio gave the table a gentle tap. 'If I may, sir?'

'Of course, Marcus; go ahead.'

'Well, sir, if the party's gone for any length of time, we'll need reinforcements ourselves; we're already below strength, and we can't risk not being able to respond to trouble somewhere else.' Or to defend ourselves and the town here, if it comes to it, thought Marius grimly.

'Good point.' He motioned to the scribe. 'Write up a message to the commander at Brocavum and ask him if he can spare us half a century in a hurry; he'll be able to draw troops down from further east if he needs to, but we'll confirm it when we know more. Write up your notes for me; I want a record of everything that was said. And we'll double the patrols in town and on the roads; but otherwise we'll keep it all low-key – and I'll take a good look round myself, see how things lie.'

He glanced once more around the table, then stood up decisively. 'Gentlemen, you have your orders; the Senate and the People of Rome rely on us to do our duty.'

XXVIII

Messalina sat up with a start, woken by the pounding at the door and the sound of rough voices calling out in Latin. Clutching her tunic she padded across the floor and put her eye to the peep-hole, then stepped back in fright as the door shook under the weight of repeated blows.

'Open up. In the Emperor's name.'

'Gods, wait. I'm coming. Get out of the way, you useless slut.' Bran, his nightgown only half on, clumped down the stairs, his bronze bedroom lamp held high. In his hurry he missed the bottom step and grabbed at the wall to keep himself from falling; the lamp clattered to the ground, spreading a little pool of blazing oil across the floor; in moments the rushes had taken light.

For a moment Bran was terrified into silence; his voice when it came was hoarse as though from long disuse. 'Jupiter and Minerva. Quick, beat it out.' But he and Messalina both had bare feet, and could only watch helplessly as the flames spread.

Messalina screamed twice, then once again as the door finally burst open under the force of repeated blows and kicks. As it sagged back on its hinges two soldiers pushed into the room, shoved Bran and Messalina to one side, and stamped out the fire with their boots; then the taller one pushed Bran against the wall while the other snatched away Messalina's tunic with a grin and grabbed her breast.

'You trying to burn the place down? Bloody fool. If you can't be safe with fire, don't play with it. Gods, in Rome we'd have you in the arena for that.'

He shook his head in disgust, then went on, 'Associate of yours – name of Apuleios or something like that. He here?'

Bran shook his head in mute terror, then recovered enough to whisper, 'Lives near the west-gate, over the cobbler's booth; whatever he's done, I don't know anything about it.' Then, with a sudden recollection of the rules of commerce, he called to the other soldier, 'Hey, you have to pay to play with her.'

The man sniggered, then tossed Messalina's tunic clean over her head and onto the floor, then smacked her backside as she bent to pick it up. 'Right, then. We'll go looking for your friend; and you, keep your nose clean. If we can't find him we'll be right back.'

The two stepped to the doorway, looked in once more, then with a final, 'And get the bloody door fixed.' they strode off into the gloom. Bran shook himself as if trying to clear his mind of a bad dream, then gave Messalina an absent-minded cuff. 'Can't you look after the place properly? What in Hades do you think we keep you for?' He bent down to pick up the bronze lamp, then muttered in fury, 'Dented. And it cost more than you did. Come on, help me shove the door back and make it safe before we're all murdered in our beds.'

♕ ♕ ♕ ♕ ♕ ♕ ♕

Niamh sat silently at the entrance to her cave, watching carefully as the light slowly spread over the sky and the stars faded. Only when the ring of Caer Arianrhod had finally faded in the light of the brightening dawn did she turn to look over her shoulder at the sleeping form of Cybele.

'Child, get up. You have work to do.'

Cybele sat up slowly, rubbing her eyes. Niamh reached back to grasp the girl's hair, and gave it a sharp pull. 'Come on, sluggard. This is no time for sleep. Fetch water.'

Still drowsy, Cybele fumbled for the wooden bowl that served for pitcher, drinking vessel and divination cup, then picked her way yawning to the stream.

'Fill it. To the brim. There are things I must know. Hurry.'

With the brimming bowl set carefully at the entrance to the cave, Cybele sat in front of it as she had done before; but before she lowered her head to gaze into it she looked up into Niamh's face, shadowed against the growing light.

'Why do you not look, Mistress?'

Niamh was silent for a long moment, then answered reluctantly, 'The gods have taken the gift from me and given it to you. One evening not long ago when I came to look into the water, I found that I could see nothing; for a long time I sat and stared, willing the vision to come, and when it failed I wept for the gift I had lost. The gods give, and the gods take away, and no-one knows the time of either giving or taking. So you must be my eyes, and I must teach you all that you need to know.'

'I never knew there were pictures in the water. Do the gods send them, Mistress?'

'To those that they favour, yes, though they cannot be bidden. But do not trust them. They tell of things that are now or of things that will be; and they never lie, but the truth they tell can lead the careless astray. You have much to learn.'

Almost tenderly she went on, 'I never asked your name, child. What are you called?'

'Cybele, Mistress.' She paused, then added, 'My master called me that, Mistress; my mother gave me no name that I ever heard. But I like the name he gave me anyway.'

Niamh laughed mirthlessly. 'Cybele? In their ignorance they named you well, child. The Great Mother, the witch-goddess of the woods and hills. Child, my own name means Brightness; even between us it seems that the old story goes on, for you are named for the wild wood, and it is Urien who watches over you as it is Lugos who watches over me.'

Her voice suddenly hardened. 'And you are young and I am old, and I think I shall not stay to see how this story ends. And, child, I hate you for it – never forget that. Now, tell me what you see.'

Cybele lowered her head and stared unblinkingly into the water; after a moment she rocked backwards and forwards as though trying to focus the image, then murmured, 'Only water, Mistress. Wide, wide water; and men, Mistress, so many men.'

XXIX

The little maid had piled cushions in the corner of the garden by the ancient oak tree, and now Verica was sitting on them, so absorbed in reading a scroll, moving it back and forth to catch the best light, that she didn't hear the approaching footsteps, and only a soft cough finally made her lift her eyes from the writing.

'What is it, mother?'

'Hesiod. *Εργα και Ημεραι* – Works and Days, if you prefer.' She made a face. 'My Greek's getting rusty. Gwydion reads it well enough, but he speaks it like a barbarian. You should let me practise it on you. Here, sit down and listen to me read.'

'You could hear all the Greek you want in Rome, mother. And have all the books anyone could desire, in Latin or Greek or Hebrew or who knows what else, and it's not so far to Rome these days.'

'So you've told me before. But this is my land, and here I shall live and die.'

Lugos shrugged. 'So Cartimandua would have said of Brigantia, mother. But now her bones are buried somewhere outside Neapolis.'

'So I carry on her work here. As you will one day carry on mine.' She paused, looking closely into his face. 'What are you thinking? What's going on in your mind?'

Lugos at last squatted down beside her. 'Do you remember what happened to the kingdom of the Iceni, mother?'

'Of course. Boudicca fought against the Romans, sacked Londinium and Camulodunum; no-one knows quite how she died. And then the Romans annexed her land.'

Lugos shook his head. 'Not quite, I'm afraid. When her husband Prasutagus died, the Romans ignored the will he'd written and just walked in and took over the land for themselves. Then the famous Seneca and the other money-lenders back in the great city asked for their cash back, and she decided that enough was enough. Didn't do her any good in the end, though, did it? Oh, the soldiers raped her daughters too – I nearly forgot that bit.'

Verica shrugged. 'All ancient history. You have a lesson to teach me, boy?'

Lugos flushed briefly but went on doggedly. 'Only that when the time comes, mother, I don't think that your friend Marius will be very happy to see me in any sort of authority here. Oh, I know you're sweet on him, and him on you – I saw the way you both touched hands when that altar was dedicated, and so did Gwydion. But in what, ten years' time, twenty at most, this land will be as much part of Rome as Gaul or Lusitania is today. Can you really not see that?'

'You think you see the future more clearly than Niamh. And so you prefer to give up now and run away?'

Lugos nodded. 'Indeed I do, mother. I have a simple choice: as it is now the Senate will give me a pension, enough for me to live a pleasant life as a private citizen with a decent estate, a villa somewhere in Umbria, perhaps, with a local girl for a wife and enough slaves to keep me comfortable, and I'll still have a worthwhile inheritance to pass on to my children; or I can stay here and have nothing at all, perhaps. What choice is that?'

Verica's face was white with shock. 'And that is what you want? To be a farmer?'

Lugos smiled for a moment. 'Mother dear, I remember what you yourself said only a few days ago: I was a farmer's daughter. The very words. And to live in Italy, with the sun and the blessed warmth, not the perpetual rain and fog we have here. With grapes, and pomegranates and melons.' He suddenly knelt on one knee and took his mother's right hand in his. 'Will you not come? Come to a new life with me. And you can have all the latest

Roman fashions to take your pick of.'

For a moment Verica seemed uncertain. She shook her head, ran her left hand over her hair, then looked wildly around the garden. At last she spoke firmly but quietly. 'This is my place. This house, this garden, these people. How can I leave them? What would I be in Rome? Some nameless foreign curiosity for people to stare at?'

'Mother, you would be honoured. As the great Cartimandua was. What harm can there be for you to follow in her footsteps? If she were here today, she would tell you so.' He glanced at Gwydion, standing silent and impassive. 'Would she not, Gwydion?'

But Gwydion was silent and the moment of indecision had gone. Verica stood up abruptly, pulling her right hand free. 'Go where you please, Lugos – or Lucos, or whatever name you want to go by. Take what you want, take two of the men-servants for your companions, and go – and go quickly.'

She turned away, facing the garden wall where a young apple tree was growing as an espalier. 'Go. I do not think we shall meet again.'

Lugos stood unmoving for a moment. Then he took his mother's hand in his own again, bent to kiss it, turned abruptly and left. Behind him Verica stood unmoving until his footsteps had died away. Then she sat calmly again on her pile of cushions. 'It is all as Niamh foresaw; and now there's only Gwydion to help me practise my Greek,' she said to herself, and bent back to her scroll.

☙ ☙ ☙ ☙ ☙ ☙ ☙

Gracchus halted his men at the end of the beach and stared over the flat expanse of the Ituna estuary; dotted here and there little groups of men and women were bent over, digging in the sand for cockles, their donkeys waiting patiently by them. Everywhere was calm, with only the slightest of warm breezes from the west, though he fancied that he could see a smudge of smoke still rising from a point on the northern shore.

'It looks easy enough. It can't be much more than a mile or a mile and a half.'

Apuleios gave a slow smile and leant on the pole he was carrying. 'Then I'll let you take your chances on your own. But I'll tell you this for free: there are three channels cut deep, and you need to know the fording place of each; and there's quicksand that will swallow you whole and never leave a trace. A mile, you say? The shortest route, maybe – the shortest route to drowning.

'There's the tide as well; it goes out slowly enough, but it comes in at a run. If you want the guide, you pay me now; if not, I'll just sit on my backside here and watch you drown in your own good time.'

Gracchus shrugged. 'Ten denarii was agreed, and ten denarii will be paid – when we're all safely on the other side.'

Apuleios grinned and shook his head. 'I'm not falling for that one. It's cash in advance, or do it yourself. And don't think of trying the old half now, half later trick either. You see, you have to trust me; but I don't trust you further than I can see you. And I wouldn't take too long about making your mind up, or the tide'll turn and you'll drown whether you've paid or not.' He spat copiously on the sand, narrowly missing the hind hoof of Gracchus' fine Spanish stallion.

Gracchus gave a sidelong glance at Eburnus, but he seemed to be preoccupied with the cinch of his saddle. With a look of fury Gracchus pulled open the money-bag hanging at his waist and counted out the coins, then tossed them contemptuously onto the sand; Apuleios gave a broad wink, then bent over and carefully picked them up, meticulously turning each one over as he did so; when they were all in his palm he muttered, 'I reckon that'll pay the ferryman for all of you,' then went on aloud, 'Don't forget what I told you: keep in single file, half a spear's length between each one; anyone gets into quicksand, just call for help and I'll come, but whatever you do don't start thrashing about and shouting. The first quarter-mile or so should be easy enough; after that it begins to get interesting. One rider up front, the other at the back, and everyone keep their eyes peeled.'

As they tramped over the firm sand the little clusters of cockle-hunters stood to watch them, then bent back to their digging; two men in one group raised their arms and shouted a greeting to Apuleios, but otherwise they passed in silence, the sand muffling the beat of the soldiers' boots and the horses' hooves.

When they had left the cockle-hunters behind, Apuleios began to walk more cautiously, thrusting his pole deep into the ground at every step; the ground was wetter here, making puddles around the men's feet and the horses' hooves as they moved on; a flock of greylag geese honked at them and moved reluctantly away as they approached.

For perhaps half an hour the group trailed across the estuary, the soldiers staring around curiously while Apuleios kept up his even pace, still probing the sand from time to time. The breeze had died and there was real warmth in the sun now, so that the heat reflected back from the glaze of water on the surface of the sand, making the distant shore swim in the haze.

Then, without warning, they came to the edge of a deep channel, cut perhaps ten feet below the main level of the sand and perhaps twenty feet wide, with water still flowing strongly down it.

'The first channel. It's shallow enough to wade through here, but you'll need to take care on the other bank. Follow me.'

Apuleios scrambled down the nearer side of the dip, leaning on his pole as he did so; at the edge of the stream he paused, scooped up some water and tasted it, then nodded with satisfaction. 'Sweet. We're doing well. You can stop and drink if you want, but don't take too long about it.'

He felt the bottom of the channel with his pole, probing to left and right before settling on a fording point and waving the men to follow him, then waited as they squatted down and drank. As they waited, Gracchus pulled up beside him, leaning down from the saddle.

'Can't you be quicker? I thought you knew the way.'

Apuleios grunted. 'The way changes from tide to tide, shifts this way and that. If you think you know better, you go on ahead.'

Gracchus turned again, glanced towards the coastline behind him and then ahead; it was overcast now, and in both directions the shores were only a rumour in the haze. They'd covered perhaps a third of the way, he guessed, with two more channels still ahead. 'How long before the tide turns?'

'Half an hour, perhaps a little more; it runs up the channels fast, but everywhere else it just rises through the sand and turns it to quicksand. Listen. What do you hear?'

Gracchus turned to one side for a moment, then shook his head. 'Nothing.'

Apuleios smiled. 'That's right; there's no sound out here; this is the dead land, even the birds don't come here. This is where most of the quicksands are, so follow me carefully – not a step to right or to left of the track I mark, and we'll all be fine. And keep the men quiet; I need to listen to the sand as I go.'

He turned abruptly and began to walk ahead, probing the ground at every footstep; twice he stopped and retraced a few steps before trying a different route, casting always a little further to his left as he went. At one point he stopped and pointed to the rotting ribs of a boat, half-covered in sand and weed.

'See that, the *Puella*, that was. Nice little fishing boat she was, till one day the owner managed to miss the channel and beached her on a spring tide. If he'd waited a few hours she'd have floated back up and no damage done, but the fool thought that he'd walk back to shore. He made it for about a hundred paces, I'd say, before he got himself trapped in the quicksand; the cocklers could hear him screaming for help, but they had more sense than to try to save him. Must have been yelling for an hour before he went under, calling on every god you ever heard of and a few you haven't. He's still down there, somewhere, I suppose.'

Gracchus shook his head angrily. 'You can save us the horror stories, man. Get on with what you're paid to do.'

Apuleios smiled slowly, then gave a curt nod and set out again; the haze was all around them now, a thick curtain that hid every feature of the landscape.

The second channel came sooner than Gracchus had expected. It was shallower than the first but wider, and held standing water; as he had done before Apuleios scooped up a palm-full of water and tasted it. 'Tide's well on the turn. No time to waste. Over you come.'

He watched while the troop crossed, then gave a grim smile. 'This is a bad patch too, and there's not a lot of time left. Let's go.'

He stepped out carefully, probing with the rod every few paces, moving a little quicker than he had before. Only when he heard shouts from behind did he stop and turn; one of the men, perhaps more heavily built than his fellows or maybe carrying a bigger load, was already sinking up to his knees and calling out in terror. Eburnus had calmly reined in his horse and was motioning the men near him to silence.

A fleeting look of alarm passed over Gracchus' face but he mastered himself quickly. 'What do we do? What's the routine?'

Apuleios shook his head. 'You need rope. But first make him get down on his back; it's safer to lie flat, it doesn't drag you in so much. And he can throw away his kit, unless he wants to take it down to Annwn with him.'

Now that the first shock was over, good discipline reasserted itself in moments; a coil of rope was unhooked from Gracchus' saddle and at Apuleios' direction a loop was quickly but efficiently tied in it.

'Right, now throw it to him; throw it past him and pull it back, that's right. For all the gods' sake don't any of you get any closer to him, or you'll be down there with him.'

Eburnus had dismounted now, and carefully took the coil of rope and sent it snaking over the sand; the second throw brought it within the man's easy reach as he tried to lie flat on the sand, though terror was written plain in his face.

'Pass it over your shoulders, man. That's the idea. Now, hold tight and we'll have you out in no time.' Eburnus tied the free end of the rope around the horn of his saddle and then walked the horse slowly forward.

'Gently does it. That's the stuff.' The man came free with a sucking sound, then lay still and shaking from shock, his legs and thighs still caked in wet sand and his feet raw where his boots had been pulled off.

'Pull yourself together man. The gods have decided to let you live a bit longer, so mind where you're putting your big feet from now on, or you'll be down there keeping your boots company.' Apuleios cast a glance around and went on, 'Tide'll be on us before long, there's no time to hang about. Look lively.'

He moved faster now as though more certain of his way, though every few paces he still probed the sand with his pole. The going was noticeably wetter now, and for much of the time the men were ankle-deep in salt water.

Peering ahead from the back of his horse Gracchus could see the northern shore emerging from the haze. Then suddenly they were at the third channel, with the land rising sharply beyond it, and trees standing thick and tall on the far side. Gracchus permitted himself a smile of relief.

At the edge of the channel Apuleios stopped and shook his head. 'We've wasted too much time; look how it's filling up. And listen – the sand's singing. There's not many get to hear that and live.'

It was true; the ground beneath their feet was beginning to whistle softly; as they stood there astonished the sound grew louder, seemed to come from all around them. Then as they watched, a wave, no more than an a few inches high, ran in past them; and suddenly everything to the west was already under water and the tide was rising fast.

Quickly Apuleios waded in to the channel; the water here was already at his waist, and flowing strongly. Supporting himself with the pole he waded across, then scrambled up the northern bank.

'Right, lads. Safely delivered as promised. Over the channel and up the bank and you're home and dry. If you can, that is.'

Behind Apuleios a troop of men had materialised out of the woods that fringed the beach, armed with spears and slings, and dressed for the most part in old Roman battle-gear; Gracchus glanced to left and right, but the line stretched unbroken as far as he could see.

Apuleios stepped forward, cupped his hands around his mouth and shouted, 'Not many people hear the sand sing and live to tell the tale. Say hello to Arawn for me, you bastards. The third time will be the greatest. Tell him I said that.'

Blind rage made Gracchus unable to speak for a moment. The old, old story – betrayed by native scouts. Almost without thinking he bellowed, 'Eburnus, to me. Double column, lads, form up behind us. Swords out, no quarter.' He flashed his own sword over his head, shouted 'Rome. Rome. Rome.' He waited until the men had taken it up as a battle-cry, then urged his stallion into the stream as the slingers' stones flew around them.

On the bank Apuleios watched dispassionately as they struggled to get over the channel and up the bank. Then, without waiting to see the end, he turned away and walked calmly into the forest, whistling and jingling the coins in his purse.

XXX

Verica shivered; the day had started fine and sunny, but the gathering haze had brought a chill to the garden where she sat idly watching the carp in the pool.

She motioned Iras closer. 'Fetch me a wrap, girl.' She scanned the sky, then went on, 'The fine cream wool one, with the golden threads in it. And be quick.'

She watched the girl hurry away, then turned back to the pool. 'Do you feel the cold, little fish?' A sudden fancy took her. 'How many lives have you had, little fish? What were you before, that made you come back in such a funny shape?' She laughed briefly. 'Cold maids, perhaps, frightened of a kiss and never bedded?'

She trailed her fingers in the water. 'And what shall I be in the time to come? I think I should like to be an otter, little fish, so that I could come here and eat you all up in one gulp.'

A sudden shadow fell across her. Expecting the maid she turned to let the girl drape the wrap over her shoulders; but it was Gwydion who was standing there.

'You were laughing, my lady. Do you feel easier now?'

Verica shook her head. 'I was discussing rebirth with the fish; they had little enough to say about it. Gwydion, it seems to me that to be born again is nothing without those we love around us. And so many have gone: my mother and father both, simple farmers that they were – he, killed in a boar hunt and she dead of some pestilence while I was far away; then Venutius, who came to take me away from home as a fosterling, though I had little love for him in the end; and the great Queen Cartimandua, who was another mother to me. And now my son as well, and his body burnt to ashes on some Roman pyre.'

Gwydion nodded. 'My lady, whatever I may think of the Romans, this at least I will say to their credit: that they give due honour to the dead, and commend them with all ceremony to the gods of the underworld.

'But, my lady, I have some news for you; the guards at the gate are full of this story: that soldiers have marched out from the fort the day before yesterday, and that they are headed north, to Caledonia, to avenge some outrage that has happened there.'

He paused, his eyes fixed firmly on Verica's face. 'My lady, it may be that Niamh's words are coming true, and that the gods are stirring men's hearts to war. My lady, you spoke a moment ago of Cartimandua; soon, I think, you will have to choose your friends, as she did in her day.'

He paused at the sound of approaching footfalls, then waited as the returning maid laid the wrap on Verica's shoulders, before going on in an undertone, 'If it comes to war, my lady, will you side with the Romans, now that they have killed your son?'

'Killed my son? It was the gods who took him, Gwydion, and if he had never left my side then perhaps they would have taken him here. Hunting for boar like my father, perhaps, or falling from his horse, or drowned at some ford; who can tell? Death hides in many places, Gwydion, and none of us is wise enough to avoid his pitfalls.

'When I first heard, then indeed the anger was fierce; and for that time, I hated Marius and all his kind. But the storm has blown itself out, Gwydion.'

Suddenly she stood, her eyes blazing. 'This is not war as it used to be, tribe against tribe, fighting over a fertile valley or the theft of a drove of cattle or over some imagined slight, a tussle between a few dozen men brawling to give their bards something to sing about and to make their names remembered. No, this would be war as the Romans wage it; and I have seen such war, seen a legion rape and kill in its fury, and I will not loose that fate on my people. You told me not long since that the gods want blood, Gwydion.

They will not make me their accomplice. You will not speak of this again.'

Gwydion stood for a long moment in silence, then bowed deeply. 'As you command, my lady; I will only say that beyond these walls, the drums may already be beating; and such is the common talk among the guards at your gate.'

Verica nodded, and answered in a low voice. 'I know; and so I know where my duty lies. Some of us are born to face hard days, my friend.'

'Things have changed here, I see. It's good to see a man making his way in the world. How's the new enterprise working out? No other customers yet? What have you got for my noon-meal? Something hot, I think.'

Bran gave Senorix a wary look, then beckoned him to one side. 'Got my fingers burnt, didn't I. The old bugger took his pots and pans away with him. And nowhere to buy more round here, so I'll have to wait till the pot-man shows up and Jupiter knows when that'll be. I'll lose my shirt if he doesn't come soon. Still, I can do you some nice ewe's cheese and fruit, and the bread's as good as ever. And there's some pickled herring too, if you want. There you go.'

Senorix took the platter with a smile and sat carefully on one of the stools. 'Ah, that's the way with commerce these days; got to keep your wits about you, or they'll open your purse with one hand while they're greeting you with the other. The stories I could tell. But it seems I've got some good news for you; the pot-man's on his way; I passed him just inside the North Gate, bargaining with some housewife. I'd get in there quick if I were you, or he'll have nothing decent left.'

For a while he ate silently, watching the comings and goings in the market-place. Then with a sigh he stood up, wiped his lips and handed back the platter with a little bow. 'And now I'll be off round the corner to see your lovely wife. Good luck with the pots.

And don't worry, I shan't say a word to the little lady.'

Bran watched him out of sight, then turned back to his counter. And that's not the only thing I didn't think of, he grumbled. With the old woman on her own looking after the Eagle, all the takings go straight into her pocket; and she can't sell the good stuff because she doesn't know about it. And the gods know how much I'll have to spend on those blasted pots.

'Ah, the lovely lady of the house. And how are you, my dear?'

Morrig scowled briefly. 'Still full of clever talk, I see. And a purse still full of silver, I hope. Do you have more cattle to sell? The way you keep turning up there can't be that many left to bring.'

Senorix shrugged. 'A man can trade in many things, my dear, and find a profit in all of them if he's clever enough. I'm only passing through now, though, but I couldn't pass up on a chance to tickle that little whore of yours. Are you sure you won't be willing to sell her to me? She won't be worth as much tomorrow as she is today, you know.'

Morrig grunted. 'No use talking to me; it's himself that thinks he knows all about money these days. All these years I've looked after the cash, made sure he can come up with the taxes when they ask, pay for the wine, keep us all in food; but now…'

'You don't like him running the cook-shop next door? And there was me thinking he was making a success of himself.'

Morrig shrugged, then suddenly decided to throw off the weight on her mind. She went to the door and glanced up and down the street to be sure that no-one was listening, then burst out, 'Come and look at this. What d'you make of it?' She led Senorix down the alley, then pulled back two of the amphorae stacked there to show what lay behind.

Senorix leant forward to read the labels gummed on the jars hidden at the back and whistled quietly through the gap at the front of his mouth. 'Now that's good stuff, from what I've heard. Better than the rot-gut you usually sell, I'd say, though I'm a beer man myself.'

'So where did he get the money? And enough to buy that caupona, too? What's he mixed up in? Did he get it from some fancy-woman? Someone with more money than sense. That's what I think anyway. And there's something brewing up at the fort, too. Twice we've had them chasing around here looking for people. Some runaway slave-girl the first time, then that old drunkard Apuleios, and in the middle of the night too. They're not here, I told them, neither of them, so you can go away and let us get our sleep.'

Senorix shrugged. 'Ah, that's the soldiers for you. Still, they're good customers, aren't they? And I'm not one to interfere between a man and his wife – not if I want to be comfortable with either. But money's the thing these days, that's for sure. Himself should watch the bankers, though. Oh, they'll lend pleasantly enough; then when the time comes for them to have their money back, it's quite a different story – worse than any soldiers, they are.'

Morrig shook her head. 'Who'd lend money to that fool? Ah, I'll get to the bottom of it sooner or later – but don't tell him I said anything. At least he's got less time for his fishing these days, if that's what he was doing. Quite the little man of business he is now, with that caupona to run as well as the Eagle. Would you be wanting the girl now? Before she gets busy?'

Senorix nodded. 'Aye, send her out to the shed here, I'll let you have her back when I'm done with her. Cash in advance, wasn't it?'

He pulled the purse off his arm and counted out the coppers, then ducked into the stable and lay back on the straw, thinking of what Morrig had said and wondering why does everyone want me to listen to their troubles? It's none of my business anyway. And I'm buggered if I'm going to lend any money to anybody.

But even when Messalina came in a few moments later, pulling her tunic over her head as she knelt down and kissing him full on

– 229 –

the lips, he found that Morrig's question kept going round in his head. Gently he pushed the girl away, laying his fingers on his lips as he did so.

'Now stop your fussing. I told you I'd be back, didn't I?'

'Have you got more money for me? Can you give it to me now?'

Senorix laughed. 'All in good time, girl. No, you'll get no more out of me today, but maybe another time. Now tell me, what's this I hear about your master and his new money?'

Messalina pouted. 'Let's do it first and I'll tell you afterwards. Mistress had me scouring pots with sand, I'd much rather do this. Hey, look what some Roman taught me to do.' With a giggle she lay back on the straw and pulled her legs up high, struggling to cross her ankles behind her head.

Senorix watched her and burst out laughing. 'Silly girl. I can show you better tricks than that.' Suddenly serious he went on, 'She hasn't found your money again, has she?'

Messalina shook her head, then said, 'She says she'll have me branded, though. I don't want that. She says it would stop me running away like some girl the soldiers came looking for.'

'Aye, your mistress told me about that. Said they came looking for your master's friend Apuleios, too.'

Suddenly Messalina was whispering confidentially, 'I know. In the middle of the night. Master nearly set the place on fire when he dropped the lamp. You'll never guess what the soldiers told me the next day.'

Senorix yawned theatrically. 'Go on, then, girl, if you must.'

'They said that a whole century had been sent over the river somewhere. And that before long there might be some new soldiers coming instead of them. From Bravo-something-or-other. It'll be nice to see some new faces.'

'Faces? Lass, I know you and it's not their faces that you'll be interested in. Maybe you'll be gone by then, though. I've offered to buy you, but your mistress won't give me a clear answer, not just yet. Now, lass, we'll let you earn your keep in a few minutes, but first tell me about your master and his money.'

Messalina shrugged, then went on in a sing-song voice, as if she was explaining something to a rather slow child. 'It's no secret, he borrowed it from someone; there's a big man comes to collect something from him every Saturn Day morning out in the forum. He calls himself Amicus – that's a silly name.'

No mysteries are safe from slaves, thought Senorix. 'And your mistress doesn't know? He's kept that a secret from her?'

Messalina tried and failed to keep a straight face. 'Oh, he thinks he has, but she knows more than she'll tell. One day she'll bring it up just when he doesn't expect it, and then he'll really be in the shit.'

Before Senorix could say anything else, Messalina grabbed him between the legs, then pulled him on top of her; and he thought no more about it for a while. But afterwards he remembered what Crotos had told him about his father's farm and what had happened to it; Bravo-something-or-other. I think I could put a fuller name than that to the place.

XXXI

'Drowned? Trapped by an ambush and then drowned? Two days ago? By all the gods, what were you thinking of?'

Gracchus stood to rigid attention before Marius, his helmet clasped firmly under his left arm. 'We were betrayed, sir, by our guide. We had no way of knowing what he would do.'

By the guide I arranged for you, thought Marius, but he pushed the thought to one side. 'Go on.'

'There was a large war party waiting on the northern side of the firth; they caught us just as the tide was coming in. We charged them, but they had the advantage of higher ground and the situation was impossible; most of the men were carried away by the water – there was a wave, a bore, that came sweeping in and swamped them.'

Marius stood up and banged his fist on the table in frustration. 'Drowned. Just at the shoreline. A very Celtic way to kill their enemies. Tribune, you well know what happened to Publius Varius' men in the Teutoburg Forest: slaughtered as they marched to winter quarters, hunted down to be butchered at the sides of rivers and streams, their bodies dedicated to some Celtic river god or other. And here are my men, killed in the same way; and only you, it seems, alive to bring me the news.'

Gracchus' eyes were fixed on the wall behind Marius' head. 'I was mounted, sir, and my horse was able to carry me to safety. I am a Roman and a patrician, and I deny any suggestion of cowardice.'

Marius tried to contain his fury, but found the words coming unbidden to his lips. 'It seems to me that when disaster struck you rode off like Numonious Vala at the Teutoburg. By Jupiter, this is not what Rome expects of its soldiers. Do you think I'll stand here banging my head against the wall like the Divine Augustus shouting to have his legions back.'

He stopped, hearing a sudden clatter on the stair, and the door flew open. Marcus Asselio was there, his face black with rage but with a grim smile just appearing. 'Sir, we have more survivors. Three more men have just made it back into camp, and there may be others.'

Marius turned to Gracchus. 'Stay here, Tribune. I'll talk to you later. Marcus, take me to them.'

Two of the men were already in the sick-bay, both half drowned and still shaking with shock and horror; in the confusion of the moment Eburnus had managed to haul both across his horse's neck and ridden through the tide to safety. He was now quivering with anger, much of it directed at himself, as Marius forced him to sit down and have hot *mulsum* poured down his throat.

'I had no choice, sir. I couldn't save any more; the tide was too strong, and the horse was foundering as it was. The water just swept them away – they were loaded with equipment, they didn't have a chance.'

He bit his lip and made the worst confession. 'And the *vexillium* went too; all swept away and lost.' His shoulders shook and he suddenly burst into tears.

Marius waited until his sobs had subsided, then spoke plainly. 'You saved two men, and others may have saved themselves; we shan't know for a day or so, perhaps. No-one could have done more; you saved your comrades' lives in the face of a cowardly enemy, and brought them back safe. I did nothing half so brave at your age. The gods will surely reward you.'

He paused, then went on, talking almost to himself, 'We'll have to mount full patrols on both sides of the firth, well-armed and prepared for action; and perhaps a punishment raid in a few days' time to draw a line under this. So like you suggested we'll need more men than we have here, and there won't be enough at

Brocavum, so for sure we'll need to draw from Bravoniacum. I hear that they have archers there, from Syria or some such place – we can find work for them, perhaps. Though the gods know how long before we get them.

'And Hades, we daren't leave our rear unprotected; Eboracum will have to know, and I can just imagine what the brass there will have to say. In the meantime we'll call a general parade, make proper sacrifices to the gods, stamp out any loose talk before it has a chance to grow.' He turned to Marcus Asellio, standing stolidly at his shoulder. 'See it done, Marcus. One hour, everyone – everyone, *immunes* and all except for the gate guards and the sick-bay people – in parade dress, turned out for full inspection; anyone who isn't perfect will be on fatigues for the next month.

'I'll get the scribe to draft a letter to Eboracum, and I'll handle the usual formal requests to the other forts for assistance. Eburnus, wipe your eyes and go and see the men you saved – and remind yourself that you saved not only them but their unborn children for all the ages of the world as well.' He clapped his hand on the young man's shoulder. 'I'm proud of you lad. We all are.'

As they stepped away, Marcus whispered, 'Who will you send to Eboracum? It'll need to be someone with a bit of clout, but I'd rather stay here and face the fun if it's all right with you, sir.'

'I have someone in mind, Marcus. Gods, if he stays here much longer I'm apt to disembowel him myself after what he's done. Clumsy, arrogant young fool.'

Marcus Asellio nodded, then went on, 'It's luck that he lacks, sir; Fortuna seems to have bestowed her blessings on Eburnus instead. And well-deserved, I'd have to say. But I'd hate to see the slant that the noble Tribune will put on things when he's delivering your report.'

'I have no choice, Marcus; if he stays here then frankly I can't guarantee his safety after what's happened; he wasn't popular to start with, and too many men will have lost comrades in this bloody fiasco. It wouldn't take much: an 'accident' in a melee somewhere, even a knife-blow on a dark night here in camp, or a drowning in the baths. And then I'll have an even worse problem on my hands. No, I'll feel happier when he's well out of my way.'

Marius stopped and turned to face the centurion. 'Look at it from my point of view: he's competent – you've said so yourself – and he certainly has connections somewhere up the chain of command – he may even know the Emperor, or carry some sort of imperial orders in his rucksack – why else would they send a senior tribune to this little outpost? In theory he's exactly the sort of man that any commander would be delighted to work with – and in fairness, if he'd pulled off this expedition, we'd all be singing his praises.

'But he was too confident, and walked right into a trap – a trap that he should have been prepared for. He knew he was in potentially hostile territory, he knew that there were clear signs that one of our forts had been attacked within a few miles of where he was, and yet he blundered right into an ambush even though a few hours earlier he'd been talking about the dangers of being caught on the road.

'He's a good book soldier, Marcus, but he's not safe in the field. He's read about ambushes – he'd be wary of being attacked on his flank, with the way ahead and behind blocked, but he never expected to be trapped out on the open sand, with the sea coming in. He should have known better.

'I can't keep him here, for two reasons: first, I don't trust him, or his judgement; and second, I can't protect him. We're all better off if he's out of my sight – and the sooner the better. Well, I'd better tell him so.'

Gracchus was still standing motionless where Marius had left him; he might have been carved out of stone. Marius wondered for a moment how long he would have stood there waiting.

'Tribune, we have three more survivors; your centurion Eburnus and two of your party that he managed to rescue – which was two more than you did, I may say – and brought them to safety.

Tribune, I will bring no accusation against you; but I will charge you with carrying a report of what happened to our superiors in Eboracum. The report will be brief and truthful; I have no doubt that you will wish to add your own interpretation of it.'

Gracchus flushed but was silent. He won't say anything, Marius suddenly realised; this is the old sort of Roman who would scorn to tell a lie even to save his own skin. By all the gods, I can't abide the man and I certainly can't think of keeping him here; but he's the true old breed for all that.

'Tribune, is there anything you haven't told me? Any detail that I should add to my report?'

Gracchus thought for a moment. 'Only one thing, sir; when our guide had betrayed us, he shouted something. I didn't quite catch it all at the time, but I've had a chance to think about it since, and I think it was the same thing that that thief we crucified a few weeks ago yelled before he died. The third time shall be the greatest, something like that. It didn't make any sense at the time – well, either time – but I suppose it could be important.'

'The third time shall be the greatest,' Marius repeated, and shrugged. 'Means nothing to me, but I'll ask around. Anything else?'

Gracchus shook his head. 'No sir, you have it all.'

'Then tell me this for my own curiosity: Eburnus managed by sheer courage and skill to save two men, but you saved no-one. Tribune, I'm willing to believe that you're no coward; was there no more you could have done to rescue your men – or the *vexillium*, which is either floating around in the sea, or perhaps captured by the enemy?'

Gracchus nodded. 'I might have saved some, sir, yes. Not the banner, which went under the waves almost at once – I think the standard-bearer must have been hit by a sling-shot, he went down right at the beginning and the water swept the flag away. But my duty as I conceived it was to report back so that appropriate action could be taken, and I did not feel that I should take any step which might jeopardise that. Sir, I still feel that.'

Marius stared at him for a long, hard moment, then said, 'Dismissed.' As Gracchus returned his salute and marched out, Marius shook his head thoughtfully. A hard man. We may need many more hard men before we see the end of this. And now I suppose I have to write that report.

A polite cough roused him from his reverie. Flavius was standing in front of him, an apologetic smile on his face. Marius raised an eyebrow.

'I know you have a lot to worry about, sir; but I have some news that you may be pleased to hear. It seems that Cybele was seen, a day or two after she ran away, wandering down to the south somewhere. Some country-people saw her; but they didn't know she was a runaway until they came in for the market and heard people talking. That's what they said, anyway; perhaps they're just after the reward, though.'

Marius gave a short humourless laugh. 'Ah yes, Cybele. I'd almost forgotten her. How simple everything was a few days ago when she was still here – then away she ran, and nothing's gone to plan since. It's almost enough to make you think that she was carrying our luck with her.'

He dismissed the thought with a shake of his head, then turned to more recent worries. 'Tell me, Flavius – does the phrase "the third time will be the greatest" mean anything to you?'

Flavius considered gravely, then shook his head. 'Not really, sir. But I can ask around. Someone's sure to know what it means.'

 ⚜ ⚜ ⚜ ⚜ ⚜ ⚜ ⚜

'Sit still, girl, and stop wriggling.' Niamh pressed Cybele down on her knees as she hacked a lock from her hair with her knife, then tied it up with a piece of scarlet thread.

'Now stand up – and don't slouch. I have a task for you that you must do alone, tonight by the light of the new moon. Listen to me.

'You must follow the stream back the way I brought you until you come out in the little meadow; the walking along its bed is good and firm and you can support yourself against the cliff-face, so you will not stumble. In the meadow near where the stream rises you will see three trees growing together in a group: an oak, an ash and an alder. Do you understand?'

Cybele nodded, but without conviction. Niamh went on, carefully explaining. 'The oak is the greatest, and it has the lowest branches. You must circle the oak three times, turning sunwise, and with your eyes fixed on the ground; then you must tie this hair to one of the lowest branches of the tree, and then come back here as soon as you can, and without looking behind you. Is that clear?'

'Should I say any words, Mistress? Will I see anything? Why can't you come to see I do it right?'

'Child, you already see many things that are hidden from me. Yes, there are words you should say; and I will teach them to you. And you must do this in secret, and then as your hair fades you will gain new power from the oak tree.'

Suddenly tender, Niamh went on, 'This I did, many years ago; I had a fine teacher, and these were the words he taught me.' She lowered her voice and whispered the incantation into Cybele's ear, then went on, 'Those words I said three times as I went around the tree, and then – and then I came here, and here I have been ever since. Can you remember the words, Cybele?'

Halting at first, Cybele repeated Niamh's invocation. Then she was silent for a long moment before asking, wide-eyed, 'And will I be here for ever too?' But at that Niamh turned her face away and would not answer.

XXXII

'So where's the money?'

Bran shifted uncomfortably. 'Had to spend it, didn't I? On new pots. There'd been a misunderstanding about them when I bought the place. Thought I'd have made it all up by now, but trade's been slow.'

Amicus raised an eyebrow. 'Slow? That's your problem, not mine. And not having the money's your problem as well. And you really don't want to make it mine.'

He settled his bulk on a stool and studiously began to clean his nails with his knife, then at last looked up with a smile. 'Look, I can cover for you for a week or two, but that's all. Glaucus trusts me, he won't ask for a full account. But you'll have to make it worth my while, understand? I don't mind doing favours for my friends, I'm a very friendly fellow. That's why they call me Amicus. You'd like to be my friend, wouldn't you?'

Bran thought frantically, then grabbed at a straw. 'There's the girl. You could have a go with her. Free, gratis and for nothing. She's good. I can go get her.'

'That skinny little bit of skirt you've got in the tavern? I prefer a girl with something I can squeeze.' He raised an eyebrow, then realised that no better offer was forthcoming. 'All right, I'll take what I can get. Fetch her round and let's try her out. And then we'll be big friends, you and me. That'll be nice, won't it.'

Bran hesitated for a moment. 'And Glaucus?'

'Don't you lose any sleep over him. I always look after my friends. For just as long as they are my friends. Now, fetch the little tart and let's see if she's worth all the trouble you've put me to.'

In the tavern, Senorix was just finishing a bowl of porridge before taking his leave.

'It's fine porridge you have. Good ballast for an empty belly.' He scooped the last of the oatmeal from the wooden bowl with his horn spoon, then ran his finger round the rim and licked it clean. Morrig gave him a scowl that had more of habit in it than malice, then watched him pull his pack onto his shoulder and swing through the door, almost colliding with Bran as he hurried in.

Senorix paused for a moment listening, then shrugged and stepped out into the street. The haze of the last few days had lifted and the day promised to be fine, though a few swirls of dust were dancing in a light breeze. He glanced at the sun; nearly the second hour already, and beginning to get hot.

Pulling his hood over his head – didn't need to do that while I still had some hair, he thought – he turned into the forum and bought two loaves of flat bread from the baker's stall, pushed them into his pack and then walked briskly to the south gate, passing through with a genial wave to the soldiers on guard. Without waiting for possible companions he hurried past the tombs which lined both sides of the road, then stepped on at a fast pace like a man intent on covering as much ground as possible. The road was busy with little groups of country people heading into town; some were carrying baskets full of eggs or cheese, two or three had lambs held tight across their shoulders, and one farmer, perhaps more prosperous than the rest, was driving an ox-cart with his plump wife and plumper daughter sitting at the back resting their feet on half-a-dozen trussed-up piglets, and each holding a sack from which a goose's head and neck stuck out.

Senorix strode on, pausing only once, by where Verica's palace stood back from the road. He stood there as if deep in thought for perhaps as long as it takes to count slowly to twenty, then shrugged and continued quickly southwards.

After perhaps another three or four miles he slackened his pace and began to whistle to himself. At last he spotted a milestone at the side of the road; he made a show of reading the inscription on it before sitting on it rather theatrically and stretching his arms and legs as he watched the passing crowds. After a few moments he pushed back his hood to enjoy the sun.

Perhaps half an hour had passed when he felt a tap on his shoulder. He looked up and smiled. 'Well met, Iatta,' he said, then went on, 'you look like you've been sleeping in a hedge somewhere.'

'And you smell like you've been sleeping with that tart again. And had a decent breakfast into the bargain.'

'A bit of porridge, that's all. And I brought you these.' He pulled out the loaves and held them up to Iatta. 'Better?'

Iatta squatted down beside him. 'It'd be a bad morning if I couldn't find something to eat for myself. Still, it's the thought that counts, they say.' He pulled the bread apart, then offered a piece to Senorix, who shook his head sadly.

'No, keep it for yourself. It's good bread, but it'd be better if I still had my front teeth. How did it all go up there after I'd left? I see you managed to stay alive anyway.'

'Me and all the rest of the lads, thank Belenos. It was as easy as skipping stones. They never knew what had happened.'

Senorix was thoughtful for a moment. 'Like skipping stones, eh? That takes me back, that does. Any of them make it out?'

'The mounted ones did, and I think a few others, but it was hard to tell in the confusion; that's a wicked tide they have there.'

'And afterwards? Did you do what I told you?'

'We did indeed. Tickled the lads' fancy quite a bit. I wonder what the Romans will make of it when they find it?'

'And Apuleios? Out of the way now?'

'Won't be bothering anyone again. That's right, isn't it?'

Senorix nodded shortly. 'He was a killer before I ever met him. Fate has a way of catching up with people like that. How's that bread, by the way?

Iatta shrugged and bit off a hunk from one of the loaves, then mumbled, 'Pretty good. Perhaps there's something to be said for town life.'

'You shouldn't talk with your mouth full. Gods, didn't your mother teach you anything?'

He gave Iatta a good-natured poke in the ribs. 'Crotos seems to have vanished too. Neither hide nor hair of him around the place. Shame, though; the man's local. He's farmed round here, he'd know the countryside like the back of his hand – man, until I came scouting up here a week or two back I'd not been round these hills for years. But as it turns out, we don't need him. The little girl came up with the goods again; worth every penny, she is.

'You know the way the Roman military mind works: when in doubt, send for reinforcements. Makes sense. Never get into a fight if you don't have superior numbers and weaponry – and a good tactical position as well if you can manage it. Only a fool gets into a battle that he's not pretty certain of winning.'

He paused while a heavy ox-cart laden with amphorae lumbered past heading northwards, then went on conversationally, 'What do you suppose they've got in those pots? Olive oil, fish sauce, wine perhaps? And it'll all find a buyer in the town, my friend. Things there are changing, and no-one even notices. Even mine host at the Eagle's selling some decent wine these days. Borrowed a load of cash to buy it, it seems, then maybe having trouble paying it back.

'Iatta, it's all very well fighting the soldiers, but it's the money-men that frighten me. Once you're in their claws you might as well be strung up on a cross – except that the bankers let you dangle there for longer, the bastards. They say it was because of them that old Boudicca thought she'd take her chance against the Romans after her husband snuffed it – she saw a chance of not paying his loans off, and took it. A bit of a chancer, she was – but the third time shall be greatest, eh?'

Iatta gave a non-committal grin. 'Maybe. But you're a bit of a money-man yourself, if it comes to that.'

Senorix grinned but let the sally pass and stood up. 'And now, if you've finished stuffing yourself I'll tell you about where those reinforcements are coming from, all information courtesy of that lovely little tart herself.'

☙ ☙ ☙ ☙ ☙ ☙ ☙

'Four patrols in all, Marcus – two for each bank of the Ituna Estuary with about thirty men in each, with a good centurion in charge of each one. They're to hunt for survivors, render any necessary assistance – you know the drill. And be sure they know it's not a punitive expedition, and the local people mustn't be treated as hostile without good cause; I want this fire to burn out as soon as possible, and any idiot who goes about fanning the flames will get a damn good flogging with the short whip. When the Ninth Hispana went wild all those years ago, it took us years to undo the damage they caused. So pick lads who can keep their temper on a tight rein.'

Marcus Asellio nodded. 'I'd like to volunteer to lead the first patrol to the north, sir. Those bastards killed good men, and I'd not want to pass a chance to settle accounts with them. Not my kind of soldiering, though, trapping people out on the sands and watching them drown while you jeer at them. Makes me sick to think of it.'

'Sorry, Marcus. I need you here.' Marius shook his head grimly and went on, 'Not their kind of war either, usually; the big set-piece, that's always been their thing, whether it was giving the Divine Julius a hard time with chariots on the Downs, or lining up in neat rows to get butchered at Mons Graupius. And we have better discipline and better weapons, we can beat them at that game every time. It seems that they're getting smart at last. And we can't do what they do; they know every inch of the woods and the rivers, all the places for an ambush or a quick hit-and-run attack, and they can run rings round us the whole time.

'The whole Empire's a kind of confidence trick, I think; we kick off with a quick campaign against some forsaken tribe of savages, with plenty of good battles to give a consul something to put in his memoirs; then we start taming them, give them wine, baths, gladiators and the whole deal, and before you know it they're asking us for protection against their barbarian cousins on the other side of the mountain. And after a while they pay their taxes and think of themselves as Romans and talk what passes for Latin and work out how their sons can get into the Senate.'

'And if we can't tame them?'

'Then we send in the legions, and get ready for the long push, like in Judea. Here, my old friend, a long push is just what it might turn out to be; but our first job is to keep our own people safe.

'Remember what happened when that bitch Boudicca marched into Londinium? Old men, women and children flayed alive just for blood-lust, the whole town burnt to ashes around them, and the legions nowhere to be seen. Well, it won't happen here, Marcus; not on my watch or yours. And that, my friend, is why I need you here. I want you to take a dozen of your best men, check our defences – camp and town both. Put yourself into an enemy's shoes, and then work out the best defence. Take your time – a couple of days, let's say – and then let me have your full assessment: supplies, weak points, the lot. And then we'll start some serious planning.'

He gave a grim smile. 'A few days ago I thought I was going to end my career working as a country-town policeman. At least this looks a sight more interesting.'

XXXIII

Prid. Id. Ivn – June 12th

'What a fuss the Romans make about their laws.'

Verica nodded. 'Indeed, Gwydion; and the Senate keeps making new ones to keep their lawyers in business. But what do you have there?'

Gwydion laid the scroll carefully on the ground. 'Some sort of commentary that your son brought back from Rome with him when he returned; I thought it would be interesting to understand more of it; but, my lady, it goes on for ever, with so many divisions and sub-divisions. How can anyone ever remember all of it? Public law and private law, written law and unwritten law, common law and singular law; there seems no end to it.'

Verica laughed. 'I've heard it said that in the olden days, any Roman man could be a judge if the two parties could agree on his name; things have become much more difficult since, and now it's all work for the professionals. *Corruptissima re publica plurimae leges* – the more laws a country has, the more corrupt it is. But are we so very different? We have the laws of the court, and the laws of the country, and the laws of men and the laws of women. And I remember it was said, Gwydion, that even our law would take a man ten years to learn.'

Before Gwydion could answer, Verica turned away to face her major-domo, who was bustling in from the gate. He bowed briefly, then went on, 'A petitioner, my lady; I told him he should come back on the proper day, but he seems quite set on seeing you.' He raised an eyebrow and went on, 'He says it's important.'

'Every man's business is important to him; and every woman's too. Well, send him in; it may be more interesting than our discussion about Roman law. No, wait, get my proper magistrate's chair and put it under the oak-tree, then wait until I'm sitting there in state and let him come in. One has to make something of a show, after all.'

As the major-domo hurried off, Gwydion remarked with an ironic smile, 'My lady, this much of Roman law has come even here. I mean that chair of yours.'

'As always, Gwydion, I will use what seems good to me, and leave everything else untouched. The chair seems little enough to take from them after all.'

Gwydion watched with a quizzical smile on his face while the chair was fetched and Iras fussed around Verica as she sat down, carefully draping her robe around her, then scurrying off to fetch the supplicant.

Verica watched him approach, and waited for him to bow, before she spoke up. 'We have a time set aside for such matters, my friend; it would be better if you were to come on the allotted day and take your place with others, rather than to disturb us when we have other business.'

'My lady, I ask your pardon; I have come before at the right time and spoken with you; but I have urgent news that I think you will not hear from anyone else. Do you remember me, my lady? My name is Crotos.'

Verica glanced up at Gwydion, who bent and whispered in her ear, 'He came here about a land matter, my lady. Down in the south. He said that the Romans had dispossessed him of his father's land and built a camp there; they call the place Bravoniacum now, I believe. I think he has been here twice before, once at the last session but one of your court and once some time before.'

Verica nodded. 'Now I remember; and, Crotos, I remember my judgement in the matter, which was that the land in question is beyond the borders of my realm, and so I can do nothing. If this is what brings you back, then I can only give you the same judgement again.'

'No, my lady; though there might be a connection. My lady, I have a friend named Apuleios; he was a guide across the Ituna Estuary back before the Romans built their road, and it was a good living for him. But now everyone uses the road, and his living has gone, like mine.

'My lady, a few days ago we both met a man who told us that he could find a way to get *galanas* for us from the Romans; and I and Apuleios both agreed with him. But four or five nights ago the Roman soldiers came looking for Apuleios, and took him away, and no-one has seen him since. And now I'm afraid that they will come for me as well.'

'Why would they come for you? Have you any guilt on your conscience? It may be that they had some good purpose in looking for your friend – perhaps they even meant to use him as a guide, as they used to do in the days before the road was built. That would be cause for joy, surely, not fear?'

Crotos swallowed nervously. 'Then why hasn't he come back, my lady? Even when he was busy he never stayed away for more than one night. He used to guide people over and bring others back the next day as the tide suited, but he'd never stay away longer. He was always hanging around the forum or the tavern. No-one knows what's happened to him.'

'So you think that the Romans have heard that someone offered to find *galanas* for him and have done away with him? And now you think they might do the same to you?'

Crotos nodded. 'What else could it be? This man who came, I think that he was only trying to stir up trouble, and then to sell us to the Romans.'

Verica paused for a moment as a thought struck her. 'This man that you met; did he tell you his name?'

'Yes, my lady; it was Senorix.'

For most of the way the patrol clung close to the shoreline, only moving inland to avoid marshy ground or to find a fording point for the many rivers that ran down into the firth. They moved in close order, wary of an attack from the forest that came down within a bow-shot of the water; but all was peaceful and calm, the silence disturbed only by the occasional call of a bird and the perpetual rippling of the water.

After perhaps a dozen miles Eburnus called a halt, shielded his eyes and looked out over the firth to the south. The tide was well out now, leaving a vast expanse of gleaming sand; and from where he stood he could clearly see the three channels which the rivers had carved out. In the distance the ground rose only slightly above the level of the water; but there was no sign of human presence to be seen there except where an infrequent column of smoke rose up straight from some cottage or farmhouse.

His *optio* stepped up beside him. 'Much further, sir?'

Eburnus shook his head in puzzlement. 'It's hard to tell; there was a thick haze over everything, when we were in the middle we couldn't see either shore; and one bit of beach looks much like another.'

He gestured at the receding waters. 'The tide's so strange here; it goes out so slowly, but it came in like a slingshot. It doesn't make sense. Anyway, I suppose I'll know the place when we get there. Let's keep moving – and keep your eyes and ears open. Any sign of an attack and we form a square at once, don't wait for my order. Right, let's go.'

Cautiously the patrol continued their way along the strip of coarse grass between the trees and the beach, pausing at every little headland to scout the way ahead; but still everything was quiet and peaceful. They know we're here, Eburnus thought, they're just letting us put our heads into the lion's mouth. He muttered a prayer to Mithras and clutched his sword a little tighter as they rounded yet another little promontory.

But no attack came; only a sudden call from one of the men. 'Sir, there's something in the woods. Just a couple of spear-lengths in.'

Eburnus stopped and looked where the man was pointing. At first he saw nothing; then a slight movement caught his eye. In the darkness of the forest it was hard to make out what it was, but at last he was certain. 'It's our *vexillium*. It looks like it's just been left there; but I saw it carried away in the tide. It must have drifted to shore.'

'Shall I get it, sir?' The *optio* was almost pleading for permission.

Eburnus shook his head. 'It's a trap. Why else would anyone set it up there? They know what the flag means to a Roman soldier, and this is just the cheese in the mousetrap. None of us is Germanicus, setting off to recover the legions' lost Eagles.'

He turned to scan the foreshore and his eyes caught a glint of metal on the edge of the water. He gestured to one of the squad. 'You – what's your name?'

'Arminius, sir.'

'Right, lad, see that thing shining down there? Go down and get it; we'll watch your back.'

Without a word Arminius scrambled down the grassy bank. He bent low, then called back, 'It's half buried, sir. It'll take a moment.' He knelt down and scrabbled at the ground; as he watched the young man, Eburnus had a sudden mental picture of himself as a child playing on the wide sandy beach at Ostia, his nurse standing at his side fretting that he was getting his tunic dirty.

'Got it, sir.' Arminius pulled himself back up the bank and handed his find to Eburnus, who took it gently in his hand and brushed the damp sand from it. As he did so the image of a stylized face emerged; he gave it a final blow to remove the last grains of sand, then polished it on his sleeve before taking a careful look at it. It had once been round, but part of it had been roughly cut off, as if by a blade, leaving behind a jagged edge.

'It's part of a *phalera* – a bravery medal. Why would anyone wear that when they were on a mission?' He shook his head in surprise, then handed it back to Arminius.

'Right, pass it round. Anyone recognise it?' There was a general shaking of heads as the medal was taken from hand to hand. 'Someone who didn't want to leave it behind, I suppose; he must have had it in his purse; he certainly shouldn't have been wearing it. We'll take it back with us and see if the Commander knows who it belonged to.'

He slipped the piece carefully into his own purse, then took a careful look around; the ground at the top of the bank was scuffed and torn, and in many places the turf had been wrenched loose.

'This is the spot, all right. And nothing to mark it except for our vexillium propped up in the woods and a broken medal on the beach.' He shook his head in exasperation. Are they watching us, he wondered; will there be a sudden attack out of the forest? But the woods were still silent and motionless. Suddenly he made up his mind.

'I need three volunteers. One to get that banner back, two to cover him.'

A dozen men stepped forward, and he quickly picked three. 'Keep it as quiet as you can; we'll give covering fire with our spears if anything happens – if anything goes wrong, just keep low and get back as quick as you can, with the banner or without; and be careful where you tread – there might be caltrops or poisoned spikes, that sort of thing.'

He took a last long look at the dark woodland, then nodded. 'Mars Victor be with you. Go.'

As he watched the men tread carefully through the undergrowth Eburnus was suddenly aware that he was holding his breath. He forced himself to breath normally, then glanced around the rest of his troop and realised that they were similarly spell-bound. Stupid, he thought, guard your flanks. This will be when they attack out of nowhere.

But still nothing happened; the little group of volunteers had reached the lost banner now, moving with extreme care, listening for any sound that might betoken an ambush; but the silence was still unbroken. Eburnus watched as the leader leant forward and plucked the banner from the bramble bush into which it had been thrust, then saw one of the others bend down to pick up something from the brush. Then with a sudden oath the leader dropped the banner, and as he did so Eburnus saw something else hanging from its pole.

In a moment the man had mastered himself and caught the flag before it had fallen to the ground. He and his companions stood for a moment as if thunderstruck, then one of them pointed at something that Eburnus could not see. After a moment's hesitation the group hurried back with their trophy, and now Eburnus could see clearly what new thing was hanging from the pole alongside the banner. It was a man's severed head, and the distorted features were not those of any of the soldiers who had crossed the firth with him, but rather those of the guide who had led them to their doom.

XXXIV

Prid. Id. Ivn – June 13th

'There were half a dozen heads altogether; the party carried them back all wrapped up in their cloaks. The heads of my men, or some of them anyway, and of the guide I'd hired for them as well – his head had been tied to the *vexillium*. And there were pieces of broken swords and helmets and Nataero knows what else littering the ground right across the clearing. What do you make of that, my lady?'

'No, Commander, tell me first what you make of it.' So Apuleios got his promised *galanas*, and paid for it with his life.

Marius nodded, his face hard. 'As you wish, my lady. I know enough about Celtic customs to understand what's happened here. They were dedicated to some bloodthirsty native god in a shrine in a woodland clearing – men, broken weapons and *vexillium*, all there together. What else could it be?'

'Let me be sure I understand, Commander. One of your fortlets along the northern shore of the Ituna Estuary was attacked in some sort of hit-and-run raid, and you responded by sending reinforcements across the firth with a guide to help them. And when they were near the northern shore, they were overwhelmed by both the tide and some brigands who were lying in wait for them, was it not so?'

'They were no brigands, my lady. This was a carefully laid trap, planned and executed with some skill; and in any case, brigands would strip the dead and then withdraw to their lair. I can imagine such people trying to ransom the *vexillium*, not leaving it unguarded for my men to stumble across it, and without even an attempt at an ambush.'

'And there I think you have it, Commander; your men stumbled across it. It was deliberately left where they could hardly fail to find it. No shrine would be so easily found; nor would it be unguarded. And I am as much at a loss as you are; perhaps they will attack again; perhaps not.'

Marius shook his head. 'They would not succeed in another such attack, my lady. I've already sent for reinforcements, and I understand there will be a company of Syrian archers among them; these things take time, but I hope they are not too long delayed. And in the meantime we are working to strengthen the ramparts of both town and fort. We may not be many but we are stronger and better disciplined than any force that these thieves and cut-throats can put together. You can sleep soundly; Rome will see to that.'

Verica raised a cold eyebrow. 'Thank you, Commander; if I should ever need protection from my own people I shall make sure you are informed in good time.'

Marius clenched his right fist in exasperation. 'Madam, your own people, as you see fit to call them, have just murdered a century of my soldiers as well as one of the townsfolk who are under my protection. If this meets with your approval you had best say so now and I shall know what action to take.'

'So it's Madam now, is it Commander? And you dare to suggest that I approve of this outrage. I would remind you that I am Queen here by marriage and by treaty, Commander, and you would do well to remember that before you issue charges and threats that should see you summoned to account for yourself before the Senate.'

Before Marius could answer, Gwydion gave a polite cough. 'Sir, my lady, may a mere poet and singer say a word? Remember the song of Efnisien in his anger, how he offended the people of Hibernia and kindled an enmity that lasted for many years. And that hatred had its beginning at a feast for friends.'

He waited a moment, and hearing no objection went on, 'Commander, your men were killed in a skirmish on the very borders of Caledonia. These things happen in such debatable lands. Give the dead due honour, Commander, but rest assured that the living need have no fear of such a thing happening again. We here shall mourn the dead with you and your men, Commander; but you need not fear that another war is about to break out.'

Marius looked irresolutely from Queen to bard and back again. 'My lady, I apologise for my blunt words; I spoke in haste and in passion, as your good friend here has seen. I shall hope that he is right, and that there will be no more killing. How foolish it would be of anyone to think they could safely pull the she-wolf's tail.'

He paused, then went on thoughtfully, 'Perhaps you can cast a little light on something. The fellow who led our troops to their death and then paid for his treachery with his own life – I hear that he shouted something to the effect that 'The third shall be greatest', and one of those crucified thieves shouted the same thing. My lady, do those words mean anything of importance? It seems strange that both should shout the same thing.'

Verica shrugged, puzzlement written on her face. 'Our bards often talk of things in threes, Commander – Three things it is hard to restrain: the flow of a torrent, the flight of an arrow, and the tongue of a fool. I think it helps them to remember their verses. And many of our gods and goddesses also are three-fold, like the *matronae* that I know you have seen, though I will not talk further of their mysteries here. But perhaps Gwydion knows more?'

But Gwydion only shrugged in his turn, and Verica shook her head. 'If more comes to our ears, Commander, I shall be sure to let you know.'

When Marius' departing footsteps had faded, Verica turned to her maid. 'Lie down, Iras, under my feet. You must be my footstool. Now, Gwydion, you see I am quite unofficial. You remember, I am sure, who last spoke those words he quoted, here in my own garden. My dear Uncle Senny, no less.'

Gwydion sighed. 'Indeed, my lady, it seems he may well be

behind it all, and who knows what other mischief he still has up his sleeve. And Crotos mentioned his name as well. It was a black day when he visited you.'

'Then why did you tell Marius that there would be no more killing? And remember what Niamh promised too – the gods themselves are preparing for war. And yet you stood there and dissembled, and told Marius what he wanted to hear. As perhaps you tell me what you think I want to hear as well.'

Gwydion raised a hand in protest, but Verica would not be silenced. 'He has come here, when he no doubt has more important work to do, to assure us that we shall be safe; he has lost soldiers, comrades, murdered by the plotting of a man whom I loved when I was a child, and you think to lie to him, to lead him on? In my dream he led me safely out of Hades.'

'My lady, I do not understand you. When your son died in Rome you were calling out for Roman blood. And now when that blood has been spilt and Toutatis has given you the vengeance you prayed for, and there is the promise of more blood to come, you are suddenly full of regret. And you too dissembled and did not tell him the truth. I will not bear the blame alone, my lady.'

Verica stood up wildly, pushing the maid away with her foot. 'I am in two worlds, Gwydion, and I want them both. Do you not see that? Do you not see that I love the gods and the language and customs of my people? And do you not see that I love all that Rome has given me – given us all: its poetry, its art, its strength, its confidence, its grandeur. Why must you, or Senorix, or anyone, make me choose?

'And I can solve the riddle he set the Romans, even if Commander Marius cannot: it was a challenge, and a warning that he will strike again when they least expect it. I will not permit this. Go. Wherever he is hiding, find Senorix for me and bring him here. And you, girl, get out. Oh, leave me be.'

Gwydion bowed, his brow black with foreboding, and slipped quickly through the doorway; behind him Iras scuttled, still half-crouching, her face besmirched with tears. When she was sure her mistress could not see her, she tugged at Gwydion's gown.

'Will my lady be all right? What does she want? Should I stay here?'

Gwydion nodded. 'Yes, stay until she calls for you. What does she want? I think perhaps she wants the man who has just left; and I think she will never have him. Not in this world.'

𑇐 𑇐 𑇐 𑇐 𑇐 𑇐 𑇐

'You didn't make it up this far then? In too much of a hurry to get back to that tart of yours?'

Senorix shrugged. 'Didn't have time to get to all the places I'd have liked, did I? So tell me about it. The camp must be somewhere up there then? And this will be the way those reinforcements will come?'

Iatta nodded, then squatted down to wait while Senorix mopped his brow before taking a long and critical look around, muttering under his breath as he did so.

'To think I used to know all this land – gods, it must be forty years since I was here. Not changed much, I suppose; more ploughing than there used to be, but still plenty of woodland around. And the road, of course – that's new since my day. And a decent ford. I'll say this for the Romans, they don't stint on their engineering. The valley's not that deep – say seven cubits at a guess – but they had to swing the road round to find the best fording point, I suppose. Not much tree cover – I suppose they cut it back when they built the road. What do you think?'

Without waiting for an answer he stepped into the ford, feeling the bottom carefully with his staff as he went. 'Not as much flow as I'd have expected. River's about a cubit or a cubit and a half deep at the most, I'd say, though I suppose it gets higher after rain.'

He stepped back out of the ford, took off his boots and shook the water out of them, then stood out of the way while a laden ox-cart lumbered slowly past, the beasts straining and slipping on the wet slabs as they tackled the steep rise away from the river.

Senorix grinned 'And a nasty climb each side of the ford. Not a good place to get caught in a flash flood.'

Iatta gave a slow smile. 'I can see what you're thinking. Leave it to me; if you go back and get a hundred or so lads to drop what they're doing and give me a hand, we should be all set before too long.'

'I will. But not the ones who had so much fun on the Ituna – best give some of the others a turn. The more of them we can get blooded, the better. And a taste of victory does wonders for your digestion.

'Now, how long will you need? That Julius fellow they go on about only took three weeks to build his siege-walls round Alesia, and they were miles long.'

'He had more men than we do, and better disciplined too. Some of ours would cut each other's throats as soon as a Roman's. How long have we got?'

'A week at the outside, I'd say. I'll get your men here by the day after tomorrow if the gods are favourable, with enough rations to last.'

Iatta whistled then grinned. 'In the hands of the gods then.'

☙ ☙ ☙ ☙ ☙ ☙ ☙

The little hunting party had set out at first light, but up here in the hills the game had been scarce. The dogs – fine native Agassians, bred equally for hunting or for war and capable, so it was said, of breaking a bull's back – had picked up only a few scents. Now Tetricus and his friends were trudging back to camp, the hounds with their tails disconsolately between their legs, the men joshing one another about last night's dice game and the slave-girl that one of them had won for the evening.

Even with the recent dry weather the little meadow was still boggy and loud with the buzz of insects, and the men were treading carefully to avoid the wettest parts, their eyes fixed on the ground. Suddenly one of the dogs gave a low warning growl, then a louder whine.

'What is it, boy? What can you see?' The youngest of the men bent over and laid a hand on the animal's back and felt it vibrating with tension. There was another low growl, then a snuffle of excitement. The man looked around, then finally spotted a fine hare sitting unconcernedly on a dry tussock perhaps a bow-shot away, scratching the back of her head with a powerful hind leg.

The man winked at his companions, then gave the dog an encouraging pat. 'Go on, boy, kill.' In an instant the dog was away, splashing happily through the puddles, with the others right at his heels.

For a moment the hare seemed unconcerned; then at the last instant she flashed away, zig-zagging across the meadow, timing each turn to perfection, always keeping much the same distance between herself and the pursuers. The men watched, laughing with pleasure as much at the hare's run as at the dogs' frustration.

Gradually the hare worked her way higher across the meadow, to where a little clump of trees stood: an oak, an ash and an alder, all growing in a grove with their branches woven together. Here she paused, standing stock-still on her hind-legs; then, suddenly, she was gone.

Defeated, the dogs ran backwards and forwards, desperately trying to pick up the scent. Still laughing, their masters squelched their way to join them, then started to tread down the undergrowth looking for the hare's hidden form; but indeed the creature seemed to have vanished utterly from the face of the earth.

At last one of the hunters muttered, 'There was this story I heard…'

Tetricus turned and looked at him, his eyebrows raised. 'Go on.'

'It's about this hunter who wounded a hare on the leg and chased it into a bush like this one; to begin with he couldn't find where it had gone, but then he found a door into the hillside, and when he opened it there was a great hallway inside, with a girl sitting there, and a hurt on her leg.'

The others glanced at one another and smiled. 'And you believe that, do you?'

The man shook his head, but went on obstinately, 'But everyone knows hares are magic; they say that witches can turn themselves into hares and run round and find things out, and watch people.'

'Witches? No witches round here, boy. Just a clever hare that managed to fool us all.'

'Then what's that?'

Tied to the oak tree with a wisp of scarlet thread was a lock of human hair, swinging gently in the breeze. The men looked at it for a long moment, then all three stepped back, unwilling to touch it.

'That's witch magic for sure. I've heard they can put their souls into things like that so that they never die. Perhaps there's already a curse on us – perhaps that's why we couldn't catch anything.'

There was a long moment's silence; then Tetricus shook his head. 'Roman gods can beat any British witch – and Roman steel can kill one. We'll go back to camp and tell them what we've seen; then perhaps we'll get a chance to hunt witches instead of hares and boar. Hunt and kill. Come on, lads, let's get back.'

XXXV

'Egyptian my arse. Comes from Arbeia – I've seen her and her lad around before. Fond of jugglers, are you?'

The friendly voice in his ear made Bran spin round, but before he could move away a heavy hand on his shoulder was already steering him gently but firmly out of the crowd. 'Glaucus. Haven't seen you around.'

The grip on Bran's shoulder was vice-like now, but Glaucus was still smiling happily. 'You know how it is for us folks in business. We have to come and go. Man's work, that is, always looking for a new way to turn an honest copper or two. So round the Empire I trudge, always on the lookout for a good investment opportunity.'

He stopped and turned round, pointing with his chin at the juggler tossing coloured glass balls in the middle of the forum. 'Now, look at her. Good figure, knows how to get a crowd watching, dab hand with the kohl, and calls herself Egyptian – always in fashion, that, thanks to Auntie Cleopatra. Not doing badly out of it, I should think. Oops, nearly dropped one then. And just look at her lad with his collecting box. Knows what he's doing, big smile on his face, good line in repartee I should think. Makes you just want to give him money, doesn't he. But she'll still be sleeping in some barn tonight, and one day soon she'll start to go to seed, put on a bit of weight. Or perhaps she'll get pregnant, or lose her eye and start dropping the balls. Wouldn't take much to put her out of business, and then – well, it's turning tricks in the whorehouse for her, or shacking up with an old sugar-daddy with more cock than sense. Not a sensible business opportunity, really. Not one for me to invest in, anyway.'

'You, now, my old friend, you didn't seem like that. When I looked at you first I saw someone who knows how many beans make five, someone who understands how to make money work for him. Nice little business, room for expansion in a growing town, I thought to myself. Just goes to show how wrong I can be. Because when I send my associates round for my share, I kind of expect they'll come back with the money.'

Bran wriggled desperately in Glaucus' iron grip. 'I'll pay you, I swear. All I need's a little time. Another couple of weeks and I can get everything all clear.'

Glaucus smiled gently. 'Of course, my friend. And time you shall have. But just in case you forget about your debts, I'm going to ask my colleague Amicus here to help you remember.' With his free arm he waved the enforcer over from where he was standing on the steps of the temple of Mars Victor.

'You've met Amicus, haven't you? A fine fellow, but a little too keen on chewing garlic for my taste. Good at his work, though, and that's what counts. Now, Amicus here let slip that you bought him off last week by letting him have a quick shag with your girl. And thinking of doing the same today, I shouldn't wonder. No profit for me in that, is there. Right, Amicus, break one of his fingers for me, will you? Left hand, middle finger, I think. Neatly, now.'

Amicus nodded slowly and reached for Bran's hand, but Bran snatched it away and clutched in terror at the skirts of Glaucus' tunic. 'No, by all the gods no. I'll pay you, I swear I will.'

Glaucus shook his head imperceptibly and Amicus stood back. 'My friend, trust is the foundation of all business. I trust that when I lend you money, you'll pay it back. And if you don't, you can trust me to ask Amicus here to break your neck next time. It's just like breaking a finger, really; no fuss, no bother, just a quick snap and the job's done, and before you know it you're down below telling Minos what a fool you've been.

'Still, I'm willing to give you one more chance, just to be

friendly-like. Let's see, you've been paying fifteen denarii a week, haven't you? Well, not paying it more like, that's the problem. So, let's call it twenty from now on, shall we? Or I can ask Amicus here to do his thing? Up to you, my friend.'

Glaucus took his hand off Bran's shoulder, gave him a companionable slap on the back, and walked away whistling quietly to himself. Amicus trailed after him, then turned back with a grin and made a snapping motion with his hands before disappearing with his master into the crowd.

🐚 🐚 🐚 🐚 🐚 🐚 🐚

'Child, tell me what you know of the gods? Do you remember all I told you?'

Cybele knelt down, her head bowed. 'I think so, Mistress. But it's hard to learn. And I feel so sick.'

Niamh shrugged. 'There are worse pains to come. Your belly shows already. Tell me what you know of Epona.'

Cybele frowned in concentration, then spoke in a sing-song voice. 'Epona is the ruler of horses, Mistress, and all horses are sacred to her. Some say that she guides the dead to the place where they await rebirth, and some that she makes the harvests fruitful.'

'And what else?'

But Cybele clutched at her stomach and began to retch. Niamh looked at her dispassionately for a moment then pulled her upright by her hair.

'This is no time for your self-indulgence, child. Why is Epona worthy of worship? What is her fitting sacrifice?'

Cybele shook her head. 'Mistress, I don't know. Mistress, my belly hurts, I can't think.'

'Learn. She is the goddess who leads men to war. Her sacrifice is the blood of men. She is goddess of chariots and battle; her son is Arion whom the Greeks worship, and she has a daughter whose name is secret to all except those who have been taught the mysteries. I have whispered the name of her daughter to you; see you have not forgotten it.

Cybele wiped her mouth with the back of her hand. 'I remember it, Mistress. It is…'

But before she could say it Niamh slapped her hard across the face. 'Do not speak it aloud under the sky. Now, tell me what you know of Nert.'

Cybele rubbed her cheek to take away the sting, then recited, 'Nert is Mother Earth; her image is carried abroad in a wagon screened from the sight of all men, and then there is peace throughout the land. When she wishes to return to her sacred grove, her image is taken to a secret lake and washed by her slaves, and then the slaves are drowned.'

'Good; you see that even Mother Earth demands the sacrifice of men. Now, tell me of Esus.'

'Esus is the carpenter-god of woods and groves, Mistress; some say he has horns on his head, and some say that he drew the *afanc*, the water-monster, from the deep. He led his people from the Land of Summer. His fitting sacrifice is…'

'…is the blood of men.' Niamh stood up. 'Learn this well, child. Some say that the gods wish for this or that sacrifice; some offer corn or flowers, and some the blood of animals, others burn incense to them. But no god will reject the blood of men, for that is the most pleasing sacrifice of all. And the gods honour those who offer them blood, and see that their names are long remembered on earth.

'And I saw long ago that a time of blood was coming, and now I think it is at hand. Learn the ways of the gods, child, and they will be your friends – your friends for a little while.'

She paused and put her head on one side. 'Did you hear that? It was the cry of a hound. There are men not so far away who hunt with them, for boar and deer and other game; but I think that now they are hunting for us.'

Cybele's eyes grew large. 'Mistress, will they find us and kill us?

Tear us to pieces? Or give me back to my master?' She shook at the thought, then retched again and again.

This time Niamh waited until the spasms had stopped. 'They will not find us, child. We are under the protection of the gods, and this hiding place is secure, for now. But we do not have much time, and you still know too little.

'Let me warn you once more of what you see in the water. Some of what you see has already happened, or is happening as you watch it; some things will happen soon. But sometimes it only shows what you want to see or fear seeing, or perhaps things that will never happen, or not in your lifetime or mine. Use the water, child, but do not trust it. It is a faithful servant, but a dangerous master. And for you, as for me, a time may come when you can see nothing. The gods give, and the gods take away.

'And there are some things I cannot teach you; a true druid, now, could show you divination by slips of yew, with Ogam letters cut into them; but they never told the secret, and now they are all dead. How strange it is that the Romans, who augur and divine the future in so many ways, should hate the druids so much; or hate their knowledge, perhaps.'

The baying of hounds was louder now. Niamh smiled. 'Divination by blood, now – that I can teach you. All we need is a sacrifice, and it comes to me that we shall have one before long.'

XXXVI

AD XI Kal. Ivl. – June 21st

'Surprising what you can learn when you have a good poke round. Seems the place started out as a marching camp in the middle of nowhere, but they've tidied it up a bit since then. There's a big detachment of cavalry and a rather nasty bunch of irregular archers from the gods know where. Plus the brass – there's quite a big nob in charge, I think – and all the usual hangers-on you'd expect where there's money to be made. So, what have you and the lads been doing since I left you?'

'Come and see. It's a bit of a scramble, though. It's easier if you get in the river to start with.'

Senorix grunted in reply, then followed Iatta up the stream. Once away from the cleared area by the ford the trees ran right down to the water, with a dense undergrowth of bramble and this-tles; gorse-bushes gleamed yellow wherever there was enough light for them to grow. The river-bottom was rough and uneven, and the climb steeper than he had expected; in two places the way was blocked by shallow waterfalls which they had to scramble round. At last Iatta turned with a broad smile and pointed ahead. 'There we are. What do you think?'

Senorix looked past him, then shook his head dubiously. Iatta laughed. 'Look again. The trees make it hard to spot, don't they.' Twenty paces ahead of them, the valley was blocked by a tall weir of turves and logs, over which the water was cascading.

'By all the gods, that's neat. Iatta, you could have signed up for an engineer with the Romans. Esus himself couldn't have done a better job. Let's have a closer look.'

Senorix splashed up to the foot of the weir, which stood above his shoulders. Behind it a wide pool of water spread out, and only a double line of half-submerged trees to left and right marked the limits of the river's original course. As Senorix took it in, a king-fisher flashed past him and dipped into the pool, then flew back in a twinkle of silver and blue.

'How long did this take you? There must be a week's work here.'

Iatta shook his head. 'Two days, that's all. While you were poking round the camp we were getting the trees cut and shaped and moved into place. We'd have been quicker if we'd had horses to help move the timber, but some things the gods let you do on your own. Most of the timber's just there to keep the water back; the real weight's taken by the netting in front, and that's securely anchored to trees on both sides; cut the ropes and the weight of water'll be enough to push the dam down. Didn't that murdering bastard Nero have a collapsible boat built so he could get his mother drowned when she sailed in her? Same sort of idea: cut the ropes and down comes the flood. And look at this.'

He led Senorix to the foot of a tall pine, whose roots were in the new pool but whose head rose high above the rest of the canopy. 'From the top there you can see clear down to the ford.' Senorix grunted. 'I'll take your word for it. I gave up climbing trees years ago. Are you sure there's enough water there to do the job?'

'Enough to sweep away anyone on the ford, for sure; but it won't last long. I'd say it's best to let a half-century or so across to the western side, then cut those ropes. I reckon the dam'll be down within twenty or thirty heart-beats; then in the confusion the lads'll come out from cover, rush the ones who're already across, cut a few throats and disappear again before they can get organised. Not as thorough as I'd have liked, but we don't have the men here for anything more decisive. In and out, that's our motto.'

'And where're the lads now? Keeping out of the way, I hope.'

Iatta smiled, then threw back his head and gave three curlew calls.

'Will that be doing you?' he asked with a grin as thirty men emerged from the undergrowth, their faces and hands smeared and blackened with dirt.

Morrig let her gaze roam round the room. There were perhaps a dozen drinkers, the regular late morning crowd, washing the dust of the streets out of their throats. Townsmen, most of them, though there were a couple of heavily-built farm lads sitting quietly at the back. Messalina was slouching around with a jar of wine resting provocatively on her hips, bending forward to give the customers a good look at her breasts as she filled their cups, then pouting playfully when they tickled her or slapped her backside. Good for business, Morrig thought, though she wished the girl didn't seem to enjoy it so much.

Not all locals, she noticed; there was a soldier too, sitting alone in the darkest corner, and tossing back the rotgut as if it were as sweet as water. She watched as Messalina filled his cup, then topped it up again; finally she swept over to him and held out her hand.

'You've had enough credit. If you want to keep drinking then I want to see the colour of your cash.'

For a moment the man looked angry, then shrugged. 'Plenty here. Look.' He tipped out the contents of his arm-purse onto the table. Attracted by the clatter of the coins, Messalina drifted back and put her arms round his shoulder, then made to sit on his lap.

But Morrig's eyes were on the money. 'That's ten coppers you've spent so far. Let's be having it.' She picked out the coins and dropped them into the bag dangling at her waist. 'Right. For two coppers more you can have the girl as well. If she doesn't come up to scratch let me know and I'll see to it that she gets a good walloping. Lazy little slut that she is.'

On cue Messalina pulled the man's head back and kissed him noisily, then pushed her hand between his legs. He stood up unsteadily, then grabbed her by the hair. 'Hear that, girl? You've got to be extra nice to me, or you'll pay for it.'

Still holding her hair he staggered across the room. Halfway across he turned to face the other drinkers, pausing as if considering what to say.

At last he shook Messalina's head roughly from side to side. 'My whore, she is. I paid for her, I did. Look at her. Filthy little tart.' Again he shook Messalina's head while she whimpered in pain. 'Now I'm going to fuck her good.' He paused, then slurred in sudden anger, 'And fuck the lot of you, all you fucking murderous Brits. Killed my mates, you did. Fucking murderers, the lot of you.'

He dragged Messalina the rest of the way to her little alcove, pushed her in and climbed in after her, then tugged the curtain closed. Morrig hushed the angry muttering from her regulars and put her hand theatrically to her ear with a conspiratorial grin.

'Right, let's see how nice you're going to be.' There was the sound of a ringing slap followed by a sharp cry of pain from Messalina, then several moments of silence instead of the reassuring creak of the pallet that she had been expecting. Then there was a sudden cry of, 'Please don't. Don't. I can't breathe.'

Torn between amusing herself and protecting her income, Morrig hesitated; then she thumped on the wall by the alcove and called out, 'Hey, mind you don't damage the goods.' When there was no answer she finally jerked open the curtain; to her horror the man was kneeling on Messalina's shoulders with both hands clutching her throat; the girl's eyes were open but unseeing, and her lips were already blue.

Morrig's fury erupted. 'Get off her. Gods, if you've killed her you'll pay for her.' Without thinking she snatched at the man's arm, pulling him off balance and dragging him on to the floor.

The sound of coughing from the alcove made her turn. Messalina had turned onto her side with her knees drawn up, and was retching violently.

By the time Morrig had turned back to the soldier it seemed

that all the men in the room were standing over him. The first kick caught him in the stomach, the second between the legs. In a moment Morrig had thrown herself across him as he lay. 'Stop it, you bloody fools. He's from the camp. Do you want to end up on a cross?'

There was a sullen silence broken only by a muttered, 'It's that bastard that should be on a cross.'

'Who said that?' Morrig's eyes scanned the crowd, cowing them into submission by pure force of will. At last she stood up and pointed to two of the men. 'You and you. Get him out of here and dunk him in the fountain in the forum till he sobers up. Then you can drop him on the nearest midden for all I care, as long as he's still breathing when you've done. Just get him out of here.'

She watched as the soldier was half carried, half dragged, out of the inn; then, still furious, she turned to Messalina, who was now kneeling but still retching and trying to catch her breath. Morrig looked at her for a long moment, then grabbed her arm and hauled her up.

'There's men here waiting for wine. Get up and serve them, you lazy little bitch.'

But as Messalina struggled to stand, someone began to stamp rhythmically on the floor, a repeated bang, bang, that was soon taken up by the others. Gradually the noise swelled as fists and pots were thumped against tables, until the whole room rang with the din and the walls began to shake. Morrig stood stock still, caught unprepared by the sudden fury, then screamed, 'Out, all of you. Get out,' and listened fearfully as the rough music slowly moved into and along the street, always growing louder as it went.

Morrig bent down, her face inches from Messalina's. 'Now look at what you've done. How am I supposed to make money from an empty room? By all the gods, why do I bother to keep you?'

Messalina said nothing, but for an instant Morrig caught a flash of something that might have been defiance in the girl's eyes.

'So that's how it is. I'll break you, my girl. It's the branding iron for you. You can yell all you like, the smith knows how to deal with cattle like you.'

Senorix lay back on the turf, rested his head against a convenient tree-root and stared up at the canopy above him; a little bright sunlight filtered through as the branches stirred in the breeze. Only birdsong broke the silence – a blackbird a little way downstream, a lark somewhere far overhead, a thrush a distance up the valley, and then, as if from nowhere, the discordant *whoo* of an owl.

An owl's call in broad daylight? Senorix held his breath and listened again, more carefully. There it was again, seemingly close at hand. Moving very gently he pulled himself into a sitting position and began methodically to scan the trees.

Finally he spotted the bird, less than a bow-shot away on the other side of the pool. It fluffed up its feathers, then settled its head firmly down into its shoulders and closed its eyes. Senorix nodded to himself. Take your omens where you find them, lad.

He was dozing happily when he felt someone shaking his shoulder. 'They're moving.'

Senorix opened his eyes with a start and shook his head quickly. 'Already?' He gave the lad who had woken him a grin, then pulled himself to his feet. 'Right. You know your place? By all the gods, listen to that trumpet. They're nearly here.'

He splashed his face with water from the broad pool above the dam, then rubbed it with mud. 'Where's Iatta? Down by the ford? I'll join him and the lads. Belenos be with us all.'

XXXVII

'Just stand there. Oh, stop it.'

But the nanny-goat took no notice, twisting and endeavouring to pull away, then lifting her hind leg and trying to put it in the wooden bowl. Finally she succeeded, spilling the little milk that Cybele had already collected onto the grass.

'It's no good. I can't do it, Mistress. They take no notice of me at all.'

Niamh shook her head. 'You must learn. You must master them. Watch me again.'

She drew Cybele away and knelt down easily by the goat's side; the animal looked at her through its slotted eyes and gave a soft bleat of recognition as Niamh began to pull gently and rhythmically on the teats. She smiled as the milk spurted into the bowl. 'You see, they know me; as they must know you, and know that you master them.'

She went on, suddenly gentle, 'Poor child, you have had little enough chance to learn to master anyone; and goats are not the easiest of all the creatures the gods made to start with.'

She handed the brimming bowl to Cybele. 'Drink. It will help to settle your stomach. And tell me again what you saw in the water four days ago.'

Cybele closed her eyes. 'Mistress, there was a ford, with many soldiers crossing it; some of them were mounted and others on foot; I don't know the numbers to count them. And then there was a flood that swept many of them away; and then there were other men, and they fought for a little while and then drew off; and afterwards the river ran red with blood. And then I couldn't see anything else. And I've been able to see nothing since.'

'And so it seems that the time I foresaw is upon us. Before long the goats will be the least of your cares, child.'

Morrig looked up as Senorix pushed open the door.

'You again. Quite the bad penny, aren't you.'

'Ah, I know I can always count on you for a warm welcome. That man of yours around? And where's that pretty little tart of mine? Not gone missing, I hope.'

Morrig gave him a sour smile. 'Gone missing? Not any more she won't. Gods, the fuss the little bitch made about it, kicking and screaming all the way to the blacksmith, and yelling and sobbing all the way back. Anyone'd think she was being murdered. Tried to get off work afterwards, too, said it hurt too much. Here, you can see for yourself.' She ducked into the little scullery at the back of the room and came back a moment later leading Messalina by the ear.

'Stand up straight, girl, and stop your snivelling. The gentlemen doesn't want to listen to it. Show him your tit.'

Without waiting for Messalina to obey her she pulled down the front of the girl's tunic, revealing a livid wound on her left breast. 'I had her branded. A for Aquila, that's what it is. I told her it'll heal up nicely if she doesn't keep rubbing it. Stupid slut. Go and keep the gentleman company, girl – and don't let me hear any complaints from him.'

Senorix shook his head and sat down on one of the benches, leaning back on the table and stretching his legs out in front of him. 'Later will do. I'll have a beaker of beer first, if you don't mind. And something to eat as well – is himself working round the corner? One of those sausages of his would just do the trick.'

'You heard him, girl. Go and get him the beer.' She watched Messalina scurry into the scullery, then plumped herself down on the bench opposite Senorix.

'Everything all right, lass?'

Morrig hesitated for a moment, then, to Senorix' utter astonishment, her upper lip started to quiver and he thought for a moment she was going to cry. 'He's a fool, he'll lose us everything. He's been buying wine – not the regular stuff, that's not good enough for him. He'd got some amphorae full of it, Falernian and Alban and I don't know what. All hidden out the back. None of our customers can afford that kind of stuff. Where did he get the money?

'And the *caupona's* closed up tight, all the shutters up and the customers can go to hell. My fool of a husband walks out at first light and then I don't see him until just before they shut the gates for the night. I think it's all because of the big man that's been coming round – Amicus he calls himself. Not my idea of a friend. That's who he borrowed the money off if I'm any judge.'

Senorix spread his hands. 'Are you sure? Doesn't sound like the sort of thing a smart lad like him would do.'

'Shows how much you know him. And that's not the worst of it.' She wiped her eyes on her sleeve and leant forward confidentially. 'First there were those soldiers got drowned in the river, then we had the riot, and then they say more soldiers got killed somewhere off to the south. What's to become of us, that's what I want to know.'

'The drownings, now, I heard something about that. Tried to cross the firth without knowing the fords, wasn't that the way of it? Me, I take the road every time – safer that way. But what's that about a riot? And more soldiers killed, you say? Are you sure?'

Morrig looked at him carefully, then turned her face away. 'It was that stupid slut's fault. I told her to be nice to that soldier who wanted her, but she only went and got herself half-throttled instead. I kicked the man out, of course, you've got to look after your property, haven't you. And before I knew it half the town was banging their pots and pans and yelling blue murder and marching on the camp. Some idiots tried to push past the gate guards, and then one of them got himself knifed – they say it was the soldiers that did it, but no-one really knows. Anyway, they took him into the camp and no-one's seen him since – and then the rest of the bloody fools went crazy and started to smash up the stalls in the forum instead.

'I'd taken Messalina there, just gone to get her branded to teach her a lesson; Jupiter, the way that slut was shrieking and carrying on. The smith's just done with her when the crowd's all round us, yelling and screaming and waving sticks and hoes and sickles and anything they could get their hands on.

'We were lucky to get back here and get the door barred and the shutters up or they'd have wrecked this place as well. And then they went down the alley at the side and started smashing the empty pots and stuff there.'

Senorix shrugged. 'That's the mob for you. A hundred pairs of feet and hands and no head at all. But at least you all came out of it in one piece.'

Once again Morrig looked at him, perhaps wondering how much else to say. After a long moment she went on in a low voice, 'The pots weren't all empty. The wine that that idiot husband of mine's been buying was there, hidden under the empty jars. I'd only found out about it by accident; and now that's all nearly gone, most of the jars smashed to smithereens, the wine running down the street like a river. And now people can't face us; they turn the other way when they see us in the street, they don't come in. And look at the place, bare as a beggar's poke. Only a few soldiers come now – no-one else comes here at all, and there's hardly any money coming in. And he just disappears and leaves all the problems to me and the slut.

'What's going to happen to us? That Amicus, he's going to want paying one way or another.'

She slumped down in despair. 'I know how the law works. He'll lay his hands on my fool of a husband and then it'll be the slave market for him and me – that's what he'll do. Me, at my age, standing on the block in the market for people to poke at and sneer.'

Senorix waited while she pulled herself together. 'While there's life there's hope, lass. But what was that about some other soldiers being killed? We don't seem to get much of your news up there in Caledonia?'

'Killed at a ford away south somewhere. There was a flood, they say, and then some brigands attacked them and killed them; I don't know any more than that.'

The scullery door creaked open and she quickly stood up and turned away rubbing her eyes as Messalina came in with a mug of beer. 'What took you so long? Listening at the door, were you? I'll teach you to hang about.'

Messalina grimaced but said nothing, then squealed as Senorix pinched her backside. He winked at her and turned to Morrig. 'I'll be here for three days or so, I can pay for the girl and the straw now if you'd like. And the beer as well. It'd be cash in hand for you.'

A glint of what might have been hope or avarice shone on Morrig's eye. 'Three days? And the slut just for you? That's a lot of money. Ten sesterces. And I'm robbing myself blind.'

'Ten. That's a week and a half's wages for a working man. All that for a tumble in the hay. Six.'

'Gods, listen to you. And you made of money like you are. Eight. In my hand now.'

With a wry grin Senorix took the cash from his arm purse, counting it out carefully into Morrig's hand. 'There you are. And see you don't lose it.'

Morrig turned the coins over carefully and dropped them into the bag at her girdle, then paused and turned to Messalina. 'Looks like I'm going to have to manage without you. Some of us have it easy, just lying on our backs. Go and clean your face first and then put a smile on it, or you'll get what for from me.'

As Messalina slouched off, Morrig turned back to Senorix. 'I told you how things are. I need cash and I need it quick. Why don't you buy her? Cheaper than renting in the long term. You said you were interested once.'

Senorix wiped his mouth with an amused grin. 'Buy her? I offered to once, didn't I? But a man's entitled to his second thoughts, you know. Och, she's a good enough lass, but what would I want a chit of a girl like that chasing around with me for? There's plenty like her – oh, most of them don't have such good tricks in bed, and I have to say she's a fast learner in that department – but no, it sounds too much like settling down to me. Perhaps you can talk some other fellow into digging into his savings for her. And here she comes, all ready to comfort a weary traveller. Into the shed with you, girl, and let's give you a good seeing-to.'

XXXVIII

'Everyone here?' Marius glanced at the centurions standing around the table. Six men in all, each with a nominal eighty men under his command, ranging from the battle-hardened Marcus Asellio to young Eburnus, still coming to grips with the burdens of command. He let his eyes rest on each one in turn, then began with a formal, 'Gentlemen, we meet in the name of the Senate and the People of Rome and of the Emperor. I'll keep this meeting as short as I can, you all have your own responsibilities to worry about.

'You all know something of the situation, but there's new intelligence arriving regularly. The purpose of this meeting is first to inform you of the latest developments, to answer any questions you may have, and to outline our response.'

He nodded at Marcus Asellio. 'Marcus, a quick situation summary from you, please.'

The *primus pilus* nodded and laid a pair of writing tablets on the table. 'Sir, this came an hour ago. It's the latest report from the Bravoniacum garrison, and I'm afraid it doesn't make for pretty reading. They state that they lost thirty men, drowned or otherwise killed in the attack, and another half dozen wounded; most of them should pull through. Most of the damage was done by the torrent that came down on the ford while they were crossing it.

'As you all know, the cover story is that they were attacked by brigands and successfully fought them off, but the facts of the matter don't really bear that out. I'm sorry to say that after the attack they withdrew to their camp and that's pretty-well where they seem to have stayed. Gentlemen, for the moment it looks as if we can whistle for our reinforcements, but more about that in a moment.

'If they really were brigands then they were astonishingly well prepared and disciplined; they'd built some sort of turf dam higher up the river and then collapsed it just as the first ranks had passed the ford; the result was chaos, with men, mules, wagons and equipment strewn all over the place; that's when they attacked, a quick hit-and-run affair, in and out like Jove's lightening. It seems they just wanted to cut a few throats and leave the bodies in the water; then they faded away into the woods, neatly letting the Bravoniacum commander claim that his men had beaten them off.' He glanced round the room, noting the grim smiles that this elicited.

Marius nodded. 'One little blooding and they've gone to ground. That, gentlemen, is the way it is with auxiliaries unless they're given a bit of backbone from proper legionary troops. Any enemy casualties that we know of?'

Marcus shook his head. 'They certainly suffered some injuries – a few cracked skulls, perhaps, some broken bones and no doubt a few sword wounds as well, but probably not enough to hamper them much. I hate to say it, but they had better discipline than our own men. The Bravoniacum commander put their strength at fifty or so, but I'd guess that's an over-estimate; the defeated man counts every enemy twice, they say.'

Marius let his friend's words sink in before continuing, 'And they left our men drowned or cut to pieces right there at the edge of the river. A sacrifice to the old Celtic gods in the traditional style. And the second time it's happened in three weeks. Another ambush, another blood-offering that the druids would have been proud of. And to that we can add the attack on the fort on the Ituna that started the whole thing off; another in-and-out job just intended to tweak us by the nose. Still, I think we can draw certain conclusions.

'First, there probably aren't very many of them; they attack in small numbers, and they haven't dared a full assault on a properly defended position – even on the Ituna fort, the attack looks as if it was just intended to draw the garrison out into the open.

'Second, they have some real military expertise; they're going for our weak points, they're choosing when and where to attack, and have decent discipline. They have some archers and slingers, but no mounted men as far as we know.

'And third, they can just put down their weapons and fade into the general populace. The classic way to start an insurrection. And here we are between Scylla and Charybdis, as the Greeks say; if we're seen to do nothing then they'll be emboldened and keep going; and if we start turning over every farm and cottage looking for them, we'll create so much resentment that soon we'll have a real insurgency on our hands. Damned if we do and damned if we don't. Yes, Eburnus, you have something to say?'

The young centurion flushed briefly. 'Do you think there's any connection with what happened in town here, sir?'

'The riot? I'd guess not, though I'd welcome any other views. That seems to have started with a tavern brawl and then just got out of hand. What about that fellow who was stabbed, by the way? Any news on him?'

Marcus answered. 'A young idiot from the town, sir, all beer and bravado. It seems he was stabbed in the melee outside the gates; he was bleeding like a stuck pig by the time we got to him. He's in the sick bay; the orderlies have fed him with garlic in the usual way, and there's no smell of it round his stomach, so there's probably no serious damage to anything internal. He'll mend, if the gods are kind. When he's fit for it we'll give him a good thrashing and let him go.'

He hesitated for a moment then asked the question that Marius had been half expecting. 'Sir, we're the military power here, and as you say we answer to the Senate and the Emperor. But what about the civil power? Where does the Queen stand with all this?'

I wish I knew the answer to that, thought Marius, spreading his hands, but he answered firmly enough. 'She stands with us; or she falls with us. She knows what happened to Cartimandua; she has no strength of her own, only a handful of guards, so without us she is nothing.' But she hears things, he thought, and knows more than she tells. For all her fine Greek and Latin, she's only half ours and half a barbarian; the druids and their like still run deep in her heart. We have a courtesy guard on her gates; I wonder what they've seen and heard these last few days?

He glanced round the table. 'I sent a full report on the situation to Eboracum as soon as we knew what had happened; Bravoniacum will have done the same, no doubt with their own spin on events. I think we can expect very substantial reinforcements; they'll want to stamp hard on whatever's going on before it gets right out of hand. Indeed, I gather there are already rumours circulating in the camp about that.

'In the meantime we're going to have to manage on our own for a while, so we'll need to run a tight ship. We'll double the patrols in and out of town, and everyone needs to be aware of possible opportunistic attacks. But keep the men under a tight rein; as far as I can tell that tavern brawl only started because of some drunken loud-mouth on our own payroll, and we can't afford any more incidents like that.

'So restraint is the order of the day. If we can just keep things quiet and low-key, then with the help of the gods it may blow over. In the meantime we'll keep our ears to the ground and see if we can turn up any information.'

☙ ☙ ☙ ☙ ☙ ☙ ☙

Senorix lay back on the straw with a smile. 'Now, get your clothes off and let's have a better look at that tit of yours, girl.' He waited while Messalina tugged off her tunic and then cupped her breast in his hand and looked carefully at the brand-mark.

'It'll heal. Looks sore, though. What did she go and do that to you for? Did you try to run away or something?'

Messalina shook her head. 'Just her bad temper. It's been worse than ever the last few days. She takes it out on Master when she can, but he's not around much so she punishes me instead.'

She looked suddenly coy. 'Why don't you buy me? I don't think you'd beat me like she does.'

'That's the second time I've heard that today. What makes you people think I'm in a buying mood, eh? That's the trouble with girls – buying them isn't where the expense ends, it's where it starts.'

Messalina pouted. 'I'm sure you've got enough money. You're rich, aren't you? I like rich men.' She shook her head moodily. 'I think that Amicus must have a lot of money, but he's not much fun to play with, and he stinks of garlic. And Master hates him.' She brightened briefly. 'Master hides in case he comes, now. That's silly, Amicus will find him sooner or later.'

Senorix laid his forefinger on her lips. 'And have you thought that if your master can't find the money that Amicus wants, then the easy way out would be to let him take you instead, and next thing you know, Amicus'd be flogging you off to raise some quick cash. There's worse places you could be than the Eagle, you know, and worse masters than the ones you have now.'

'Don't say that. Just saying it might make it happen. Come on, let's get down to business, I'd like that.'

She bent down to grasp the hem of Senorix' tunic and started to pull it up, then stopped in surprise. 'What's that? What happened to your leg?'

Senorix took hold of her finger and held it firmly. 'It's just a bit of a cut. Things like that happen sometimes. Seems like we've been in the wars the last few days, you and me both.'

He pressed her finger to one end of the wound, then let her trace it upwards. 'See, it's healing nicely. And look at those stitches in it. Real fine needlework, that is.'

Messalina was silent for a moment. 'That's a sword-cut, isn't it? Some of the soldiers who come in have them just like that. Sewn up like that, too.'

'Aye, I'm sure they do. I'm just thankful it wasn't a bit higher and off to one side, or life would be a lot less interesting to me just now, lass.'

'Did someone try to steal your money? Is that what happened? They say there's been brigands around not far from here.'

'Something like that, aye. But they've gone to a watery grave, lass, so don't worry about them. You see I can look after myself. Here, get my tunic off and help me forget it.'

Messalina tugged his garment off, then knelt by Senorix' side. 'I know a secret. I can tell you, if you like?'

'Can't be much of a secret if you tell everyone who beds you.'

'It's a special secret just for you. One of the soldiers told me. Don't you remember, you asked me to remember the things they told me and said you'd give me more money if I did?'

Senorix gave a rueful grin. 'You're right there, lass – a *duponius*, wasn't it? Ha, this is turning out to be an expensive trip. Come on, then, out with it.'

'Money first, secret after.' After a pause she added a coy, 'Please.'

'Secret first, cuddle second, cash third. Or I'll wallop your little backside.'

'You can if you want to – that's extra.' She made a moue, then leant forward and whispered in his ear.

'Is that so? Well, well. Not a surprise, I have to say, but it's something to chew on. Now, on your back, lass.'

'Mind my tit, won't you – it's still ever so sore.' She shivered briefly. 'It was horrible; I never knew anything could hurt so much. And the man did it right there, right in the forum – I was so frightened that I wet myself, and then Mistress was even angrier.'

Senorix moved to cup her wounded breast in his hand, but as he did so the shed-door was flung open.

'The man himself, eh? Somehow I thought we'd find you here. The lady of the house said you might have your hands full, and it looks as if she was right.'

The voice was familiar, but for a moment Senorix couldn't put a name to it. He turned onto his back and shielded his eyes, but it was impossible to make out who was standing against the light in the doorway. Carefully his right hand slid towards his discarded boots, but the newcomer stood to one side and let in another, taller man who simply stepped forward and placed his foot firmly on Senorix' wrist.

'Let him go. He hasn't done anything.'

Senorix gave a rueful smile. 'Not yet I haven't, anyway. Is this a time to be bothering a man, now?'

'As good a time as any. You know, this could be your lucky day. That's a nasty wound you have on your leg there; I wonder how you came by it? And there's another lady who wants to speak to you; very eager to talk to her Uncle Senny, she is. So I think it would be a good idea for you to come to her right away and without making any fuss at all. Not a good time for you to attract attention, is it?'

Light suddenly dawned on Senorix. 'Gwydion. I never thought to meet you in a tavern.'

'Inspiration comes in many places. So let's get you dressed and then we can be off.' He nodded to his companion, who bent forward and picked up Senorix' boots, and then turned them over and shook them out; the thin dagger which had been wrapped in a piece of fine yellow silk and stowed inside one clattered onto the floor.

Gwydion picked it up and examined it carefully. 'Very nice. Silver-chased, too. You can't beat quality, can you? You can have this back later, when the Queen says so. Adeon here will look after it for the moment. Let's go.'

Messalina watched open-mouthed as Senorix stood up and pulled on his tunic, then took his boots back and slipped his feet into them. Only when the group was already at the door did she suddenly call out, 'Hey, you haven't given me that *duponius* yet.'

Senorix turned back with a shrug. 'You'll have to put it on account, lass. I'll make it up to you later. Now get your things back on like a good girl.'

XXXIX

AD V Kal. Ivl. – June 27th

Cybele stood up, walked back to the stream and carefully tipped the contents of the wooden bowl back into it. 'Mistress, I still can't see anything in the bowl. Have the gods taken the gift away from me? Like you said they have from you?'

Niamh looked up from her milking and smiled. 'The gods have purpose in everything they do, and it is not for us to question them. But no, I do not think that you have lost the gift; indeed, I think that they have many gifts that they will give you in their own good time. You must wait for them, that is all.'

Then, with a sudden change of mood, she went on, 'Look, your tunic is stained where you have been ill. You should wash it. Go and do that now. No, not in the stream here. Take it back to the place where you tied the threads in the tree, and strip yourself there and wash it in the brook. The day is warm and no-one will see you. I will stay and milk the goats and then tether them; later you can tend the herbs.'

Cybele hesitated for a moment and Niamh gave a bitter laugh. 'Child, you were the Roman's whore. He did as he wished to you. You carry his whelp. And now you are ashamed to strip naked when I tell you. Obey me, or by all the gods I will mark you for life.'

She watched as the girl fled, then turned quietly back to her milking.

Verica settled herself on the currule chair, glad of the shade from the over-arching oak tree. 'Iras, you stand there, and you, Gwydion, come and sit here by my side; we shall watch together to see what he has to say for himself.' She turned to her major-domo; 'Fetch him now; and remember that he is an honoured guest, and not a prisoner.'

When they were alone Gwydion shook his head. 'Is this truly wise, my lady? To ask me to bring him to you, that was good and proper; but to keep him locked away when indeed we have nothing against him but the word of one man – I wonder what good that will do.'

Verica shrugged. 'We shall know soon enough. And here he is. My dear old Uncle Senny, we have indeed met again in this world.'

Senorix bowed, the usual Celtic bob of the head, then twisted his head to wink at Iras before turning back to Verica.

'My lass, I must thank you for making me so comfortable these last two days. Ah, that bed. Better than straw, any night. And I can't remember when I last ate and drank so well. Though I prefer beer to wine myself, you understand. Still, when in Rome… And I see you still wear that little trinket I brought you.'

Verica's lips twitched in a brief smile and her hand crept up to touch the brooch. 'Of course – I wear it often. But Gwydion tells me that you have been injured. A battle injury of some kind, it seems. Will you not tell me about it? A hero should be honoured for his valour, after all.'

Senorix inclined his head again. '*Infandum, regina, iubes renovare dolorem.* O Queen, you order me to revive a terrible woe.'

A flash of anger lit Verica's eyes before she mastered herself. 'Why does everyone want to quote Vergil at me? No, my dear Senny, it will do you no good to bring him here. How can you compare Aeneas' woes to yours?'

'Our cases agree somewhat, my lass. He had lost all his patrimony to his enemies, and the gods in their pity took him to a land whose Queen entertained him kindly. Is that not true of me also?'

He gave Verica a look that was almost shy. 'And every child knows how Dido's story ends; when Aeneas sailed away to Italy, she killed herself for love.'

Verica hesitated. 'Only a fool dies for love. She died for honour. And so began the long enmity between Rome and Carthage.'

'So they say, though I'd be inclined to look for a more down-to-earth reason. But you kindly asked about my wounds. They are no secret, and have been painful to me for many a long year. See. My front teeth were knocked out by a Roman's sword-hilt, and I've not been able to bite into an apple or a loaf of bread since. Is that what you were so concerned for?'

Verica's anger was plain now. 'Senorix, I had you brought here partly because you seem to me to be a danger to the peace of my land, and partly because when I was a child I loved you dearly, and I would not now see you nailed to a cross. And yet you bandy words with me and think to take me for a fool.'

Then a thought struck her and she smiled. 'I've wondered more than once why you were ever at Mons Graupius; when I was a little girl and thought you were my uncle, we lived happily enough with the Romans. What drove you to fight them?'

Senorix gave a grin in return. 'When you were a little girl. Ah, they were good days, my lass. One time we went to the beach and I showed you how to skip stones over the water. It was a grey day, but the sea was calm enough. I remember everything about it; the lines of weed on the beach, the curlews calling somewhere behind us, and you with your tongue out as you tried to spin the stones. Strange how some days fix themselves in your memory. Good days indeed. We understood each other like thieves at a fair, as they say. I fear that we've grown apart since, my lass.'

For a while Verica was silent; then she shook her head as if to clear her mind of its memories. 'Senny, that was then and this is now, and perhaps today we are different people. I have no time for guessing games. Many brave men have died, on the Ituna and near Bravoniacum, and I make no doubt that you have played a part in both – and no minor part, if I judge you truly.'

She turned to Gwydion. 'Gwydion, what was it you said to me

a few days ago? Something you had read that was written by one of the Hebrew seers, I think?'

Gwydion nodded. 'Indeed, my lady, I remember the line; it was finely written. ὅτι ἀνεμόφθορος σπείρω καί...

'I do not think that our guest here will thank you for your Greek, Gwydion. *Your* Greek especially.' She turned back to Senorix and went on, '*For they have sown the wind and they will reap the whirlwind.*' That is the sense of it. These gadfly stings of yours will bring trouble on your own head, and on many others as well; perhaps on mine. Is that what you want? To see the land ruined by war, women made widows and children orphaned, towns plundered and farms burnt, famine stalking the land?

'This is not new to you, Senorix. We have seen it before, you and I, when the Ninth's auxiliaries went on the rampage back in the Year of the Four Emperors? You remember how they came to defend Cartimandua from Venutius? And how it all ended, with random killings and rapes and pillage?'

Her voice grew harsh. 'Do you remember what happened to that family of cottars in the valley to the south of Eboracum? By all the gods, it makes me sick still to think of it.'

Senorix nodded. 'A farmer and his wife and their three daughters. It seems that some men of the Ninth went there with no cause at all except their own bloodlust, and crucified the man against the wall of his hut and his wife on the wall opposite; and then raped the three little girls on the ground in front of them, on and on and on no doubt until the whole troop had had their fun. We found their bodies, you and I. That was a black day. And they had slaughtered the beasts as well, herded them into the barn and burned it to the ground. They had even crucified their dog.'

Verica's face was white at the recollection. 'That is what war does, Senorix. And we Britons can be as savage ourselves. Think of Boudicca, how she slaughtered old and young together in Londinium, the people of the city and those who had fled there from Camulodunum as well. Men, women and children murdered; the lucky ones had their throats cut, but most were flayed alive, their ruined bodies left in the streets for the dogs to eat. And at last she torched the town to smoke out any who had tried to hide. The fire blazed for three days, and the gods alone know how many died in the burning. That is where I fear you will take us; and that I will not endure.'

Senorix stood quietly, his head bowed, watching Verica's heaving breast. At last he shook his head and went on gently, 'Better be a slave and live quietly, is that your thought, my lass?

'It appeals, that I grant you. Yes, there in the Vale there were so many sights that a child like you should never have seen, but of course we came on it unawares. And in pity for the dead I fired the thatch and burned the place to ashes over them, and gave them a funeral pyre worthy of the name. May their spirits rest in peace.

'Strange how one remembers smells, sometimes, more than sights or sounds; and the foul stench of burned flesh mingled together with the good smell of a wood fire – yes, there are times I still feel it clinging to my cloak. A black day indeed. And now you have answered your own question, about what drove me to Mons Graupius.

'I never saw what had happened in Londinium of course, but by all accounts it was much as you say. Yes, a bad business, that I grant you.

'But see where your fears lead. Should the Romans have yielded to Hannibal for the sake of peace in the land? Then Rome would have been defeated instead of Carthage, the Seven Hills perhaps sown with salt as Carthage was, to be desolate for all time to come. No, the old proverb has it right: *Qui mori dedicit, servire dededicit.*'

Verica said, 'He who has learned how to die has learned how not to be a slave? No proverb, Senorix, but the philosophy of the elder Seneca, who did indeed kill himself at need.'

'Then he was true to his words; few of his kind are. But think

– 288 –

of our own tales; of how Manawdan would always yield, and only Pryderi would fight when their lives and livelihoods were threatened. What good could come of that?'

'You bring a bad witness to your case, Senorix. For at the end it was Manawdan's patience that won the day, and Pryderi's restlessness that almost lost it.'

Senorix shrugged, 'I see that Gwydion has taught you well. Let us agree that war comes at a terrible price; but I tell you that freedom comes at a price too; and if we are not willing to pay that price, then perhaps we are already no longer free. It was you who spoke so high of Dido and her honour earlier; what honour is there in slavery?

'Yes, with my own een I saw what the Ninth's auxiliaries did in Brigantium; and two days ago I heard a whisper that the Ninth will come here, perhaps very soon. My lass, pray that they are better governed now than they were before.'

Verica jumped to her feet, her face white with shock. 'The Ninth? Here? Who told you that?'

'A little tavern-girl I know; I'd have found out more if Gwydion here hadn't interrupted us in the middle of our discussions.'

'Just a rumour, then. A lie, as like as not.' She sat down heavily, breathing deeply as she regained her composure. 'But for all that, I will not leave you free to play your tricks, and bring the whole world down on our own heads. So I must keep you here, where you can make no more trouble. You need not thank me.'

She turned to the major-domo who had waited at a respectful distance. 'Take him back and lock him up securely. He will be my guest until I decide otherwise, and that will not be a brief time.'

Senorix bowed again, deeper this time than he had done before, then with a sardonic smile he said, 'My lady, you do me great honour. It will be a pleasure to stay here as your guest, though truth to tell I'll miss the company of that little tavern-girl I told you about.' He gave Iras another wink and smiled as she blushed, then bowed again to Verica and, head erect, strode out of the garden, the major-domo trailing behind him.

After they had gone, Verica remained in her chair, her head bowed. At last she turned to Gwydion. 'Do you think he told truth, Gwydion? About the Ninth?'

'Who knows? But I am sure that he believes it; indeed, it may be what he wants – squads of angry soldiery roaming about the land would soon rouse the whole people to rebel against Rome and all that she stands for.

'And remember, my lady, what Niamh said; she told us that the gods sat in council, and that war would soon be unleashed whether we wished it or no.'

He sighed and went on, 'And I notice that he confessed to nothing, my lady. Indeed, he is able to turn the conversation any way he wishes. And perhaps it suits his purpose to be safe and comfortable and out of sight here for the time being; and when he is ready to leave and create more havoc, no doubt he will find some way to slip our leash no matter how securely he is locked up. It comes to my mind that rather than delaying war, my lady, we may have brought it closer.'

Hearing a muffled sob he turned to face Iras and saw that a sudden fit of trembling had taken her, and tears were running down her face. 'Does the thought of such a war frighten you, girl? But this is how the world goes; peace follows war, and war follows peace; so also death follows life, and after a time of waiting new life follows death. Of old it was said that those awaiting rebirth are quite as anxious as those who are waiting for death, but with this fear in addition, that they can dimly see into their future lives whereas we in this world see only the present and the past.'

Iras still sobbed gently, though her mistress seemed not to hear her. For a long time Verica sat silent and unmoving; a thrush sang somewhere in the garden, its notes mixing with the faint splash of water in the fountain. At last she rose, pulling her hood over her head to shield it from the sun. Moodily she stared round the garden, then smiled at the others. 'We have no more business here today. But you spoke well now, Gwydion. Soon we shall see what the future brings.'

As Niamh had promised, the meadow seemed to be deserted. Cybele pulled off her tunic, then stretched naked to let the sun warm her body.

As she did so, a sudden movement in the grass caught her eye. For a moment she was startled; but it was only a hare, standing on her hind legs just a spear's length away and watching her with fearless eyes. Cybele laughed, then bent down and began to scrub the stains out of her tunic, rubbing the garment on one of the flat stones in the stream.

After a while she lifted it out and looked at it critically, then gave it another rub. Finally satisfied, she wrung the water out of it, gathered it carefully in her arms and stood up. The hare was still there, her eyes on every movement; then, as Cybele watched, the animal turned away and scampered up the slope to disappear in the undergrowth. How much I've learned. Cybele thought. Now I know about hares, how they're sacred to Ceridwen. Ceridwen, the witch-goddess; and Mistress said I was named for another witch-goddess. I wonder what that means?

Still pondering, she began to paddle homewards along the stream, happily unaware that hidden eyes had observed everything.

XL

Morrig looked up as the tavern door creaked open and Amicus stepped inside, his bulk briefly eclipsing the afternoon sun.

He nodded pleasantly at Morrig and Messalina, who was wiping down one of the tables with a rag, looked round the empty room and lowered himself carefully on to one of the benches as if uncertain if it would hold his weight. At last he smiled and stretched his arms over his head.

Morrig felt a chill clutch her heart, but Amicus seemed to be in a good mood. 'Very quiet today. Wine, I think – your good stuff, not the usual varnish-remover.'

She gave him a suspicious look, then nudged Messalina. 'You heard the gentleman. Get him what he wants.'

'There's not much of the good stuff left; that mob smashed up most of it.'

For answer Morrig gave her a ringing slap across the face. 'Don't argue with me, girl.' She turned apologetically to Amicus. 'Stupid slut doesn't know what's good for her. Get on with it, girl.'

She waited until Messalina had scurried out of the door, then sat meekly down on the bench beside Amicus. 'It's him you want, isn't it, your honour? He's not here; you should find him at the *caupona* next door.'

Amicus shook his head. 'Not there either, I'm afraid. It's all locked up, shutters down and no sign of him. I never seem to be able to find him when I want him. You'd almost think he was avoiding me.'

Messalina reappeared, staggering under the weight of a full amphora, and Amicus put up his hand to check her. 'Wait there, girl. Let's have a look at the label.'

He peered at the lead tag hanging around the neck of the jar, spelling out the words carefully, then read the painted inscription on the amphora itself. At last he nodded. 'In the consulship of Quintus Aquilla Niger. When was that? Two years ago?'

He gave a good-humoured smile. 'Very good stuff if it's what it claims to be. Right, we'll be off then. I'll be back for more things later. Come on girl, you belong to me now. And carry it carefully. It's worth nearly as much as you are.'

Morrig opened her mouth in astonishment. 'You can't just walk out with her. And the wine. It's ours. She's ours – look, I've marked her.' She tugged down the top of Messalina's tunic, revealing the blistered skin and the branded 'A' on her breast.

Amicus looked at it carefully, then shrugged. 'A for Aquila or A for Amicus? Who cares?' He reached across, pulled Messalina's tunic off the other shoulder and looked at her appraisingly. 'Skinny, and I've seen better tits, but I'm sure she'll earn her keep for me – well, for my boss, really. Glaucus. But he's a fine fellow, I'm sure he'll let me have a turn when she isn't otherwise employed, he's very generous that way. And then when she starts to lose her looks, he can just sell her on.

'And just to clear things up between you and me, nothing's yours any longer; not the slut, not the wine, not this place nor the caupona next door, and probably not the clothes on your backs either.' He gave Morrig a critical look, then shook his head. 'You can keep yours on, though, dear, I don't go for the mature sort and you're fat enough to turn Glaucus' stomach. He's delicate like that.'

He stretched out his arms expansively. 'It's like this, you see, Glaucus lends money to folks, and then some of them make a lot more, and some of them lose everything; but whether they win or lose, Glaucus always wins, one way or the other. That's what being a banker is all about.'

'You can't just take her. There's a law.'

'Oh yes, you're so right. There's a law. Do you know what it says? It says that debtors can be sold or locked up until they pay.

So why don't you go to the magistrate and complain and get yourself and your precious husband locked up or sold. If there is a magistrate in this flea-blown town.'

He spat copiously on the floor, just missing Morrig's foot. 'And anyway, you're not a citizen, are you? So you can take the law and stuff it. Right, girl, let's be going.'

As he started to lever his bulk up from the bench, Messalina's mind was racing. What about all the tip-money I've been hiding? What about the duponius that Senorix owes me? In sudden desperation she shoved the heavy amphora at Glaucus with a 'Here, catch' and ran out into the street.

Once outdoors she stopped for a moment. Which way to go? To the right was the city gate and the open country beyond, but there were soldiers there who would certainly stop a running slave-girl, and anyway the street was crowded with passers-by and carts. The forum, round the corner to the left, was a better choice, and behind it there was the little altar to the god Lugos. If she ran fast enough she could put her arms around the altar, and pray that the god would grant her sanctuary.

As she still hesitated there came a loud crash from the tavern, followed by a yell of fury and a long and fruity oath. Messalina bolted towards the forum, desperately pulling up her tunic to cover her breasts as she ran. Behind her was a shout of 'Stop her, she's a runaway slave.'

She risked a glance over her shoulder, and saw Amicus rounding the corner, his white tunic stained red all down the left side. Frantically she put down her head again and cannoned right into the solid form of Licnos, Marius' cook, who had just turned away from the butcher's stall with a flitch of bacon in his easy grasp.

Before she could think or dodge, Messalina felt Licnos' right hand close firmly about her wrist. 'Runaway, are you?' he rumbled, 'What's all this about, then?'

When Cybele was well out of sight, Tetricus the hunter carefully parted the long reeds in which he had been lying hidden and thought carefully about what he had seen. A naked girl washing. So there's our witch. Some witch, and she paddled away down the stream. No wonder the dogs hadn't been able to pick up any scent.

Very softly he raised himself to his feet, and suddenly noticed the hare standing on her back legs only a spear's length away and watching him intently. If only I'd brought the dogs. Well, I might get better game than that.

At the edge of the stream he paused for a moment and looked about him. There's the hare again. She's followed me. Witchery. His left hand automatically felt for his *fascinus*, the phallic amulet he wore on a leather thong around his neck as protection against the evil eye. Gently he pulled it off, then held it in front of him, 'Shoo. Get away. Leave me alone.'

But the hare at first seemed to take no notice; then she turned her back, lay down in the grass and began unconcernedly to wash her ears and whiskers, meticulously licking her front paws and rubbing them over her face. Only when Tetricus took a cautious step towards her did she make a leisurely move.

Unsure whether he was laughing at the hare's antics or at his own fears, Tetricus stepped quietly into the stream. Still clutching the amulet in his left hand and now holding his dagger in his right hand he moved quietly along the stream.

☙ ☙ ☙ ☙ ☙ ☙ ☙

Amicus puffed up, visibly out of breath, his tunic stained and dripping with red wine. 'All right, I'll take her now. Well done. Little bitch that she is.'

Licnos gave Amicus a long slow look, then, still holding Messalina firmly in a hand as big as a ham, nodded. 'Yours, is she?'

Before Amicus could answer, Messalina tugged with her free hand at Licnos' belt. 'No, I'm not his. He's not my master. I'm the tavern girl at the Eagle. You saw me there.'

Slow recognition dawned on Licnos' face. 'So I did.' He put down the flitch, leaning it against the side of the butcher's stall. 'Got a bill of sale, have you? Show it to me and she's all yours.'

Amicus had regained his breath by now. 'She's settlement for a debt, part-settlement, anyway.'

'So you took her by mutual agreement?' Licnos ignored Messalina's frantic head-shaking, and seemed about to hand her over; then he pulled her back. 'Show me the agreement. Otherwise she's disputed property.'

'Disputed property? By Juno herself, I'm a respectable banker. I only take what the law allows.'

Licnos pondered for a moment, then sniffed ostentatiously and rumbled, 'A respectable banker? Now there's two words that don't go together very often. And in my experience most bankers don't go around stinking of wine and looking as if they've just washed their clothes in it.

'You see, because I'm big and I talk slowly and move slowly, some people think that I'm stupid. But I always get there in the end. So let's go through this nice and gently, you and me.

'She's part payment for a debt, is she? Right, then what you have to do is this: you go and see the magistrate, and you tell him what this is all about; if it looks like you might have a case he'll serve a summons on whoever it is you're complaining about, and then he can defend himself; and if he loses then you can claim his property. Not before.

'There aren't any proper magistrates in town of course, they haven't got round to elections or anything like that yet, but my commander acts as *praetor* if anyone needs him to. Most people round here don't bother, they go to the tribal Queen and sort things out the old way. So it's your choice, Citizen Respectable Banker. But you'd better change your clothes first, he doesn't like to deal with folks who stink like a winery on a hot day.'

He scratched his belly and waited calmly for a response, then shrugged as Amicus turned away with an angry curse.

'Looks like he doesn't think he owns you any more,' he told Messalina. 'Let's get you back home.'

'Mistress will kill me. She will. It's all my fault that the amphora broke and the wine went everywhere; and it was the good stuff, too. It was worth nearly as much as me.'

Licnos paused, 'Is that why you were running away?' He looked at her more carefully, noticing that a bruise had started to form where Morrig had slapped her. 'By Ceres, girl, you're as thin as a rake. Don't they feed you? Here, have this.'

He reached inside his tunic and pulled out half a loaf of flat bread. 'You can have this; you look like you could do with it. Now, you just come along with me.'

He picked up the flitch again, then still holding Messalina firmly by the wrist he led her across the forum to the temple of Mars Victor and sat her down on the steps before sitting companionably beside her and resting the meat by his side.

Messalina stuffed what was left of the bread into her mouth with a mumbled 'Thank you', then added 'If we can find somewhere quiet I could make it up to you.' She gave him a coy look. 'Would you like that? I know lots of tricks.'

Licnos looked thoughtful, then shook his head. 'I prefer boys myself; but thanks for the offer. Now, tell me how this all started. None of my business, but characters like Citizen Banker get on my tits, if you'll pardon the expression.' He looked at her, then grinned. 'I think mine are bigger than yours, lass. Tits, that is. My name's Licnos, by the way. What's yours?

'Messalina. That's what Master and Mistress call me, anyway. It's an important name, it used to belong to an Empress, they said. I think I must have had another name before they bought me, but no-one calls me that any more.'

She smiled at him. 'Have you got any more bread?' .

'Story first, girl, then bread. Fair offer?'

Messalina nodded. 'He said something like that, before they

took him away. He still owes me a duponius.'

Licnos raised his eyebrows in disbelief. 'A duponius? No-one tips a tavern girl that sort of money. Not even one named after an Empress.'

'Oh, he does. And he gave me another one before, but Mistress found it and took it. I hide my tips better now, but all I usually get is a copper or two. He's much more generous.'

Licnos sighed. 'More money than sense, some people. He must be rolling in it.'

Messalina nodded in happy recollection. 'Oh yes, he's got lots. More than I've ever seen. More than Master and Mistress have, I'm sure of that. And I didn't even have to do anything special, just tell him what the soldiers were saying.'

Just tell him what the soldiers were saying? A faint suspicion began to surface in Licnos' mind. 'Good looker, is he?'

'No, he's old. And his front teeth are missing, too. But I don't mind that.' She stretched languorously. 'He's really good in the sack, though.'

And he pays a duponius a trick. But it wasn't her tricks that he was paying for. I may talk slowly and move slowly, but I always get there in the end.

'Sounds like a good man to know. I have to be getting back to camp with this meat, but I'll keep a look-out for him and tell him you're waiting for that money; a promise is a promise, after all. What did you say his name was?'

'Senorix. But I know where he's gone. Some of the Queen's men came for him, so I suppose he's down with her in that big palace they say she has.'

She sighed enviously. 'I saw her when that altar was dedicated – she's really beautiful, isn't she? I wish I could be like that. And rich, too.'

Licnos stood up slowly and hoisted the flitch onto his left shoulder, then gently pulled Messalina to her feet. 'You should come along with me. I know a man who'd like to talk to you. And I think he might like to give you some money too.'

Messalina tagged along happily, then tugged at Licnos' belt to remind him. 'And you said I could have more bread, too.'

At last the ravine opened out, revealing a fair-sized patch of level ground surrounded by cliffs. Tetricus stopped and stooped low, taking in the scene: two goats tethered, a little patch of garden, and a girl, still naked and with her back to him, kneeling and spreading out her tunic to dry in the sun; no-one else was around.

Grinning to himself, Tetricus hung his amulet back around his neck and stepped softly forward.

XLI

'You sent for me, sir?'

Marius looked up from the tablet he was reading and smiled at Marcus Asellio. 'Informal, Marcus.'

He motioned towards a stool. 'Take the weight off your feet for a moment. I have news – it seems I've been promoted.'

Marcus jumped to his feet again and clutched Marius' hand. 'That's wonderful, sir. Well done.' He paused for a moment, taking in Marius' expression. 'It is cause for congratulation, isn't it?'

Marius pulled a face and waved his hand towards the stool again. 'Of sorts, I suppose.' He held up the tablet. 'This came from Eboracum about an hour ago. Confirmation of what I told the meeting this morning – we'll be getting a couple of cohorts from the Ninth by way of reinforcement.'

'The Ninth? So the whispers were right – the camp's been buzzing with that story for days.'

'*Haud semper errat fama* – rumours aren't always wrong. They're to set up a full-scale marching camp south of the town, and I've been given overall command of them once they arrive, which should be in three or four days. It's just a pro tem promotion, no more pay, just a lot of extra work. And it gets worse.'

Marcus frowned. 'Go on.'

'It seems that this is just the advance guard; the rest of them will be coming over once the camp's established. Looks like they're going to settle our little problem once and for all.

'You remember that Lucius Aninius Sextius Florentinus has just been appointed Legate to the Ninth? He's a good man from what I hear; if anyone can keep them in order then he can. But it's still going to be a hard sell to talk Queen Verica around; they could be almost within sight of her palace, a whole camp full of the very legion that she loathes more than anything else on Tellus' the very legion that she loathes more than anything else on Tellus' Earth.'

'She'll be well protected, then, that's for sure.'

'And I know what she'll say to that. That she needs no protection from her own people; she's already told me as much in so many words.'

'But why a whole legion? A cohort or two would be plenty to strengthen us and the other local garrisons; what's behind it?'

'My guess would be some sort of punitive raid up into Caledonia; Lucius Aninius hasn't been in post for more than a few weeks, he may want to send a warning message to anyone who thinks that they can take advantage of the new boy. Personally I'd avoid kicking the hornet's nest. But then perhaps that's why I'm a humble garrison commander and he's a legionary legate. Be that as it may, and just to rub salt into the wound, the advance party will be under the command of – go on, guess.'

Marcus stroked his chin. 'Not Gracchus? Our former tribune?'

'The man himself. A decent soldier, but not a lucky one, I think. Why him, that's what I keep asking myself?'

'Perhaps they just want to get shot of him for a while. He cost us the lives of a complete century, pretty much – who knows what he's managed to do there? Though in fairness, if it hadn't been for that particular fiasco in the Ituna I'd have said that he was competent enough. Just unlucky, like you said.'

Marius shook his head decisively. 'Luck matters, Marcus; it shows that the gods are with us; at least, that's how the men see it. Think of the Divine Julius; oh, he was always careful to take the auspices before going into battle, but even if they'd turned out badly his men would have followed him to Hades if he'd asked them to, and built a boat-bridge over the Styx for him into the bargain. He was lucky, Marcus, and they knew it.'

'And then he ignored one prophecy too many.'

'Yes, I've often wondered about that. At the end I think he knew that he'd be killed on the Ides when he went to the Senate, perhaps even knew who most of his killers would be, though

Brutus came as a nasty shock. He'd faced death often enough before, it didn't frighten him; he went consenting, a willing sacrifice for Rome. Which, I suppose, is just what we ask of all our men.

'Still, to look on the bright side of things, at least I'll be able to keep Gracchus away from our camp. I still wouldn't trust some of our lads not to slit his throat on a dark night if they thought they could get away with it.'

'Have you picked a spot for the camp, sir?'

'I've been looking at this map; here, take a gander yourself. This area just a couple of miles south of the town and a little to the west of the road seems a likely candidate: good communications, a decent stream to provide a reliable water supply, and it looks like it should be easily defensible; that's all flat ground. But that means that it might be boggy, or there may be some other problem I can't see from the map. So I want you to take a surveying party down there to check it out. And you'll need to take local considerations into account.'

'The Queen?'

'Her too; this won't be that far from her palace, though I think it'll be out of her sight at least. No, really I'm thinking of the locals – the farmers and such like. They may have crops growing there, spelt and rye and who knows what else. Better to avoid cultivated land as far as possible; if you can't, tell them that they'll be paid fair compensation for the crop. I think that's about it. Good luck.'

As Marcus left he found Flavius waiting nervously outside the door. 'Is the master free? I don't like to trouble him over something so trivial, but…'

'Well, he's got a lot on his mind, but perhaps he could do with a distraction. Keep it quick, though.' Flavius nodded and went in, coughing apologetically as he did so.

'I hate to trouble you, Master; it's about Licnos; he says he has something very important for you to see.'

Marius shook his head decisively. 'I can't be bothered about menus now. Tell him to fix whatever's easiest. And if he's got some *mulsum* on the go, he can send it up, my throat's as dry as a desert.'

'It's not about the food, sir; he's got a girl with him.'

Marius smiled with relief. 'Cybele? Someone's found her. She'll get a good whipping when I have the time.'

'No sir, another girl; I think it's the tavern-girl from the town. He says she knows something that you ought to hear about spies or something. He's got her waiting down in the kitchen; she's stuffing herself with his best bread.'

Marius raised an eyebrow. 'The local good-time girl? What the blazes has he brought her here for? And feeding her with our rations? Never thought he was the sort for girls, now I come to think of it; takes more after the Emperor, by all accounts. Wonders will never cease. Oh Flavius, pity your poor commander who's dealing with a legate one minute and a tavern tart the next. All right, wheel her in.'

He turned back to his desk and rolled up the map with a sigh, then glanced again at the wax tablets with the message from Eboracum before shutting them with a bang. A moment later Flavius popped his head round the door. 'She's gone. There's no sign of her.'

♛ ♛ ♛ ♛ ♛ ♛ ♛

Tetricus looked around carefully, making sure that he was unwatched; but apart from the tethered goats and the girl kneeling near them and with her back to him, there was no sign of any living creature. Reassured, he stepped forward, his dagger held lightly in his hand, making no noise on the closely-cropped sward.

The girl stood up when he was perhaps ten paces away from her; unconcernedly she turned to face him, paused in shock for a moment, stifled a scream and then tried to cover herself with her hands. With a grin, Tetricus held out the dagger, making sure that she saw it. 'I came looking for a witch and it looks like I found a bit of fun instead. And her with her clothes already off. That should save time. Come on, darling, you be nice to me and I won't hurt you.'

Cybele sidled away so that the goats stood between her and

Tetricus. 'Go away. Leave me alone. I'll scream.'

'Scream all you like, darling. I like a girl who yells a bit. Shows they're enjoying it.'

He stepped forward again slowly, talking quietly the whole time. 'That looks like a nice body you've got there, girl. You don't want to keep it to yourself. Share it around, let everyone have a bit, that's what I say.' He suddenly lunged between the goats and grabbed her right arm with his left hand, then brought the dagger up to her throat, pricking the skin and forcing her to pull her head back. 'See, better not to fight, isn't it. Now, let's play.'

He dragged her towards him, then tossed the dagger onto the ground and with his right hand caught her by the hair and pulled her backwards and off-balance before she could kick him. Legs flailing she fell on her back, jolting all the breath out of her.

Now she tried desperately to turn over, but he was already on top of her, forcing her legs apart, holding both her arms to the ground above her head.

Tetricus laughed. 'Don't put up much of a fight, do you? You like it really, all you girls do.'

For answer Cybele spat in his face.

'Bitch.' He slapped her twice then pulled up his tunic, but her constant thrashing around made it impossible for him to enter her. 'Lie still, bitch. Or I'll slit your throat.' He fumbled on the ground for the dagger, then stiffened as a shadow fell across him.

'I am Niamh; and you have found your witch.' Moving easily she knelt down and he felt the prick of his own dagger at the back of his neck. 'Fool. I have eyes you know nothing about, and I have watched you every step of the way. The punishment for a rapist is death, and I could kill you now, with one thrust of this knife; but I think we will put you to use first.'

XLII

Marius slammed his fist on the table in frustration. 'Jupiter, wasn't anyone watching her?'

Flavius looked embarrassed. 'It seems that Licnos had promised her something to eat if she came and told you her story; then he left her in the kitchen eating bread and came looking for me. When he went back for her, she'd disappeared.'

'And she's not somewhere else in the house? How about the privy? Has anyone looked there?'

Flavius shook his head. 'Not in the house as far as we can tell, Master; but Licnos says she's only a slip of a thing, we'll need to do a careful search room-by-room in case she's hiding in a cupboard or something.'

'Do it. And tell one of the centurions that my orders are that he's to organise a small search-party to go through the camp, too; she must be around somewhere. Not Marcus Asellio, though, he's got other fish to fry.'

He gave a rueful smile. 'A stray tavern girl isn't exactly likely to have gone unnoticed in a camp full of soldiers, is she? And I suppose a lot of our lads know her?'

Flavius nodded. 'I gather she was popular, yes, Master. I'll do as you say at once.'

He bowed deeply, and was halfway through the door before Marius called him back.

'Flavius, you'd better send Licnos up, if he hasn't done the disappearing trick as well.' Better for him if he has, thought Marius as Flavius bowed again, though he wouldn't find it so easy to squeeze that bulk of his into a cupboard.

In fact Licnos appeared only a few moments later, looking crestfallen and shamefaced. He stood silently with his head bowed and his hands clasped in front of him, waiting for the eruption. But Marius was deep in thought. I've lost men, drowned or hacked to death to appease some Celtic god; good men, tricked and betrayed, their spirits left to wander with no funeral rites. And all the time this was going on under my nose.

At last he looked up. 'So you met someone with information about spies, Flavius tells me, who evaporates before she can be properly questioned. I could have you whipped for this. And she'll get a good whipping too when we finally lay our hands on her.

'But that'll have to wait. Tell me what she told you. And if you want your back to survive unbeaten then you'd better make it interesting.'

Licnos raised his head slowly. 'I can only tell you what happened, Master. I was in the forum, buying a flitch of bacon for our supplies here – the stuff we get from the contractor isn't nearly as good as you can buy in town, and the local stuff's better value too. Not all fat like the contractor sends; it's all to do with the breed of pig, you see.'

Marius drummed his fingers on the table-top. 'Forget the pig, man. The pig isn't important. The girl, remember.'

Licnos' face brightened. 'Sorry, Master. Yes, she came round the corner at a run, with this fellow a few steps behind shouting for someone to stop her. So I did. I grabbed her by the arm. Thin as a rake, it was. Poor little mite.' He paused, rubbing his hand over his face, before going on. 'Anyway, Master, he said she was a runaway, and then she said that she wasn't his slave anyway and that's why she was running. Something like that, anyway. And then he came up with some story about him being a banker and seizing her for a debt.

'Well, it all looked a bit dodgy to me, so I told him to come and see you if he wanted to start a case. Or to go to the Queen if he'd rather. Anyway, I kept a hold of her, and in the end he pushed off on his own. That's when she started talking. It seemed important, so I thought you ought to know about it and I brought her back here. She was half-starved, I thought she'd be happy enough sitting in the kitchen stuffing her face while I found Flavius. But when I went back to get her, she'd upped and gone.

'I'd never thought she'd run away. But she wasn't on her own for long, she can't have gone far.' He shook his head mournfully, then stopped as Flavius stuck his head around the door.

'Master, I thought it would be a good idea to check with the gate guards first. It seems she just wandered out. The guards all know her, it seems; she'd come in freely enough, they didn't see any reason to stop her leaving. We know where to find her, what's the problem? That's what they told me.'

'If she has gone back to the tavern, that is. Even if she does in the end, she's sure to lie low until the fuss has died down. All right, Licnos, just tell me exactly what she told you, the whole story.'

Licnos considered slowly. 'Well, Master, when I come to think of it, there wasn't that much really. Just that there was a man called Senorix, an old man with his front teeth missing, who gave her money – quite a bit of money, it seems – to pass on anything she heard about the soldiers. She'd done that a few times, she said; they all chat to her after they've – well, you know.'

He coloured with embarrassment, then went on, 'Then it seems that the Queen's men came looking for him and took him away; her nose is out of joint because he hadn't paid her for the last tip-off, she said. Where he is now, she doesn't seem to know. Lying in a ditch with his throat cut, as like as not.'

'Did she say when this was? Think, man.'

Again the slow shake of the head. 'She didn't say.' He considered carefully, then shook his head again. 'Not long ago, I suppose, but I don't know.'

Marius stood up abruptly. 'Right, nothing else to be done until we find her. We'll check her owners first, then hunt through the town; when we've got her we'll question her properly. Under torture if necessary. I need to know the whole story.'

Quite unaware of Licnos' discomfort, Messalina sat on the ground at the mouth of an alley and watched the people passing while she chewed the last hunk of bread that she'd taken from the camp. Then she wandered over to the fountain on the forum and drank, bending down and cupping the water in her hand and turning over the events of the last hour in her mind.

Licnos was kind to me she thought. I hope he won't get into trouble. Or be angry with me, and he didn't even want me to be nice to him. But I was frightened. The house was so big. And I think he was wrong when he said that someone else would give me money. Perhaps they were going to lock me up, or give me to Amicus. But where can I go now? Master and Mistress will beat me if I go back, after I broke that wine-jar. But no-one else will take me. And I've been branded, so everyone will know I'm a slave. And if I'm caught stealing I'll be crucified like Mistress said.

Nervously she shuffled along the street to the closed door of the Eagle and stood there, listening; angry voices came to her ears, her master's and mistress' among them.

And then she remembered. I don't need to steal anything. I've got money. I can just run away. She eased her way into the barn, raising the latch quietly and lifting the door to stop it dragging on the ground. No-one had heard her. Quickly she clambered up into the roof and pulled down the little bag that she'd kept well-hidden in the rafters and hung it round her neck under her tunic, then crept back to the door and pulled it open, so carefully.

No-one had heard anything. For a moment she hesitated in the street. Where to go?

Not anywhere in town. That Amicus might come looking. And not through the South Gate; that's where the tombs are. There are ghosts there, they say; and anyway, that's where Master and Mistress would be sure to come hunting for me.

Without making a conscious decision she tip-toed back past the Eagle and across the forum, then, feeling increasingly bold, set off along the street leading to the North Gate. This was new territory; she knew that beyond the gate the road went straight towards Caledonia, miles and miles away; but what was between here and there was a mystery to her. Well, she would find out. And as if the gods had decided to applaud her choice, she found a little party of travellers ready to set out on the same road: two drovers returning northwards after selling their beasts, a farmer and his fat wife heading home after shopping in town, and a tinker with his pots and pans strung over the back of a skinny donkey.

She tagged along with them as they passed unchallenged through the gate, wondered briefly how far they were all going, then found to her horror that the road led directly past the execution ground, where the tattered remains of the two thieves still hung on their crosses, now crawling with maggots and blow-flies and stinking in the hot summer air. She and her fellow travellers covered their noses and made the sign of the evil eye as they passed them. Her mistress' words came back to her: that's what happens to a thief; you get stripped and whipped and nailed naked to a cross in front of everyone, and then the ravens come and peck out your eyes.

And then you rot and stink and fall to pieces, she thought, and that's the end. But I'll never steal, no matter how hungry I am.

XLIII

AD III Kal. Ivl. – June 29th

Tetricus slowly woke and rolled over in an attempt to ease the ache in his arms and legs and to get the blood flowing in his hands. Daylight already. For two days he had been trussed up like a chicken in the market, given no food and only water to drink and left lying in his own filth day and night. At first he had tried to call out, but any sound above a whisper had been met with the prick of his own dagger just below his ear. His friends at the mine must have missed him, but in this wild fell country he could have gone anywhere. Why didn't I tell people what I was doing and where I was going, fool that I am, he wondered

The two women's voices came to him; they seemed to be talking earnestly, but he couldn't make out any words; it wouldn't have been Latin anyway, but some barbaric local language that no-one outside the island ever bothered to learn.

He tried to call again. 'Let me go. I can give you money. I swear by any god you like that I won't give you away.'

The talk stopped and the older woman – the one who called herself Niamh – stepped into his range of vision. 'You are awake, then. We have food for you. Simple food, but safe to eat, and good for a long journey. And we shall feed you as you lie there, wallowing in your own dirt.'

She turned away and called to the other girl. 'Fetch the bowl and give him food.'

Obediently the girl came over and knelt beside him, an earthenware pot in her hand. She dipped a wooden spoon into it and scooped out a fragrant porridge, flavoured with herbs. It was hot, but he swallowed it greedily as she spooned it into his mouth as gently as any nurse feeding a young child. The older woman stood watching them, her arms folded.

When the bowl was empty she spoke again. 'You are a rapist, and no doubt would have been a murderer as well. You came here of your own free will, and you have consented to eat the *viaticum*, your food for the journey. And now you will die for your crimes as a sacrifice to Esus and Taranis and Teutates, dying in the three ways ordained, by drowning, by strangling and by wounding. This is justice; and your body will be trampled into the bog where only the gods of the underworld will ever find it.'

For a moment Tetricus was silenced by the simple horror of what she was saying and her matter-of fact manner. Then, as he opened his mouth to plead or to scream, she bent forward and touched her forefinger on his upper lip, muttering something inaudible as she did so before adding, 'You have spoken your last; I still have some power remaining.' She turned to the young girl. 'Cybele, help me carry him to the side of the stream.'

Between them they half carried and half dragged him to the edge of the water. He tried frantically to scream, could feel the air rushing from his lungs, but not a sound came out of his mouth. They laid him down on the bank, his head only inches from the water; then, to his surprise, they stopped and moved a few paces away and sat down on the grass to talk calmly to each other.

'Today you will learn a great lesson, girl. Remember what I have always told you, that what the gods most desire is blood – and not the blood of animals alone, but of men and women. The Greeks and Romans believe that when such blood is offered, then the pale spirits of the dead will appear and drink it and they can then be conjured to reveal what they know of the world beyond, or of the past or the future.

'This is ignorance and folly. It is not the spirits of the dead who come flocking, but the gods themselves. I have seen them once before at such a time, though perhaps they will not appear to me today. But they may show themselves to you, for you will wield the knife. If they speak to you, answer them with reverence. Three

questions you may ask them and no more. They will not lie to you
– but they may not tell you all the truth either. That is for you to
discern. And now, to our work.'

She undid her rope girdle, knelt by Tetricus' head, and looped
it quickly around his neck while he thrashed backwards and forwards and strained to speak, though only spittle came out of his
mouth.

She turned to Cybele. 'I shall pull the rope tight and hold it
so; you must slash his throat, so first fold up your sleeves, for your
wrists and hands will be foul enough by the time we are done.
Then together we must pull him into the stream so that his blood
runs into the water and then push his head down. If he has any
wisdom he will go consenting – but I think this one is a fool. Greet
the gods for me, fool.'

She pulled the rope tight, watching closely as Tetricus' face
turned first red and then blue, and his tongue started to protrude
from his mouth.

'Now, girl. Cut him, and let the blood flow free so that the gods
will come.'

Almost in a trance, Cybele knelt down, and as methodically
and calmly as if she was slicing turnips she slashed Tetricus' throat
almost from ear to ear, smiling as the blood spurted onto her
hands. Then together they slid him into the water and held him
down until at last he was moving no more.

At last Niamh pulled the lifeless body out of the water, smiling
as the mixed water and blood poured onto the grass. She bent
down and pulled the bloody amulet from the ruins of Tetricus'
neck and looked at it quizzically for several moments, then held it
out to Cybele.

'Look, he scratched his name into it. Tetricus. He will not need
it where he has gone. Take it for your own, girl. Now we must
trample him down into the mire.

Cybele took the charm automatically and hung it around her
neck, then stood up silently and turned away, her arms, reeking

and crimson, held out before her. Niamh watched her for a moment, then smiled. The gods had come indeed.

☙ ☙ ☙ ☙ ☙ ☙ ☙

The audience had taken longer to arrange than Marius would have wished, but he had used the time to change the honour guard that was always maintained at Verica's palace and to question the men who had been relieved. There had, it seemed, been much coming and going over the last week or so, though not more than usual; if an old man missing his front teeth had been taken in, then they had not noticed him – certainly no-one had been wearing fetters, or in any other way looked like a prisoner. In a ditch with his throat cut perhaps, thought Marius, though I didn't think that was her style. But she has seen enough blood shed, a little more will not matter to her if she needs it to secure her position.

Once again she greeted him courteously, without a hint of *froideur* in her manner, and with Gwydion and Iras as always in attendance. As before she sat bolt upright on her currule chair, the little lapis brooch on her shoulder, apparently all innocent attention.

'I did not expect to meet you again so soon, Commander. I trust you and your men are all well? Do you perhaps have some news from Rome?'

'None from Rome, my lady; Rome seems content to leave us well alone these days.'

'And why not? Everything in this great province is peaceful and prosperous enough, is it not? Apart from those brigands I have heard about, and no doubt you and your men will bring them to book soon enough.'

Is she playing with me? Not a hint of that on her face or in her voice. But I know that she knows something. 'My lady, those brigands, as you call them, are the reason I have come here today.'

'Commander, you almost alarm me. Am I in any danger from them, do you think?' Wide eyes, an expression of complete innocence. What do I make of it?

'No, my lady, I think you are in no danger from them.'

She nodded, seemingly relieved. 'Then this great camp your surveyors are preparing has nothing to do with them? Surely you did not think I would not notice. It is barely a mile away.'

'My lady, it is a matter of military necessity; a marching camp only, and it will not be occupied for long. Any losses will be properly compensated, you have my word for that.'

'Commander, I had truly thought better of you.' The voice was harsh now, the eyes flashing. 'The Ninth Hispana will be there, will they not? Not that any of your men had the courtesy to say such a thing; I must be kept in ignorance, it seems, while that band of cut-throats and murderers are lodged on my own doorstep. Small wonder you come here so late, who had not the honesty to tell me what you had planned.'

'My lady, this is unjust. This is not my plan, as you seem to think, but that of the Ninth's new legate. They say that he is a good and brave man, Lucius Aninius Sextius Florentinus. The Ninth now are not what they were in those bad days that have passed.' She knew the Ninth were coming; what else does she know?

Verica gave a sudden smile, like a ray of sunshine breaking through thunder clouds. 'Commander, you must forgive us if we have been too hasty. I know that Rome is the guarantor of our peace and security, and her brave soldiers are always ready to stand in our defence. Tell me, do you know how long these valiant men will be camping here, almost on our own doorstep?'

The Royal We. Her claws are velveted now, but for how long? 'I cannot tell, my lady; that will depend on the military situation. But they will not be on your doorstep, as you put it, but a clear mile to the south; you should hardly know that they are there.'

'No doubt then we shall get accustomed to them. We suppose at least we must thank you for your visit, though it seems that it would have been a greater courtesy for you to attend on us before this work began. You had no other cause to seek us, we believe.'

Verica stood up and made to walk away, the little maid quickly falling in behind her, forcing Marius to interject, 'There is another matter, my lady, on which I would be most grateful for your assistance.'

She stopped and stared at him. 'This new discourtesy amazes us, Commander; first you plant a new military base on our own doorstep – and we will not disavow that word – and then you come seeking favours from us. Speak quickly, and do not try our patience too far.'

She plumped down in the chair with an ill grace, then gestured with her hand. 'We are waiting, commander.'

Marius spread his hands in apology. 'I will be as brief as I can, my lady. It has come to my ears that in Luguvalium a man – Senorix, by name – has been seen paying for information about our troops and their movements; spying, in other words. My lady, it has been reported to me that your own men arrested him at the tavern there, and I have to say that he has not been seen since. It is my painful duty to ask what you know of this matter?'

To his surprise, Verica laughed out loud. 'Commander, here, seated on this very chair and beneath this sacred oak, I give judgement to all those who come to me asking for justice under the ancient laws of my people. But I know the laws of Rome as well, and even Gwydion here has been reading them.

'Tell me, Commander, what would you in your role as *praetor* make of a claimant who came to you saying that things had been reported to him, or that they had come to his ears, but who presents no oath or other evidence to back up his claim? I think you would have him thrown out of the court, and even the most inexperienced *aedile* would do the same. So come, Commander, bring forth your witnesses and let me see them.'

Marius shifted uncomfortably. 'I had a witness, my lady, a girl from the tavern in Luguvalium; but she went unaccountably missing from my camp before I was able to question her.'

Now Verica's scorn was plain. 'A tavern girl? Who went missing from your camp? Commander, are you sure you have not discovered an unknown play by Plautus? Is she hiding under your bed? Perhaps in the fourth act she will crown you with your own chamber-pot?

'No, Commander, this will not do. Your evidence, as you call it, and with which you dare to question a Queen, all comes from the mouth of a slave-girl that you cannot even find. Why should I waste my time on such nonsense?'

'My lady, I beg you to listen to me. When the Ninth arrive in a few days' time, they will be led by Gracchus; and I am very sure you remember him.'

'Gracchus. Oh yes, I remember him very well, Commander. What were his words again when he thought that none were nearby? Why should we Romans, who govern the whole world, have any dealings with this woman and her little kingdom. She calls herself a Queen, and governs hardly more than one valley and its little tribe of barbarians, and yet we build her this villa – which she calls a palace – and treat her with as much honour as if she were the governor of a province. She is nothing.'

Marius stood open-mouthed, then bowed his head. 'You are right, my lady; he indeed said those words, or words very like them; and if they came to your ears then it may be by arts of which I know nothing. His views are his own, and neither I nor the Senate and People of Rome share them, and if you will accept my apology for his ill manners then I shall be in your debt.

'But it is just his scorn which puts you in most danger, my lady.' He paused, then spoke more forcefully. 'Look at me, my lady. Two generations ago, my family were plebeians; my grandfather, by dint of hard work and service to the imperial family, was able to rise to the knightly rank, and so I wear the gold ring to which that entitles me.

'But not only is Gracchus of senatorial rank; his family have been of that class since time immemorial. He has great influence in Rome, my lady, hot headed and foolish though he is, and he will not hesitate to use it.

'My lady, to speak plainly, Gracchus will be here within two or three days, and he will not hesitate to have your palace searched if he believes that you have concealed that Senorix I spoke of somewhere about the place; oh, there will be a most almighty diplomatic furore, I make no doubt, but he will justify it in Rome by saying that he is looking for the spy who was responsible for causing the deaths of almost a whole century under his command.

'If he finds no-one, my lady, be sure that he and his family have the power to smooth it over; but if his search is successful, then he will crow about his achievement like a cock on a dunghill, and the plebeians will love him for it.

'For myself, I believe unquestioningly in your loyalty to Rome, and I know of your grief at the loss of our soldiers; but I will ask this of you, my lady: will you swear an oath by whatever gods you will that you know nothing of where this Senorix may be? Such an oath will make it impossible for Gracchus to take any steps that either you or I would greatly regret. My lady, will you do this one thing? For Rome, for you, and indeed for me?'

Verica was silent for some moments, her chin resting on the forefinger of her right hand. At last she spoke, so quietly that Marius had to strain to hear her. 'Commander, friendship is a strange thing. Oh, I know what Cicero has to say of it, how true friendship cannot exist without virtue. Yes, I came to know Senorix many years ago, when I was a child. We met at the court of Cartimandua, and there he became my true friend and guide. He was not young then, and he must be nearly seventy years old by now.'

She smiled at a recollection. 'He taught me how to skip stones over the water; I have never forgotten that. In my childish way I called him Uncle Senny, though there was no kinship between us. In my eyes he could do no wrong. But I have learned to see him with clearer vision now, Commander. It is true that I had heard he was in town, and that I sent Gwydion and another of my men to fetch him; and he came here, and we spoke, though he said nothing of any wrong he had done you or your men. But then, Commander, he went away, and I have not seen him since; where he may be, I cannot tell.'

She half turned in her chair and laid her hand on the trunk of the oak tree. 'And so, Commander, I swear on this sacred oak tree by Esus and Taranis and Teutates and all the gods by whom my people swear, that I know nothing of where he may be. And may my life and honour be forfeit if I am forsworn.'

She turned back to face Marius. 'Will that do, Commander? Let me say this: I spoke of my friendship for Senorix, long ago, but I took this oath only because of the friendship that is between you and me. Yes, Commander, I am certain you know what I mean; and there is no more to be said on that score.'

She stood up, suddenly regal once more. 'Farewell, Commander. I wish you all joy in your dealings with your Gracchus.'

After Marius had left, Gwydion shook his head in disapproval. 'I did not expect you to forswear yourself, my lady. Was that wise? The gods you named will have heard your oath, and now your life and your honour are in their hands.'

Verica shrugged. 'I had no choice. Let the dice fall as they may. Where is Iras? Ah, here she comes.'

The little maid was running along the garden paths, breathless with excitement. 'Mistress, I hope I have not done you wrong. When I heard the Roman talk of the palace being searched, I slipped away and let the old man go free; he went out of the postern gate. I do not think they will find him. And he kissed me as he went. Kissed me on my mouth.'

Verica laughed and turned to Gwydion. 'So it seems I was not forsworn at all. How strange are the ways of the gods.'

XLIV

Messalina slowly opened her eyes. The air was already full of bird-song and there was a sweet scent of hay.

Where am she? A shed of some sort, made of wooden boards, with the sunlight coming through the cracks and making patterns on the straw and promising a hot day to come. She sat up, brushing the straw away from her eyes. Her owners must have found her. How did that happen?

But most of yesterday was a blank. There had been that business with Amicus and the amphora, and then she had run away; but after that there was only a great hole where memory should have been. She started to laugh, quietly at first and then almost hysterically before pushing her fist into her mouth to muffle the sound.

Too late. The door creaked open, dragging across the cobbled floor, and an old woman limped in and smiled at her.

'Nearly noon. You'll want to wash. No-one about, go down to the river and get your face clean. There's food if you can eat it.'

Messalina inched away from her, then stood with her back to the wall like a wild animal at bay. The woman looked at her with amused concern. 'Cat got your tongue? Fair enough. All right, I'll bring some food in to you – good stuff, won't do you any harm. Wait and see.'

She shuffled off again, and Messalina heard the bolt on the outside rasping home. Quickly she started to explore her prison, looking for a weak place in the wall; but the planks were sound and solidly nailed together and the roof was beyond her reach.

Locked in, then; how long before her master and mistress would come to claim her, no doubt with a reward for the person who had caught her? And then – she could imagine the whipping she would be given.

Once again she heard the bolt sliding across. She retreated into the furthest corner, shrinking herself down into a little ball; but it was only her captor, and this time she was carrying a bowl of something whose smell made Messalina realise how hungry she was.

The woman set the bowl on the earthen floor and put a wooden spoon by it, then sat awkwardly down by it, blocking the doorway. 'Eat up, girl. All good food – goat's meat and turnips, herbs for flavour. Take it easy, though – hot, don't burn yourself.'

Messalina inched forward and snatched the bowl, spilling some of the hot stew on her hand. She licked the spot where it had scalded her. It was good. And yes, there really was meat in it, meat like she had never eaten before.

The woman watched her eat, smiling the whole time but saying nothing. Only when Messalina had emptied the bowl and licked both it and the spoon clean did she break her silence.

'Slave girl, are you? No shame in that, I say. You can stay for a while, if you want; I won't tell on you. I was a slave, once, till I ran away. People like us should stick together, that's what I think.'

Messalina eyed her suspiciously. 'Master and Mistress will come looking for me. They'll beat me when they find me, I know they will.'

The woman shrugged. 'They'll have to find you first. Keep you out of the way for a while. Change how you look, too.' She hesitated. 'Don't trust me, do you?'

Messalina shook her head candidly. 'Not much. How did I come here? Who brought me?'

'You brought yourself, girl, on your own two legs. There was a whole bunch of folk with you headed up the road, and you all stopped off here for a dram, the way people do.'

She smiled. 'You might fool some people, girl, but you can't fool an old slave like me. You walk like a slave, with your head down and your shoulders bent; only old women and slaves go like that, and you're no old woman. There's someone who could do with a spot of help, I thought; so I doctored your poteen, and you went right off to sleep and let the others go on without you.

'I'm not as strong as I used to be, but I can still lift a little slip of a thing like you, so I hoisted you over my shoulder and dropped you down in the barn here. By all the gods, girl, you were snoring like a trooper. Remember a bit more of it soon, I dare say – my drams take some people like that if they're not used to them. We've not been introduced – what do they call you, girl?'

Not 'What's your name?' Messalina thought, just 'What do they call you?' Slaves have no name but what someone calls them. She understands that.

'Messalina.' Feeling more confident she looked straight at the other for the first time, noticing with a start that her left ear had been cropped.

The woman laughed. 'Everyone sees that, but most people are too polite to stare at it. Slave-punishment, you see, for running away, so next time I ran I made sure they wouldn't find me. Still looking perhaps. Doesn't bother me much these days, don't usually listen too much to what other people are saying anyway. Privileges of age, girl – sorry, that's Messalina, isn't it.'

She put her head on one side and nodded slightly. 'I can guess why they called you that. Whore, are you? Named you for one, anyway.'

Messalina was surprised to find her face flushing, but she nodded. 'In the tavern by the forum; I didn't mind, really.'

She hesitated, then asked boldly, 'You didn't tell me your name.' But the woman only gave a crooked smile and muttered, 'That's true, I didn't. You can call me Anand. Anyway, stand up straight and let's have a look at you. Come on, slip that filthy tunic off and let's see if we have something a bit better.'

Messalina reluctantly did as she was told. Anand looked at her blistered breast and shook her head. 'Bastards. Master did that to you? Got some ointment that might make it heal faster. Stay here, I'll get it. Get you something else to wear, too.'

She didn't bolt the door. But she took my tunic away, so I can't leave. What does she want? Why is she keeping me here? Messalina stepped cautiously to the door, opened it a crack and peered out. Here the light was dazzling, mirrored back from the river that flowed past only a stone's cast away, and at first she could see nothing clearly. Once her eyes had become used to the glare she could make out a small field – a paddock, really – with hurdles around the edge; a coracle was leaning up against the barn wall, its paddle thrust neatly through the carrying loop.

Hearing halting footsteps, Messalina moved away from the door. It was Anand again, now carrying a red tunic over her arm and with a small jar in her hand. She dropped the tunic on the floor and plumped down clumsily beside it, then motioned Messalina to kneel by her.

'Good stuff in this jar. Make it myself. Mugwort pounded in honey. Poison, though, so don't think of sticking it in your mouth. Right, let's have a look at those blisters. Done with a cattle-brand, was it? Gods, that must have hurt. To get a good cure I really ought to put the ointment on the brand as well as the burn, it heals better that way, but this is the best I can do. Stay still, girl, stop wriggling. There, you can rub it in yourself now. Remember, don't lick your fingers when you've finished.'

She held out the tunic and gave it a critical look.

'Might be too long on you, but try it anyway. That's linen, that is, good hard-wearing stuff for all that it's a bit frayed in places. Go on, slip it on.'

Gingerly Messalina slipped the garment over her head; it fell almost to her ankles, and Anand clucked like a hen and shook her head. 'Too long. Thought it would be. Used to be mine; best I've got though. Don't wear red when I'm old. You'll do. Now, go and wash your hands in the river.'

A sudden thought struck Messalina. 'Where's my money? It was in a bag hanging under my tunic. Someone's taken it.'

'I did. Safe here.' She lifted the cord from her neck and passed the little bag over; Messalina grabbed it quickly, and Anand laughed. 'All there. I'm no thief. Know what happens to them.

Now come out.'

Once out of doors Messalina looked around curiously. 'I think I remember a little about coming here now. There was a horse in that field then, wasn't there? A brown one.'

'Bay, girl, not brown. Yes, big brute. Friend of mine likes to leave it here sometimes when he goes into town. Came for it last night, when it was just getting dark and you were already fast asleep and locked in the barn. Not a good time to go riding, but seems he was in a hurry and he had another fellow with him so he'll be safe enough. Right, if your hands are clean then you'd best come into the house and we'll talk.'

Messalina hesitated. 'I think my old master comes up to the river here sometimes; he likes to go fishing.'

Anand lifted her eyebrows dismissively. 'He's a man. I've never met a man who could tell you what his wife was wearing or how she'd had her hair dressed that morning. We'd better give you a new name, though, that's true enough.'

She paused then laughed. 'So your old master called you after an empress who could turn tricks better than any professional, did he? Then I'll name you after a Queen who was famous for smith-work, to honour that brand on your tit. How does Brigid sound?'

Messalina tried the name and nodded. 'I like it. But I think I'd still answer if someone called me Messalina.'

'Ah, you're young. Come quickly enough to you, you'll see. A lady should always have a spare name or two, in case the one she's got gets a bit shop-worn. So walk with your shoulders and your back straight, and remind yourself that you carry a Queen's name.

'Now, come in and help me. Not as young as I was. But not my slave, understand? Free to go if you want, or free to stay. But if you stay, I'll teach you how to make poteen like I do. Not as much fun as turning tricks in bed, but lasts a lot longer.

🐚 🐚 🐚 🐚 🐚 🐚 🐚

'Can you speak yet, sister?' Niamh stroked Cybele's brow gently and looked into her eyes.

For a long time there was no answer; Cybele's eyes were open indeed, but seemed to be looking far away. At last she sighed and shook her head gently.

'The gods came to me. To me. Mistress, they came and spoke, and I heard them and spoke with them.'

Niamh nodded. 'Girl, I am no longer your mistress and you are no longer my slave. Now you are my sister, my equal in the eyes of the gods.

'Now, can you tell me what they told you? Or did they lay a charge of silence on you?'

Cybele shook her head. 'No, I can tell you. You'd said I could ask them three questions, so I did. First I asked them about the child I carry and what his name should be; he comes from the legion, they said, so name him for the legion – name him Myrdd, which means Myriad.

'Will he be famous? I asked. His name will endure when Rome is only a memory, they said.

'Will he live long? When he is old he will die the triple death, they said. And then they spoke no more.'

Cybele passed her hand over her eyes. 'It seemed to be over in a moment, but it must have lasted for hours.'

'All night and longer, sister. That is the way of the gods, whose days are not as ours. Sister, it seems to me that my time is done; your time is beginning. And if the gods told you true, your time too may be brief, but your son's name and renown will last into an age we cannot imagine.

She sighed. 'So much for the affairs of the gods, sister. But we have a body to trample down in the mire, filth to filth for all eternity. Shall we do it now? Ah, listen to the dogs. His friends are looking for him, but they will not find him.'

🐚 🐚 🐚 🐚 🐚 🐚 🐚

Senorix woke with a start. The sun was already high enough in the sky to shine directly into the little woodland glade, and Iatta was standing a few feet away, bending over a little fire of twigs and dry grass; two horses, safely hobbled, were grazing contentedly a little way apart.

He turned as he heard Senorix stir. 'I thought you were going to sleep all day.'

'And why not. We were riding most of the night. Thank Arianrhod there was a good moon. We must have done twenty miles at least.'

Iatta nodded. 'All that and more.' He grinned. 'I can see why you wanted to get off the road before it was light. They'll be looking for you, my friend, by name and by description, but you should be safe enough now. Here, have something to eat.'

Senorix sat up and stretched. 'I have to face it, Iatta, this sleeping out of doors isn't good for my old bones. What have you got? No, I can guess – a few bannock cakes to eat and burn-water to wash them down with.'

'Better than nothing. I kept some for you. Here, catch.'

Senorix easily fielded the cake with his left hand, broke off a piece and put it in his mouth. 'Gods, Iatta, they're stale. How long have you been carrying these in your saddle-bag? A fine quartermaster you are. You should take lessons from the Queen. She knows how to entertain. Good wine, Iatta, and she doesn't stint it. And the best meat, and fine white bread. That's the way to live.'

Iatta gave a cynical snort. 'You could live like that whenever you decided to. You've plenty of money in your purse, and more safely buried; you could sleep on a goose-feather bed and drink yourself silly with Falernian if you wanted to, and have half the lasses in Caledonia lining up to put one hand on your purse and the other on your cock.

'Anyway, if you were so happy lodging with the Queen why didn't you stay there? No-one made you leave, did they?'

Senorix stood up and yawned. 'Pressure of events, my lad, pressure of events. May all the gods bless that little Iras. I tell you, Iatta, a smile and a wink are cheap enough to give, and more often than you'd think they come back with good interest. But you're right, I'll have to stay away from there while the hunt's on for me. That Roman knew my name, Iras said. How the devil did he hear that, that's what I'd like to know. Still, the Queen stood by me it seems, for he went away empty-handed, there's that to be thankful for.

'But I must know what they're doing, Iatta, so I need you to go back and keep a weather eye on things. I'll head on north, I need to look over a few places, get the lie of the land crystal clear in my mind, then I'll be back to the usual meeting-place. Look for me there in two weeks from now.

'And I nearly forgot – I owe money to that little lass at the inn; here, take this and slip it to her if you see her. Messalina, they call her; good name for her, too.

'I owe her a good seeing-to as well, since I paid for my fun and never had it.' He sighed. 'Half the lasses in Caledonia, you said? She'd beat the lot of them, Iatta. I'd even thought of laying out good money to buy her, but thank the gods I came to my senses soon enough.'

Iatta shook his head. 'You're mad, always wanting what you can't have.'

Senorix paused and put his head on one side; there was a quizzical expression on his face. At last he nodded. 'I suppose you're right. But listen, I have a lifetime of watching these Romans. I know where they are strong, and where they are weak; and even better, I know where we are weak. I can trap them, Iatta, I can lead them a merry dance and then strike so hard that they will never dare give us open battle again. That's all I truly want. Not too much to ask, is it? If the gods are good and the omens are favourable then afterwards I'll retire in peace and put my feet up, and know that at least we've avenged Mons Graupius.

'When I was younger I thought I might live to see the whole island cleared of the Romans, but that's too big a mouthful to swallow. So I think I'll have to leave that to my children and their children after them; but I can make a start, at least.' He stared unseeing at the ground. 'I'll come to my grave soon enough, Iatta. Seventy summers I've seen. I can't go on for ever, old friend, I must leave someone to take up the fight after me. I still have time for that.'

'Children. Grand-children. Setting up a line of succession now, are you.' Iatta paused. 'That's not like you, man. You be careful. Once that fey mood takes you, you're apt to go and do something foolish. Still, I'll head back and see what I can hear; if it's true that the Ninth are really going to come up this way, then the whole town will be buzzing with it.'

He stamped the fire out, clapped Senorix on the shoulder, and readied his horse. Then with a grin he swung into the saddle, raised an arm in farewell, dug his heels into the animal's flank, and was soon lost to sight among the trees.

XLV

Marius wiped his brow. It was hard to remember that only a few weeks ago he'd been fretting about the cold and damp, but now it was so hot that even to stand in the blazing sun for more than a short while was uncomfortable. It was an oppressive, heavy heat, he thought, bouncing back at him from the cobbles of the little forum, and without even a hint of a cooling breeze from the sea. The stalls were quiet, and the *caupona* near the tavern seemed to have shut up shop completely. A dog was sprawled along the steps to the temple of Mars Victor, pink tongue lolling out of its mouth. Only the distant clink of a chisel on stone showed that the stone-mason at least was still at work; Marius reflected that the un-healthy weather might bring him more than enough business; can't keep the dead waiting, Marius remembered him saying, or who knows what they'll do.

The advance party from Eboracum would already have ar-rived at the ground Marcus Asellio had marked out for their new camp; Marius felt a twinge of sympathy for the troops sweating there, digging ditches and building up ramparts, laying out tent-pitches, bread-ovens and roads. No doubt Gracchus would be keeping them busy, confident that hard work would keep their dis-content at being dragged away from their women and friends at Eboracum to a minimum. The men in his own depleted garrison, he reflected, already had their hands more than full, what with the increased patrols along the roads and along both shores of the Ituna estuary, a more marked presence here in the town, and daily weapon drills to make sure that they were at their peak of effec-tiveness.

His stroll brought him to the altar that he'd raised only a

couple of months earlier. After that sudden hailstorm which had marred the dedication, the god had honoured his promise; one dry day had followed another, and now it seemed as if good old Pluvius, so regular in his bounty earlier in the year, had decided to take a well-earned rest from his watery labours.

There were, he noted with pleasure, fresh flowers around the altar. He ran his hands over the carved lettering, remembering how they had stood there and their hands had touched; a different world, two months ago.

A sudden voice broke into his reverie. 'Commander.'

A tall man, almost a head higher than Marius and perhaps twenty years younger, dressed in a plain white tunic, clean-shaven and with his hair neatly trimmed. Marius stared at him for a moment before his memory came up with a name.

'Lucius Aninius – Legate! We were not expecting you, sir. We would have prepared a formal military welcome.'

The legate smiled. 'I arrive officially in three days; in the interim I shall be a ghost, flitting unseen hither and thither. Commander, I need three things: your own assessment of the situation, your suggestion for future action, and your candid view of a certain young tribune who arrived back in Eboracum with his tail between his legs and a long story of grievance. We shall walk around as we talk.'

He suddenly broke off and looked carefully at the altar. 'Your gift to the town? That was well done.'

He read the inscription, sounding out the words in flowing Latin. 'It reads well, Commander. And the god is no doubt happy to be thus honoured. Sadly our tribune was less happy with the turn of events afterwards. I have heard his version of what happened at the crossing of the estuary; what is yours?'

Marius considered for a moment before speaking. 'Legate, from what I know of the man I suspect that he would have told you nothing but the plain truth; he would hold anyone who failed to do that in utter contempt. To me, Legate, he seems to be a

Roman of the old days who holds virtue to be the highest good. I sent him back to Eboracum simply because his presence here would not have been conducive to the good order of my men.'

The legate's calm blue eyes were fixed on Marius' own. 'In other words you thought someone would knife him. You were probably right; our men are not happy bedfellows with failure, are they, Commander? So why did his mission not succeed?'

Marius viewed the cold water and decided to plunge straight in. 'I sent him with an unreliable guide, Legate. We were both deceived by the man, who has now been murdered himself; so there has been a small measure of justice in the matter.'

The legate's silence invited Marius to continue. 'And we found that a local tavern girl has been passing on information to a man who seems to have some connection to these attacks; just soldiers' gossip, of course, but of possible value to an enemy. And now she has vanished too. And the man she was talking to as well; they're probably all stowed away somewhere in the wilds of Caledonia.'

'Ah, Caledonia. I wondered when that place would be mentioned. A cistern full of rebellion, that we need to empty and clean out once and for all, would you not say, Commander?'

Marius saw the pit open at his feet and decided to side-step it. 'That would be one approach, Legate. I have no opinion as to its advisability.'

'Of course you have, Commander. You're the man on the ground. Come on, speak up. I've never punished a man for giving me his honest opinion, and I'm not about to start now.'

Marius took a deep breath and plunged on. 'Legate, a few months ago one of my men broke his leg while he was cutting timber for spear-shafts. It didn't seem much at first, but then it festered and turned to poison.

'In the end, the orderly asked my permission to amputate it at the knee, and that's what he did. The soldier lived to tell the tale and draw his pension, and now he's settled, with a native woman somewhere down south. My judgement would be to do the same in this case – isolate the poison, limit the movement between here and Caledonia.'

'Interesting.' The legate raised an eyebrow and went on, 'So the empire has reached its limit here, has it, Commander? Just as the River Rhenus provides a natural border between the barbarians of Germania Libera and our own provinces, a border beyond which we barely attempt to go except for the odd raid or punitive mission, so here there is a natural border between the province of Britannia and the barbarians of Caledonia? But here no convenient river divides us from the painted savages to the north, and no impenetrable mountain range renders our lands safe from their incursions.'

He was silent for a while as if considering, then suddenly broke off at a tangent. 'The town doesn't seem very busy, Commander. There was a caupona just there, was there not? Closed now, it seems. And the stalls in the forum aren't exactly heaving with customers, are they? What's the problem, Commander? Just the natural indolence of the natives when the weather turns hot? Or something worse? Are they frightened that we might turn on our heels and abandon them to the wild hordes of murderous barbarians from the north?

'Look at the town with their eyes – or with the eyes of the Caledonians, perhaps. Wood and thatch. The place would go up like tinder, especially in this dry weather. And you have no *vigiles* trained to deal with such an event, have you, Commander? There would be panic, women and children trampled down in the streets, looting and murder.

'Even Rome was once not safe from such predations. When Brennus and his Gauls attacked at night, only the sacred geese on the Arx raised the alarm and so kept the Capitoline Hill at least free from the pillaging hordes who had already occupied the rest of the Great City, as you well know.'

He paused in his walking and turned to face Marius. 'Reassure me. Persuade me that my nightmare is only that and nothing more. Convince me that this town of yours is safe.'

Marius shook his head. 'Legate, I cannot do that. I can only promise you that my men would give their lives for the safety of the people under their care, and so would I. We are well-trained and ready to serve the Senate and the People of Rome to our last breath.'

The legate nodded but said nothing, then resumed his slow walk. After a few steps he broke his silence again. 'Once I am here officially, protocol demands that I should pay a courtesy visit to the local Queen. There is no reason why I should not, is there?'

'Indeed, Legate, you must surely call. But you should know that when she was much younger and living as the foster child of Queen Cartimandua in Brigantia she saw how the Ninth lost their discipline and rampaged through the land. Of course that was many years ago; but I must say that although she is most surely the friend of Rome, she has little cause to be the friend of the Ninth.'

Again the legate turned to face Marius. 'Commander, the Ninth – like every other legion – exists to defend the Senate and the People of Rome. Now, most of our people live their daily lives never once thinking of the legions which keep them safe from the barbarous Scythians or the bloodthirsty Parthians, or any of the other savage tribes which still live in those lands which fringe the Empire. And so they trade and marry and have sons and daughters, they create poetry and carve statues or cast fine bronzes, and so the grandeur of Rome grows and flourishes; and yet the legions are never in their thoughts from one year's end to the next.

'While the legions do their work, Commander, and the hordes of which I speak are kept at bay, it matters little whether the people they defend think well of them or otherwise. So let it be with this Queen. I will visit her as protocol demands, and she will greet me with an equal courtesy, or show that she is less than Rome's firm friend. I do not have to like her, Commander, nor yet does she have to like me. I have heard something of her from the

– 332 –

Tribune, Commander, and when all is said and done, she is no more than a generation removed from barbarism herself. An ignorant old woman ruling an ignorant people, barely raised above the level of the dirt.'

Marius bowed his head in acceptance, thought his mind was racing. She infuriates me and charms me. I have never known anyone like her. She is beautiful and graceful, and speaks pure Latin and decent Greek. She has the poets and orators of both tongues at her fingers' ends. She will surely eat him alive. But sometimes it is better to be silent. He said only, 'When you visit her it might be as well to take the Tribune with you. As you say, they have met together before and so he may help to ease your meeting.'

The legate nodded. 'A good suggestion. And since we are talking of him again, I must tell you that his situation is shortly to change.'

Marius kept his face carefully blank. 'May I ask in what way, Legate?'

Lucius Aninius nodded. 'You will hear this officially before long, I am sure, but for the moment it would be better if you kept it to yourself. I have been recalled to Rome; I will be leaving in a week or two. Apparently our Emperor wants an assessment of the situation on this northern flank of the Empire, and I hear that similar orders have been issued in other frontier regions.

'I shall therefore be advising the Divine Emperor on the situation here, and on our possible future strategies; I may mention your own suggestions to him along with those of others whom I have also been sounding out.'

'And the Tribune?'

'He will command a large portion of the legion on a raid into northern Caledonia. He has particularly urged me to let him undertake such an operation, and I see no good reason to deny him. You have said yourself that he is a Roman of the old school, and I certainly have no cause to doubt either his courage or his skill.'

He raised a hand to forestall Marius' interjection. 'He was

unlucky once, that is true; but you too, Commander, hardly have an unblemished record; by your own admission, it was you who found him that treacherous guide who led so many men to their deaths. My mind is made up on this matter; within three weeks he will set out for Caledonia and teach the barbarians there a lesson that they will not soon forget.

'Now, when I say that I have been recalled to Rome I must add that my senior staff have been recalled with me; clearly the Divine Hadrianus wants a proper in-depth analysis of the situation and perhaps fears that he will not get it from his legates alone. This, of course, will cause certain problems for that part of the Ninth which will be engaged on the mission I have outlined to you. It would be deemed a considerable favour on your part if you could release one – no, let's say two – of your own senior men for attachment to the Ninth. There would be no command responsibilities, I'll fill those with internal promotions, so it's purely a staff role. I would suggest perhaps someone who already has considerable combat experience and with him a younger man, someone looking to gain valuable experience that might well see him promoted ahead of his contemporaries. Who can you offer me?'

For a moment Marius was stunned into silence; the politely-phrased request was in truth an order that he could not refuse. And yet two names leapt at once into his mind, and after a brief pause he suggested both. 'For an experienced man, sir, I'd suggest Marcus Asellio. He's *primus pilus*, and an old friend, with plenty of battle experience; and frankly I think he'd probably jump at the chance if it were offered to him. And then there's young Eburnus; he's not long made up from *optio*, and one of the most competent and courageous young men I've had the pleasure to work with. The experience would be very useful to him; but I'll certainly miss them both.'

The legate nodded. 'Then an appropriate approach will be made to both men, with your approval, Commander. Both men, of course, will receive an additional allowance and will be on the

Ninth's payroll for the duration.'

For the duration. I wonder if I'll ever see either of them again. After this tomfoolery is over, the pair of them will pick up some nice cushy number in Eboracum, or my name's not Marius. After a few moments Marius decided it would be politic to change the subject.

'May I ask where you are staying, Legate? Your arrival was certainly a well-kept secret.'

Lucius Aninius gave a cold smile. 'A secret that Rome's enemies would wish to have known, as like as not. As far as anyone knows, I am a humble civil servant taking tallies of taxes paid and due. As you can imagine, that does not make me a popular figure, so people go out of their way to avoid me and don't ask questions that I might find tricky to answer. They talk little and guardedly, and make the sign of the evil eye when they think I can't see them. What fools people are.

'I've found lodging a little way to the north of the town, a little cottage by a bridge where once there was a ford. An old woman runs the place with a young girl to help her, and there she makes the most astonishing liquor that you or I ever tasted – it would truly take your breath away. It'll do for the next few days – I've certainly stayed in worse places.

'At a guess, I would say that the owner was a slave once, her ear has been cropped. She may be a runaway, but that, fortunately, is none of my business at the moment.

'To speak candidly, Commander, I wonder what is going on in Rome. I was only appointed to my post as Legate of the Ninth a few weeks ago. And then before I really get to grips with the new command I've been pulled out and sent off to liaise with the High Command; and they haven't even got a successor to me lined up yet. Well, that's the army, I suppose.'

Suddenly smiling, he clapped Marius on the shoulder. 'We shall meet formally in three days, Commander. You have done good work here. Farewell.'

He strode smartly away and turned the corner without a backward glance. Marius was left alone, standing by the fountain in the forum. After a moment he sat down on the edge of the basin and trailed his right hand into the cool water, then splashed it over his face and pondered the turn of events.

So that's how politics works, is it? Until an hour ago, I thought that it was me who'd sent Gracchus off on that fatal expedition over the Ituna. How can I have been so naive? It was what he wanted all along, and by hinting that Eboracum would find out that I hadn't been forward enough he persuaded me to give him his head. And I thought I'd been so clever. What a fool I was.

And now he's pulled the same trick with the legate, no less. If the Ninth don't chase up into Caledonia, then his friends in Rome will drop hints in the Imperial ear that Lucius Aninius isn't taking his new command seriously enough. And with the legate called off to Rome, who does that leave to take on this 'important mission' but Gracchus himself? And when he's burned down a few native huts and taken a couple of hundred women and children to sell as slaves in Rome, his friends will shout about the great victory he's won. How the people will love him.

And I've lost two good men to this tomfoolery. Pray the gods that they come back safe.

But even as the thought entered his mind an unwelcome sound came to his ear. For an instant he persuaded himself that it was only the noise of a cart rumbling over the cobbles; but there it was again, beyond doubt now – on his left hand there was the foreboding rumble of thunder, coming out of a clear sky. *Absit omen*.

XLVI

'Taranis is busy again. Hear his chariot wheels rumble in the sky. Three days already. And this heat. When there is such war in the heavens, then war on earth must follow soon.'

Niamh paused in her hoeing of the little garden and wiped the sweat from her brow. 'Since the gods came to you, sister, I have been able to see nothing further than what these two eyes tell me.'

She shrugged. 'I knew it was coming; perhaps it has come sooner than I had expected, but when the gods decree, man must obey. You are the one who must lead us now.'

Cybele looked up from milking the goats. 'I'm not ready, mistress – sister. There's still so much I don't know.'

'Girl, look at the animals. Just days ago they would fight and kick and bite when you tried to milk them, but now they stand patiently and let you do as you will. The gods have given you that gift, as they will give you others. But I still have time to tell you some things, I think.'

Cybele hesitated as if embarrassed, then blurted out, 'You told that man, Tetricus, that you had eyes he knew nothing of. What did you mean? How did you see him? Or was that just a trick?'

Niamh laid the hoe carefully down and began to pick at her hand. 'I have a splinter; I must stop while I take it out. Come and sit with me; I think the goats will wait patiently enough.'

Cybele waited until Niamh had sat down, resting her back again the warm cliff-face, then settled herself by her feet. After Niamh had gently sucked the sliver of wood from her palm she pointed to a kite, hanging motionless in the sky above them.

'A trick? Perhaps, but it is a trick I can teach you I think, though I cannot do it myself any more. You see that kite? Watch it closely.

Ride the air with it. Down here there is no breeze, but there is a little up there; feel that breeze under your wings, feel your wings flex and move.'

Swiftly she put her hands over Cybele's eyes. 'Now see through its eyes. Ride it, girl, ride it through the air. You can do that. Yes, you can do that.'

Cybele gasped. 'I'm so high.' She suddenly laughed. 'I can see you and me sitting here in the little garden. We're so small. I can see everything. Oh.'

She jumped to her feet as the kite suddenly plunged to the ground perhaps half a mile away. 'I thought I was falling. I thought I was going to hurt myself.'

Niamh smiled and stood up effortlessly. 'You see how easy it is. But only for those to whom the gods grant the gift. But yes, it does take practice. Be warned, though – to ride the mind of a bird or a hare is easy; others will perhaps come with time.

'But though you can ride them, you must not try to steer them. They are not your servants, but the servants of the gods who feed them in due season. So go gently with them.'

'Was that how you knew to find me at the stones after I left my master? For how long had you been watching me?'

Niamh shrugged. 'Perhaps. But there are other gifts that you will learn when the gods decide it is time for you to learn. Look, you have lost your amulet, the one we took from that man.'

Cybele's hand flew to her throat. 'The cord must have broken. It was weak where the knife nicked it when we killed him. I never felt it go; it could be anywhere.'

Niamh shook her head. 'Not anywhere, but where the gods bade it fall. They work their purpose out as slowly as the stars wheel in the heavens; and like the stars, they never fail. Listen. Do you hear the thunder again?'

Senorix mopped his brow and envied his horse for its ability to fend off the midges with a swish of its tail. He was beyond the end of the road now, though still not beyond all remnants of Roman presence – every twenty miles there was a marching camp, long-since abandoned and left rent-free to sheep and cattle, and the occasional signal tower, now rotting and gently toppling back to nature. Soon only the foundations will be left, he thought, and then the ages to come will send grass and trees to bury those as well.

And then, seemingly out of nowhere, there was a whole cohort in good order swinging southwards along the trackway, standard held high at the front, a sensible rear-guard, centurions on horseback posted along the length of the column, their eyes carefully scanning the edge of the forest for any signs of trouble. From one of the big river-supplied forts on Bodotria, Senorix supposed, though why they would be heading south like this was more than he could imagine. Just a show of force, perhaps, a reminder to the native tribes that this was still land that Rome claimed as her own; or maybe sent to combine with the Ninth in their push northwards. That was something he would have to consider.

He urged his horse to the side of the track as the soldiers thumped past, their hob-nailed boots raising a cloud of dust, and raised a hand in greeting to each centurion as he rode by. What did they make of him, he wondered. Certainly no word could have reached them to put them on the look-out for him. When they were safely out of sight he spurred onwards, still looking for a place that he knew he would recognise, though he had not laid eyes on it for perhaps thirty-five years.

He found it later that evening, in the last sunlight of a long summer's day; the lazy river winding through water-meadows, deeper in truth than in appearance, the great stack of rock on the right-hand side rising up like a platform built by mortals to assault the gods; and opposite, crowned by woodland, a smaller hill, the sides still steep enough to make an assault on it difficult. The upper reaches of Bodotria, he thought, and the lowest fording-point on the great river that flowed there. He smiled grimly; this was a place that he remembered well.

Turning his horse, he studied the great crag in careful detail. Above the scree which surrounded its lower half the rock rose, bare and almost vertical. Only to the south did an approach to the summit seem possible, though there too the ground was steep and covered in brambles and thorns. On his first two attempts Senorix failed to find a practicable way to the summit, but at last he managed the ascent, his horse's hoofs sending cascades of stones falling as it sought for a firm footing.

Arriving at last at the bare crown of the rock, Senorix noticed the faint marks of trenches and ramparts. There had, he thought, been a hill-fort here long years ago, but there was no sign of recent habitation.

Carefully he rode to the very edge of the precipice, looking down at the broad spread of the lands laid out before him. To the east the river widened on its long run to the eastern sea; to the west the land was broken and easily defensible, while in the north the mountains reared up, snow-free now but treacherous in the winter. Mons Graupius was there, he thought. Here and there, smoke rose from hearth-fires, with a whole cluster of fires to the north showing where a village had sprung up; scattered assarts had been cleared in the forest, with long-horned cattle roaming and barley ripening in the sun. This is what it must be like to be an eagle, riding endlessly on the streams of the wind; or like a god, perhaps, surveying the little world of mortals, pondering disinterestedly which of the insignificant creatures below to favour and which to kill.

And then he saw what no Roman had seen and what perhaps no man had ever realised before; the ford below was the disregarded key to the mountains to the north and the fertile lands to the west. Only own this ford, he thought, and you could split Caledonia in two; only own this ford, and all the lands to the northward were as securely yours as if you had set a garrison in every hamlet. How good are the gods.

He suddenly felt eyes on him and swung round in the saddle, but saw nothing at first. He shook his head, then shielded his eyes from the rays of the setting sun and looked more carefully, letting his gaze rest on every feature of the landscape in turn. At last he saw it, almost within his reach – so close, indeed, that his gaze had passed clear over it before; an owl sitting motionless on a rock, staring unblinking at him.

Take your omens where you find them, he told himself. The owl, if not Blanaid herself then surely her creature, the harbinger of chaos and disorder. Senorix raised a hand in salutation and grinned as the bird lazily spread its wings and flew away, barely skimming the ground until it was lost to sight in the gathering dusk.

In the faint evening breeze, Cybele left her body leaning against the cliff-face while her mind looked first through the kite's eyes and then roamed further, from bird to bird, until the little garden she shared with Niamh was only a distant blur. As the sun sank and the sky grew dark she reluctantly returned, and found that she was shivering in the sudden evening chill. So that is freedom. One day perhaps I shall fly like that again and never come back.

XLVII

The parade had, Marius acknowledged, been a great success. The Ninth – the whole legion as well as a *vexillation* of auxiliary cavalry – had marched through the town, bringing gawping crowds out to watch them and applaud. The thump of the soldiers' boots and the clatter of the horses' hooves, the brazen roar of horns and trumpets, and the splendour of the centurions' parade-dress, would certainly have made a lasting impression on anyone lucky enough to be there. This is Rome. Strong, eternal, unshakable.

And there was Lucius Aninius Florentinus at the head, glittering despite the heat in his legate's formal armour, his scarlet *cincticulus* tied around his waist with an elaborate bow, proclaiming him the personal choice of the emperor himself. And, should there be any doubt of the source of the legion's power and authority, there behind him was the *imaginifer*, carrying the image of the Divine Hadrian himself as a reminder to civilians and soldiers alike of where their loyalty as citizens lay. Truly a wonderful display. And how grand had been the formal burning of incense at the temple of Mars Victor, an offering to ensure the god's lasting protection. Even the occasional rumbles of thunder added to the magnificence of the occasion, assuring the world that Jupiter himself was watching from the skies.

If there was a worm in the apple, Marius reflected, it was the way that Gracchus was riding at the legate's side, his fine Spanish horse fully the equal of his superior's; and where Lucius Aninius rode bolt upright, his eyes firmly fixed ahead of him, Gracchus smiled and nodded at the cheering crowd as though its plaudits were due to him alone. Remember that you are mortal, Marius thought, then found himself muttering the word politician as though it were a curse. Did the legate notice? He must have done, but chose to ignore it. Two politicians together, I suppose. Well, may the gods bring them a good reward.

Now at the formal reception in the legate's pavilion in the new camp, Marius munched the inevitable honeyed pastries, nursed the watered wine in his cup and studied the other guests. Clearly Gracchus had been put in charge of drawing up a list of suitable civilians, and had decided to pick those townsfolk who were most ostentatiously wealthy. It made sense, after all; these were the people who would have most to lose if the town were to be attacked. Glancing from face to face, he faintly recognised a bald and rather plump man dressed in an expensive town-dress that must surely have come all the way from Italy; he had last seen him walking in that funeral procession a month or two earlier.

He was talking animatedly to another man whom Marius knew he had seen before, though his memory refused to tell him just where and when. He was about to edge closer to see if he could join their conversation when Gracchus politely touched his elbow.

Marius turned to face him with a smile. 'Tribune, a most successful day. You have certainly all made an impression on the locals.'

Gracchus nodded, clearly pleased with himself. 'The splendour of Rome, Commander. It does them no harm to see it. What other people in the world can equal it?'

Well, the Parthians for one, let alone the mysterious silk-people of the distant east, thought Marius sourly, but he contented himself with another smile, then noticed that the tribune seemed to have something on his mind.

'Are you ready for your great command, Tribune?'

'Into Caledonia? I think we will be ready soon; we've sent messages to some of the northern garrisons there, around Bodotria and so on, to send men south to meet us as we push north.'

He smiled confidently. 'This time we shall be very

well-prepared. The legate and I have organised a proper joint naval and military operation. Our triremes will land soldiers from Legio II Adiutrix at the mouth of the Bodotrian firth, then row up-river to give any necessary assistance as they move westward on both banks; they know the area already, of course.

'And my own legion will head north within the next week and – after we've met up with the force coming south – our joint army will aim for the upper reaches of Bodotria and advance down-stream. I gather there are old marching camps along much of the way we shall take, so that should make things easier – and faster, of course. There's no settlement of any size to worry about along the way, of course, so we shan't need *onagers* or heavy artillery, just the usual *scorpiones* and *vespae*. All-in-all we should be well-equipped to deal with any trouble we meet, we can take hostages, and carry out such punitive action as may be necessary to impress the power of Rome on these savages.'

My own legion. thought Marius wryly, but he contented him-self with a congratulatory smile and then went on, 'I thought that the Second Adiutrix had been withdrawn from Britain? You clearly know more than I do about these things.'

'Yes indeed, the Divine Domitian recalled them to Rome some years back; but we have secured the promise of a substantial vex-illation of their veterans. The noble legate knows how to set up these things. They should be arriving at the mouth of the firth at the same time that we reach the headwaters of the river, so as both forces advance we will surround the rebels and crush them like cob-nuts in a vice.'

If they're there to be caught, thought Marius, but again he simply smiled. 'Well, may Mars and Mercury go with you. And I think you will have met the Queen again?'

'Yes, the noble legate paid her a formal visit yesterday and was gracious enough to invite me to accompany him.'

Thunder rumbled in the distance as he shook his head sadly. 'I fear that things have much changed there since I last met her,

Commander. Her Latin seems to have almost deserted her, and that tame poet of hers had to translate everything into their barbarian doggerel. Perhaps the gods have struck her, or something? Either way, she had almost nothing to say for herself.'

Man, thought Marius, she mocked you to your face and you have not the wit to see it. But Gracchus was already chasing another thought.

'Oh, I nearly forgot. She'd sat herself in a proper magistrate's curule chair. She has no right to that. The noble legate suggested that you should insist on its removal, Commander. Not that it's for me to tell you that, of course,' he added with a sudden frown.

'There was one thing, though. When the legate explained that she need have nothing to fear from these savages once we'd dealt with them, and informed her that we would be heading north soon, and hoped to have everything settled by the August Kalends or thereabouts, that poet of hers had the gall to tell us that that was an unlucky time. Superstitious nonsense, of course, but it might unsettle the men if they came to hear about it.'

He glanced round with a nervous expression. 'Do you know what it's about? Some native celebration, or something?'

'I'm no expert, Tribune, but the Prefect in charge of the cavalry detachment that was here before I came left me a briefing note about it. Apparently it's one of their biggest festivals; I gather that they believe that there are four times in the year when time and eternity touch: the kalends of May, which they call Beltane; and then the kalends of August, November and February. At the August Kalends they'll be celebrating the beginning of the harvest, and those who have travelled away will try to return to their homes for the feast. They say that even the spirits of the dead return on the night before the festival, to share in the rejoicing with their descendants.'

There was another rumble of thunder, closer at hand this time. Gracchus glanced up, then laughed, 'The dead can stay in their graves, as far as I'm concerned. But the living will be right where we want to find them. A poor harvest they'll have of it this year, when we've burnt their crops and taken hostages. And some of those little red-haired Caledonian girls should brighten up the knocking-shops in Rome no end, shouldn't they, Commander?'

Smugly satisfied, he bowed and then turned to scoop a handful of pastries off the tray that a servant was carrying past before catching sight of someone that he apparently needed to talk to. He bustled off, leaving Marius standing in silence. Until a moment ago, I saw you as a Roman of the old school, he thought, stiff-necked and proud, but noble and honest. True, I have never liked you, and for that I was perhaps to blame; but with those last words, Tribune, I think you have earned my lasting contempt.

Moodily he held out his wine cup for a slave to refill while he listened to the thunder, seemingly further away now. A gentle tap on his shoulder made him turn; it was the man whose face he had been unable to place earlier, and it bore a worried expression.

'Commander, I understand you act as *praetor* if there's a case to be brought? I appreciate that this isn't the best time to bring up this sort of thing, but an associate of mine was in town a little while ago with a matter that he should have brought to your attention. But apparently it was *dies nefastus*, a day when legal proceedings can't be brought. You'd know more about that than I do, of course. But I should come and see you on the next proper day, so I thought I should take this opportunity to introduce myself: my name is Glaucus; I'm a banker.'

So that's where I've seen you. thought Marius. But before he could answer, all conversation was rendered impossible by an ear-splitting crack of thunder right overhead, and then the sudden roar of rain as the weather finally broke.

☙ ☙ ☙ ☙ ☙ ☙ ☙

Senorix brushed the flies away from his face and resumed his probing of the water-meadows. He cursed as his feet sank into the wet ground, but forced himself to continue right to the river's edge, leaning heavily on the staff he'd cut from an oak tree as he'd climbed down from the summit of the great crag.

At the water's brim he stopped to get his breath back, then plunged the staff into the stream. At the brink here the water was only a hand's-breath deep, and barely flowing, but it grew rapidly deeper and ran faster as he moved gingerly across, still supporting himself on the staff. At the middle of the stream he stopped; here the water was almost up to his waist, and moving with enough force to make him fear for his footing.

Grunting with satisfaction he retraced his steps. When he reached dry ground he sat down on a tussock and pulled off his boots, tipping the water out of them and finally hanging them round his neck to dry.

One job done, one to do. Still leaning on the staff and panting a little he set off for the summit of the little wooded hill that he'd remarked on the previous day. There was plenty of cover here to hide a substantial force, he thought, but the undergrowth was tangled and thorny. By the time he reached the summit the sweat was pouring from his forehead, and he sat down again to catch his breath. What I told Iatta was the truth, he thought, I'm getting too old for this. Settle down, that's what I need to do.

He used the staff to pull himself to his feet again and looked more carefully at the way the ground fell away from the summit. Easily defensible, and a good place to mount an attack from, apart from that thick undergrowth. We'll have to do something about that.

Satisfied at last he turned to go. I shouldn't have left the old nag at the top of the crag. he muttered to himself. Let myself into a pig of a climb there. He clambered up the scree-slope, stopping now and then to get his breath back and to check that he was on a practicable way to the top. At last he reached the summit and whistled tunelessly to call the horse. Used to be able to whistle properly when I was a lad. The things you lose along with your front teeth.

There was a smattering of relieved laughter as the thunder-clap died away. Marius blinked, then shook his head. 'If you're going to bring a case then I really shouldn't talk to you about it here. But to be frank I thought that you people generally used more... direct means of recovering debts.'

Glaucus raised an eyebrow, then waved the objection away with a smile; his hand was adorned with no fewer than three finger-rings and a thumb-ring, Marius noticed. 'It's true that we sometimes reach – well, let's call them informal arrangements with our clients; we find that that's usually in everyone's best interests. But there are other concerns here.'

His voice dropped and he leaned forwards to whisper confidentially into Marius' ear. 'Commander, I have a lot of money invested into various interests in this area. There's no grave danger of any barbarian incursion, is there? I could stand to make serious losses, you realise.'

Marius gave him a cold look. 'You have no need to worry. If the worst comes to the worst, I'm sure that my men and I will be happy to put our lives on the line to secure the safety of your investments.'

But the sarcasm was apparently lost on Glaucus, who merely nodded his thanks before turning away and holding out his wine-cup to a passing waiter.

XLVIII

'Sister, the time I foretold has come. Sit down by me and listen; we only have an hour or so.'

Cybele obediently left her weeding and sat down at Niamh's feet, her eyes wide with concern, but Niamh simply stroked the girl's hair, as one might calm a nervous pony.

'There is nothing for you to fear. Or for me, either. Indeed, the gods have been good to me and have given me back so many of the gifts that I thought had gone for ever.'

Cybele laughed with delight, but Niamh quietened her. 'Listen, sister. The gifts that the gods give are all granted for a purpose, even if we cannot tell what that purpose might be.'

She paused, then went on hesitantly. 'Within this hour the friends of that man Tetricus will search the meadow and find the trinket that fell from your neck, and then they will surely find the way to our secret place. Indeed, I have seen them do so – remember how I warned you that some of the pictures you will see in the divining bowl are of things that will surely happen, but others are of things that may be avoided. And so I must prevent them coming here, and to do that I must lead them far away. And I am very sure that I shall not return to you. But this I promise you, that they will not lay hands on me.'

Cybele's face was a perfect mask of horror. 'You're leaving me? Now? Alone. What shall I do?'

Niamh gave her a comforting smile. 'You will do as I have shown you. And what I have not shown you, the gods will show you in their own good time.'

Cybele looked down at her growing belly. 'But I'm going to have a child. How will I manage?'

Niamh smiled again and stroked her hair once more. 'It will be hard, but you will bring your son to birth and he will rise to manhood; this at least is ordained. You would do well to fear the pain and the loneliness, but at the end it will happen as I told you. But listen. For two evenings now I have watched you as you soar with the hawks and the kites; and now I must give you my last warning; heed it well.

'You ride the mind of the birds, and you look down at the world and its little people, and you think you have found freedom. But that is not the work you were brought here to do. Your freedom lies in choosing to do the work set out for you. As it does for all the world's people.'

But Cybele was almost in hysterics, clutching at Niamh's feet. 'I'll be alone. I've never been alone. Don't leave me. Let me come with you.'

Niamh watched her in silence for a moment, then softly wiped away the tears from her eyes. 'Child, I am old and you are young. For you to be left alone is the way of the world. You will grow used to it, and the pain will grow less though you will not believe that now.

'Dear child, you have your own task now, and I have mine. Be sure that we shall meet again, and know one another – and that sooner than you might think.' Suddenly tender, she bent forward and kissed Cybele on the lips, then put her hand on the girl's head in a final blessing, before adding, 'And now, dear sister, give me your blessing too.'

She bowed her head while Cybele stumbled through the words, then murmured, 'The gods will be with us both. Now I lay this charge on you, that you do not follow me. Is that too hard? Then sleep.' She lay her fingers on Cybele's eyelids and closed them, then rose easily to her feet, leaving the girl stretched out unmoving on the ground. She glanced around the garden for the last time, then stepped into the little beck and followed it into the larger meadow, before climbing up the fell-side until she was outlined against the sky. There at last she closed her eyes and sat down to wait.

It seemed to her that only moments had passed before she heard from below the bay of hounds and the shouts of men, confused and indistinct at first, but rapidly becoming louder and clearer. 'Tetricus' amulet. There's blood on it.' 'Witchcraft.' and then at last, 'There she is. At the top of the hill. There's the witch.'

At last Niamh opened her eyes. There were five men and perhaps half a dozen Agassian hounds, all straining at the leash, their voices raised at the sight of the quarry. She smiled and stood up, tall and untroubled, then set off at an unhurried pace down the slope behind her.

The gradient here was steeper, with tangled brushwood, bracken and brambles, but she walked through it easily. When at last she glanced around, the men and the dogs had cleared the crest behind her but were now tangled in the undergrowth and swearing with fury. She laughed, loudly enough for the men to hear her, then set off again across a landscape of broken scree and tumbled stones, always breathing lightly and with a grim smile playing about her lips. Only once did she look up, to see a great eagle holding station in the air above her; and seeing it she again laughed out loud.

Senorix rode easily, his head up, savouring the scents of the forest, pine mixed here and there with the sweeter odour of heather; the storms of a few days earlier had cleared the air, and the woodland was full of birdsong. A blackbird was singing its heart out, and he stopped for a moment to listen to it before shaking his reins and moving on.

A fine bird, the old blackie, he thought; there's no singer like it. The sweet notes continued as he turned off the road and down the broad track to the shallow ford where he had met Iatta's men two months earlier. As he had hoped, Iatta was mounted and waiting for him; but otherwise the clearing was deserted

It was Iatta who spoke first. 'I have news. The town is full of it.'

Senorix laughed. 'And so do I. But mine can wait. Tell me yours. But give me something to eat first; I've ridden starving the last day, and that's no pleasure for a man who likes his commons.'

Iatta pulled some bread and a crumbling honey-cake from his saddle-bag. 'You should look after yourself. Oh, and here's a sup of your favorite dram as well, from that carlin at the river-crossing.'

'Good man. Now, tell me your news.'

Iatta paused to put his thoughts in order. 'First of all, it looks like you'll have your wish. Most of the Ninth seem to be set on some sort of raid into Caledonia, though it seems that there's a cohort or two will stay in camp down south. And they'll have cavalry with them. They looked right bonny as they paraded through town, all pomp and trumpets. And the people all cheering and shouting for them.'

Senorix gave a cynical shrug. 'Rioting one day, cheering the next. And if our men had paraded through the next day, they'd have cheered them to the echo too. They like a good show, and they know better than to wear their colours on their sleeves. How long have we got?'

'Two weeks before they leave, I'd say. I'd think they'll take their time once they're on the march, taking it from camp to camp as they go. They'll have that young fool of a tribune in charge, it seems; the legate's been called away.'

Senorix scratched his head. 'Tribune? Remind me.'

'You've met before. Remember how you drowned his men on the Ituna Estuary?'

'Ah, the same fellow, is it? Perhaps he'll have taken the lesson on-board. No teacher like experience, eh?'

'That's not all. There's a couple of cohorts have come down from the north to join up with them. They're already in camp south of here, I rode past them on the way up.'

'Aye, you don't surprise me; I met some of them on the road a few days back. The lad's not going to go blundering into the unknown this time, then. So, all in all, a full legion with cavalry. Man, I've been waiting for this day since Mons Graupius. Anything else I should know?'

'Only that I've got your money back for you. No sign of that girl you're so keen on; seems she ran away and no-one knows where she's gone. I'd say you're well out of it.'

'That's a pity, now; I like to pay my debts, and the lass was worth every copper.'

He sighed theatrically, and then grinned as Iatta shook his head in wry amusement. 'Ah, you can laugh if you want to. Still, I have another debt to pay – in blood this time, and it's been waiting a long time. Tell me, how many mounted men can you give me?'

'That's more like it. In two weeks I can round up maybe three hundred, perhaps more. Not the best fighters, maybe, but then they've not had a lot of practice lately.'

Senorix nodded. 'That's good; I could find room for maybe fifty more, if you can manage it. And on foot?'

'An easy thousand, more if I can rouse them; but they won't all be well-armed; and it's not much fun facing swords and javelins when you've nothing more than mattocks and sickles to fight back with. And your black knife, of course, but you need to get close before you can use that.'

'And how many archers or slingers among them? At a guess.'

Iatta pursed his lips. 'Slingers – that's easy enough. Every lad knows how to use a sling. Of course, there's plenty can shoot, too, but spitting a roebuck for your dinner is one thing, facing up to a legion with their shields up and their spears out is a different kettle of fish altogether. That's a hard thing to ask.'

Senorix nodded. 'These horsemen – would they be good at running away, would you say?'

Iatta frowned. 'I hope they'll do better than that.'

'Well, I don't think I'll need them to. Think, lad, what is it we've done time and time again when we've been face to face with the legions? We've fought bravely enough for an hour, and then we've run away; and that's when they've slaughtered us. Think of Boudicca's lads trapped between the Fourth and their own wagons. Killed in their thousands, they were. And that old rogue Julius found that the Suebi did the same thing in Gaul, let themselves get cornered with no way to retreat. Well, that's one lesson I've learned – leave yourself with a good way out.'

He grinned. 'Did you ever watch a cat when a dog's after her? She'll run, sure enough; but she'll always retreat to a place that she can launch an attack from. A good lesson, that.

'Now, there are two big fords on the road north of here. I want both of them defended; small detachments of horse, not more than fifty or a hundred men in each. No brave last stands, though. Once they've shown the flag, they can just disappear into the forests. We need to tempt the enemy on, make them think that this is going to be a pleasant country stroll.'

Iatta nodded. 'And the rest of the men?'

'Send them up to meet me at the upper reaches of Bodotria. I have plenty for them to do before the Romans ever come close. I'll tell you what I've found…'

☙ ☙ ☙ ☙ ☙ ☙ ☙

For perhaps an hour the chase continued, Niamh always the same careful distance ahead and yet almost always within sight, the men and their dogs for ever struggling through brambles or boggy ground or scrambling up loose scree which slipped under their feet and threatened to send them tumbling into yet another morass.

And now at last, it seemed to the men that their quarry stood at bay. She had stopped at the very summit of a slope with a sharp drop behind her, and now turned to face them, apparently calm and unafraid.

And now the men paused too, certain that only a powerful

witch could have outpaced them so easily and suddenly nervous of what new power she might unleash.

For an untold time the hunters stood there irresolute, until at last one of the men, perhaps braver than his friends, urged the dogs on to attack their prey. They ran now, baying and belling over the open ground, mouths slavering, and at last the men found their courage and ran to follow them.

But while the dogs were still a spear's-throw away from her, Niamh looked up again at the eagle and let her mind ride it through the air and away, away to the glory of the sun. And her body fell back and vanished into the ravine, and was lost for all time.

XLIX

The formalities had been – well, formal. The currule chair had been set under the ancient oak, and Verica was already sitting there, apparently deeply immersed in reading, when Marius arrived, and she carefully had him wait until she was ready to take notice of him. Despite the warm summer's day, there seemed to be a marked chill in the air.

At last she carefully rolled up the scroll and passed it to Gwydion, who was sitting as usual on the ground at her side. The little maid seemed to be missing this morning; Marius wondered briefly where she had gone.

'Good morning, Commander. Do you have any news for me?'

'Nothing of note, my lady. Town and countryside alike are quiet and peaceful, for which we can surely both be thankful.'

'Of course. And now we have a whole legion here to enforce that peace. How fortunate we are. The famous Ninth, who distinguished themselves so splendidly at Verulamium and Mons Graupius. And Eboracum, too, as you no doubt know.'

For perhaps the first time in Verica's presence, Marius felt far out of his depth. He spread his hands deprecatingly. 'They will soon be gone, my lady. By the August Kalends they should be far away.'

'Ah yes, the kalends. He told me so, that legate you spoke so highly of. Why did he come here? I had nothing to say to him, and he bored me till I was weary of his endless jabber. Well, let him begone, and his men and his mules with him. And may he have joy of the kalends.'

'Your harvest festival, is it not? The tribune asked me about it, but I could tell him nothing beyond that.'

'Once again, Commander, Gwydion could tell you more than I can; but you are right. There are three great festivals in the autumn. The first is the August Kalends, when we celebrate the kindly first-fruits. The second is that time when night and day are equal; and the third is our new year, at the November Kalends. I seem to remember that we spoke of that some time ago. Like Beltane, the August Kalends are sacred to Lugos, who is the sun and who gives us all growing things; but as the wheel of the year turns, it is also the time when Urien and Blanaid begin to show the power of darkness and chaos. Is that not true, Gwydion?

Gwydion nodded. 'Indeed it is so, my lady; you have spoken well. Commander, I think that this, when the powers of darkness begin to spread their wings, might not be a propitious time for the legate's campaign. I told him as much, but do not think he was willing to hear me.'

'Neither he nor the tribune, it appears; but by the kalends, the legate will be well on his way to Rome and the tribune will be in sole charge. With two of my best men. May the gods keep him and all of them safe. By the way, my lady, I've had rather a roundabout instruction to ask you to give up that magistrate's chair; the legate thinks you're not entitled to it. For my part, I feel I have done my duty in passing on his message.'

'Ah, what a fine man he is to be sure. Nothing escapes his gaze. Truly a great leader of men. Know that this chair was once the property of the great Queen Cartimandua, presented to her by the imperial senate no less, and it has now descended to me as her foster-daughter. The legate seems to be lacking in both knowledge and courtesy.'

Suddenly she passed a hand over her face. 'But when all's said and done, it's only a chair. And a most uncomfortable one, it must be said. Let him take it, if he wants it so much.'

She sighed. 'Commander, for the first time in my life, this morning I feel old. Events seem to be slipping out of my grasp; it is not a pleasant feeling.'

Marius nodded. 'Things have changed in the last three months, my lady, and not in a way that any of us would have foreseen. When I met you here before the May Kalends, the worst we had to fear was that there might be trouble over the crucifixion of a pair of thieves. But since then, I have lost a century of my men, drowned not many miles from here, and more good men have been killed in the hills to the south-east as they marched to reinforce us. And now as you say we are near to the August Kalends, and I too feel that our troubles are not over.'

'And in that same time I have lost two sons, Commander. One has left me to lead a farmer's life in Italy – and he does not write. And as you know, the other has descended to serve Arawn in his kingdom of shades.' She added silently to herself, 'I sought him there, and in my dream it was you who took my hand to guide me through the gates of the Underworld and bring me back to life. Will you not take my hand now to save me in this waking world? Ah, but it was the lying gates of ivory through which you brought me.'

She gave a wan smile and shook her head. 'So I administer justice as our law has it, and I honour the gods, and I ask myself what of good remains in this world for me.'

'My lady, to serve the gods and to be just are all that anyone can aspire to; and at that last assize, those deeds will be rewarded, I have no doubt. But, my lady, you talked of giving justice as the law has it. Now, I know our own law well enough to pass judgements in such cases as come before me as *praetor*; but I am curious to know what judgement you would give in a case of debt.

'It seems that one of the townspeople has bound himself in debt to a banker – a money-lender, to be blunt; and now he cannot pay back what he has borrowed. Our own law is clear enough; at the end of the process, he and all his property are at the disposal of the lender, to do with as he wishes. Would that be your law as well?'

Verica shook her head. 'Commander, we had little truck with

money in the days when our law was created. A man might lend a ploughshare or an ox, or a slave maybe, and then come to me for redress if they were not returned as promised; and if the case were proved then the debtor would have to name a surety, who would stand honour-bound to see that the loan was repaid within a month. And if that were not done, then the surety would make good the loss himself.

'Our law was made for simpler times, Commander; but I would guess that this townsman of yours would struggle to find anyone to stand surety for him? Then our law can be no more lenient than yours. But still my heart goes out to him; for a free man – and his family as well perhaps – to be taken into slavery over nothing more than money is a troubling thought to me; I will consider if anything else can be done for him, though in truth I have little hope.'

'You are right, my lady, it is a troubling thought indeed; but the law expects that a man will have his eyes open when he walks into debt.'

He smiled. 'Then I think our business this morning is at an end, my lady; we should meet again before the kalends, and perhaps we shall have more news by then.' He glanced around at the garden, then added, 'When I talked of the events of the last three months, my lady, I forgot to remark on how well this garden has grown in that time; I would not have believed that such a thing was possible in these northern climes; it must give you great pleasure.'

Verica followed his gaze. 'It is indeed beautiful. Even at the worst of times, I take great pleasure in this fine house, this fruitful garden, and the words of the great poets and orators. What does Cicero say? *Si hortum in bibliotheca habes, nihil deerit,* is it not? With a garden and a library, nothing else is needful. How right he was.' And here I sit alone, she thought; does he not see that?

When Marius had gone, Gwydion caught Verica's eye. 'My lady, I can put a name to the debtor that the Roman mentioned; when Adeon and I were sent to find Senorix and bring him back here, we tracked him down to the tavern in the town; and the whisper is that the owner and his wife had borrowed deeply to buy the caupona, and then find themselves unable to repay the debt. I am sure that the man he speaks of is the tavern-keeper Bran; and his wife is called Morrig.'

Verica considered for a moment. 'Then he must repay his debt, or be in the hands of the lender; I think I can do nothing for either of them.'

But Gwydion was deep in thought. 'You remember, my lady, how the story of Urien and Lugos goes, and how it tells that the children of Branwen are alive to this day. Bran is of that line, and if my lore is true he is the last of Branwen's descendants living in this land; and he has no children, and is not like to have any.

'My lady, by all accounts the man is a weakling and a fool, and in thrall to his wife. But even so, the last of an ancient line should not be left to die as a slave.'

'An ancient line? Gwydion, we are all children of the great oak-tree that the gods fashioned into men and women long ago. What was I? Nothing but a poor farmer's daughter, turned Queen by fortune – ill fortune, it sometimes seems to me. Think of Iras, a foundling child brought up in my court, who will no doubt one day marry well. Which reminds me – is the girl ill? She waited on me this morning as she should, but I have not seen her since.'

'I shall look for her, my lady; she has not been herself since she let Senorix escape. She will surely not have gone far. And Bran?

Verica sighed. 'One of the tasks of a Queen, it seems, is to rescue fools from their folly. You may go to him tomorrow and see what help you can give; but be careful that this money-lender does not catch you in his toils.'

Marius let the cob trot easily back to the camp and let his thoughts roam free. Dying – now, dying is nothing; it comes to all of us. But suppose we were to know beyond doubt that a day or two after our own death, Deucalion's Flood were to come again, and this time not even Pyrrha and Deucalion himself were to be left alive. Then there would be nothing left of us in this world, no-one to inherit anything after us, and nothing left for us to do in our remaining time but to count the hours and days until we too 'come where Tullus and where Ancus are.' And to think I never used to like Horace.

Isn't that her case? The gods have cast her adrift, alone, while petty fools like Gracchus try to belittle her and snatch at her dignity. And me? Oh, a comfortable pension of course, enough to buy a little farm and live out the rest of my time in comfort; but still alone, counting out the hours and days as she does. Still, 'Thaw follows frost...'

☙ ☙ ☙ ☙ ☙ ☙ ☙

Anand closed the door of her cottage behind her and looked up at the darkening sky. Messalina was already sitting on the riverbank, staring up at the first stars.

'Another fine day. Good it's a bit cooler, though. You tired? You should rest.'

Messalina nodded. 'Yes, Mistress. Should I get you something?'

Anand clucked like a mother-hen. 'Silly girl. Not your mistress, remember. Free now. Free to look at the stars, where the gods live. Most of them, anyway. Now, see that.'

She waved at the great band of the Milky Way, slowly emerging into view as the night deepened. 'Caer Gwydion, that is. Two great castles in the heavens: Caer Arianrhod, up there to the north, and Caer Gwydion, stretching across the whole sky to reach it. See everything from there, the gods do; whole world is like an arena to them.'

Messalina sighed. 'It must be wonderful to be a god. Or a goddess, of course.'

Anand grunted. 'Not what it's cracked up to be. Most things aren't.'

'I never knew much about them; but I heard that Urien and Blanaid have come back to earth. Have you ever seen them?'

'Maybe. I see all sorts of things. Nasty pair they are, going around making trouble. We can do without them. Huh. I could tell you stories.'

'My friend talked about them to me; the one I was telling you about, the one who owes me money. He said that when they'd come, they'd make us free. And now I am free, so they must have come and it's all true.'

'Girl, there's free, and then there's free. Means whatever you want it to. Now who's that?'

And indeed the deep silence of the evening was broken by the sound of someone paddling up the river. Anand stood up and stared downstream, then whispered. 'You've got better ears than me. Hear anything? Too dark to see anyway. Best keep your voice down.'

Messalina shook her head, then jumped to her feet in panic. 'It's my old master. I'm sure it is. He's come for me.'

'Stuff and nonsense. No-one knows you're here. Still, best go back indoors and keep quiet. It's far too dark for him to recognise you, even with the lamp lit.'

Anand made to push the girl into the cottage, but she hung back, peering into the gloom and listening intently. Mixed with the splash of the paddle there was a voice now, muttering drunkenly.

'It is him. I know his voice. Hide me. Please.'

'In the house. Quick. And don't speak, in case he hears your voice. And remember, your name's Brigid now, not Messalina. Go now.' Anand shoved her into the cottage and pulled the door closed, then retraced her steps to the edge of the bank. The shape of the man could be clearly seen now, pulling his coracle up onto the riverbank and making a terrific noise about it; once he lost his footing and almost fell into the water. But at last he turned from the river and climbed the bank, moving on all-fours. Only when he had reached the top did he stand up.

'Anand's voice rang out. 'Stay there. I've got a knife. One step closer and I'll cut your throat.'

'I fell asleep while I was fishing. The town gates will be shut, they won't let me in. Let me sleep here, I won't hurt you.'

Anand considered, then relented a little. 'Come closer, where I can see you. Yes, I know you. You're forever fishing in the river. Catch anything?'

'Salmon and sea-trout. I'll give them to you.' Bran stumbled back to the coracle and lifted out the two fish, then scrambled up the bank again, holding them in front of him like a shield.

Anand looked at them critically, then nodded. 'Take them as payment. Wait here. Get you a dram of something warming, then you sleep in the barn.'

She disappeared into the cottage with the fish and came out a few moments later with a beaker in her hand. 'Here, drink this down. Best poteen there is for a good night's sleep.'

She watched as Bran downed the liquor, then watched as he slouched into the barn, and waited until she could hear his snores. Finally she called Messalina out to her.

'He's well away now; gave him some of the same stuff that I gave you – never fails.'

She motioned Messalina into the barn, and pointed at Bran, lying spreadeagled on the straw. 'Little beauty, isn't he? That the bastard who had you branded? Here's my knife. Want to slit his throat?

L

In the first light of false dawn Anand dragged Bran's coracle up the bank; then she and Messalina carried his limp body out of the barn and laid it in the little craft, confident that they were unobserved in the thick morning mist.

Then Anand stood up stiffly, put her hands on her hips and took a deep breath. 'Gods, he's heavier than you'd think. I couldn't have done that on my own.'

She shook her head and went on, 'Why didn't you kill him when you had the chance? One quick cut and it's all over; and he'd be none the wiser till he woke up in the underworld.'

But Messalina was still getting her breath back and said nothing. At last she bent over the sleeping form and looked at it closely. 'It wasn't him that had me branded, it was my old mistress. He used to slap my bottom a bit, but he was never cruel like she was. He doesn't deserve to die.'

'Girl, he turned you into a whore for anyone with a few coppers. Still, blessed are the merciful for they shall be shown mercy.'

'Who said that?'

Anand gave a cynical grunt. 'No god you've ever heard of. Left to myself I'd have done for him then and there. Now, let's see what the gods have in store for him. Tide's well on the turn, we'll just let him float out into the firth; by the time he wakes up he'll be far away. If the gods are as merciful as you are, he'll come to shore somewhere safe – if not, then so be it.'

'When he wakes up, won't he remember coming here?'

Anand shook her head. 'Not properly, not after what I gave him. Be like a dream; come on, let's get him on his way.'

The women slid the coracle and its cargo easily down the bank and into the river, then stood watching as it spun gently in the current, then moved slowly out of their sight.

'Good riddance to him. Come on, girl, let's have that salmon for breakfast.'

Morrig swept the floor, smashing the besom against the tables and benches in her fury and muttering curses under her breath. 'First the stupid girl runs away, then that fool of a husband disappears, and I'm supposed to do everything myself. Sweep the floor, serve the customers, make my breakfast, fetch the water, empty the piss-pot, put up my own hair, throw out the rubbish. And wait for that money-lender to show up and take it all away from me. Curse him and everything he ever did.'

Still muttering, she clumped up the stairs and came down moments later with the chamber-pot in her hand. She dragged the door open, looked up the mist-shrouded street, and tossed the contents into the gutter. Then she picked up the big ewer and strode out into the street, pulling the door shut behind her.

Despite the early hour the little forum was already busy with slaves and slave-girls fetching water. Grumpily Morrig joined them, making sure that none of them came close enough to touch her. At last she filled the jar at the fountain, hoisted it onto her hip and turned away.

It was then she saw the girl – hardly more than a child – huddling against the wall of the caupona. Her predatory instincts were suddenly alive: well-dressed, but out here on her own – out here all night, perhaps. A runaway, for sure, and from a house that wasn't shy of spending money on slave's clothes. Controlling her excitement, she walked slowly over to the girl and bent solicitously over her.

'Are you all right, my dear? This is no place for someone like you.'

But the girl shied away, like a puppy that fears another whipping. A slave for certain. 'It's all right, my dear, I shan't hurt you.

Why don't you come with me and I'll get some food into you. How does hot porridge sound?'

The girl looked anxiously around, but finally stood up slowly. 'Come on, it's not far. We can get on very well together, you and me. You see, I'm all alone too. Oh, I must remember my manners. My name's Morrig. What's yours?

The answer was so quiet that Morrig had to ask for it to be repeated; but when she had heard it at last she smiled and said, 'Iras. That's a lovely name.'

☖ ☖ ☖ ☖ ☖ ☖ ☖

Senorix looked up at the looming bulk of the great crag and wiped the sweat from his face. All around him the first of Iatta's promised battalions were hard at work clearing the brushwood from the upper reaches of the wooded hill, while others were dragging the rubbish clear and heaping it up in two great piles.

'Great work, lads. Remember, I want all the decent branches kept separate, and the bramble and suchlike all together. And no cutting within a stone's throw of the bottom of the hill. I want it to look as uninviting as possible.'

Satisfied that the work was being done satisfactorily, he set off across the water meadow, watched by the curious long-horned cattle. Around the meadow the river flowed in a long, easy loop; but before he was more than half-way across the ground became marshy, and the mud sucked at his feet as he walked. He counted his paces to the brink of the river itself, then pulled off his boots and began to wade across, still tallying as he went; by the time he was half-way across, and with the water reaching almost to his waist, the current was threatening to pull him off his feet, so he turned and retraced his steps.

'Deepest on the other side of the loop. Fastest, too. But sodden wet long before you even reach the river.' He sighed. 'How many men can I afford to lose here? Will they take the bait? By Belenos, I wish it was all over.'

He was still probing at the wet ground with his bare feet when he became aware that he was not alone; in front of him was lounging a man in prime middle age, with a young lad – perhaps his son – standing a little further away.

Senorix looked carefully at the man: big-boned, red-faced, and with well-muscled arms showing beneath his tunic. His right hand was holding a massive hammer, which he hefted easily as he stood with his legs firmly planted in the wet ground. A blacksmith, thought Senorix, and probably pretty handy with that hammer.

When he spoke the man's voice was a rumble which carried a distance in the still air. 'I came here to fight Romans, not to clear hillsides. I don't do farmers' work, and neither does he.'

He pointed to the lad, who was standing in the same posture as his father, though the look on his face was rather less belligerent. Around the pair, Senorix noted, a growing knot of men had come to watch what happened.

Senorix smiled indulgently. 'And kill Romans you shall, man. But I'd like to send you both home alive at the end of the day; so we'll do it my way while you're here.'

'And what's the way of an old goat like you? Running away and bleating? I'll fight in my own way and use my own good cracker.' He tapped the head of the hammer threateningly in the palm of his left hand, then folded his arms defiantly.

'Old?' said Senorix, as if the thought were new to him. 'I suppose I must have learned a lot of ways to stay alive, then.'

He shrugged amiably and half turned away. Then with a lightening flick of his body he landed a merciless kick between the blacksmith's legs, and as the man toppled forward he brought down his right fist in a vicious rabbit-punch on the back of his neck.

In a moment the man was lying face down on the ground with Senorix kneeling on his shoulders and with his left hand twisting both the smith's arms high behind his back. With his right hand he forced the smith's face into the muddy ground and held it there.

'I can keep you there till you choke. But I'd rather send you home alive, and your lad with you.'

The man's legs flailed wildly, but Senorix held his position. 'Don't think about it, lad,' he warned the son. 'Your dad's a fine fellow, and I'm sure he'll come round to my point of view in a moment or two. Unless he'd rather I stifled him, of course.'

He pulled up the smith's head by the hair and went to, 'Or I could break his neck, if he prefers. It's easier than you'd think, and he wouldn't be the first.' Then he pushed the man's face back into the mud and held him there until at last he lay still.

At last Senorix stood up and hauled the smith back onto his feet. 'Fight Romans? You can't even fight an old goat like me. But you're strong enough, I'll grant you that, and you're heart's in the right place. Now shake my hand. And then get your face clean.'

Shamefaced, the smith grasped Senorix hand, then pulled him quickly off balance. As Senorix went down, the smith was above him in a moment, one leg drawn back for a kick. But the kick never came; Senorix was already sitting up, a broad smile on his face and his silver-chased dagger pricking his opponent's genitals.

'Fine lad you've got there. Knows when to stay out of things. So if you don't need the gear in your kecks to make more like him, just kick me and see what happens. You might enjoy singing with the lassies, but by Toutatis you won't be doing anything else with them. Now, shake my hand properly and have done with it.'

He stood up and laughed, then clapped the smith on the back. 'Don't know when you're beaten, do you. I like that in a man. Now, if you're a smith like I'd guess I have a special little job for you. And the rest of you can get back to work. Unless there's any-one else who'd like a tumble with this old goat.'

☙ ☙ ☙ ☙ ☙ ☙ ☙

Iras looked wide-eyed around the main room of the Eagle. 'Don't worry, dear, there won't be anyone here for a while yet. My cus-tomers aren't early risers. Now, you sit down and I'll get you a nice cup of mint tea and some porridge. And then you can go up and have a nice sleep in my own bed if you want, you look exhausted.'

She bustled into the kitchen, poured fresh water from the pitcher into the kettle and blew up the fire. 'Won't be long, love.' she called over her shoulder, then went on, 'It's a rough old town, this. Pretty young thing like you, you need to be sure you're not going to get hurt.' *Where did she come from? Is there a reward for her? Or shall I just grab her and put her to work? Quiet little mouse, I could easily force her. And the customers would pay well for a new girl. Ah well, hasten slowly as they say.*

Whistling cheerfully she carried out the steaming porridge and a beaker of hot mint tea, but Iras was already asleep, leaning back against the wall with her head lolling to one side. Morrig shook her gently, then swore under her breath. But as she went to shake her again the door opened and Glaucus stepped in, with Amicus at his elbow.

Morrig looked at them, ashen-faced. 'He's not here. And I don't know where he is. He's not been home all night.'

Glaucus shrugged. 'I've got a *libellus conventionis* here; that's a statement of claim.' He waved the tablet in her face. 'Normally I shouldn't have to serve it myself, but it seems they're too busy up at the camp to look after the affairs of honest businessmen. Amicus, see if you can find him – try upstairs, then round the back, and round the town after. And when you find him, bring him here; you can use as much force as you like.'

Morrig opened her mouth to protest, then realised that it would be pointless. As Amicus clattered up the stairs, the banker sat down on one of the benches. 'We can wait. All day if necessary.'

He gestured at the sleeping Iras. 'And where did she come from? Been laying out the cash, have you? Better quality than I'd expect to find in a dump like this. Fancy clothes. Face like a pan of milk, though.'

A sudden thought occurred to him. 'Virgin, is she? Why don't

I take her off your hands? If that husband of yours doesn't show up, perhaps we could come to a deal, just you and me? Cut my losses. Think about it. I'll be waiting outside.'

He stood up, picked up the bench and carried it into the street, then sat on it with the air of a man who had nothing else to do all day.

Bran slowly came to his senses and sat up groggily, nearly upsetting the coracle and tipping himself into the water. A thick heat haze had come down, and the little boat seemed to be floating in a featureless expanse in which shore and sky were both invisible.

He tried to gather his senses. He'd been fishing – he vaguely remembered making a catch – and then he must have gone to sleep, lulled by the heat and the motion of the waves; but now the water was a dead calm, and the pearly light made it impossible to tell if it was morning or afternoon. He dipped an experimental hand into the water and raised it to his lips: salt. He must be well out from the coast.

He looked around the coracle and saw that the fish had gone, and the paddle was missing too; he could do nothing but drift aimlessly on the surface. He shouted for help; but the haze muffled the sound of his voice, so in a panic he called on every god whose name he could remember. And finally he began to cry in sheer terror.

LI

It was early afternoon when Gwydion found Verica reading in her private chambers and bowed to her. She looked at him quizzically and noticed that a subtle smile was playing around his lips.

'So, Gwydion, you went to meet Bran? And by your smile, it seems you were successful?'

Gwydion considered for a moment and then shook his head slightly. 'Not in every way, my lady, and yet the gods directed me to a good end, and my labour was not altogether lost.

'I must begin with Bran. I went back to the tavern where, you will remember, Adeon and I found Senorix. But Bran was not there, and it seems from what his wife told me that he hasn't been seen for a day or perhaps longer. She told me that he often spent time fishing, though from the way she said the word I suspect that she really thinks he has another woman somewhere.

'Be that as it may, it seems certain that he has either run away where the money-lender cannot find him, or has perhaps suffered some mishap.'

'And his wife? This must be sad news for her?'

Gwydion smiled again. 'Her name is Morrig, my lady. In truth I think that she would be glad to see the back of him. Indeed, I found her in high spirits, as if a load had been lifted from her mind. At first I thought it was only because her husband had vanished, but she was so full of her news that it all tumbled out whether I would hear it or no.

'It seems that in the morning early this money-lender and one of his muscle-men came calling, waving a formal court claim and asking for Bran; but, of course, she could tell them nothing about his whereabouts. Such men, of course, will not usually let that stop them – I hear that they think nothing of taking any property they can lay their hands on as settlement, and will use any necessary violence to achieve their ends. But now, my lady, with a whole legion encamped south of the town and the people nervous of what the next month may bring, they seem reluctant to resort to such measures.'

'Then the whole claim will surely fail? If the debtor has not been summonsed according to their law, then the *praetor* will dismiss the case, will he not? And the *praetor* here will be Commander Marius, who I am sure will act justly.'

'That is true in law, my lady, and I am sure that the moneylender knows it; but seeing that his claim might go unanswered, he found another way to recoup his losses, as he thought. And it was that that made the lady so cock-a-hoop.

'It seems that shortly before the lender turned up at her door, she had taken in a young girl that she found homeless on the street. I think there was no kindness in the deed, only that she saw there might be some advantage to her in it; and, indeed, before the morning had run its course, she had sold the girl on to the lender in return for his sworn and witnessed note that the debt was cancelled.'

Verica frowned in puzzlement. 'Gwydion, you cannot mean that she took it on herself to sell this girl – whom she did not own and of whom she surely knew little – in order to clear her husband's debt?'

'Indeed, my lady, that is just what she has done, and she boasted of it to my face, as if she had scored a great triumph. She waved the lender's note of settlement in front of my eyes. So that's an end of that, she said, and that little slut Iras will find life getting a lot harder. That'll teach her to show up here sponging off honest working-people.'

Cold horror ran through Verica's veins. 'Iras! What was she doing there? How can this have happened? We must save her!'

'She is safe already, my lady. I have left her in the garden here, hanging her head in shame and embarrassment. You remember how we missed her and no-one knew where she had gone? It seems the silly child had run off looking for Senorix, who you remember had turned her head with his smiles and winks; he had even kissed her for letting him out of the postern gate. Of course when she could not find him she was so frightened that she dared not come back. Who knows what might have happened to her if Bran's wife had not happened to take her in?

'At all events, I searched quickly through the town and found the banker ready in his cart to take him and his latest acquisition away to the south; and sitting there in the cart was poor Iras, frightened out of her wits but otherwise unharmed.

'I challenged him at once, as you can guess. That girl, what are you doing with her?'

'New goods,' says the banker, with his eye on a quick profit. 'Not much to look at, but I can let you have her for a decent price.'

'She's no slave, said I, but the Queen's free servant. Abduction is a serious crime; you could be flogged in the market-place for this. The whipping post in the forum is ready for you.

'That soon changed his tune, my lady; he could hardly throw her out of the cart quickly enough. But I cancelled a debt for her, he says. Then you made a poor bargain, I told him, and left with Iras before he could think of a retort. And it was on the way back that I winkled out her story of how she had gone looking for Senorix.'

Verica shook her head with relief. 'I shall see that the silly child is corrected. Don't worry, Gwydion, I shall be gentle – I think she has suffered already. And wherever there is trouble, it seems that Senorix is somewhere at the back of it. But Bran's wife; she must be punished, surely. What she did was evil. What does our law say?'

'That compensation should be paid to the girl's father, my lady; but Iras has no kin, being an orphan and reared as your free servant. But under the law of the Romans, Morrig would be as guilty as the banker, and like him would be whipped.'

Verica nodded. 'Then I will make sure that such a case is brought against her. At least some justice will be done.'

The haze showed no sign of clearing, and Bran drifted alone and lost in his tiny cockle-shell of a boat, at the mercy of the uncertain wind and waves.

Nothing to eat, nothing to drink, lost in the middle of the sea. How long have I got? Quicker to go over the side now. All be over then. By all the gods, what a mess I made of everything.

He leant over the side of the coracle and dipped his hand into the water. It was cold. He pulled it back, shivering uncontrollably, and imagined the chill creeping up his body, soaking his clothes, a great weight pulling him down into the unspeakable depths.

The sea. That was where the giants lived, and where the great sea-god Manannan ap Llyr had his home. They called the haze that surrounded him Manannan's cloak, drawn around the coasts and islands to hide them from sight. He shivered again and felt the god's presence close about him, bringing not comfort but only a greater terror.

I won't die now he told himself. I'll live. Somehow I'll come to land. There must be land somewhere near. The gods won't let me die, won't let my bones be picked clean by the crawling things at the bottom of the sea.

But the hours seemed to pass without any movement of the boat, without any change in the pearly light. And so, at last, utterly drained of every feeling, even of fear, Bran prepared to die.

Once the decision was made, the rest was easy. He tensed himself, muttered a last prayer to Arawn, and jumped into the water. The coracle bucked as he went, then drifted away beyond his reach. That's done it he thought. I'm dead now for sure.

But drowning was harder than he had expected. His body fought against the water, forced him spluttering to the surface, thrashing wildly. He opened his mouth to scream, convulsed as water flooded into his lungs, and then finally surrendered to the blissful darkness.

Gradually he became aware that he was lying on hard shingle. He retched, vomited water from his stomach, tried to clear his lungs, then lay down exhausted. At last his body went into a hard spasm, voiding clear liquid from his chest; now he could catch his breath and raise his head to look about him.

The haze had cleared, and he was lying just above the reach of the waves on a little beach. In the evening light he could make out only trees, growing almost down to the edge of the beach, bearing a fine early crop of…

…apples. Ynys Afallen – The Island of Apple-Trees. The Isle of the Dead, some called it. So it was all true.

There was the sound of hurrying footsteps on the shingle, and he sensed rather than saw someone bending over him. A voice called, a woman's voice. 'He's alive. Help me lift him up.'

Strong hands pulled him to his feet, but as soon as they let him go he collapsed again to the ground. More cautiously this time they helped him first to his knees and then at length lifted him upright. Two women, dressed in white. Spirits, to be sure.

At last Bran was able to see them clearly. They looked alike, both with a quiet beauty and the same reddish tint to their hair, which they wore long down their backs – sisters, perhaps, with no more than a year or two between them. How should one talk to the gods? Would he have to confess all his misdeeds? Could he even remember them all?

He hesitated, trying to find words that would be both pious and respectful, but when he finally opened his mouth all that came out was, 'So I'm dead.'

To his amazement the older girl lifted her eyebrows in surprise while the other burst into peals of laughter. 'Dead? For sure you're not.' She laughed again, her eyes twinkling with merriment. 'You must be a very wicked man if the sea-god won't take you.'

Now both girls took him by the elbows and led him gently away. The older had an air of tranquillity about her, but the younger was happy to chatter. 'Come, you must meet our father.

He'll be so interested to see what the water's thrown up today. And what's your name? I'm Branwen.'

LII

AD XVI Kal. Aug. – July 17th

Morrig bustled around the Eagle, planning a carefree future for herself. No debts any more, and no husband either as far as she could tell, and now the tavern and the caupona next door, neglected for weeks, were hers and hers alone.

He might come back – she thought briefly about the possibility, then dismissed it from her mind, certain that he had gone off with his imagined girl-friend at last and wishing he'd gone years ago.

Or course, there were things that she would need before she could make the Eagle a success again – a little whore to keep the customers happy, that was the main thing. A shame to let that little bitch Iras go, but it was worth it in the end. She'd find another soon enough, there's plenty of little beggar-brats around. And after all, she'd feed them and clothe them, so they'd be better off there than if they were dying on the street.

She looked up and smiled as the door banged open and two soldiers from the camp walked in. Early customers, she thought, but instead they took her by the arms and pulled her out into the street, ignoring her protests.

'You've been summonsed. The *praetor's* waiting.'

At that she went willingly, certain that the wretched banker was behind this again, sure that she only needed to show his letter cancelling the debt and all would be in order once more. She put up a hand to straighten her hair, wished that she had washed her face more carefully – how hard it all was, without a slave to fetch and carry.

Marius had had a space cleared of stalls in the centre of the forum, not far from the fountain. He was sitting on a plain camp-stool, with a small retinue of soldiers clustered around him; a scribe was waiting by his folding table to take a record of the proceedings, and the curious townsfolk were already clustering around. Justice, as always, was to be done openly, and Morrig relished the thought of public vindication. Head held high she shook off her escorts' grip and walked confidently forwards, then bowed low.

Marius nodded in return, then spoke formally. 'The court is now in session. Your name for the record, please?'

Morrig answered, then added, 'I'm afraid my husband isn't here, your honour; he disappeared a few days ago and I don't know where he's gone.'

Marius raised an eyebrow in apparent surprise, then went on, 'I have here a formal complaint from Queen Verica that you were involved in the attempted abduction of one of her maids, a freeborn girl named Iras. This is her written charge.' He held out the tablet, then asked, 'Can you read it, or do you need someone to read it to you?'

Morrig felt the blood drain from her face, but managed to answer. 'I can read it for myself, your honour.' She read the charge aloud, prompting gasps from the nearer watchers, then handed the tablet back hardly believing this was happening and wondering why the wretched girl didn't say anything.

Marius took the tablet and handed it to the scribe, who carefully copied the details down. When he was certain that had been done, Marius turned to face Morrig again.

'This is an extremely serious charge; selling a free woman into slavery counts as abduction, and would certainly leave the victim vulnerable to all sorts of other abuse, including rape – doubly serious in this instance as the Queen claims, as you have read, that the girl Iras was a virgin. That she remains so is, it appears, no thanks to you.

'You are not a citizen, and so I could simply announce a summary verdict. However, Rome stands for justice and so the court will hear your own version of events before coming to judgement.

However, I must warn you that your oral evidence would not normally be allowed to prevail over a written claim, unless you are able to bring witnesses to confirm what you say or unless you are in a position to make a written counter-claim.

'Now, take your time and tell the court what happened.'

Morrig felt her throat tighten; her right hand was beginning to shake uncontrollably, and she pressed it against her side to stop the trembling.

'It's just a misunderstanding. Your honour, I went out for water from the fountain in the morning, our girl had run away so I had to do it myself. I saw her there, poor lamb, all alone on the street, looking so frightened. Your honour, I couldn't just leave her there. Anything could have happened to her.

'And I could tell that she was a decent girl in trouble, she was smartly dressed and ever so quiet and polite. So I took her in, I took her back to the tavern – there weren't any customers there, it was too early, so I knew she'd be safe. She came willingly. I never forced her to do anything. Anything she did, she did quite freely.

'And she was so tired that she went to sleep right there, just sitting on the bench in the Eagle. I went and made her some nice peppermint tea and got her some porridge, but she was so tired she didn't even notice. And then I stayed with her while she was asleep, to make sure she was safe. I didn't do anything bad to her, I swear by all the gods.'

Marius signalled to her to wait while the scribe wrote down her words; he was using Tironian notes, but still needed a few moments to catch up. At last he looked up and nodded.

'You can go on now. What happened afterwards? According to this complaint, you passed her on to a man named Glaucus, who calls himself a banker, as payment for your husband's debt. What do you say to that?'

'Your honour, that was all my husband's fault. If only he was here, he'd tell you so. Nothing to do with me. It all happened after our slave-girl ran away.'

'Don't prevaricate. Now tell us all quite plainly what happened between you and this Glaucus?'

Morrig's heart was thumping so strongly she was certain that Marius could hear it; behind her in the rapidly growing crowd she could hear some men whispering, placing bets as to whether she would be acquitted, while someone else, who clearly thought he was a legal expert, was loudly explaining the procedure to anyone willing to listen.

'Glaucus, yes, of course your honour. Sorry, I've lost the thread of what I was saying.'

Marius nodded. 'Madam, calm down and take your time. Now, had you met this Glaucus before?'

Morrig grabbed at the straw. 'Yes, your honour, of course. He used to come by quite often, but sometimes he sent his associate. He's called Amicus.'

The name raised a snigger in the crowd, but Marius was unmoved. 'He came to drink? To use a woman? Or what?'

'For money, your honour, though sometimes Amicus had the girl instead if my husband didn't have the cash ready. Your honour, it was all my husband's fault. He'd borrowed money and was having trouble paying it back.'

Marius nodded. 'And this Glaucus came to me and swore out a statement of claim against your husband, and then rushed round to serve it himself instead of decently waiting for a bailiff. I presume he called on you almost immediately?'

'Yes, your honour. Your honour, he lied to me. He said you'd refused to send a bailiff.'

Marius shrugged. 'I note what you say, but of course Glaucus is not on trial here today, and you are. Do go on – did you come to some arrangement to make him go away?'

Morrig was desperate now. 'Your honour, I'm a poor woman running the tavern on my own. My husband has disappeared, gone off with his fancy-woman I think; and my slave-girl ran away too, though we treated her like our own daughter, gave her the best to eat and fine clothes to wear. She lived better than we did, your honour.'

This drew a disbelieving laugh from the spectators, but Marius pointedly ignored it. 'I will repeat the question: did you come to some arrangement to make him go away?'

Morrig looked around, all her neighbours were clustered about her, watching intently. Trapped at last she tried to put the best construction on what had happened.

'Your honour, I was all alone in the tavern; anyone might have come in and harmed the poor girl, and I wouldn't have been able to stop them. Glaucus told me that he'd look after her, he said she'd be safe with him. Your honour, she went willingly. I swear; no-one laid a finger on her, not me or Glaucus, or Amicus either.'

Marius waited until the scribe had finished writing, then steepled his hands in front of him and considered. At last he spoke.

'I accept what you say, that no physical force was used to put the girl into Glaucus' power. But did he give you anything in return for her? Money, for instance?'

'No, your honour, he never gave me any money. Not a penny. I did what I thought was best for her.'

Marius nodded, then produced another writing tablet and held it up. 'I have here a further deposition from the harpist to Queen Verica, a gentleman and a Roman citizen named Gwydion. Read it please.'

Morrig took it in her shaking hand and read it aloud; when she came to the part where Gwydion asserted that she had shown him the letter cancelling Bran's debt, her voice fell into silence. But Marius insisted that she should continue.

'…and she showed me a letter from the said Glaucus, cancelling the entire debt owed by the said Bran.' Her voice was dry and Marius had to lean forward to hear her words.

'So there at last we have the truth of the matter, I think. From what I've seen of this Glaucus, a man who rushed off to deliver his statement of claim without waiting for the bailiff, he would not go around cancelling the debt out of pity or good humour, but only in return for some valuable commodity; and the commodity in this instance was the girl Iras, was it not?'

Morrig shook her head but said nothing; around her the crowd was waiting for the inevitable verdict with quiet anticipation, while someone who had lost his bet on the outcome was already counting out his forfeit.

Marius stood up. 'The court considers that the charge is proven. You will be whipped as a punishment for you and a warning to others who may think that abducting young girls is an easy way of getting out of their financial difficulties. Centurion, strip her and whip her.'

For a moment Morrig was unable to speak, then as her gleeful words to Messalina *some men like watching that kind of thing* of a few months earlier came unbidden into her mind she screamed 'No. Not here. Not in front of everyone. No.' But Marius was unmoved, and in moments the centurion had torn Morrig's tunic from her to the accompaniment of whoops and whistles from the crowd.

She had half collapsed on the ground in terror and humiliation, trying desperately to cover her breasts and her genitals, but he pulled her up and dragged her over the cobbles to the whipping post and tied her hands high over her head, forcing her onto her toes. In a daze she kept reciting the same words over and over again, as if they were a charm to keep her safe. 'Not me. It was my husband's fault, it was the slave-girl's fault. Don't whip me. Whip them.'

Then as the first blows fell she began to scream, wordlessly at first, then yelling, 'Stop, stop, you're killing me, I can't stand it.' But the centurion kept on, carefully working the ox-hide whip down her back and her buttocks as the blood began to flow and drip onto the ground, each fresh blow bringing a raucous cheer from the crowd.

After thirty vicious strokes she slumped unconscious and the screaming ended. Marius signed to the centurion to stop, then said, 'That's enough. Cut her down. And let that be a lesson to everyone.'

With the bonds released, Morrig fell senseless to the ground; the watchers gathered round her now, and a man spat on her face, though another more kindly fetched a bucket of water from the fountain and poured it over her, then gently laid the ruined tunic over her to hide her nakedness.

As she slowly regained consciousness those nearest her could hear her still muttering the same words over and over: Not me. It was my husband's fault, it was the slave-girl's fault. Don't whip me. Whip them.

✙ ✙ ✙ ✙ ✙ ✙ ✙

Anand found Brigid sitting on the doorstep of the cottage, her hands clutching her stomach.

'You all right? What's up?'

Brigid turned a pale face to her. 'I'll be fine. It's just my monthlies; they only came on a couple of months ago, and I'm not used to them.'

'Couple of months? How old are you, girl?'

'I don't know; fifteen, perhaps, maybe sixteen. No-one ever told me.'

'Girl, you were put to whoring far too young. And out of it just in time, I'd say, or you'd be farrowing bastards every year.'

She sat down by Brigid and cradled her head in her arms. 'It'll pass. Things do. And don't worry about your old master and mistress any more; no more trouble from that quarter.'

'How do you know?'

Anand looked uncomfortable, then shrugged. 'Female intuition, call it. Look, you've got blood on your tunic; get yourself another from my chest; bring your old one too. We'll need to find you some blood-rags as well.'

When Brigid came back, Anand was listening intently with a hand raised to her damaged ear. 'Hear that? Soldiers coming. Hark to them tramping. Quick, give me that thing you had on, I'll wash it.'

Anand took the blood-stained tunic to the river's edge and had just begun to swill it in the stream when the advance-guard appeared, heading northwards. She paused to watch them, aware that behind her Brigid was watching too and probably waving at them, but she remained unmoving while cavalry, soldiery and finally the baggage-train and rear-guard went past. At last when the road was quiet and the dust was settling she turned back to her washing, and then lifted out the wet tunic and draped it over the bushes bordering the paddock.

'Dry fine there. All done.' She shook her head almost regretfully. 'All done indeed. Poor bastards, not many of them'll come back. They'd have known that if they'd seen me washing off the blood in the stream.'

A feeling that something was happening that was utterly beyond her understanding flooded Brigid's mind. She shook her head and finally asked, 'Anand, who are you?

The older woman gave her a piercing look, then grinned. 'Once they'd have called me the Watcher at the Ford. But then the buggers spoiled it and built a bridge, didn't they?'

LIII

There was no reason to hurry. The promised triremes weren't expected at the mouth of the Bodotrian Firth until the August Kalends, still almost two weeks away, so the progress of the Ninth into Caledonia could be measured and cautious. Gracchus sat back at the entrance to his tent and watched with pleasure as his men set about the well-ordered business of refurbishing this old marching camp.

Even so, he was starting to ask himself if he was being more careful than necessary. After three days on the march, they were still only forty miles or so from their starting point, and so far they had encountered no resistance at all.

But they had been busy, nonetheless: one deserted marching camp twenty miles to the south of them had already been reoccupied, the fallen ramparts restored, and half a century left as a temporary garrison, with a good *optio* in command. When they moved on from the current camp in a day or so, they would do the same again. Stronger garrisons would have been better, he admitted to himself, but the land seemed peaceful enough, and he knew that he would need as many men as possible once they reached the upper reaches of Bodotria – the push down-stream in that carefully planned pincer-action with the sea-borne troops, that was the main course, and he wasn't going to spoil it with an over-elaborate *gustatio*.

No resistance? Actually that wasn't quite true, he confessed. Just a few miles back they had had their first encounter with the enemy, though it was hardly a proper battle. He lifted the wine-cup to his lips and took a sip, then laid it down again as he reviewed the action.

He had sent out scouts, of course, carefully probing the territory ahead. He could still conjure up the scene when two of them returned, warning that ahead of them there was a wide clearing in the endless forest, with the road crossing a shallow ford on the far side before rising up the flank of a great hill. And the ford, the scouts had warned, was guarded by a strong party of armed natives.

And so he had done it by the book, horribly aware of how easily he could be ambushed in this dense forest. First he had brought up the bulk of his men into the clearing and set them to guard his flanks, and then ordered the rearguard to take up a defensive position along the line of the road. Only when he was certain that his defence was sure did he finally ride out himself with only a single centurion – that new man, Eburnus – as companion to investigate.

He had reined in a long bowshot from the river and surveyed the scene. From the scouts' report he had expected that there would be archers or perhaps slingers, but none seemed to be in evidence. There were, he estimated, perhaps fifty riders on the far side of the ford, mostly on native ponies though one or two had better horses; every man of them was wearing Roman armour, no doubt looted from some earlier outrage, and they all carried lances and long native swords.

I have to get this right. What have I forgotten? What will they do when I attack? My flanks and rear are secure, what can go wrong?

He ran through the options in his mind. We'll ride them down with the cavalry; a wedge-formation should do it, and follow them up with the troops in the vanguard if necessary, but I won't commit them right away. And so he had given his orders, and so it had happened, as smoothly as a hot knife sliding through butter. The Caledonians hadn't even stayed to fight; the moment they saw the cavalry riding towards them, they had turned tail and galloped away, whooping as though they had won a victory.

The cavalry had been a nuisance, though; he'd ordered the *cornicen* to sound the recall as soon as the ford was cleared, but in the thrill of the chase the horsemen had taken their time about returning. That was something that would have to be sorted out before the next encounter, if there was one.

He took a deep draught of wine and chuckled to himself as he remembered how easily the victory had been won and how foolish his fears had been. Will they try it again? There's that big ford where the road crosses the Clutha, which we should reach tomorrow. Well, at least we know they're not up for a fight with proper troops. Cowards, the lot of them.

♛ ♛ ♛ ♛ ♛ ♛ ♛

Huctia stood by the bread stall, one hand firmly in the grip of the baker's wife and her rag doll tucked under her arm. Her other thumb was stuck in her mouth. Exhausted by the journey, she was beginning to get tearful and fractious; at last she took her thumb out of her mouth to ask, 'Why's Daddy so long? He said he'd be back quickly.'

'He won't be long, love. He'll be back as soon as he can. You've been such a good girl, come and have a treat – you can choose whichever one you want.'

Huctia wiped away her tears with a grimy hand, then stood on tip-toe to pick a cake from the baker's stall, her fingers hesitating over the various delights on offer. At last she plumped for the biggest sweetmeat she could see and pushed one corner of it contentedly into her mouth.

She was still chewing away when Bris came back round the corner and squatted down in front of her. 'You all right, chick? Got yourself a present, did you? Did you say Thank you like a good girl?'

Then he shook his head dolefully. 'You were right, it's all locked up, no sign of life. What's been going on?'

The baker's wife looked meaningfully at him, then turned to

her husband. 'He'll tell you. You've missed all the excitement, you have.'

The baker smoothed his hands on his apron and gestured towards the locked caupona. 'Couldn't make a go of it, could he? Went missing a few days ago, his wife reckoned he'd run away with another woman, but I don't think he had enough spirit for that. Who'd have any spirit left after being married to that old shrew, that's what I'd like to know. Saving your presence, dear. Then someone said that yesterday morning his boat – that old coracle he used to go fishing in, you remember – it turned up on the beach miles from here; no nets, no paddle, no gaff and no Bran either.'

He lowered his voice. 'Some people think that he went and drowned himself. I'm not so sure.'

He tapped the side of his nose conspiratorially. 'I think it all got to him and he went mad and forgot who he was and everything, and just went wandering off all crazy. He could be anywhere. Shame he missed the big event, really, it would have done his heart good to see it.'

He dropped his voice even lower and pointed to the whipping post. 'His wife got what was coming to her at last, just three days ago. Stripped naked and beaten till the blood ran, and all for kidnapping a poor little chit of a girl and trying to sell her to some Greek fellow. I tell you, the whole town turned up to watch and cheer. Jupiter, the backside on that woman, never seen anything like it!

'And her girl ran away, as well. You remember her, that cute little tart Messalina. A lot of lads are missing her, I can promise you.'

He glanced at his wife, and went on, 'Not everyone's happily married, like me.

'Sorry, I'm not making much sense, I'm telling the story all backwards, the girl ran away first. And no-one's seen much of Morrig since the whipping – she slunk out of town the same afternoon, and good riddance to her I say. Shame about the Eagle, though, we could do with somewhere round here to have a drink and a dice-game with the lads of an evening. And I used to get a lot of business from you when you were running the caupona. So, anyway, what made you come back?'

'Mother died, all of a sudden. Hale and hearty one day, felt a bit under the weather the next, and then that night she just popped off in her sleep. Mind you, she was getting on a bit, but even so. Huctia was in hysterics for days after that, frightened to go to sleep in case she died too. Anyway, I laid on a decent funeral for the old lady, took stock and decided to come back. All my old friends are here, after all, and Mother's place seemed so odd without her in it. I thought we could stay at the back of the Eagle for a day or two till we got settled; even after I'd paid for the funeral I've still got most of the money I got when I sold the caupona, I thought I'd be sure to find a way to get by. Now I'm not so sure.'

The baker tapped his nose again. 'Why not force the latch on the caupona – that's what I'd do. No-one'll stop you, we'd all be pleased to see you back there. Course, if Bran turns up out of the blue you'll have to tell him you were just looking after it for him. But between you and me, I think we've seen the last of the pair of them.'

He hesitated, then suggested, 'If you can get some help, you could try to open the Eagle again too. Why not give it a go? Give me somewhere to rinse my throat when the flour gets in it.'

☙ ☙ ☙ ☙ ☙ ☙ ☙

The fires could be seen for miles, but there was no helping that; and at least the smoke was helping to keep the midges away. The upper part of the wooded hill had been cleared of underbrush, and most of the the brambles and thorn bushes were rapidly being reduced to ash, with the remainder carefully woven into an impenetrable barrier all along the base of the hill. Behind that barrier, the lower branches of the trees had been lopped down, so that a rider could gallop down and clear the thorny fence at one jump.

Senorix prowled round with a broad smile on his face. In the shade of the trees the smith and his son were working busily together, bending long iron nails carefully harvested from old Roman signal towers together to make caltrops and stacking them in a pile, only breaking off from time to time to shoe a horse or sharpen a dagger; and perhaps four-score men were hard at work laying a low hedge of cut branches the length of the water-meadow and a good bow-shot away from the track. All around was the bustle of preparation as thousands of others sweated at sword or archery practice, and rehearsed simple drills with spear and shield.

Senorix looked up at the sound of hoof-beats, then relaxed as Iatta cantered into view, reined his horse to a stop and slid quickly down.

'They're on their way. They left camp three days ago. Not that they seem to be in much of a hurry. I've had men shadowing them, and the fords are guarded as you said. I'd say we've got three or four days before they get here; is that enough?'

Senorix whistled. 'It's a bit tight, but we should make it. There's good hard work going on here, it's a fine set of lads you've got me.' He slapped his face. 'Blasted midges. The smoke helps, but they still bite. What the blazes were the gods thinking of when they made them?

'Now, we'll need to get a better guard on the road; I've posted a lookout a few miles south, but I've tried to keep as many of the men as I could working up here. I've got about three thousand all told, about five hundred of them mounted, and I suppose we'll be facing about five thousand, but we can work the terrain to our favour, and that should even the odds. By Taranis, I certainly hope so. I've been promising the lads that they should be safe to go home afterwards, and I'd hate to be wrong about that. I want Roman blood on my hands, not our own fellows'.'

Iatta looked at the activity and nodded. 'Good to see them working so well; no clan troubles? Some of those fellows would cut their neighbour's throat as quickly as the enemy's.'

'We sorted it. Afterwards they can fight among themselves as much as they like. If it all works, there'll be plenty of booty for them to scrap over, and if it doesn't then they'll have other things to worry about.'

'And where will you go afterwards? I'm all right, I've got a wife waiting for me, a nice little assart carved out of the forest, and a nephew who fancies himself as a harper to sing about what a hero I've been; what else could a man want? But you? You won't go back to trading cattle, that's for sure.'

Senorix slapped at another midge, then turned away. 'Not thought about it, really. Just wanted to have this one big chance, and to do it properly; and when it looked as if the gods were on our side, I thought we'd go for it. Now I wonder if Blanaid and Urien were really there when we celebrated Beltane; I suppose we'll find out soon enough.'

Iatta smiled to himself and slapped Senorix on the back. *And he still hasn't said what he wants to do afterwards. I'll have to watch him, or the fey mood will take him and he'll get himself killed for no reason.*

LIV

AD XI Kal. Aug. – July 21st

To Gracchus' secret relief, the night had passed quietly, disturbed only by the challenge and counter-challenge of the sentries patrolling the ramparts of the marching camp. Apart from the single encounter at the ford a few miles back there had been no sign of the armed insurgency that he had been expecting and, to be honest with himself, had been rather hoping for. No doubt it would be all very well to harry a few villages along Bodotria, take slaves and hostages and generally ensure that the name of Rome was properly feared, but something more martial would certainly not come amiss, and would serve him well in his future political career.

That business on the Ituna still rankled; like a fool, he'd allowed the guide to lead them all by the nose, and had been helpless as his men drowned or fell under a hail of missiles from the slingers. He remembered Commander Marius' words before he'd set out – 'Take the auspices, it always heartens the men.'

That, he now realised, was the problem right there. To the commander it seemed that taking the auspices was just one of the endless little tasks that needed to be done, like filling in troop and expenditure returns for Eboracum; and that was how it had been done, no more than a quick and comforting ritual that made you feel better when it was over.

Not that he thought the commander was an impious man, of course; there had been that altar that he had commissioned and paid for himself, after all. But how could a sensible man set out on any serious course of events without taking great care to ensure that the gods approved of it?

Now, under his command, it would be done properly. He owed it to his men, after all. Not, of course, that all of them would see it like that; the legion was bound to have some followers of the Mithraic mysteries. There might even be some Nazarenes, though he rather hoped not; it was the hypocrisy of that cult that particularly infuriated him, the way that some of them would refuse to burn as much as a pinch of incense to the Divine Emperor while others would cheerfully swear him allegiance and serve in his legions. Their loyalty, it appeared, depended on whether they were being paid or not. You could understand it of Greeks, but what a way for a free Roman to behave. Bunch of unprincipled bastards.

And so, as every day, they held a full parade before setting out, with the sacred chickens in their coop brought out for all the men to see, and the *pullarius* tossing bread and cake-crumbs onto the ground in front of them. His relief at seeing the birds rush out to peck at the food must have communicated itself to the men, because they started to cheer and laugh at the sight. And then the birds actually began to perform the *tripudium*, the sacred dance, flapping their wings, rushing around in circles, taking up the food and then letting it fall to the ground. There could hardly be a better omen.

And so the parade dismissed, the men hurrying to break camp, load the mules and find their places in the line of march, certain that divine favour was guaranteed, at least for this one day.

☙ ☙ ☙ ☙ ☙ ☙ ☙

'The ancients used to say that *gwyddbwyll* represents life itself, my lady, with all its trials and tribulations reduced to a board and a set of playing-pieces.'

Verica looked up from setting out the pieces on the board with a smile. 'Perhaps. But all the challenges in gwyddbwyll are over in an hour or less; the others take – well, a lifetime. But the first game was mine, and now we must see if I can win the rubber. I shall have fewer pieces now, but at least the advantage of the first move.'

She turned to Iras, who was sitting cross-legged on the floor watching the proceedings. 'You must learn the game, girl. You would do better to spend your energies on playing this than on running away after Senorix. Come, see how we play.'

Iras blushed scarlet, but Verica affected not to notice and went on with the lesson. 'See, here in the centre is the king on his throne, guarded by his loyal friends just as I am by mine. And around the edge of the board, these pieces are his enemies, who wish to capture him and in doing so win the game. We move in turn – the king first, as is only right – and any piece can move any number of squares in a straight line, provided only that they cannot move corner-wise or to a square which has another man already in it.

Iras studied the board for a while, then nodded. 'So the king has to avoid being captured?' she ventured at last.

'Just so; and to do that he must find his way clear to the edge of the board. That can be a hard battle, and many men will fall before he either succeeds or fails. For if any man is trapped just between two enemies, then he is captured and taken from the board. It is harder than you might think – here, if Gwydion will let you take his place we shall play slowly, you and I.'

But before Verica could make her first move, the major-domo scratched gently at the door and then stepped silently into the room and with a bow handed Verica the tablet which he was holding. 'A letter, my lady, brought here only a moment ago. The superscription shows it is from your son.'

At once the game was forgotten. 'And I said that he did not write. And yet his letter was already on the way to me. May the gods forgive me the injustice of my words. Quickly, open it.'

But the string holding the tablets closed had been sealed with rather more wax than was perhaps necessary, and it was some time before the major-domo was able to unpick the knot. At last Verica opened the leaves and began to read aloud, exclaiming delightedly, 'And, by all the gods, he has written in Greek.'

Lucos to his dear and noble mother greeting. Know that I am in good health as are all those who came with me. The gods of our people and of Rome have favoured me greatly and by their kindly office the Senate have granted me a pension and land not far from the great city of Mantua. Dearest mother you will know that the immortal Vergil himself was a Mantuan and his fame is still great hereabouts.

Know also dearest mother that I have agreed to marry a girl of Senatorial family descended from C. Valgius Rufus. Her name is Priscilla though she is most often known as Prisca. Like you my dearest mother she is a great lover of books and of gardens and she has given me much joy as indeed I hope you will be joyful at my news.

Dearest and most noble mother I entreat you again to leave wet and foggy Britannia and to come to this most fair country where the vines and olives grow in great profusion. The only sadness in my life is that you are not here to share in my pleasure…

Verica broke off her reading and closed the leaves with a snap. 'I shall read the rest later. At least it seems he is not asking for money, or not yet. And now there is something I have to do.'

And with that she walked purposefully into the garden; but when Gwydion looked up some time later, she was sitting upright and motionless by the fountain, her right hand trailing in the water, and with her eyes closed.

☙ ☙ ☙ ☙ ☙ ☙ ☙

It was going well, the men singing their hearts out and the sun just warm enough to cheer the spirit. On the road led, straight as an arrow on its strong embankment through the forest, the trees cut back for a bowshot on each side, though here and there undergrowth was beginning to encroach on the cleared area. Have to get the men to deal with that later, he thought no hurry now, though.

And then, with no warning, out of the forest to the left came the unmistakable call of a Roman *cornu*, a patter of notes that lasted for only moments before it faded into silence. Then, away to the right, an answering call on a *buccina*, repeated time and time again before it too finally ended with a loud single blast.

Gracchus felt the hair prickle on the nape of his neck. He nodded to Marcus Asellio to keep trotting on, then nervously reined in at the side of the road, letting the rest of the vanguard and the first ranks of the main contingent march past him. The singing had died away now, and the men were eyeing one another in puzzlement; Gracchus noticed that some of the veterans were fingering the hilts of their Spanish swords.

Quickly he spurred back down the line, calling as he went to every centurion to redouble his vigilance; but there were no more trumpet calls, and at last he galloped back to resume his place in the vanguard.

Twice more that morning the calls were repeated before they reached the ford of the Clutha: a *cornu* first, on the left, then an answering *buccina* on the right. Are they keeping pace with us, whoever they are? How can that be possible in this wild forest? Is this witchcraft? He filed the thoughts away in his memory, and felt relieved when at last the road emerged from the trees into a wide plain, with the Clutha winding across it, still a fairly young and shallow stream rather than the great river that they said it became in its later course. Even wider than the Ituna before it meets the sea, came the unwanted thought.

A thin column of smoke rose up a mile or so to the west, marking the huts of a native village on the far side of the river, and he could see fenced fields of barley and rye, and small black cattle grazing on the banks.

And, just as he had anticipated, the ford was defended: perhaps fifty horsemen again this time, with lances and swords, though still with no foot-soldiers among them.

I've seen this before, but I won't take it for granted. The cavalry can ride them down, but I'll still safeguard my rear and my flanks first. What do they think they're playing at?

As before, Gracchus took his time over the disposition of the men, carefully consulting with Marcus Asellio before he took any action. Then, with the baggage-train brought up and well-defended and both flanks carefully covered, at last he had the cornicen sound the charge, and watched with delight as the auxiliary cavalry galloped forward in tight formation.

But this time the enemy seemed about to try a different tactic; when the cavalry had covered perhaps half the distance to the ford, the enemy suddenly lowered their lances and mounted a counter-charge, advancing in a long line that quickly resolved itself into a crescent shape capable of attacking the auxiliaries on their flank. But that too was only a feint; with a sudden loud whoop they turned tail and spurred back across the ford, shouting and cheering as they went.

If they were Parthians, he thought, they'd turn and shoot at us as they pretended to flee, but these barbarians don't have any tricks at all; they just run away. No guts, no backbone.

Around Gracchus the men were roaring with laughter and yelling catcalls and mock challenges at the enemy, who were clearly high-tailing it to safety. At his signal the *cornicen* sounded the recall, but once again the cavalry had their blood up and were in no mood to return.

Remember what you were taught. Cavalry is like a ballista bolt: treat it as if it were a missile that well-aimed can scatter your enemy to the four winds, but once you have fired it, it has gone for ever.

No matter. He led the cheering centuries over the ford and drew them up in ranks on the far side, though still in a careful defensive formation. And then at last he could ride up and down the ranks, enjoying their plaudits; somewhere in his head he could almost hear them shouting *Imperator.*

A dangerous thought. He put it out of his mind. 'A good morning's work, lads. And you'll be rewarded for it.' He waved his sword at the little village. 'There are the people who dare to stand up against Rome. There are the men who ride out to challenge the power of the Divine Emperor. There are the women who practise spells and witchcraft. To the sword with them. To the sword with them all.' From the corner of his eye he caught a glimpse of Marcus Asellio's stony face, then shrugged and put it out of his mind.

LV

'Most of the women and the smallest bairns had hidden before the soldiers arrived; just the men and the lads were left. No-one had a chance, of course – the soldiers rounded up everyone they could find and killed most of them on the spot. Then they burnt the place to the ground, slaughtered the livestock, fired the fields. The mighty power of Rome.'

Senorix shook his head. 'The Ninth reverting to type, it seems, Iatta. I've seen it before, in the country round Eboracum, long before you were born. This won't be the end of it, either; there'll be more villages burnt, more men and women killed, more farms destroyed. Nothing changes. *They make a desert and call it peace.*

'And Verica would blame me for it. What was it she said? Sow the wind and harvest the whirlwind? Something like that anyway. I hope to all the gods that it won't be me that the whirlwind strikes, Iatta. Now tell me, what else have we learned?'

'He's no fool. He's careful; defends his flanks and his rear before taking any action, and takes time to make sure that he understands the lie of the land. Then it's been the cavalry both times. And he's careful not to let down his guard afterwards; he won't be an easy nut to crack, my friend.'

Senorix nodded. 'I never thought he would be. We caught him with his kecks down once, he won't let it happen again. And think of the advantages he has: experienced officers, hardened men, better weapons, greater numbers. And what do we have? Only this place that we've chosen. Iatta, we've thrown the dice twice and won each time, but the stakes were small enough. Do we dare throw again? Or shall we take our little winnings and go home? It's not too late to do that. Iatta, for the first time since Mons

Graupius, I feel we could lose.'

'Quit now? Then the killing and the burning won't stop, my friend. Other villages will go up in flames, all the way from here to the sea; crops will burn, the young will be slaughtered or enslaved and the old will starve. Better fight. By nightfall tomorrow they'll be here. Be ready to meet them.'

This place is mine. It was an unfamiliar thought, but Cybele was beginning to relish it. She looked round the little garden with pleasure, sensing the life flowing through the plants as they stretched up towards the dawn sun.

On a sudden thought she fetched the wooden bowl – my bowl now, she thought – and dipped it into the stream, filling it to the brim with clear water, and wondering if she could see the pictures in the bowl again. And so for the first time since Niamh had left her, she carried it carefully to the shadow of the cliff and bent over it, watching for movement in its depths.

The vision came quickly: a deep forest, with tall, unfamiliar trees spreading in every direction. Then, as if in a dream, she found a path through the wood and followed it as it twisted and turned between the ancient trees, always heading upwards. At last the trees were left behind and she was standing alone on a bare hill-top.

And then she was not alone; another woman was there, standing a few paces away and looking into the distance. At last she turned to face Cybele; and she was Cybele's own image, but somehow at once both older and ageless.

She smiled, and in her vision Cybele found herself kneeling before her, but the woman stretched out both hands and raised her gently to her feet. In the silence that followed, Cybele felt rather than heard the words: 'You were named for me, but I have many names beside Cybele. I am Astarte and Selene and Artemis, and many more. You are welcome here.'

'The witch-goddess of the woods?' Cybele blurted out the words, then blushed red.

The woman laughed. 'She called me that, did she not? Niamh, named, as she owned, for the light. The unchanging, burning light of the sun. And you and I are named for the soft, changing moon, now nothing, now a crescent and now a full orb. I am the eternal maiden; you, child, will soon be mother; and there is the third, dressed in black, that I shall not name.'

'Why am I here?'

'Because you offered a sacrifice to me by one of my other names, many changing moons ago: lamb fat, burned secretly in a lamp, where none but the gods would see.'

A memory flashed into Cybele's mind of a life that she had almost forgotten. 'My master was going to whip me for that. He thought it was evil magic.'

The woman in the vision shook her head sadly. 'These are women's mysteries, and men do not understand them. So they call them Witchcraft and Evil at the same time that they acknowledge their power. Through all the ages to come, these secrets of the Bona Dea, the Good Goddess, will be hidden from them.'

She smiled, and the hillside below them was suddenly wreathed in light. 'Have you seen trees like these before?'

Cybele shook her head. 'No, never. Not when I was awake. But perhaps in a dream once?'

'They are cypress; they are sacred to me, and to the dead.'

A sudden suspicion formed in that part of Cybele's consciousness that was not immersed in the vision. 'What is this place? Is it real?'

'It is real – in your mind. You may rest here when you have need; and from this hill-top, you can see far. Now I shall leave you; walk freely.'

Alone again, Cybele wandered down from the hill-top and was soon back among the trees. They grew close together, and the air between them was green and warm; where the grass failed, the earth was red and soft. As she walked, her mind ran back to the time when she had stood in the market-place, one slave among many, offered body and soul to anyone with enough coin. Did I mind? Not really; that's how the world is. Better that than to starve in the gutter. Then his steward came, poked at my breasts and stomach, pinched my arms, pulled back my lips to see my teeth. 'How much do you want for her? Does she speak Latin? No, that's too much, she's not worth more than half that.' Then they spat and shook hands, passed over coin, gave and received a note of sale. Owned. And a strange house, full of soldiers, with an owner who hardly noticed me except as a household drudge and an occasional whore.

A brief picture of her one-time master passed across her mind. Sometimes he was kind. He gave me wine once; then he had me, right there on his table with the dinner-dishes still around. I could have died of shame, but he didn't notice. And now I will have his child – his son, Niamh said – and he will never know.

Cybele suddenly remembered how she had run away – without purpose, but unseen – and then had walked day after day along the river-side until the great stones had drawn her. The woods had been alive then with bird-song and the perpetual scurrying of small creatures, and once there had been that face, half-glimpsed in the leaves – indeed, half-made of leaves. Strange. There are no animals or birds here, she thought. And then, as if the vision had been waiting for her imagination or memory to bring them to life, the air was suddenly full of the liquid notes of a thrush, a cuckoo was calling somewhere in the distance, and a rustling in the undergrowth spoke of little lives hiding as she passed.

And then Niamh found me – came looking for me, and was sharp with me because she had been waiting for me. And so I became her slave, beaten with a hazel-switch if I was slow to understand. But she taught me well, and I shall always think kindly of her. Niamh's face drifted into her mind, but her features were already beginning to blur in Cybele's memory.

Her walk had brought her back to the bare summit of the hill, and she somehow felt sure that any path she had chosen would soon have returned her to this same place.

What had she said? 'From this hill-top, you can see far.' Cybele stood on tip-toe and looked around, but as far as she could see the cypress-wood stretched level and unbroken in every direction. She shook her head in amazement: 'I, bargained for and sold in the market-place, now walk with gods. But for all that, I still have to milk the goats.'

The sudden memory of the every-day made the vision fade, and Cybele looked around and found that she was back in her garden, and the sun had risen no higher in the sky.

'Cybele.' Marius woke with a start and sat bolt upright in bed. The dream had been so real that he felt he could slip back into it; but even as he tried to remember it, the urgency began to fade.

He shouted for Flavius, who came in almost at a run, his face full of concern. Marius waved a hand to calm him. 'No, I'm fine. Flavius, I've seen Cybele. In my dream. Flavius, she's dead, I know it. Fetch me some mint tea, I'll tell you all about it.'

By the time the tea arrived Marius was already dressed and felt calmer; but the reality of the waking dream was still strong in his mind. 'You remember how she just disappeared, walked out for no reason? They looked for her everywhere, but there was no sign of her, just a couple of rumours that we couldn't trace.

'Well, girls like that go missing every day, with their heads turned by some stupid fairy story; they all think there's some Parthian prince waiting to rescue them and set them up in their own palace. Mostly they get kidnapped by some trickster and palmed off into the nearest brothel; either that or they run right away and get killed by a bear or a wolf. *Damnatio ad bestias*, Flavius, just for running away. Not that I wouldn't have tanned her back-side if we'd found her, of course. Stupid child. What did she have to run away from? Plenty to eat, an easy billet – there's plenty of freemen wouldn't mind having it so good, I can tell you.

'Something like that must have happened to her, poor wretch. But there she was in my dream, just like in life, but walking through a cypress-wood. Cypress, Flavius; isn't that what the Mysteries tell us? That there are tall cypress trees on the left hand as you enter the nether-world, and many others about?

'And in my dream she looked at me, Flavius, and her face was sad. Flavius, when the dead return they have some message for the living. Go quickly, fetch Acestes the augur; do it as quietly as you can, I don't want the men to think there's anything amiss. But keep what I've told you to yourself; not a word to anyone.'

☙ ☙ ☙ ☙ ☙ ☙ ☙

Brigid's screams brought Anand running. She sat by her, cradling her head, stroking her hair. 'There, there, nothing to be afraid of, it was only a bad dream. Hush, chicken, mother Anand's here and you're safe with her.'

Brigid stared wildy around. 'It was horrible. The soldiers. It was so real. And it went on and on. The blood, Anand, all the blood. And men and boys running and crying, and swords and fire and…' She broke off into loud racking sobs, pressing herself hard into Anand's arms.

At last the terror eased and she drew away and wiped her eyes with her hand. 'I'm sorry, that was silly of me. I don't usually have nightmares, I don't think I ever dream much at all. I'll be all right now.'

Anand stood slowly up, and now Brigid noticed for the first time that she had put away her usual black. 'Anand, the red suits you. You look so much younger in it.'

☙ ☙ ☙ ☙ ☙ ☙ ☙

The augur was grave – Marius had always assumed that his placid demeanour was part of his stock-in-trade, intended to inspire the men with confidence before a battle, or to assure them of the goodwill of the gods when they established a new camp. But this was different: Acestes was more careful, more meticulous than Marius had ever seen him before.

How long had the dream lasted? Had there been any other dream before it? Had he ever had such a dream before? And Cybele – had he been dreaming of the forest of cypress trees before she appeared, or had they and she appeared together? What had she been wearing? Was she standing to his right or to his left? Or in front of him? Had she spoken? Did she seem as if she wished to speak but could not, for everyone knows that the ghosts of the dead have no voice?

Marius answered the questions as well as he could, but found himself becoming more and more confused. But the augur was unabashed. No matter. Your confusion is to be expected. You were right to call me. This could be most serious. And then he turned again mumbling to his scrolls, keeping his place with his forefinger and muttering the words so low that Marius could not hear them.

At last he finished, rolled up his scrolls and piled them on the floor, then nodded in self-satisfaction. 'Commander, it is most unusual for a man in your position to dream of a slave-girl in such a way; or perhaps it would be more accurate to say that it is unusual for a slave to appear to her master – her former master, in this case. As is well-known, the gods send us dreams to warn us of dangers that may befall, so that we may be fore-armed against the perils that face us, or at least so that we may bolster our courage to face the inevitable. The foreboding dreams sent to Calpurnia on the night before the killing of her husband the great Julius are a matter of historical fact, for instance, and even the impious Nazarenes have tales about the dreams sent to the wife of the Prefect Pilatus in Judaea some years later.

'The case here seems to be this: that the most high gods have permitted this girl to appear to warn you of a great peril. But, Commander, she is not dead. I can understand how you would jump to such a conclusion.'

He chuckled to himself, then went on, 'That is the danger of a mere amateur attempting to understand these matters, if I may say so. Of course you saw the cypress trees and the rest seemed obvious to you; but no, Commander, she is only dead to you. You will not recover her – you must reconcile yourself to that. She is in the service of the gods themselves, and is far beyond your reach. But from time to time she thinks of you, as you no doubt think of her – though perhaps neither of you would be pleased at the other's assessment.

'And so she has sent you a warning of danger. Oh, she may know nothing of it; she is merely the channel through which that warning is sent. Heed it, Commander. And as she was close to you, so the danger is from those close to you. I can tell you nothing else; but if you should chance to dream of her again, be sure to recount the details to me before your memory fades.'

'If there is danger, should we not take the auspices? It would be better to know more, surely?'

Acestes hesitated. 'Commander, that is a decision for you to make; but I would not recommend it. Taking the auspices is a public matter – that is how this most ancient of arts retains its high status. We augurs speak the truth as far as we can see it, and do so in the most open and public of places: in the great Senate of Rome, in the Roman Forum, in the arena before the Games – and also before soldiers, assembled together to fight Rome's wars and to defend the Eternal City, whose everlasting imperial power was guaranteed to the good Aeneas so long ago.

'It is true that there are augurs who demean our craft, who forecast what some client – or some politician – wants them to say. No doubt the Sibyls at Cumae or Delphi were also subject to what we may call pressure. But true augury, Commander, tells the truth and tells it openly, so that with the passing of time every citizen can see how truly the augurs spoke.

'Now, let us suppose that the auguries are bad, either for your own men here or perhaps for the valiant men of the Ninth. Then everyone will know, and the effect on morale might be considerable – and yet it would be beyond your power or your orders to do anything to help. Indeed, if the auguries are bad, then taking precipitate action to make them of no account could be thought of as impiety. Commander, the gods dispose, and we must obey their will.

'Or suppose that the opposite is true, and that the auguries are good. Then would the men not wonder why you had ordered them to be taken? And so again doubt would creep in, and fear perhaps with it.

'So, Commander, my advice is this: guard yourself well; set a double watch; burn incense daily at the camp altar and at the temple of Mars Victor; and do it all in such a way that it will occasion no surprise or alarm. And be mindful of your dreams in future.'

LVI

It was a dream, a waking dream. What else could it be?

From this hill-top, you can see far. For two days the strange words had echoed through Cybele's mind, and so in the last moments of sleep before waking she found herself again standing on the bare hill-top with the dark cypress trees spreading unbroken to the horizon.

Except that now she looked more carefully, the trees were not cypress any more, but ancient pines. *How could I have got that wrong? Is this really the same place as before?* As she scanned the scene below her she suddenly noticed smoke rising from a clearing some distance away. *Are there people there? Or gods?*

With the same dream-logic that had changed the cypress-trees to pines, she found herself in the clearing, watching a group of eight men gathered around a table; and the clearing had somehow grown large enough to contain a whole marching camp, and she sensed that there were hundreds of other men bustling about their work on the edge of her vision.

After a moment she concentrated her mind on the men sitting around the table – *weren't they standing a little while ago?* – and let her eyes pass slowly from one to the other. Soldiers, every one of them, and all in uniforms of the sort she had seen day after day *before I ran away.* But she didn't know any of them.

With a sudden start she realised that wasn't true; there was one face that she knew very well. Marcus Asellio. *My old master's friend. But he can't see me.* And at one end of the table there was another familiar face, the face of the tribune who had laughed at her when she talked about the sacred stones, but whose name she had forgotten. *Why are they here? Who are the other people?*

Why can't I hear what they're saying? For they were clearly talking animatedly, pointing to what she now saw was a map on the table, measuring distances first with their hands and then with a folding bronze yardstick and a pair of dividers just like the ones they had in her old master's house.

In the dream she moved effortlessly around the soldiers, peering over their shoulders; but the map meant nothing to her. And then there was another woman with her, a woman – and she had to look twice to see that it was true – who had the face of Niamh.

Then the dream-Niamh looked at her, held her eyes for a long moment; and spoke in words that came directly into Cybele's mind. 'So you have found this place already. That was well done. I told you we should soon meet and know each other. Did you ever doubt me?'

'You're alive. I thought you must be dead.'

'I am as real as I ever was, sister. I told you there was nothing to fear.'

Cybele digested the remark in silence. 'And the goddess told me that this place was real – in my mind. Is all this just in my mind?'

The dream-Niamh shook her head. 'The men you see are real, but they cannot see or hear us; to them we are at most *idola* – wraiths, if you will, less substantial than the mist.'

'Why are we here? What will happen?'

The dream-Niamh smiled sadly. 'We are here as the proxies of the gods – their representatives, if you will. You must remember what I told you: the gods desire blood, and soon they will have their fill. We are both witnesses to the will of the gods and their agents.'

Cybele shook her head. 'That can't be right. Why just you and me?'

'No, sister; there is always the third; you must remember that.

'Think of the great world that the gods made – always there are three: there is earth, ocean and sky; the great lights in the heavens are sun, moon and stars; here, I am the maiden, you will soon be the mother, and then there is the other that I will not name.'

'The other?' And then Cybele saw that there was indeed a third there, an old woman dressed in a black cape, though as Cybele looked more closely she saw to her surprise that her clothes shimmered with red. The newcomer – though now Cybele thought that perhaps she had been there all the time unnoticed – bowed low first to Cybele and then to Niamh. And then, with a start, Cybele was fully awake.

♕ ♕ ♕ ♕ ♕ ♕ ♕

Gracchus looked around at the little group, met in what he was starting to think of as a Council of War; that term seemed to invest a particular significance to the mission. 'As far as I can see, gentlemen, we should reach the upper reaches of Bodotria at noon or a little later. We'll clearly need to establish a significant presence in that area; would it be suitable for a long-term camp?'

One of the centurions shook his head. 'Too wet; it does dry out sometimes, but it was pretty soggy when we marched south to meet you. And the thing to remember about wet places in Caledonia is that they're all plagued with midges.'

Gracchus raised an eyebrow. 'Thank you, Gaius. And you think that legionary troops would be afraid of a few insects?'

'I tell you, sir, it's like being condemned to the arena, only instead of getting eaten in one go it keeps on for weeks at a time. And they'll drive the horses mad. There are better places just a few miles further on, well away from the wet and the bugs.'

Gracchus nodded with the air of a man who concedes a point unwillingly. 'Right, a few miles further on shouldn't make any difference. We should be ready to march soon; now we're off the proper road we'll need to send out a more fully-equipped advance-guard with more scouts ahead of them, and make sure that our rear is well-defended too – Marcus, can you organise that?

Marcus Asellio nodded. 'Certainly, sir; I'll get young Eburnus on to it; all good experience for him. At least those random trumpet calls have stopped.'

There were answering grins from around the table. 'Witchcraft. I thought as much. Burning down that village by the Clytha put a stop to it once and for all.' Gracchus glanced round the table, noting the nods of approval from most of the others, though Marcus' face was impassive.

Gracchus affected to ignore him and went on, 'Right, now who can tell me more about what we'll find when we reach the upper reaches of the river? This map has no useful detail at all. Yes?'

Gaius was nodding. 'I can't say I know it well, but our whole cohort has marched past there, of course. There's a very tall hill on the eastern side – almost a young mountain, you might say. Then there's open ground with a couple of streams running through it – that's why it's all so wet – and on the left there's a smaller, wooded hill. I'd say that it's a pretty safe area, really, good and open with nowhere for an enemy to hide – the big hill would be impracticable for an army – I don't know of anyone who's ever climbed to the top, it's all scree and loose stuff – and the little hill's so tangled with undergrowth that you shouldn't need to worry about it.

'That leaves the main river. It's not particularly wide – nothing like as wide as it gets further east, of course – and there's a decent ford, the lowest one on the river. The river itself is usually quite fast-flowing, and there are trees – big ones – on both banks. The ford itself is right among them, rather than being out in the open. We should be prepared for a spot of bother there, perhaps; the place has a bit of a history.'

'History, Centurion? Well, we're all students of history, aren't we. Enlighten us.'

The centurion gave a rueful smile. 'If you insist, sir. I'm afraid the valiant Ninth had a spot of bother there a few years back, right after their famous victory at Mons Graupius; some brigands managed to get their hands on one of the wagons in the baggage train and ran off with a few thousand sesterces. Some heads rolled over that, as I recall.' He glanced at the stony faces around the table; only Marcus Asellio was hiding his mouth behind his hand.

Gracchus was clearly not amused at the recollection. 'Thank you for that little digression, Centurion. I'm sure we all found it most enlightening. I'll make sure our men keep the strong-box safe this time.'

He turned to the orderly who was plucking at his sleeve. 'Yes, what is it?'

'Ready to march, Legate. We only need to take the auspices.'

Gracchus stood up to signal that the meeting was at an end. 'Then I thank you, gentlemen; we'll see what the gods have to say and then head off.'

As the meeting broke up, Marcus Asellio drew alongside Gaius. 'A shame we didn't hear a little more about that ford; sounds like the sort of place I'd be very nervous about.'

♛ ♛ ♛ ♛ ♛ ♛ ♛

Brigid shook her head in dismay; there were so many different herbs to sort out and weigh, and she was finding it hard to tell the difference between some of them. At last she gave up and called Anand over.

'It's no good, I'm sure I keep getting them messed up. Which one of them is the marjoram? And which is thyme? I know this one's mint. And this is juniper, isn't it.'

Anand sat down beside her, her thick fingers quickly sorting through the fragrant bundles of herbs culled from the hedgerows and banks. 'That's right, that's mint and this one's juniper.' A dreamy expression came over her face. 'Lovely thing, smells gorgeous, doesn't it. Some people say it's a bit like cypress; odd that.'

Her voice tailed away, and after a moment Brigid realised that Anand's eyes were closed and she was crooning softly to herself.

'Um? Anand, are you all right?' But there was no answer, and at last Brigid plucked up her courage to first tap her on the shoulder and then, when that had no effect, to pinch the back of her hand quite hard.

Anand came to with a start. 'Sorry about that. I was miles away. In more ways than one.'

She gave a cynical grunt. 'That's the trouble with novices, they leave you in the lurch and you have to do two jobs yourself. Anyway, where were we? Oh yes, juniper. Yes, you're quite right about that, it's just the other two you need to sort out; once you're sure about it you can start to make the same brose I do; here, bruise them both with your finger-nails and have a good sniff.'

Brigid did as she was told, filling her mind with the fragrances; but when she looked up again, Anand was once more in a trance.

The ceremony began as usual: a quick prayer to the gods, and particularly to Mars Victor, and then the coop was opened and the *pullarius* began to cast crumbs of bread and cake on the ground. But to his clear discomfort and Gracchus' fury, the chickens obstinately refused to come out and take the food.

Gracchus left his place in the front rank of watchers and demanded in a whisper, 'What's wrong with them? Why aren't they coming out and feeding? They must be hungry.'

The *pullarius* shrugged. 'Sorry, sir, I don't know; I'm not a proper augur, I just look after the sacred birds. All I know is this, the better they feed, the better the gods are pleased. Bad omen that is, when they don't come out at all.'

Gracchus racked his brains furiously. 'We've broken camp. The gods have been with us every step of the way. This can't be right.' Then a sudden revelation burst on his brain. Of course. It was obvious. Why hadn't he seen it before?

Smiling grimly he turned to face the men, noting their downcast expressions. Time for a heartening speech.

'Brave centurions and men of the Ninth Hispana. And you

others, joined with us on this valiant campaign. Remember how the gods have been with us, have granted us victory whenever the cowardly enemy dared to take up arms against us. Remember too how as we marched northwards we heard the sound of those infernal trumpet calls, raised up against us no doubt by the fell spirits of Avernus and the vile Caledonian witches who serve them and call them up at their need.

'But where are those trumpet calls now? Gone, my comrades. Remember how we put the witches to the sword. Remember how they fell, cursing as they saw that they could not withstand the might of Rome and our own valour.

'But, my comrades, these dark powers of the pit have not been vanquished for ever. They have sought to bring new terrors with which to frighten us. But see how weak they are. Can they dishearten you or me? Of course not. They can do no more than scare a few chickens. Comrades, any slave-brat could do as much. They think they have shown their strength. Never. They have only shown their weakness. And so I call you, in the name of the Divine Hadrianus and the Senate and People of Rome, to scorn these evil forces, gird up your courage and march on to the victories and the spoil that surely await us.'

He unsheathed his sword and held it high. 'We march for victory. We march for glory. We march for Rome. Rome. Rome.'

As the men took up the war-cry, a great roar that grew in intensity and filled the air, Gracchus noticed Eburnus, standing in the second rank and shouting with the others, and for a moment their eyes met. And he remembered with horror how he had raised the same chant when his men had been trapped on the Ituna; and he knew that Eburnus was reliving the same catastrophe.

Absit omen.

LVII

Caution, that's the name of the game. Act confident, but by all the gods take as much care as you can. And so Gracchus had sent scouts ahead of the advance-guard, checking for possible ambush-sites, and sending gallopers back to report to him in the vanguard. And the rear-guard too were on high alert, nerves taut as harp-strings.

But there had been no sign of any enemy – no horsemen, no mysterious trumpet-calls from the depths of the forest, no attempt to create pitfalls in the road. And so, as they neared the famous ford that Gaius had warned him about, Gracchus allowed his spirits and his confidence to rise. Soon they would have crossed the river, and within a few miles they would establish their new camp, confident that the triremes with their reinforcements would soon arrive at the mouth of the firth.

☼ ☼ ☼ ☼ ☼ ☼ ☼

Marius wiped his brow as he climbed the temple steps; the dog he had noticed there earlier had clearly taken up residence, and was lolling on the steps with his tongue hanging out. Marius gave him a friendly nod and the animal responded with a cheerful wag of his tail.

From his place outside the door Marius could just see the statue of great Mars inside the building, a local copy at two or three re-moves of a Greek image of Ares, with smaller statues of Deimos and Phobos standing on the god's right and left.

Fear and Terror, thought Marius; how useful they are in war. And how infectious. May the gods preserve our men in Caledonia from their workings.

He bowed deeply before the altar, then threw a pinch of

incense on the little charcoal fire smouldering day and night in its brazier. Does the god even notice this? Does it please him? How far up to heaven does the sweet scent rise? Well, Acestes thinks it will help.

He turned to go, aware of the dog's hopeful eyes on him. But he had nothing to give him, so he merely bent down to pat the animal's head and then headed back to camp.

Time for the evening milking. Cybele squatted down and began to pull rhythmically at the first goat's teats, resting her cheek against the animal's flank and singing softly to herself. As she remembered the events of the early morning her mind began to wander. Was Niamh really there? And who was the other woman – 'the other that I do not name'? And why should she not name her?

And then the other was there, speaking straight to her mind in blunt words followed by a cheerful laugh. 'The usual three. Maiden, mother and hag. She thinks that's rude. Doesn't bother me, though. Been called worse things than that in my time.'

'Where are we? Is this the land of the gods? Niamh warned me about it, how easy it is to enter and how hard it is to leave.'

The old woman shook her head. 'Everything comes in threes. Niamh told you that, didn't she? So, there's the world of the gods, the world of men, and this place, half-way between. Tir na mBeo – the Land of the Living – some call it. Anyway, good to have you back. Always best to have three. Hate having to do two jobs instead of one with a battle coming up.'

'I remember seeing the soldiers looking at a map. Marcus Asellio was there. And the other man, I don't remember his name – and hundreds of others as well that I couldn't see.'

Again the old woman laughed. 'That's them. All thinking that their gods are on their side and praying hard that they'll win. Huh. If only they knew.'

'I don't understand.'

This time it was Niamh's voice that cut in, coldly. 'Do you still not remember what I told you. What the gods want is blood; they do not care who wins or loses, only that blood is shed.'

Cybele shook her head in astonishment. 'That can't be right. I remember my old master burning incense to the gods, and all the camp watching. That must mean something.'

It was the old woman who answered again. 'She's right, girl. The only side the gods are on is their own. Do you really think the great Immortals care for a few coppers' worth of incense?

'No, they don't care who wins or loses. Get used to it. Different with me. With me, it's personal. Now, hush yourself and watch. Things are just coming nicely to a head. And that means that he should be turning up there soon, evil old bugger that he is.'

♛ ♛ ♛ ♛ ♛ ♛ ♛

'Two miles? Here in half an hour then. Everyone's in their place, everyone knows what to do. By Toutatis, Iatta, I can't think of anything we haven't thought of. It's the waiting gets me down.'

Iatta clapped him on the shoulder. 'As I recall, the last time you went to sleep. Not sure this is a good time for a nap, though.'

'Ah, last time I saw that owl in the tree and I knew that we had the gods on our side. Blanaid and Urien – they've been with me ever since I saw them at the Beltane fire. I even saw Blanaid's owl when I climbed to the top over there. So where are they now?'

He shrugged. 'When I went to see the Queen just after Beltane, she told me she thought I was already up with the stars. Iatta, perhaps before the day's out, that's just where you and I will be.' He grinned. 'Should be a good view from up there, anyway.'

Iatta grasped Senorix by both shoulders and turned him gently to face the nearest trees. 'Is that what you're looking for?' And indeed for a moment Senorix could glimpse the shifting outline of a human face as a warm breeze stirred the pine-branches.

He smiled. 'Good man. Take your omens where you find them, that's what I say.'

♛ ♛ ♛ ♛ ♛ ♛ ♛

At first Verica thought that the *gwyddbwyll* board had been left untouched since the day before; but when she looked at it more closely she realised that some of the pieces had been moved, and guessed that Gwydion had continued the lesson that she had begun, and that he and Iras had begun a game.

Smiling at her own childish memories of learning to play, she glanced at the disposition of the pieces. Iras must have been learning by taking the defenders' side and Gwydion the attackers', and at first glance it seemed that the king could have no route to safety at the side of the board. Her attention now fully engaged, Verica sat down first in one chair and then in the other, wondering if there could be any other end to the game. But of course – it depends on who has the next move. If the next move is the king's, then he can feint here, sacrifice that man, capture that piece, and his way to the edge of the board is clear. I wonder if Gwydion or Iras saw that?

A sudden thought struck her. It all depends on who has the next move. And that is true for me also. My safety in difficult times depends on this. And I know which piece I must capture. I shall write my letter to him today.

LVIII

Bodotria at last. Gracchus called Gaius and Marcus Asselio and the other senior centurions to his side and together they galloped ahead into the fine wide meadow that lay before the ford. It was much as he had expected from Gaius' description – a wooded hill on the left, marshy ground cut by little streams on the right, beyond that the main river looping and then at last a great pinnacle of rock reaching up into a louring sky. Thunder rumbled somewhere in the distance, threatening a storm before nightfall.

The meadow itself had been trampled flat, perhaps by the cattle which he noticed scattered across the space. But Gracchus' eyes were drawn to the ford straight ahead, with light tree cover on both sides of it, and the track curving away to the left beyond the trees.

'A good place for an ambush indeed, Gaius. We'll deploy two centuries from the first cohort to occupy the ford, and to hold it until we're all across; the *aquilifer* will remain at the head of our main body. Once we've got everybody across he can lead the men in the proper way until we reach our camp-ground.'

He wiped his forehead with the back of his right hand, and glanced up into the sky. 'I didn't think it ever got so hot this far north. Cloudy too – no wonder it's so oppressive. And a storm on the way, I think – the sooner we've got everyone safe in camp the better.'

For a little longer he hesitated, sweeping his gaze carefully across the land. There on his left was the wooded hill; Gaius had been right about that, even from here he could see the tangled undergrowth under the trees. No danger from there. The turbary land to the right seemed innocuous too; there was a low barrier of greenery across it, presumably to stop the cattle from wandering into the boggier parts, but it was beyond bow-shot, far enough away that he could safely disregard it. Satisfied at last he issued his orders.

'Gaius, you will take the first two centuries forward to occupy the ford; give a flag-signal when you're in position and secure, and we'll march forward on that. Marcus, draw up the rest of the first cohort and the auxiliary cavalry ready to give support if necessary, though I must say that the place all looks quiet enough at the moment. The rest of you to your usual places; gentlemen, you have your orders.'

He waited impatiently while the commands were passed on, the two named centuries drawn out of their cohort and the marching-line reformed. Then as the two centuries advanced towards the ford the remainder of the first cohort drew forward, with the cavalry already moving into position on the left flank.

And then, utterly unexpectedly, from somewhere on his right came the brazen notes of a Roman *buccina* sounding the charge. More phantom trumpet calls. He spun round in the saddle, trying to trace the source of the sound. What in Jupiter's name are they playing at?

But this time the call was not a mere provocation but a signal meant in deadly earnest. A sudden thunder of hooves made Gracchus wheel his horse around; a long column of horsemen had appeared beyond the ford, riding hard, a barbarian horde with a tall man on a fine grey leading the charge. Even as Gracchus watched transfixed they splashed through the ford, whooping and ululating wildly, then spurred straight towards his own centuries still advancing towards the ford.

He turned to the *cornicen*, waiting at his side. 'Sound a cavalry charge. And then a general advance in three ranks.'

Already two gallopers had drawn up at his side, waiting to carry his orders – thank the gods for good military discipline. 'My orders to the third and fourth cohorts – advance in quick order to cover our left flank, it'll be vulnerable without the cavalry.'

Ahead of him the battle had already been joined in earnest. Curious how slow everything seems to be, he thought, as if time is running as sluggishly as a river in a hard frost. I can see everything in the smallest detail, notice the riders' clothing, judge their horses, see them frothing at the mouth. And it all seems to happen in silence.

The feeling lasted in truth only for a moment and was replaced by a sudden spurt of elation. Battle at last. I can win us a victory that will resound across the Empire. When he looked again he saw that under Gaius' experienced leadership the two advanced centuries had already formed squares and the men were now crouching behind their interlocked shields, forming solid walls against the attackers. At a command which Gracchus could not hear but whose import he could guess, both squares launched their throwing spears, aiming at the horses rather than the riders; the sound of the animals' screams mingled with the crash of weapons and the yells of the stricken.

And now his own cavalry was in motion, a deadly missile aimed straight at the barbarians, red cloaks flashing in the wind and turves flying from the hooves. With a crash the forces met; then, all momentum lost, the struggle degenerated into a grim melée, horsemen circling each other, slashing and stabbing, while the horses too lashed out with their hooves.

Fools, sending cavalry against experienced soldiers without infantry support. We've got them now. But already the invisible *buccinator* was blowing the recall, and the attackers were disengaging and turning back to the ford with the auxiliary cavalry in hot pursuit.

Gracchus turned to the *cornicen*. 'Signal a stop to our advance; we'll let our cavalry hunt them down.' He turned to his aide-de-camp. 'Get the medical orderlies up there as soon as you can; and I need a casualty report. If those barbarian bastards have left any of their wounded behind, I want them brought back here – no throat-cutting on the sly. Once we're in camp we'll make a proper example of them.'

❦ ❦ ❦ ❦ ❦ ❦ ❦

Cybele covered her eyes with her hands. 'It's horrible; I can't watch it.'

The old woman laughed, but Niamh's voice was hard. 'You cut a man's throat. His gore reeked on your hands and your arms. Together we trampled him down into the ground, stamping on his back and his legs and his face until he was hidden, and then you took his amulet, stained as it was with his heart's blood. This is no time for your girlish nonsense. Now look.'

'She's right, girl. This is what we do. Some of it, anyway. You'll get used to it in time; we all do.'

Reluctantly Cybele forced herself to look back; the whole meadow seemed to pass under her gaze, from the trampled and bloodied earth where the squares and the cavalry had fought off the attack to the quiet discipline of the cohorts still drawn up in full battle-order, but as yet unbloodied.

'I'm better now. How long will it last?'

'For us? Less time than you'd think – there's not that much good daylight left, really, only a couple of hours, maybe three. For them? Eternity, for some of them.'

'Who's going to win?'

The old woman shrugged and muttered something under her breath; Cybele could just hear her murmur, 'Crassus lost the Eagles at Carrhae.' but there was more that she could not quite make out. Then with a grin she turned back to the battle. 'Ah, here we go again.'

❦ ❦ ❦ ❦ ❦ ❦ ❦

A sharp yell made Gracchus turn his head. 'Incoming. On the right.'

Several hundred men were advancing rapidly from where they had been concealed, crouched down behind the greenery on the right; already in range, some were firing arrows, a high drooping shot that brought the missiles flying down from the sky; and there were slingers too, their stones crashing into bodies and faces, sending men screaming to the ground.

By all the gods, I should have seen this coming. The auspices were a warning. Why was I so stupid? No, think, man. We've got them trapped – they've got the river behind them, we can just advance and mow them down.

'Sir – what's happening there?'

The aide-de-camp was pointing away towards the ford; the pursuing auxiliaries were already far out of sight, but more barbarians had emerged from the trees on either side of the river, laden with baskets. As Gracchus watched they ran up the track, tossing small, heavy items all about them as they went.

'They're sowing caltrops. To stop our cavalry from coming back. We can clear them once we've dealt with this little sideshow. Nothing to worry about now.'

He turned to the gallopers, already waiting for his orders. 'Three lines, shields up, advance on the enemy, Eagle to the fore. No quarter.'

At his signal Marcus Asellio spurred his horse to take up his place at the front of the quickly-formed battle-line, raising his hand in salute to the *aquilifer*, standing proud and resplendent in his shining uniform, a wolf-skin draped down his back, its mouth gaping at the enemy. The she-wolf's-litter – that's us. No-one can face a Roman army and hope to live. But an insidious thought from somewhere was beginning to worm its way into Gracchus' mind: Varus lost the Eagles at the Teutoburg Forest. Crassus lost the Eagles at Carrhae. And you couldn't even keep the *vexillium* safe on the Ituna. You aren't good enough to guard the Eagle of the Ninth. Look. They could take it now.'

In his mind Gracchus answered the charges. Crassus was an incompetent politician who started a war because he was greedy and wanted to seize the spoils for himself; Varus was careless when he set out for winter-quarters. But quickly these comforting answers were brushed aside. Crassus was an able general who had defeated Spartacus, and as for wanting money, he was already the richest man in Rome. Varus was tricked by Arminius. They were unlucky. Are you a lucky man? Were you lucky on the Ituna? An impious man like you who ignored the auspices. The gods will judge you.

He pushed the thoughts to the back of his mind and scanned the front of the battle. The advance he had ordered was proving difficult; the earth was sodden, and within a few paces the legionaries were up to their ankles in the wet ground, stumbling from tussock to tussock, the orderly battle-line wavering as the heavily-armed men fought to keep their balance. The first onslaught of missiles had petered out and the outnumbered attackers were retreating slowly in the face of the Roman advance, but hampered by their locked shields his own men lacked manoeuvrability and were vulnerable to sudden lightening assaults on the line, and the boggy ground made the usual 'thrust and step forward' impossible. Where's the *aquilifer*? Where's the Eagle? Jupiter, have they got it already? And then he saw it, still borne bravely aloft in the centre of the line, and breathed freely again.

On horseback to the *aquilifer's* left, Marcus Asellio surveyed the struggle; here he could see what Gracchus could not, and was aghast at the damage the lightly-armed raiders were doing: the arrow-fire had resumed, the range now so close that the shafts could pass clean through the threefold wood and leather of the scuta, mostly not life-threatening in themselves but certainly with enough impetus to wound the shield-arms of his men and disable them. There were five, no, six places now where the solid line had broken completely and the barbarians were pressing home their advantage; and the length of their line made it impossible for his wings to advance and outflank them.

'Fall back on the second rank.' It was a standard move, letting the inexperienced men who had so far borne the full brunt of the battle pass through the second and third ranks to recover. But under constant attack on the uneven ground, and in the frantic excitement and noise of the struggle, the manoeuvre was executed clumsily, leaving a space in the centre of the battle through which the enemy could force an opening.

Gracchus saw the tumult and passed his hand in front of his face. Jupiter, we'll lose the Eagle. He turned to one of the gallopers. 'The *aquilifer* is to fall back to the third rank. We can't risk the Eagle. The Emperor entrusted it to us, it's our duty to keep it safe.'

And in the world of her own mind, Cybele heard the old woman laugh quietly to herself.

LIX

'What happened at Carrhae?'

Anand shook her head and blinked. 'Sorry, what was that?'

Brigid repeated the question. 'You said something about eagles at Carrhae? I couldn't hear it all. Are you all right?'

'Having one of my turns. Happens sometimes. Better if I go and lie down. Must have had a bad night. Carrhae, you said? That was Crassus – Roman general, back in the days before they had emperors. Tried to take on the Parthians off his own bat, took seven legions with him.

'Paid for it, of course. The Parthians beat him hollow; they said he was only after booty, so after they'd cut his head off, they poured molten gold down his throat.'

Cybele winced at the thought. 'And the eagles?'

'Seven legions – so seven Eagles. The Parthians got the lot of them. Didn't give them back for, oh, years.'

'And Varus? Who was he? You said something about him, too.'

'*Varus, give me back my legions.* Famous, that was. Another general, in Augustus' time. Three legions and their Eagles that time, over in Germania. Drove Augustus wild, they say; he used to bang his head on the wall and shout those words over and over.'

Brigid nodded. 'I never knew any history, just little tit-bits that the soldiers used to tell me sometimes. The way they talked, you'd never think they ever lost a battle. I wish I knew as much as you do.'

'Useful, sometimes; especially when I want to put an idea into someone's head. Anyway, you keep sorting those herbs out, I need to get my head down. Look at me – can't be doing without something to keep my hands busy.'

She showed Brigid the forked stick that she had picked up from somewhere; then still muttering distractedly, she wandered over to her bed and lay down. For a while Brigid could hear her still talking quietly to herself, but at last she seemed to drift off to sleep.

Marcus Asellio swore a succession of colourful oaths, but was careful to do so under his breath. What sort of fool lets the men believe their Eagle's threatened? They must think he'll call a general retreat next. Desperately he rode behind the ranks, urging his legionaries forward. 'Mind your footing. Remember, we outnumber them. They're trapped by the river. Keep up the advance. Push, stab, disengage your sword – you know the drill.'

Further along the line he could hear the other centurions shouting similar commands; from the corner of his eye he saw Eburnus, dismounted by a sling-shot that had broken his horse's foreleg, standing in the front rank with his men, his sword red with blood and a round shield taken from one of the fallen enemy on his arm. Marcus watched his plumed helmet rising and falling as he thrust and parried, and then turned back to his own grim work.

And so at last, slowly, the whole tide of battle turned. It was impossible to pinpoint the moment when the painful advance began to gain momentum, but now there could be no doubt that the barbarians were being forced back across the boggy ground towards the fatal river, leaving their dead and wounded behind them.

Gracchus permitted himself a smile of satisfaction; Roman discipline had surely won the day yet again, and his fears for the safety of the Eagle had been groundless. And then, once more, he heard the hidden trumpeter sound the charge.

There was an answering roar from behind him, from under the trees of the wooded hill that he had disregarded. Too late he realised that the undergrowth he could see was merely a hedge-like facade, that behind it under the cover of the trees everything had been cleared away, with perhaps thousands of men concealed there under the greenery. Even as he watched in horror a whole *ala* of horsemen had cleared the hedge at a full gallop and was charging towards the rear of his line, led by a tall man on a bay horse. And then behind them – why didn't I see they could do that? – men on foot were pulling sections of the hedge apart, and their fellows were streaming through the gaps, a dozen different battle-cries on their lips, all waving swords, mattocks and sickles Already the extremities of the cavalry were racing ahead of their fellows, a classic crescent aimed at turning his flanks. And now his lines were beset at both front and rear, his men falling screaming and dying as the assault gained ground.

'Horsemen. Repel horsemen.' The words were no sooner out of Gracchus' mouth than he realised that both his command and the *cornicen's* obedient signal were unnecessary; his centurions had taken it on themselves to give the same order, and raggedly but with brave determination each cohort in the Roman triple line re-formed into a square, the first cohort forming up around him and his gallopers, with wounded men desperately dragged into the safety of the centre. He breathed a sigh of relief; a Roman defensive square was almost unbreakable as long as the men could cover themselves with their shields. Security at the expense of mobility – but at least it would give him and his centurions time to assess the situation.

🐚 🐚 🐚 🐚 🐚 🐚 🐚

'Why have they stopped fighting? What's happening now?'

The old woman tutted and shook her head. 'Did you think they just kept hacking away at each other until they were all dead? Even gladiators don't do that. Everyone wants a breather now and again – regroup, lick their wounds, perhaps decide to call it a day and disappear into the forest. Not that any of them look ready to run away just yet. A coward's mother sheds no tears, they say. Not true, that, but it's what they say. Ah, told you so: here come the wasps and the scorpions.'

🐚 🐚 🐚 🐚 🐚 🐚 🐚

In each cohort men were feverishly preparing the *vespae* and the *scorpiones*, the light anti-personnel artillery now being deployed for the first time. Quickly the weapons were bolted to their supporting wooden frames and carried forward, and baskets of bolts brought up ready for use.

The *vespae*, quickly set up and capable of being handled by one man, were the first to fire, the bolts zipping through the air with the characteristic high-pitched buzz which gave them their name; the heavier *scorpiones* took longer to manhandle into place, but like the scuttling creature whose name they bore, their powerful sting was usually deadly.

The effect was dramatic; as salvo after salvo of bolts were loosed into the barbarian cavalry, so the attack wavered, and finally broke in disarray, although there were still strong pockets of resistance.

Relief flooded Gracchus' mind; now his victory was inevitable. At the *cornicen's* call, square after square and cohort after cohort reformed into a wedge and advanced against the enemy, trampling the fallen into the ground; now in the van the Eagle was borne triumphantly aloft. This was to be a victory that the Ninth Hispana had won on its own, long before they could receive any support from the galleys and their contingent of soldiers that should even now be approaching the mouth of the firth. Already he could hear the cheers of the Forum crowds.

LX

'Bugger. Thought something like that might happen. Time to stick my oar in. Like I said, this is personal.'

The old woman looked up from the battle, and Cybele saw for the first time that she had a forked stick in her hand. She smiled grimly at Cybele, then nodded to Niamh, whose face was a mask of indifference. 'Time to take *galanas*; it's due to me. I claim it as my right; will any god or man gainsay me?'

There was no answer. After a moment she nodded again, then looked at the stick in her hand and muttered something which Cybele could not hear.

'Should do it. Let's see how he copes with that.'

🐚 🐚 🐚 🐚 🐚 🐚 🐚

Senorix reined in his horse by Iatta's side and shook his head. 'A good throw, Iatta. We did our best. Looks like I was right, though. This is Mons Graupius all over again; they'll just keep coming until we're wiped out, and there's nothing we can do to stop them.

'Gather the men you can and get away; you've got your wife and bairns to look after. This is as far as I'm going. I ran away once, and I won't do it again – too old for that trick. Get that nephew of yours to make up a decent song about me. Shame I never gave that lass her money. Ah well, it's a poor life that leaves you with no regrets.'

He looked round the stricken field; the Roman advance had taken firm hold, though here and there his men were still fighting valiantly. And there in the centre of the oncoming line was the Eagle, held high and still moving purposefully forward.

Senorix grinned and pointed his sword at it. 'Now that trinket would be worth a song, wouldn't you say?' He gathered the reins and prepared to charge, but Iatta lent across and held his shoulder fast.

'Wait. Listen.'

It was faint to begin with, but getting louder with every moment that passed, a soft patter that quickly grew in volume and intensity. Hail-stones. But this was no ordinary hail: some of the stones were the size of pigeons' eggs, but others were a hand's-breadth across. As Senorix watched they fell like rocks from the gods' own artillery, moving purposefully across the field, a deadly barrage crashing onto the advancing Roman lines but leaving his own unscathed.

In an instant the fey mood evaporated. He looked up at the grey sky as if searching for inspiration, then shouted, 'The gods are with us. The gods have won the day for us. Follow me, lads, and honour the gods. With Taranis and Toutatis to the battle.'

How soon an army's advance can turn into a rout. The whisper spread along the Roman lines like wild-fire: their gods are sending this on us. We should have heeded the auguries. If the men raised their shields, they were exposed to the suddenly renewed barbarian attack; if they kept them lowered, then they would be beaten into unconsciousness by the incessant bombardment from the clouds. The wooden frames supporting the *vespae* and *scorpiones* cracked and splintered under the remorseless battering, and the legionaries stood uncertain for a moment and then began to give ground.

Now it was over almost as quickly as it can be told: the cohorts, under attack both from above and the front, retreated in decent order towards the river, only to come under fresh attack from the archers and slingers still waiting there; as the ground grew more boggy the heavily-armed troops struggled to keep their feet, then fell and were trampled into the mire first by their fellows and then by the advancing enemy; a resourceful few managed to gain the river-bank and plunged desperately into the stream, only to be dragged down by the weight of their armour and drowned, their bodies swept downstream.

Only the First Cohort managed to mount a desperate last stand. Here, Gracchus, Gaius, Eburnus and Marcus Asellio, together with the battered remnants of the other cohorts, gathered around the Eagle; and here now the celestial assault was concentrated. Doggedly that last guard stood their ground as rank after rank fell to the advancing enemy, led by the same tall man who had earlier headed the charge from the wooded hill. Gracchus could see him clearly, swinging his sword with an astonishing vigour. 'Cut him down! Him! He's their leader!'

But the tall man seemed to lead a charmed life; now he was only a spear's length away. And, as at the beginning of the battle, suddenly Gracchus was in a world of silence; he seemed to be standing outside himself, surveying the struggle with interest but without any concern for his own safety and well-being.

And then the din of battle resumed. Only one thing to do now. The Roman way. To Gracchus' surprise he found that he had no regrets as he fell on his sword; and even as he breathed his last the tide of battle swept over his body, driving the last survivors on towards the river and oblivion in its depths.

The Eagle was bravely defended to the end, but at the very water's brink that too fell; and then, as the final blows were struck and the last blood shed, the Eagle of the Ninth was trampled into the mud and vanished for ever.

♕ ♕ ♕ ♕ ♕ ♕ ♕

Senorix looked round the trampled, boggy ground, red with blood of men and horses, and shook his head angrily. 'Damn it all. I'd got my heart set on that Eagle. We'll never find it in all this filth.'

'A gift to the river-god, then. It's the old style, my friend.' Iatta was breathing heavily and bleeding from a wound on his forehead, but he could still hardly stop himself from laughing aloud with pure relief. 'And the hail's finished. Just in time, that was.'

'The gift of our gods, Iatta. It was our gods that won the battle for us. But it's not over yet. There's still that cavalry somewhere out there; you'll have to track them down and deal with them. I have other work to do – I owe it to the Queen. I wouldn't give two coppers for her safety when the remains of the Ninth down on her doorstep hear about this. I must warn her.'

Iatta shook his head. 'You're in no state to go riding that sort of distance. Come to that, the horse isn't up to it either. The pair of you need to get your wounds tied up and rest for a few days – look round, there's none of them left to carry tales back. It's all over, man. We've done it. By all the gods, we've done it.'

Senorix made to answer, but the world seemed to be spinning about him. Slowly he fell forward onto the crupper of his saddle and would have fallen hard to the ground if Iatta had not caught him and lowered him gently down.

☙ ☙ ☙ ☙ ☙ ☙ ☙

'He said that it was the gods who helped them.'

'Then he's an old fool. Nothing personal.'

Cybele ignored the warning look on the old woman's face. 'You said you were claiming *galanas*. That's compensation, isn't it? For a death or an injury?'

'Compensation or blood-feud, yes. And I'll say no more about it – ask no questions, hear no lies. Girl, you've got goats to look after.'

And Cybele was back in her little garden; and it seemed that here no time at all had passed.

☙ ☙ ☙ ☙ ☙ ☙ ☙

It was night now but the clouds had cleared and the stars were casting a faint glow over the field; a growing brightness in the eastern sky hinted that the moon would soon rise. Slowly and hesitantly Eburnus came back to consciousness, aware at first only that his body was full of hardly-bearable agony.

Silence all around, except for the night-creatures; ah, there's an owl. Gingerly, wincing in pain, he lifted his head and looked around. No movement at all; no, there's dogs over there – or wolves, maybe. At last by slow degrees he pulled himself to his knees and started to take in the little that he could see. All dead? Everyone? How can that be? Marcus Asellio? The tribune? All the centurions and the brave lads who marched with us? All gone down to the Shades? *Dis manibus.*

He racked his memory for an explanation, but to no avail; he could remember standing shoulder-to-shoulder with his comrades, glorying in the fact that even in defeat the Eagle still held its ground and was not surrendered – and after that, there was nothing, not even a memory of the blackness that must have overcome him.

Breathing was agony; he must have broken several ribs. But his arms and legs felt sound enough. Carefully he felt his face; blood had run down from the crown of his head and was matted in his eyebrows, but his nose, mouth and eyes all seemed to be uninjured. His ears too were undamaged. *The gods have saved me for the second time. Why me? And then a more worrying thought. Are the barbarians still watching? How long before they send me to join the rest of our lads?*

But no-one appeared, and as time passed and the moon slowly rose, Eburnus shook himself and began to hobble slowly away from the stricken field; at every step it seemed that his sandals touched a body, though in the glimmer it was impossible to distinguish fallen friend from foe. And then at last he was clear of the meadow. *I must find a horse. I must raise the alarm. I owe it to the dead.*

With that thought fixed in his mind he lay down in the shelter of the trees, and surrendered again to unconsciousness.

LXI

Kal. Aug. – August 1st

It was a pleasant early evening ride, but as the faithful cob trotted southwards there was a nagging doubt at the back of Marius' mind. True, an invitation to a banquet – and an invitation from a Queen, no less – wasn't something to carelessly turn down; but things were not – well, not as easy now as they had been. And the August Kalends, she had told him, marked the time when the powers of darkness were beginning to climb once more into the ascendant.

But it seemed he need not have worried; there was a sturdy lad waiting at the gate to help him dismount – *does he really think I can't get off on my own?* – and to lead the horse away; and the major-domo was waiting too, ushering him politely through the garden and towards the famous dining room with its beautiful murals. A pleasant place to dine on a summer's evening, he had thought when he first saw it; and so it turned out to be.

But if this was indeed to be a banquet, then it seemed there were to be very few guests: only four couches were ready, two on each side of the fine beechwood table. He hesitated in the doorway, and heard a lightly mocking laugh behind him.

'Unsure of your place, Commander? You will be at my right hand, of course.'

Verica swept past him and sat easily on one of the couches, letting the little maid fuss around her to arrange her dress. Ah, the dress. A Greek high-girdled *chiton* in beautiful linen; sacred to Aphrodite, a little voice at the back of Marius' mind reminded him.

She caught his eye and laughed, and he knew that she had read his thought as clearly as if he had spoken it out loud. 'Commander, it is cool and pleasant at the end of a hot day. Now, come by my side; my next two guests are ready to take their places as well.

No shyness, now – you know both of them, though perhaps you have only spoken to one of them before.'

She clapped her hands and Gwydion entered and bowed to her, then sat on the couch opposite. In his hand he was carrying a pipe of a kind that Marius had never seen before, with a wooden body and a bell of cow's horn, which he carefully laid by the side of the couch. Finally, the little maid – Iras, that was it – bowed and pattered round the table to sit on the couch by Gwydion's side.

His face must have betrayed him. 'You must not be surprised. Iras is as free-born as you or I or Gwydion there; and I have arranged this feast in part to thank you for punishing the woman who tried to sell her into slavery, and partly to assure her of how highly I think of her. I am sure, Commander, that you have servants that you too value highly, do you not?'

Marius nodded. 'That is very true, my lady; indeed, I would have set Flavius free years ago, except that he would not let me do so. But I have my revenge at Saturnalia, for then he sits in my place, and I serve him and do his bidding; and there is no-one I would serve more gladly.'

'No-one? Commander, you are telling me too many secrets. But yes, you may think of this as if it were a Saturnalia feast, where the family are gathered together to share in each others' joy; for that indeed is our custom at the August Kalends.'

She cast a theatrically sad look about the table, then went on, 'You see, Commander, the only family I now have is far away; my dear son has written and told me of how he has established himself in Italy, and he urges me to come to live with him; and perhaps one day I shall do so.

'But I have no other family still living on this earth, so I invite you as my dear friend, and with you Gwydion, whose wisdom and lore have always been a strength to me, and Iras who is my daily companion. But enough of this chatter. We should eat and drink and let all cares be far away.' She clapped her hands again and a dozen servants appeared carrying dishes for the *gustatio*: stuffed olives, a bean salad, mussels in white wine, and carrots with a spicy cumin sauce.

At first they ate in a companionable silence that was broken only by the chattering of swallows in the garden and the distant tinkling of the fountain. At last, as she dabbed her hand in her finger-bowl, Verica smiled and asked, 'Was she very severely punished, that woman who tried to sell my dear Iras?'

Marius glanced quickly at the girl, and saw she was blushing. He smiled reassuringly at her, and nodded. 'A good public whipping, which I am sure she richly deserved. At all events, she took herself off early the next day and no-one has seen her since.

'And her husband whom she blamed for all her misfortune, he seems to have vanished too. Drowned, I suspect, but no-one's reported finding his body.'

Gwydion, who had been listening intently, smiled sadly. 'It seems he was of an ancient line, and now that branch of it has died out. But there are other branches, no doubt, so some of the lineage of Bran and Branwen may still live on, though I do not know where that might be.'

The conversation paused while the first course was quickly cleared away and the *Prima Mensa* carried in. Marius looked with envy at the fine Samian tableware, and Verica gave another light laugh.

'A fine dinner-service, is it not? Ah, but the truth is that most of it was broken before it ever got here; when it was unpacked, we found that more than half of it had been smashed to pieces on the road, or while they were loading it on the ship or wherever. Or perhaps the potters took me for a rich Barbarian fool who would blame the carrier, and had only sent me their own breakages. With Gauls, nothing would surprise me.

'Now, there is duck with damson sauce, stuffed hare, and spiced lamb; and something of a special treat for the *Secundae Mensae*, so be sure the lad doesn't fill your plate so full that you have no room for more.'

The treat, when it came, left Marius frankly open-mouthed with astonishment: ice, flavoured with saffron, and topped with fruit. Verica nodded when it was served as though it were the most ordinary thing in the world, but Marius was still staring at the dish in amazement.

'We have an ice-house high in the mountains, Commander, in a shaded valley where the sun hardly comes even at midsummer. It's covered with earth and straw, and my men harvest the ice in the depths of winter and store it there, with more straw wrapped around it to keep it from melting. This is the very last of the winter's ice, Commander, so the pleasure of the dish should be all the greater as you know that there will be no more – or not for several months, anyway. The idea was the Divine Nero's, by the way. He wanted to be remembered as an artist, poor fellow, but it is for this recipe that his name is honoured here.'

And finally there was the wine, strong Alban and Caecuban vintages the price of which Marius would never dare to calculate, served unwatered, though Iras drank very little.

'Tell me, Commander, have you heard much of the progress of that troublesome young tribune and the legion he was lent?'

The question caught Marius quite unawares, and he had to pause for a moment to marshal his thoughts. 'Indeed, my lady, we have had some news, though not for several days now. It seems that he has regarrisoned several camps that had been left abandoned years ago, and carried out a punitive raid on an enemy stronghold near the Clutha. Since then we have heard nothing, though in truth we would not expect to for some time yet. No doubt he has come to the upper reaches of Bodotria and is probably awaiting news that the galleys have arrived at the mouth of the firth.'

'And so the influence of Rome continues to spread, Commander? That must be very satisfying for you. And for him, of course. I suppose that a political career will open out for him when this is over?

– 437 –

'No doubt. The crowd love to hear of military success.'

Verica nodded. 'Commander, let me speak frankly. You and I have not always agreed of late, and perhaps that was my fault more than yours. At bottom I think that our view of the world is very different: you see progress, Rome spreading her power ever more widely until in the end the whole world is Rome; and I see the world moving in cycles of growth and decay which in the fullness of time will even bring down Rome's greatness. But for all these differences, you and I should be friends, should we not?'

In a warm haze of wine, Marius could only nod his agreement. Verica smiled and waved an arm to bring Gwydion into the conversation. 'Now, Gwydion there is learned in all our lore, and of late he has been reading even more widely, and has found much of interest in the writings of the Jews and especially of their seers.'

'The Jews? The Divine Vespasian thought we could stamp out all the trouble they cause if we rooted them out of their country, but even in Rome they have still caused havoc with their endless violent disputes though they have been banished from the city no fewer than three times.'

Now it was Gwydion's turn. 'Indeed, Commander, they are a most troublesome and foolish nation, so intent on worshipping only one god that when the final disaster struck them, they had no other god to turn to for aid. And yet some of their seers had thoughts which accord with the true nature of the world, and with the Queen's encouragement I have set the words of one such, a man who called himself The Orator, to a song. As my lady will tell you, my Greek is not of the best, so I will not attempt to play the harp while I sing; instead, young Iras here will play the melody on her pibgorn, at which she is greatly skilled.'

And now the girl took up the instrument that Marius had seen earlier and blew a few experimental notes on it, then blushed. 'It needs to be warmed first. It will be ready to sing for us in a moment.'

She tried it again, then nodded to Gwydion and struck up a

haunting melody; Gwydion waited until she had played several notes, then began to declaim in a strong counter-tune:

'τί τὸ γεγονός αὐτὸ τὸ γενησόμενον…

'That which has been is that which will be, and that which has been done is that which will be done. So there is nothing new under the sun. Is there anything of which one might say, "See this, it is new?" Already it has existed for ages which were before us.'

Marius sat stunned at the beauty of the playing and the strength of Gwydion's voice. When at last the song had finished he clapped his hands in delight. Verica too was smiling; then, delicately, she stifled a small yawn.

'Commander, I think that the music marks the end of our entertainment this evening. How pleasant it has been.'

Clumsily, and aware of the effects of the wine, Marius stood and bowed. 'It has been a most pleasant evening, my lady. What can I say? The food, the wine, the entertainment, all have been… well, superb. But I think it is time for me to take my leave. Will you be so good as to send someone to saddle my horse and bring it to the gate?'

Verica looked startled. 'Commander, it is far too late for you to risk the road. I was – we were – expecting that you would stay here with us.' The unspoken *with me* hung in the air, and for one long moment Marius stood undecided. His answer, when it came, surprised him almost as much as it surprised Verica.

'My lady, my duties call me. But truly I thank you.'

Verica had already recovered her poise. 'You are right. And I have my Court to attend to in the morning. So I shall send Adeon to escort you; two are safer than one. If you would be so good as to lend him a bed for the night and send him back safe tomorrow I shall be most grateful. And, Commander, remember that despite whatever disagreements we may have had, you will always be welcome – most welcome – here.'

Afterwards Marius often wondered how different the world might have been if his choice had been otherwise.

LXII

AD IV Non. Aug. – August 2nd

The hot weather had broken at last, and the fine rain which had fallen in the night had given way at dawn to a pervading dampness. From time to time sharp gusts of wind shook the trees, sending sudden cascades of water from the leaves onto the ground below.

Undeterred, Verica sat on her currule chair under the old oak tree, the hood on her head her only concession to the change in the weather, and with Iras and Gwydion in their accustomed places. But it seemed that only one man, standing hooded and aloof, was waiting to present a case at her court. Now at her invitation he stepped forward and in one motion bowed and pulled the hood back to reveal his face.

'Senorix! You have the effrontery to come here again! I should…'

But Senorix laid his finger to his lips and shook his head. 'My lass, I am here to warn you. I would have been here some days ago, but as you can see, my wounds needed some care.'

He bared his right arm, showing a livid scar running from wrist to elbow, then went on carelessly. 'And I have others too, that I will not show. My dear lass, the Ninth are no more. Eboracum and Mons Graupius and Verulamium, all are avenged at last. But you are surely in danger, and I have ridden here to tell you so. If we go within doors I will tell you more; but this is a matter on which we should be secret.'

Verica jumped up in fury. 'What have you done? Fool. We were at peace.'

'Peace? Tell that to the people in a little village on the Clutha, butchered by the Ninth for no reason. My lass, I saw with my own een what they had done, and for shame I will not repeat it here. But this I will say: in the end it was not our lads but our gods who defeated them, battered them to the ground with hailstones such as you and I have never seen before, no, nor will see again. But when news of this comes to those still camped on your doorstep, how safe are you then?'

'But this was no doing of mine. I urged you to live in peace. Why should I pay the price for your blood-feud?'

'Why? Because they will not stop to think. They will already know that you have known me, have entertained me; and that will be enough for them. When you have two cohorts of crazed soldiery at your gates trying to avenge their fallen comrades, do you think that if you tell them you only want peace then they will go away? No, my lass; they will butcher you and everyone about you, Gwydion and Iras here and Adeon and anyone else they can find, and they will smash your statuary and burn this place to the ground. You cannot stay, my lass; or if you do, then you will surely die, and your friends with you. And the manner of your deaths will not be easy.'

Verica, all anger suddenly gone, cast a despairing look at the garden, now in its late summer glory. 'Where can I go? To hide in the hills like some criminal? To find a place beyond Rome's reach, in Caledonia or Hibernia? Is that what you want me to do?'

'My lass, you have a son in Italy; you could go to him there. Calmer counsels would soon prevail, and you would be honoured and unmolested there. There you could find the peace that you seek.'

But Verica was silent. At last, Senorix bowed deeply and strode away, leaving Verica with her eyes still fixed on the garden and her hand raised to her lips.

Gwydion lent closer to Verica and could just hear her repeating over and over again, So near. We were so near. He sat down beside her and waited patiently, until she turned to him and put her hand on his shoulder.

'Gwydion, he has played *gwyddbwyll* with me, and I have lost. And I have lost everything.'

'Not so, my lady. He has been playing indeed, but at dice with the Romans I think; and it seems that he has won his game. And if either he or the gods are playing *gwyddbwyll* with you, then my lady you still have two moves that can bring you to safety; but move you must. You cannot stay. And so you must make the choice that you have been avoiding all through the game, moving always backwards and forwards, feinting and parrying. The world of your fathers, my lady, or the world of Rome? Perhaps soon they will be the same. But the choice is yours alone; and you must make it today.'

He smiled. 'Once, my lady, he showed you how to skim stones over the water. Think how they travelled so far. Because, my lady, they barely touch the water but lightly pass over it. Be like that to the world. Touch it lightly. That way, safety lies.'

Verica was silent for a long moment, and when she did speak there was a smile on her lips as well. 'When Senorix first came here, three months ago or nearly, he brought me a gift, and I have worn it ever since. A pretty thing, this little owl in silver and lapis lazuli. But what did Niamh say? *It reeks of death. Can you truly not feel it?*'

In a sudden flash of anger she pulled off the little brooch and tossed it onto the ground. 'I shall wear it no more; all it has brought me is trouble.'

She looked slowly around the garden as though trying to fix the image for ever in her mind. 'How I love this place. How I loved his gift. Well, I will be the prisoner of neither place nor gift – see, I can cast them off of my own will. I have decided. Come with me.'

But Gwydion laid a restraining hand on her arm. 'My lady, that is bravely done. But remember what I have always told you, and the words that you bade me sing last night. That which has been is that which will be, and that which has been done is that which will be done. And so I tell you with certainty that a time will come when you will stand here again in this garden and hold that brooch, though there will be many turnings of the world before that happens. But happen it surely will.'

'Can I be cheeky?'

Anand looked up from her cake-baking. 'What's that? You asking rude questions?'

'Not rude. Not really. It's just that you seem so much happier this last few days. Baking and brewing and everything. And when I had that nightmare you were so comforting. I never really said thank you.'

Anand's voice was gruff. 'Nothing to thank me for. Just glad you're all right now.'

But Brigid persisted. 'You held me in your arms and said, Mother Anand's here. I never remember anyone doing anything like that before. You've been better than a mother to me, Anand. Anand, why did you never have children?'

A shadow suddenly passed over Anand's face. She hesitated for a moment, then began to speak in a monotonous voice, as if dredging up long-buried memories. 'Did. Had a son. Taught him everything. Little bugger went to the bad. Turned thief, then killer. Got himself crucified in the end. Deserved to die, too, but not like that. No-one should die like that. But I got *galanas* for him at last, poor soul. My fault, perhaps; I'd named him Urien. Bad name, hard fate.

'Hush now. There's someone coming. Not a word of this to anyone.'

She cocked her head to one side, then hurried out of the door. Brigid could hear the hoof-beats stopping on the road, then a thump as someone awkwardly jumped down. There was a brief conversation that she couldn't hear followed by a gasp of surprise, and then the light dimmed as a head was poked through the open shutter.

'Messalina? Is that you?'

But Brigid hunched herself up tight and ignored it. Brigid now, she said to herself. Mustn't ever answer to Messalina.

But then Anand was there, tapping her on the shoulder. 'It's all right. He told me to say he's got a duponius for you. And that where he's taking you, they'll treat you as a Queen.'

But when realisation struck, Brigid burst into sudden tears. 'But Anand, I can't leave you.' She flung her arms around the old woman's neck and clung on tight.

Gently Anand freed herself. 'Girl, people like me – well, we tend to hang about a bit. So you don't need to worry about me. And I'll always have an eye open for you. Go with your man. And so the world turns.'

LXIII

Non. Aug. – August 5th

Marius put down the pen and rubbed his eyes. Beginning of the month – so that means reports. What do they ever do with them? File them away and forget about them, I suppose. So many sick, so many attached to here or there, so much spent on cheese and pork and Jupiter knows what. Or Juno, divine housekeeper, more likely. And how am I supposed to report on the blessed Ninth when most of them must be a hundred miles away?

From somewhere nearby there came the sound of running feet, and then the door was roughly thrown open. Marius looked up in fury at the interruption, but one look at Flavius' flushed face was enough to choke the angry words in his throat.

'What is it, man? What's the matter?'

But Flavius could hardly speak, overcome with horror and shock. At last he managed to stammer out the words, 'Eburnus is here. The Ninth. Gone. Almost to a man.'

Marius shook his head in frank disbelief. 'Gone? Rubbish, man. A whole legion doesn't just disappear.'

But then Eburnus was there at Flavius' shoulder, his face white and drawn with pain. 'It's true, sir. The Ninth has gone for ever. Marcus Asellio too, as bravely as you'd expect.'

Marius took several deep breaths. 'Flavius, get wine for Eburnus. And for me. And not a word of it outside this room.' He waved Eburnus to a stool. 'Tell me everything.'

Eburnus paused to gather his thoughts. 'Everything was in good order, sir. We'd run into a little trouble at a couple of fords along the way, but it was just a feint, really; they ran away as soon as we put the cavalry up. The tribune was careful, too, not taking any chances.'

'There was something in the despatches about an attack on a stronghold near the Clutha? A punitive raid? Was there a problem there?'

Eburnus shook his head. 'There was no stronghold, sir, just a native village. The tribune ordered an attack; just blood-lust, really. Marcus Asellio would have nothing to do with it, and neither would I. It was just slaughter for the sake of it, sir. Truth to tell, I felt ashamed to be a Roman when that happened.'

Marius waited while Flavius brought in two wine-cups and a flagon of everyday wine, and let Eburnus drink deeply. 'I'm afraid the Ninth were famous for that sort of thing. But they were heroes to the mob in Rome. Go on.'

'Well, we got to the upper reaches of the Bodotrian Firth without any problems – oh, just one, perhaps: the auguries were bad. But the tribune came out with some line about how the Caledonian witches might scare a few chickens but they were no match for a Roman legion. And then, when we were just preparing to cross the ford there, they came at us on both flanks. They must have been preparing for a week or more, the whole thing was arranged like the chorus in a theatre.

'But we still managed to get the upper hand, sir. We withstood the onset and we were forcing them back, all in good order. In half an hour we'd have won the day. And then…'

He stopped and took another deep draught from the wine-cup. 'And then the gods joined the battle. A bombardment of hailstones, sir, some of them as big as your fist, and all of them falling just on our own lines. Men were falling like flies. Of course that was enough to rally the enemy; we fought bravely enough, but we didn't have a chance. They pushed us back into the boggy ground, then cut us down where we stood or drove us into the river to drown. All I remember is seeing Marcus Asellio and the tribune and a few others trying to defend the Eagle. Then I must have taken a blow to the head; when I came round hours later, it was all dark and the battle was over. The Eagle had gone, either captured or swept away in the river; and the wolves were out, howling over the dead. I managed to get away and hide in the forest, and then a few more lads managed to join me. One of them died before the night was out, but the others of us managed to get back to the last of our marching camps to raise the alarm. I don't know how long that took us; we kept off the road as much as we could.

'And then they didn't believe us either, sir. Thought we were deserters, locked us up and threatened us with execution for cowardice. It took them three days to send out patrols and find that we hadn't been lying; at least then they started to take a bit of care of us. They hadn't bothered earlier – not much point if they were going to chop our heads off, I suppose.

'Then they wanted to send word back with some of their own men, sir, but I'm afraid that I insisted on coming myself. At least they let me have a decent horse.'

'And the native gods did that to the legion? Who knew they had such power?'

'I wonder if it wasn't our own gods, sir; what had happened on the Clutha must have sickened them as much as it sickened me. They'd warned us, too, sent us unfavourable auspices, but we ignored them.'

Marius tapped his fingers on the table. 'I see. Right, who knows you're here?'

'Everyone must know by now, sir; the guards at the gate wanted to know everything about the campaign. I said I couldn't tell them anything, that I had to report to you; but the rumour that something's happened must be all over the camp.'

Marius considered briefly. 'Can you ride further? I need a companion. And you can tell me more along the way.'

Eburnus nodded. 'I'll need a fresh horse, sir, but yes, I'd be honoured to be with you.'

As they rode south, Marius thought about how he had ridden this road just four days earlier. She asked me what I'd heard about the Ninth; innocent enquiry? Or something more sinister? Did she know something? Soon find out.

But apart from his own courtesy guard at the gates, Verica's villa was deserted; and his own men had the shifty look of having been handsomely bribed to see nothing and hear nothing, and most of all to report nothing.

With Eburnus at his heels, Marius strode through the deserted rooms. It was clear that everyone had left in a hurry; chests had been left open, some of their contents spilled on the ground, and in the kitchen uneaten flat bread was still piled on the table.

Was this all of her own plotting? Did she lie about what she knew? Was that Senorix fellow part of it? Or was she an innocent bystander, a victim of circumstances getting herself out of the way of the storm that she must have known would soon break? She offered me riches, comfort, love; and like a fool I turned them down; and now I shall never know where she has gone or why.

In the garden the currule chair was still set under the oak-tree, and something glittering in the dust by it caught his eye. He bent down to pick it up; it was the little owl brooch in silver and lapis that she had been wearing every time he had seen her for months now. He turned it in his hand, letting the light play on it. *Sunt lacrimae rerum*, he murmured to himself, then regretfully he laid it carefully back on the ground.

'This place is to be guarded, Eburnus; give that order. No squatters, no thieves, no-one at all is to come in. Let it crumble to dust where it stands. She gave it back to the spirits of the place; I will honour her choice.'

Then he turned and left and never once looked back.

Dramatis Personae

The Romans
Marius (Vitellus Decimus) – commander of the detachment at Lugovalium
Flavius – his faithful steward
Licnos – his cook
Gracchus – his ambitious tribune
Marcus Aelius Asellio – his *primus pilus* and an old friend
Cybele – Marius' slave-girl
Arminius – a recruit from Rhaetia
Acestes – an augur
Eburnus – an *optio*, later a centurion
Tetricus – leader of a hunting party
Gaius – a centurion attached to the IX Hispana
Lucius Aninius Sextius Florentinus – legate of the IX Hispana, who has a glittering career ahead of him, becoming Governor of Arabia in 127

The Queen and her Court
Verica – Queen of the Carvetii
Gwydion – her harper
Lugos – her first son
Urien – her second son, now in Rome
Iras – her maid
Adeon – a member of her court

The people of Luguvalium
Bran – An inn-keeper
Messalina – his slut-of-all-work, later Brigid
Morrig – the inn-keeper's wife
Bris – owner of the caupona (takeaway) next door
Huctia – his daughter
Glaucus – a dubious Greek banker
Amicus – his friend and colleague
Anand – an old woman with an interesting line in herbs

Crotos – a dispossessed farmer

Apuleios – a disappointed expert on the Ituna and its fords

The Caledonians

Senorix – a Caledonian freedom-fighter

Iatta – his second-in-command

And...

Niamh – a seer

Notes on names and other references

Annwn/Annwfn – the Celtic otherworld, presided over by Arawn

Bodotria – the Firth of Forth

Bravoniacum/Brovonacis – Kirkby Thore, near Appleby-in-Westmorland

Brocavum – Brougham

Caer Arianrhod – The Silver Wheel; the circumpolar stars, believed to be the place where the dead await rebirth.

Caer Gwydion – The Milky Way

Camulodunum – Colchester

Clutha – the Clyde

Eboracum – York

Ituna – the River Eden; the Ituna Estuary is the Solway

Londinium – London

Luguvalium – Carlisle

Voreda – settlement north of Penrith, now called Old Penrith

Verulamium – St. Albans

Charon – the ferryman who carries the souls of the departed across the River Styx to the Underworld

Esus – a Celtic god of the forests, sometimes identified with Mercury, whose name means 'Lord'

Manannan ap Llyr – a Celtic sea-god

Minos – the Judge of the Dead in Roman mythology

Nataero – the Roman god of lost things

Pluvius – the Roman god of rain

Toutatis – a Celtic tribal god, sometimes identified with Mars

Taranis – a Celtic thunder-god

The matronae were worshipped widely in much of north-western Europe until as late as the sixth century. Little is known of them, but they are always shown in groups of three, either sitting or standing, and always depicted frontally.

Gustatio – hors d'ouvres
Prima Mensa – Main course
Secunda Mensa – Sweet course

Vespae and Scorpiones – Roman anti-personnel artillery, both very effective types of powerful platform-mounted cross-bow, used both in open battle and during sieges

Verica's judgement about the future of the Forum was precisely correct; by the Middle Ages it had reverted to wilderness and was known as Campo Vaccino (Cow Hollow).

The Roman Calendar

Romans in the period in which the book is set tended to identify years by the names of the two consuls who held office in that year, although they were also sometimes numbered after the supposed founding of Rome followed by the letters AUC – Ab Urbe Condita, From the Foundation of the City.

The months in this period had names which would be entirely familiar to us, but within the months the days were numbered not by how far they were from the beginning of the month as we do but rather by how far they were before one of the three fixed named days in that month: the Kalends (always the first of the month); the Ides (the 15th day of March, May, June and October, and the 13th day of all the others) and the Nones (always 8 days before the Ides); to complicate things a little further for modern readers, the Romans always counted inclusively, so that for instance in January the Ides would have been on the 13th of the month, the day immediately before it would have Pridie (= the day before, and abbreviated to Prid. Id. Ian.) and the day before that would been counted as three days before the Ides and abbreviated to A.D. III Id. Ian. where A.D. Stands for Ante Diem (= before the day).

Gwyddbwyll

Gwyddbwyll is a strategy board-game for two players; the aim of the first player is to manoeuvre the 'king' from the centre square to safety at the edge of the board, while his opponent attempts to stop him and capture the 'king'. In the version described by Verica, which is similar in some ways to the Roman game of *Latrunculi*, or 'Brigands' as well as to a number of 'tafl' games played by Celtic and Germanic societies throughout northern Europe, the two sides have unequal forces, and a 'rubber' would presumably therefore consist of two games, with the players swapping sides between games. The name literally means wise wood though Welsh and Irish literature both describe sets made of white and dark bronze or of gold and silver. This version is different from the mediaeval game of the same name, in which both sides have equal numbers of men; in modern Welsh *Gwyddbwyll* signifies chess.

A number of versions of this and similar games are available on the web, so you can have a go for yourself. They're not as easy as they look.